BUG BOYS

Adventures and Daydreams

Also by Laura Knetzger

Sea Urchin (Retrofit Comics)

Bug Boys series
Bug Boys
Bug Boys: Outside and Beyond

BUG BOYS

Adventures and Daydreams

By Laura Knetzger

RH
GRAPHIC

NEW YORK

Bug Boys: Adventures and Daydreams was drawn and colored digitally in Photoshop.

Text, cover art, and interior illustrations copyright © 2022 by Laura Knetzger

All rights reserved. Published in the United States by RH Graphic, an imprint of Random House Children's Books, a division of Penguin Random House LLC, New York

RH Graphic with the book design is a trademark of Penguin Random House LLC.

Visit us on the Web and sign up for our newsletter!
RHKidsGraphic.com • @RHKidsGraphic

Educators and librarians, for a variety of teaching tools, visit us at RHTeachersLibrarians.com

Library of Congress Cataloging-in-Publication Data is available upon request.
ISBN 978-0-593-30952-0 (hardcover) — ISBN 978-0-593-30953-7 (lib. bdg.)
ISBN 978-0-593-30954-4 (ebook)

Designed and lettered by Patrick Crotty

MANUFACTURED IN CHINA
10 9 8 7 6 5 4 3 2 1
First Edition

A comic on every bookshelf.

To Bob and Deb

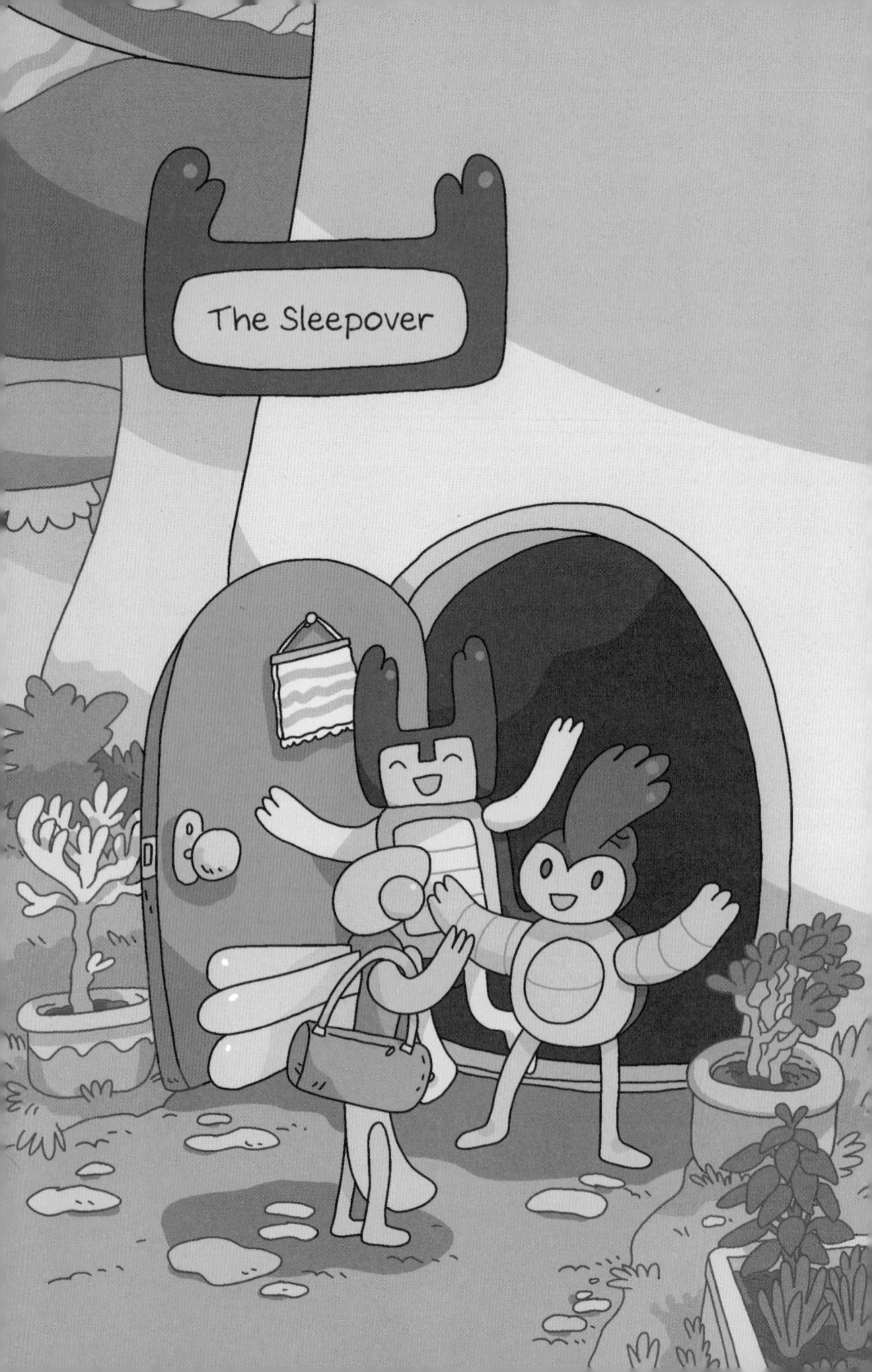
The Sleepover

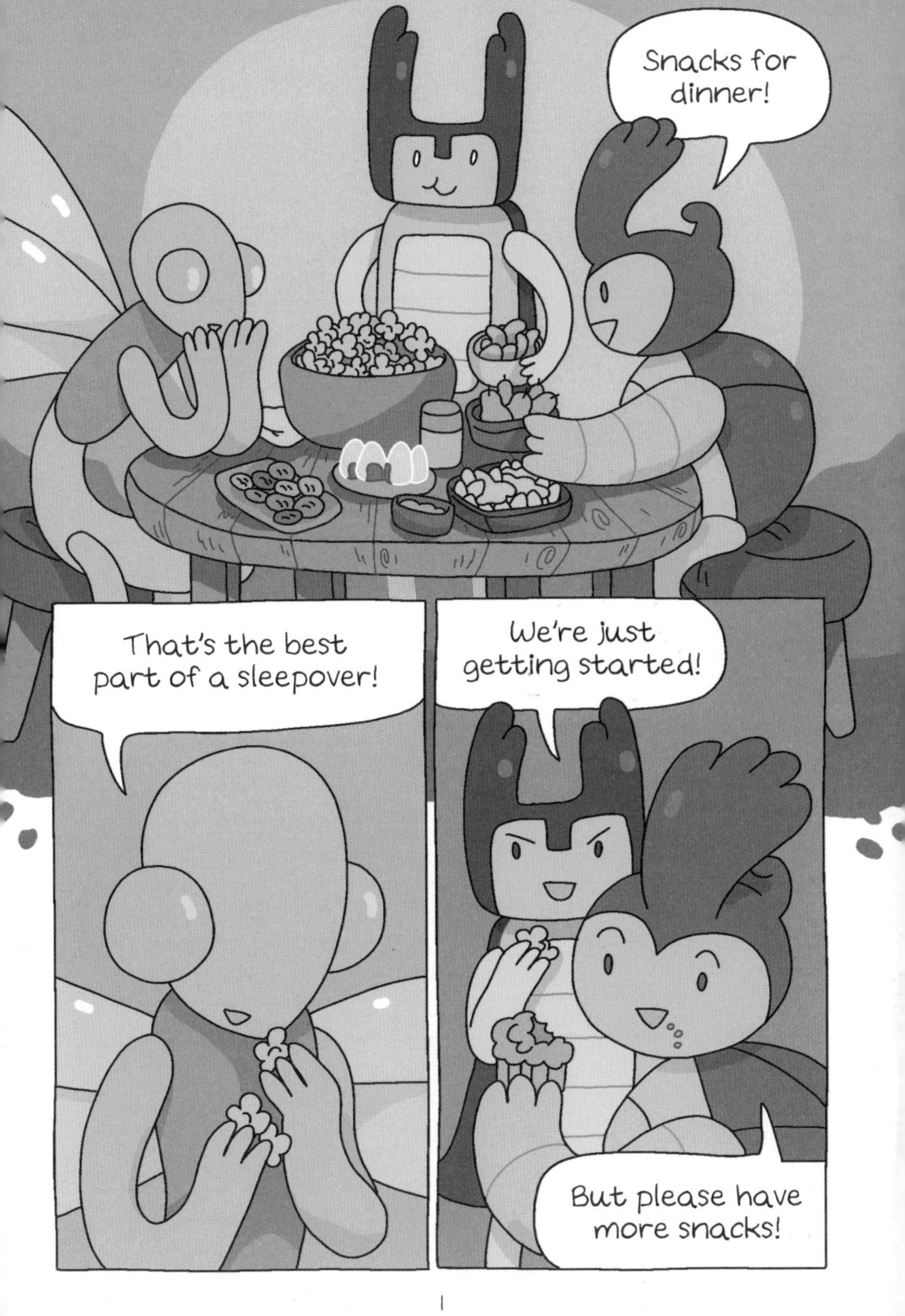
Snacks for dinner!
That's the best part of a sleepover!
We're just getting started!
But please have more snacks!

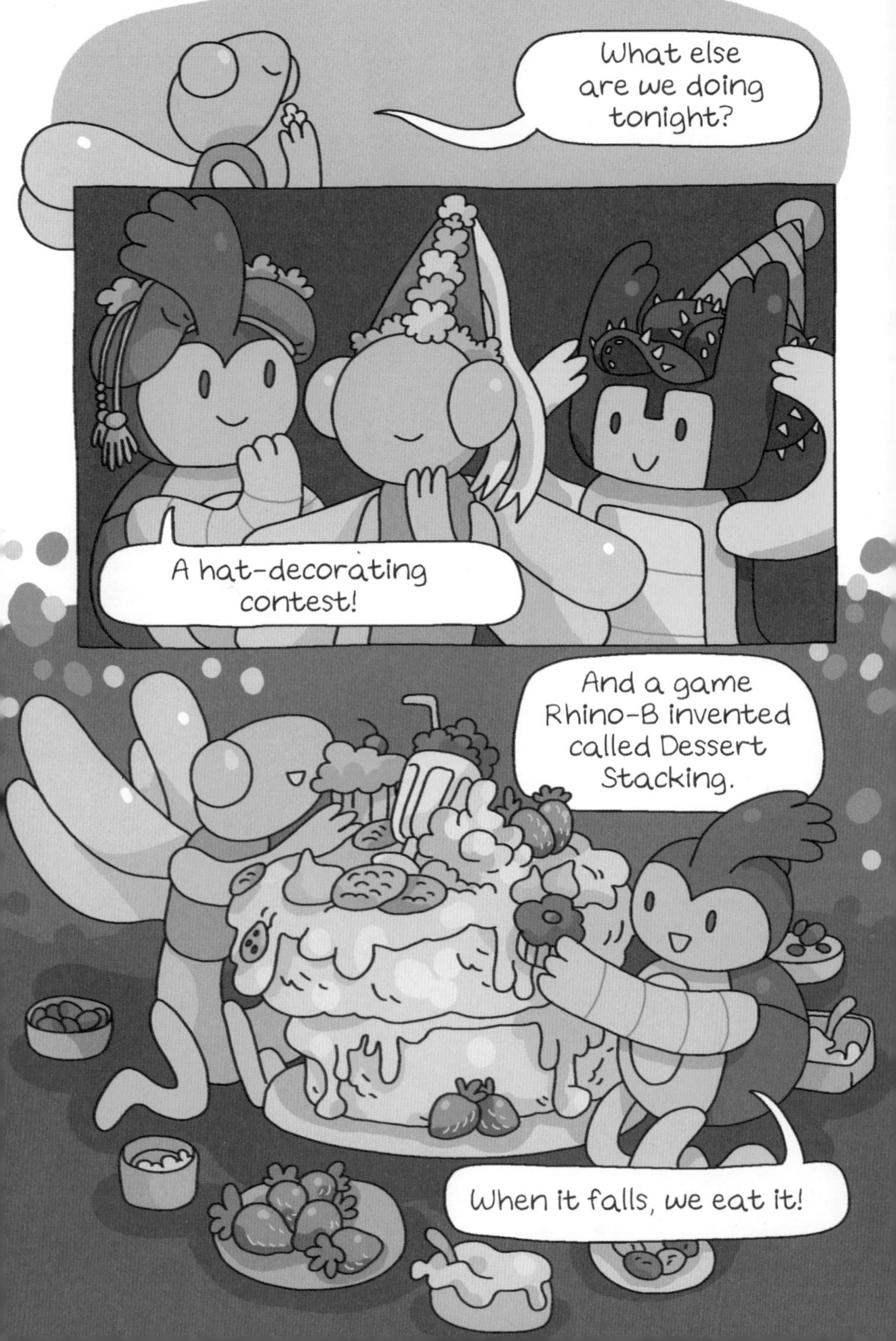
What else are we doing tonight?
A hat-decorating contest!
And a game Rhino-B invented called Dessert Stacking.
When it falls, we eat it!

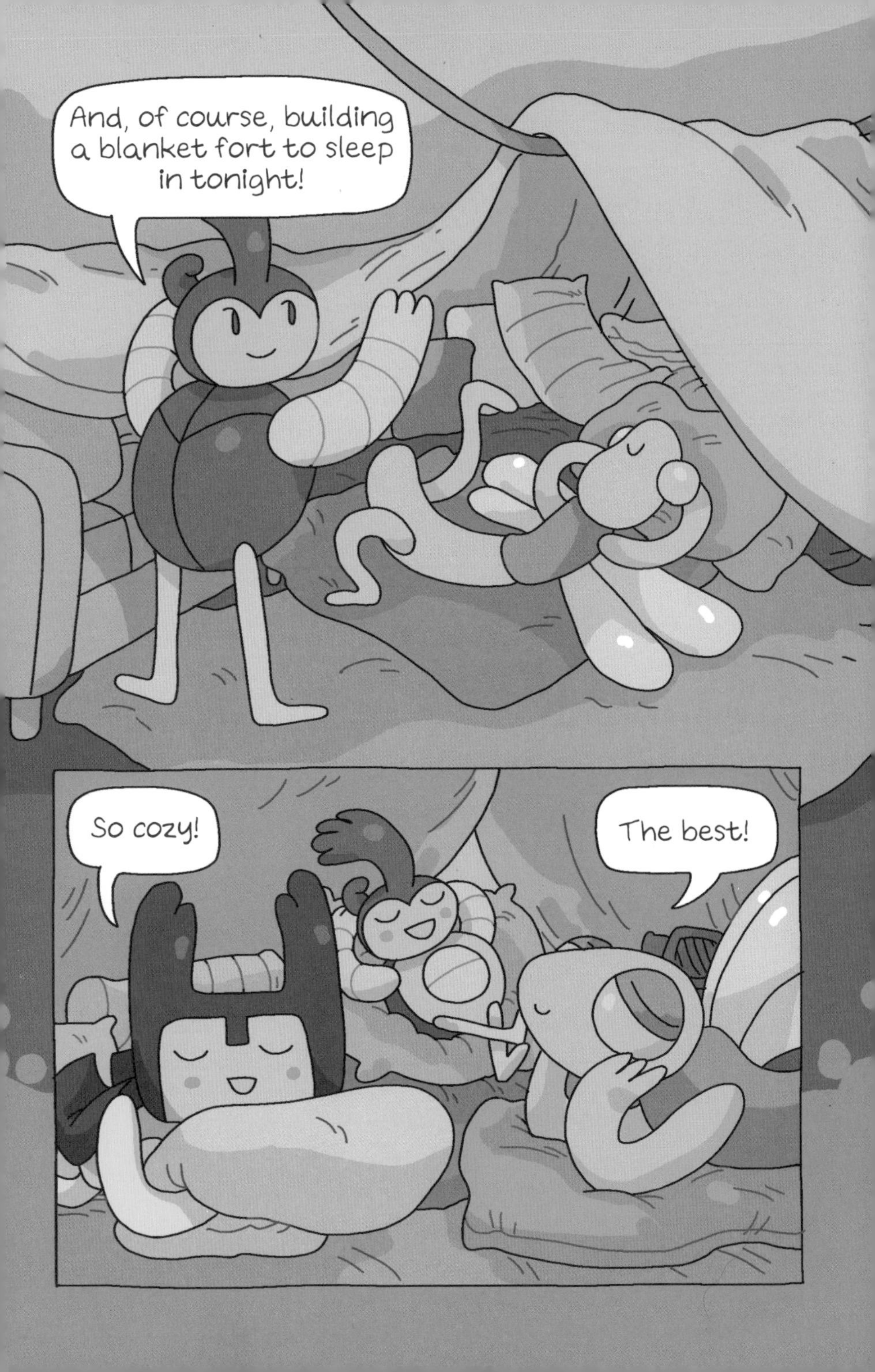
And, of course, building a blanket fort to sleep in tonight!
So cozy!
The best!

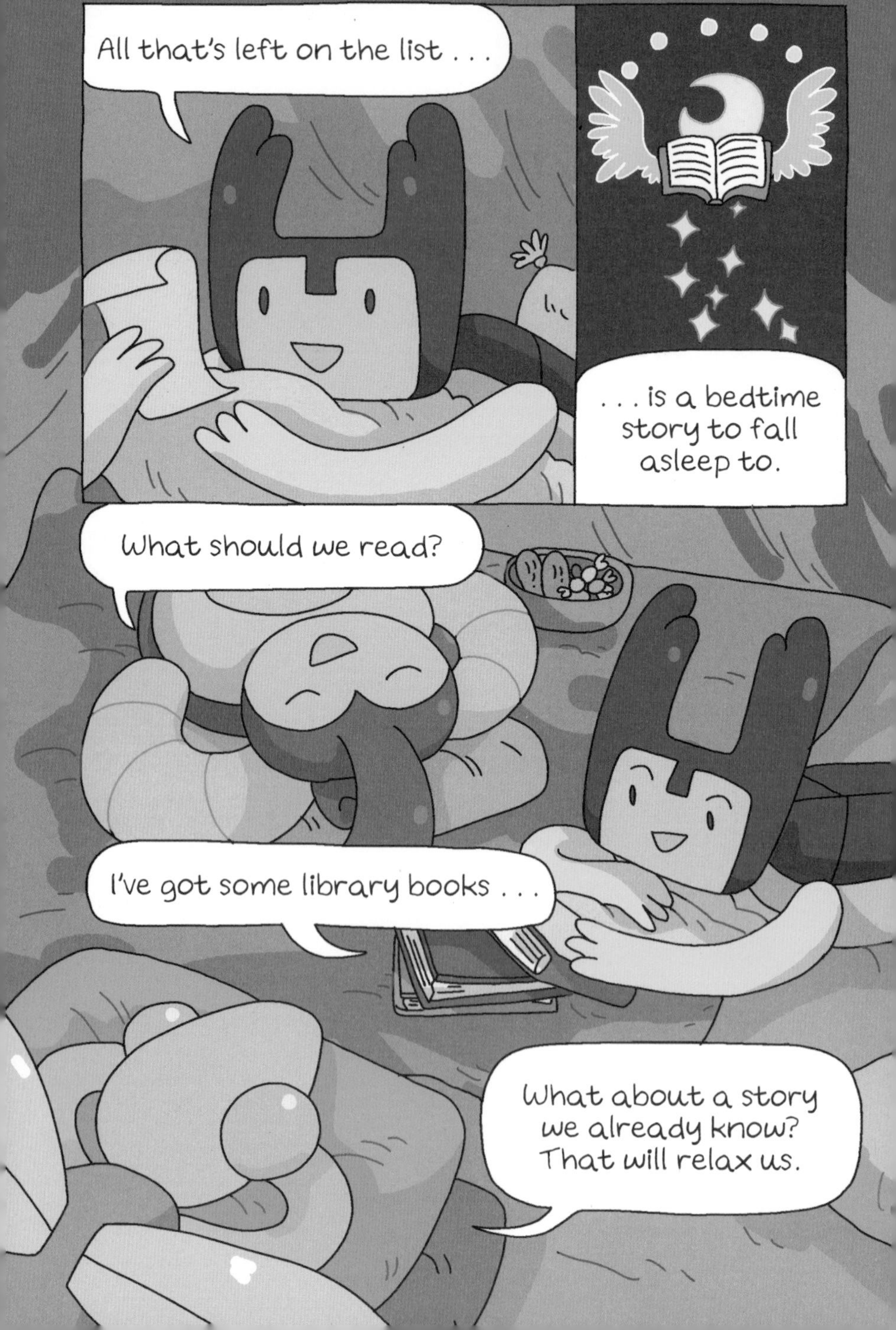
All that's left on the list . . .
. . . is a bedtime story to fall asleep to.
What should we read?
I've got some library books . . .
What about a story we already know? That will relax us.

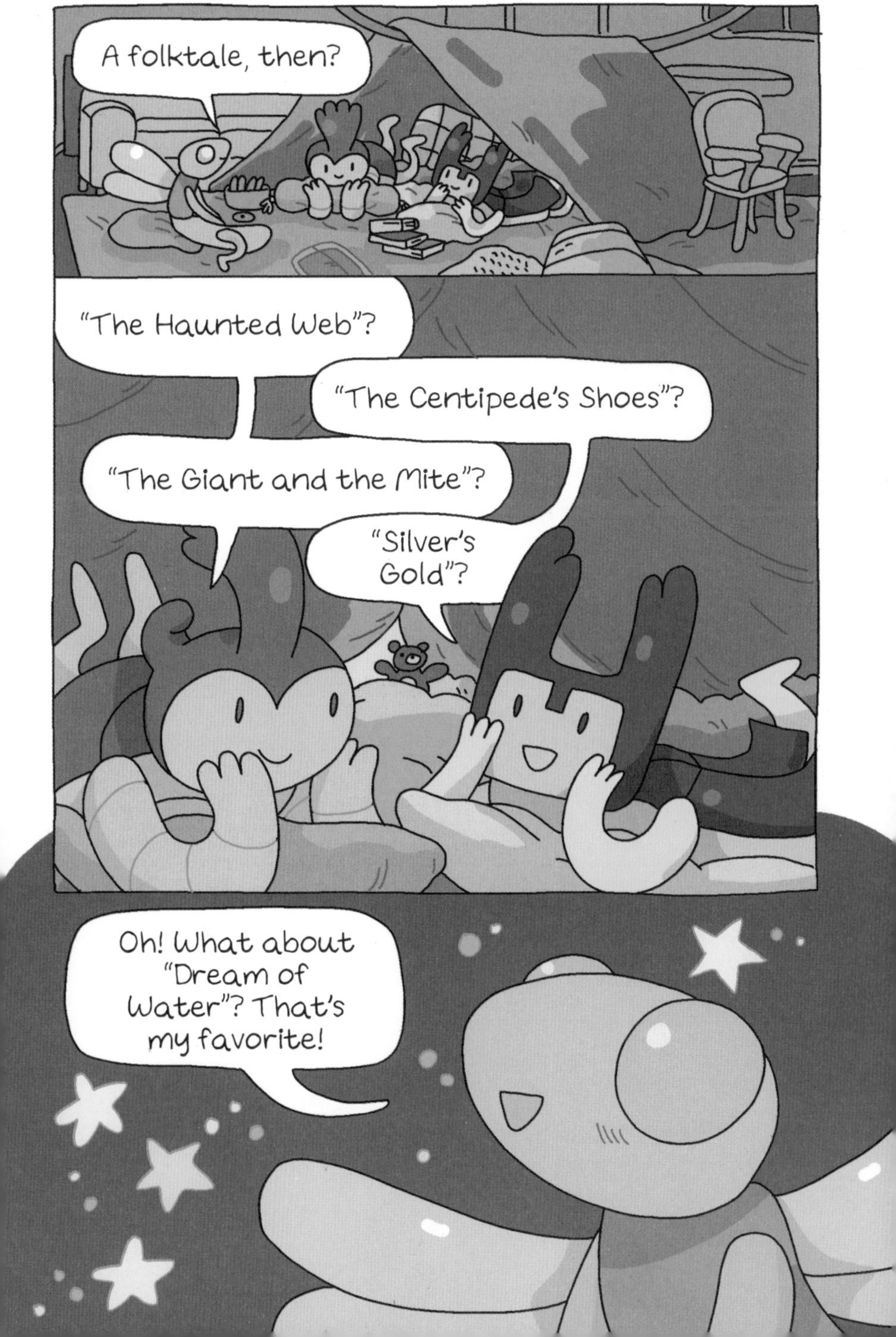
A folktale, then?
"The Haunted Web"?
"The Centipede's Shoes"?
"The Giant and the Mite"?
"Silver's Gold"?
Oh! What about "Dream of Water"? That's my favorite!

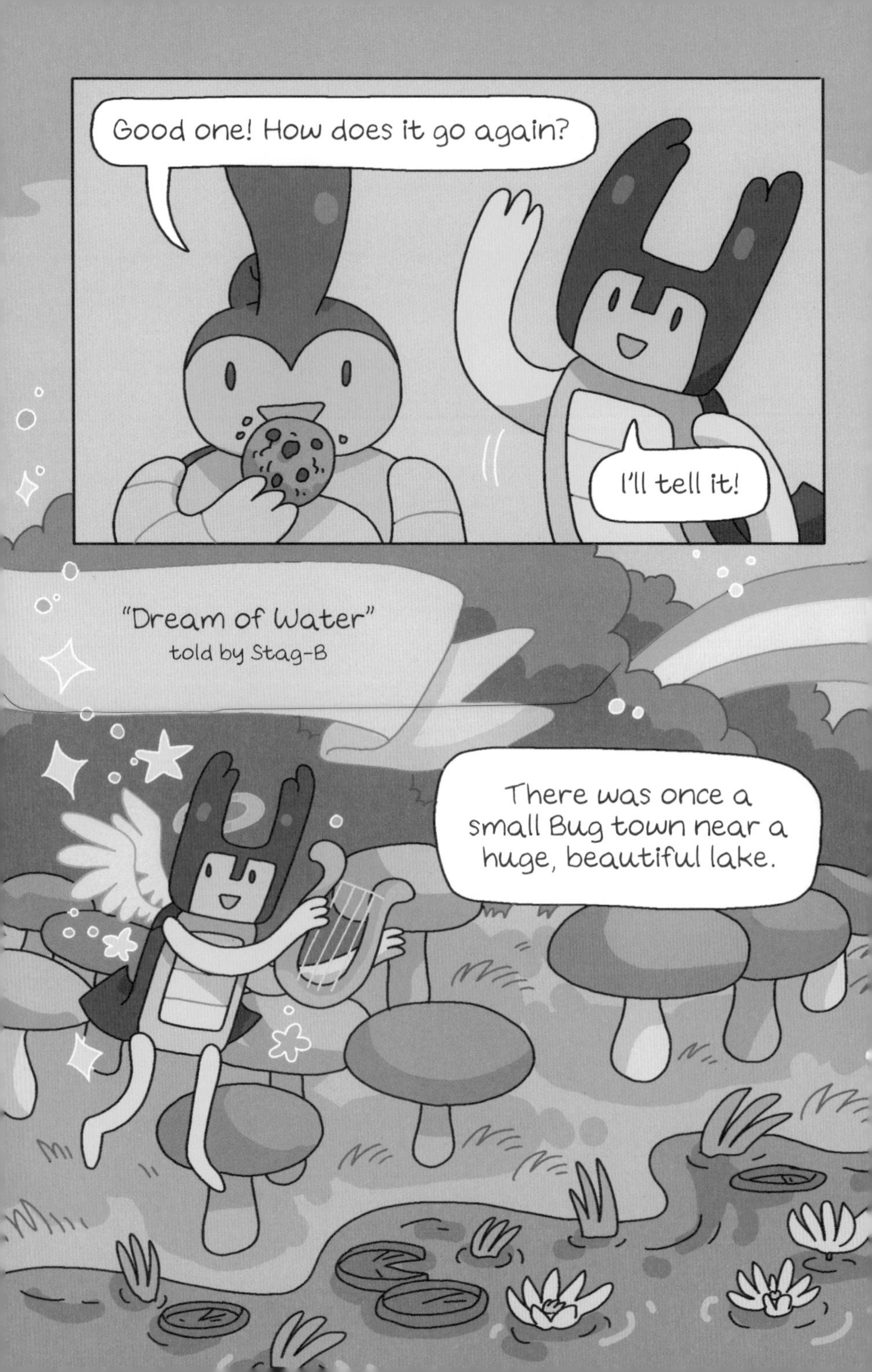
Good one! How does it go again?
I'll tell it!
"Dream of Water"
told by Stag-B
There was once a small Bug town near a huge, beautiful lake.

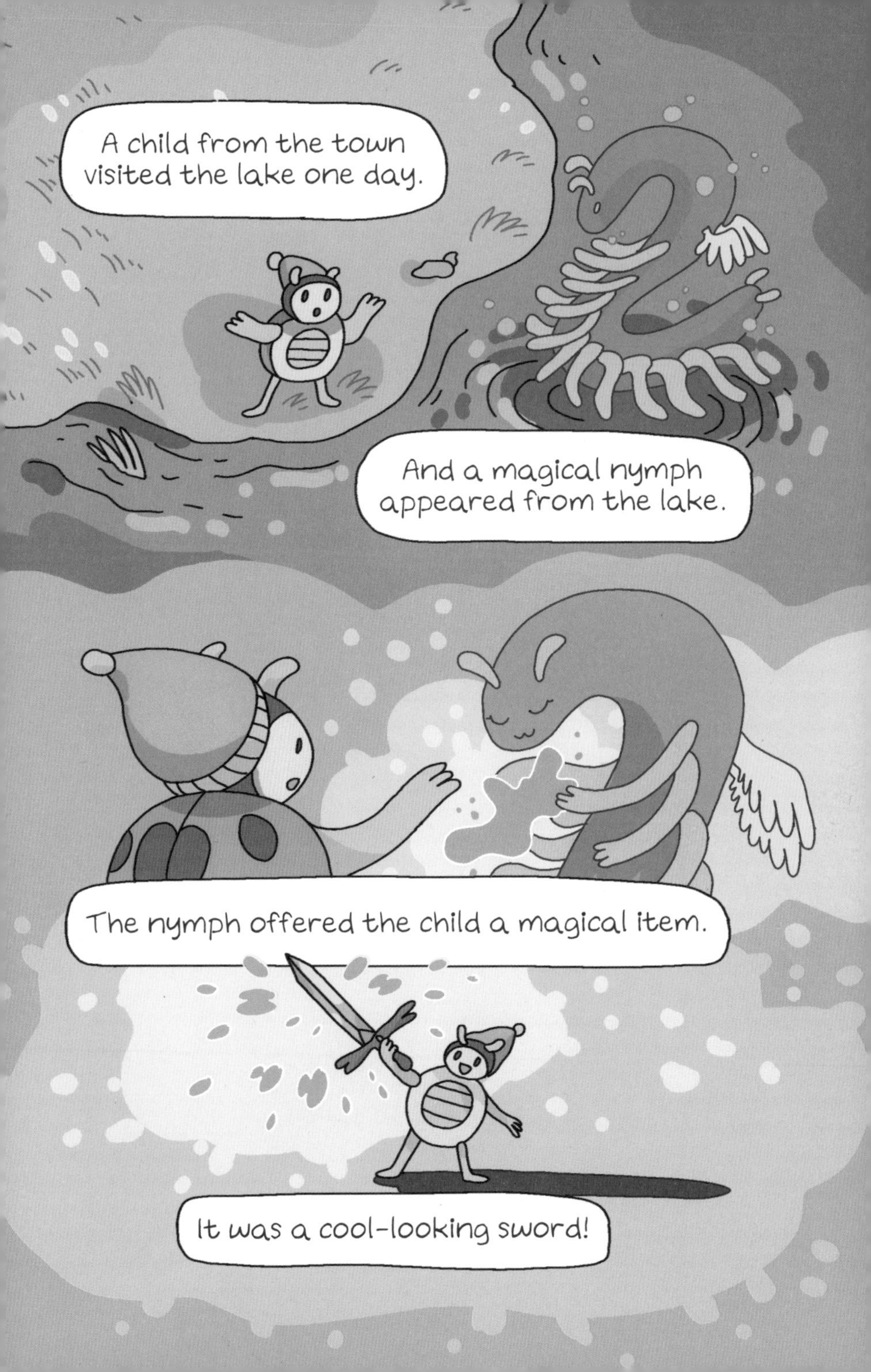
A child from the town visited the lake one day.
And a magical nymph appeared from the lake.
The nymph offered the child a magical item.
It was a cool-looking sword!

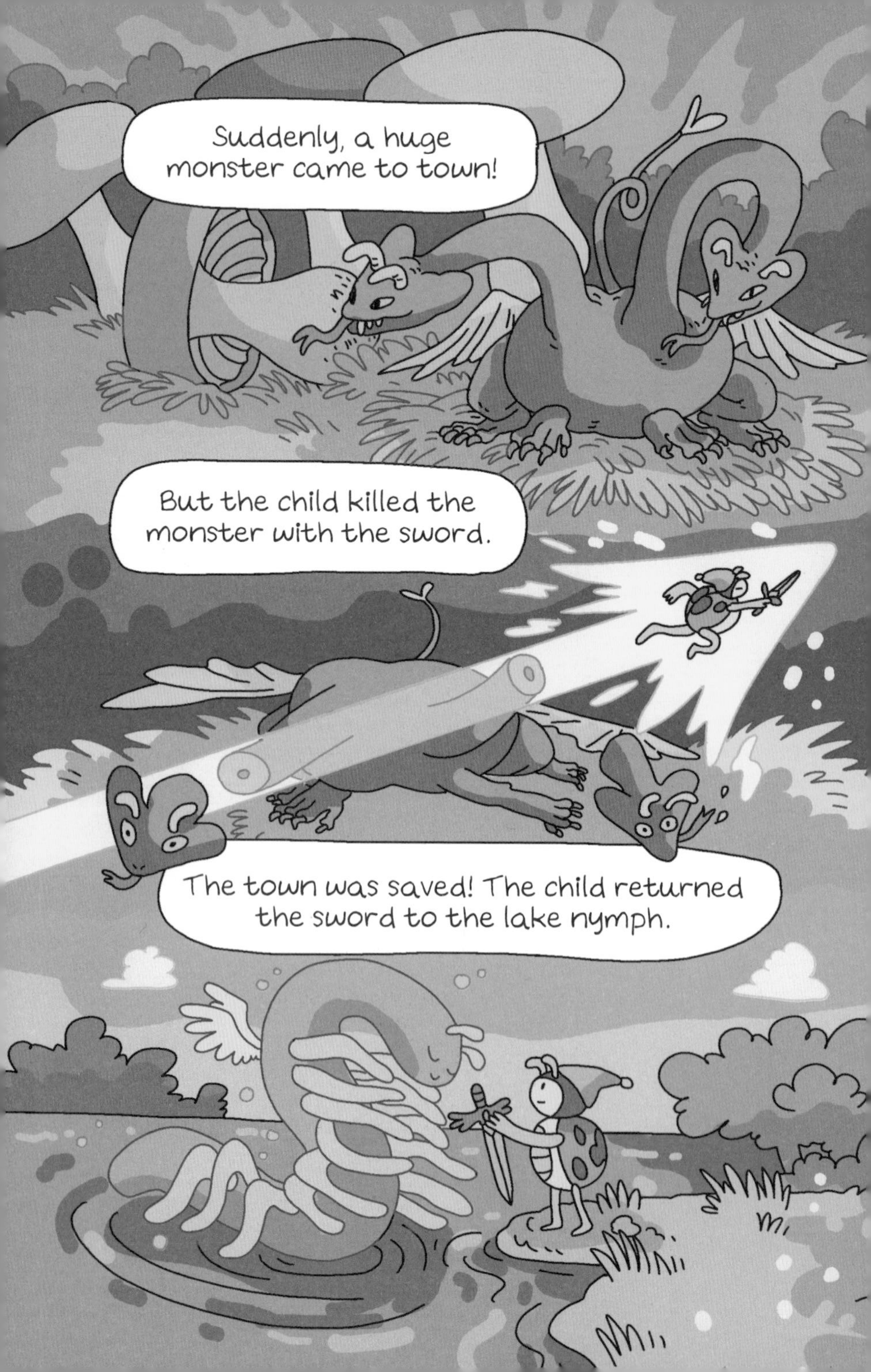
Suddenly, a huge monster came to town!
But the child killed the monster with the sword.
The town was saved! The child returned the sword to the lake nymph.

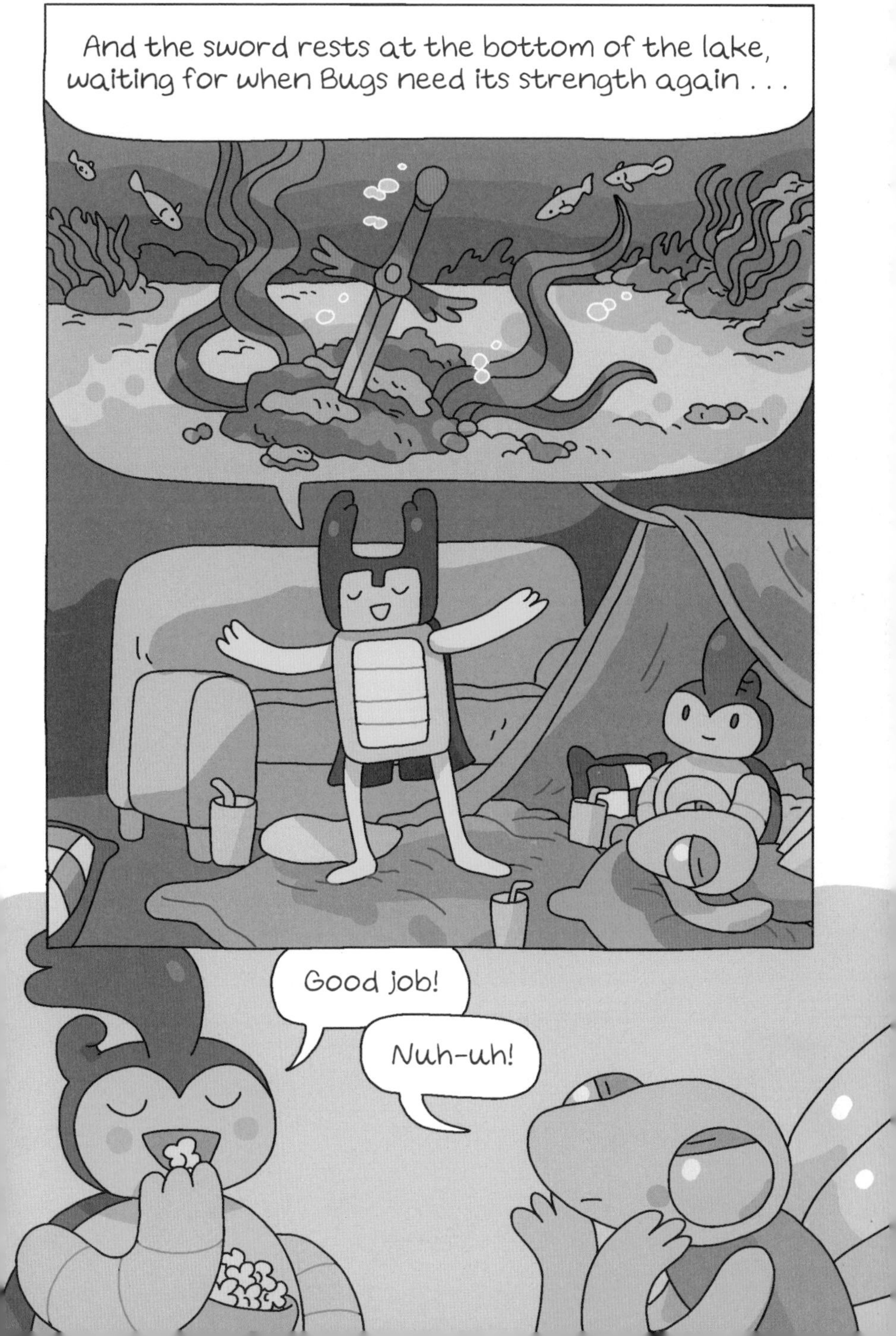
And the sword rests at the bottom of the lake, waiting for when Bugs need its strength again . . .
Good job!
Nuh-uh!

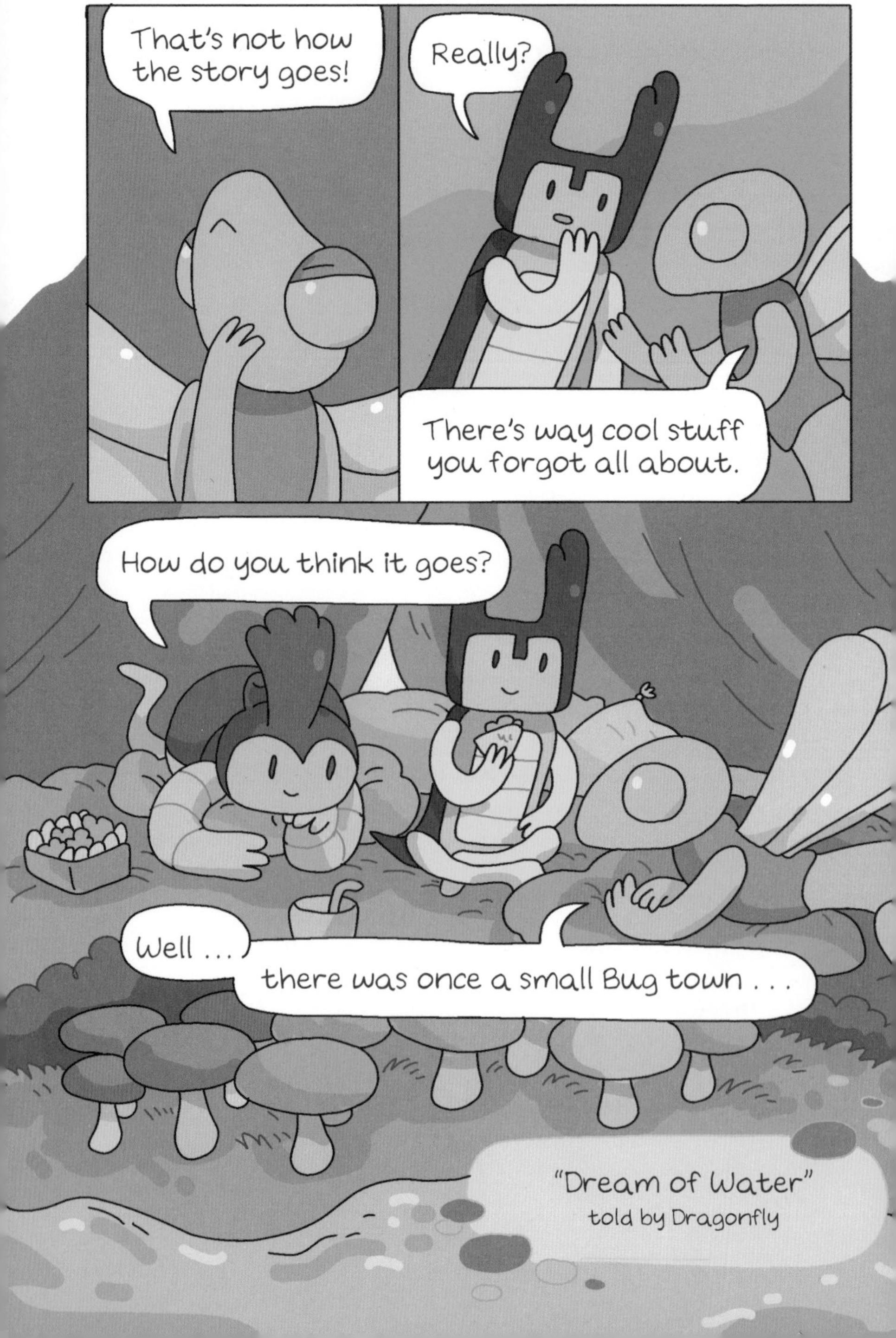
That's not how the story goes!
Really?
There's way cool stuff you forgot all about.
How do you think it goes?
Well . . .
there was once a small Bug town . . .
"Dream of Water"
told by Dragonfly

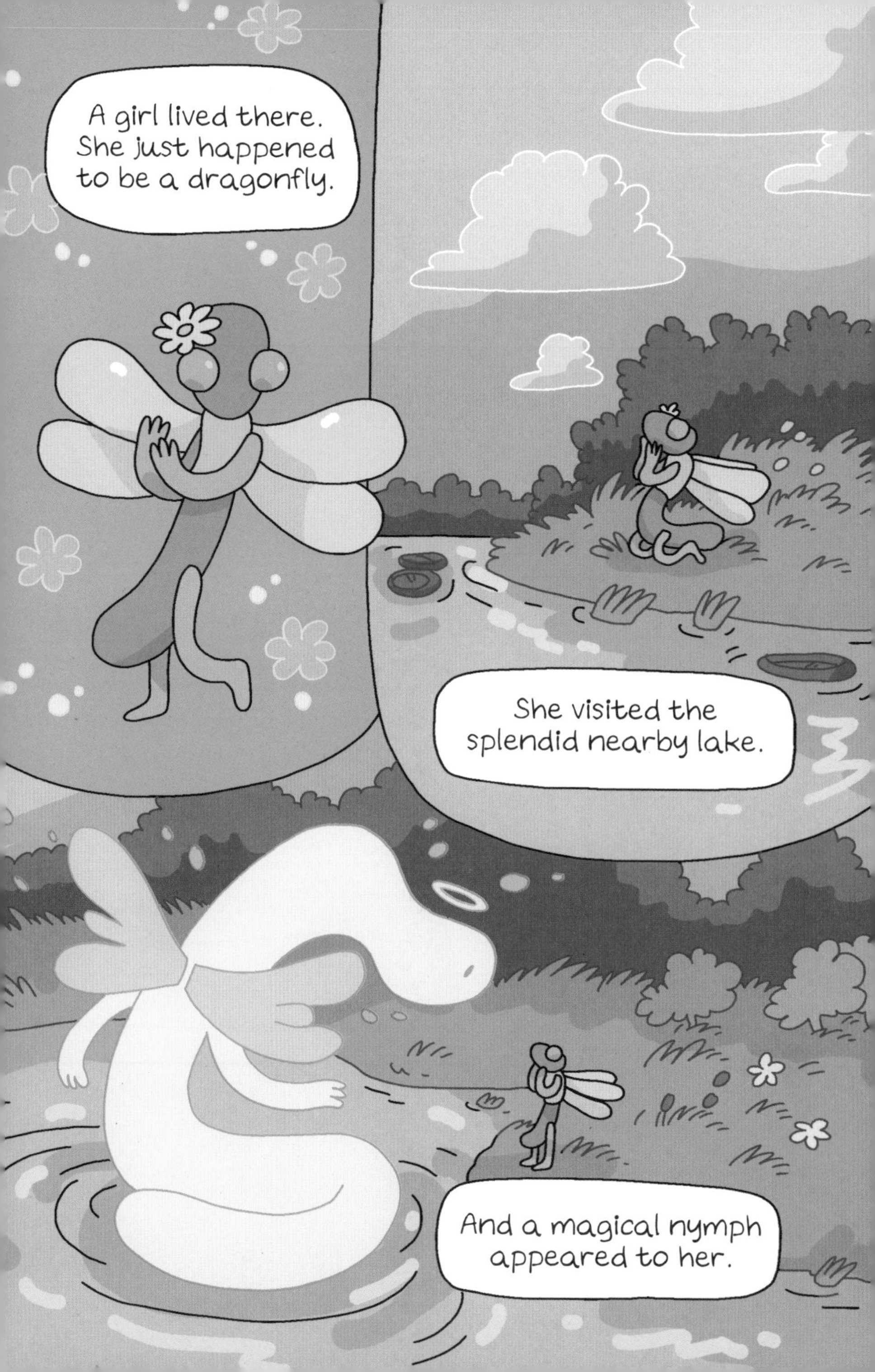
A girl lived there. She just happened to be a dragonfly.
She visited the splendid nearby lake.
And a magical nymph appeared to her.

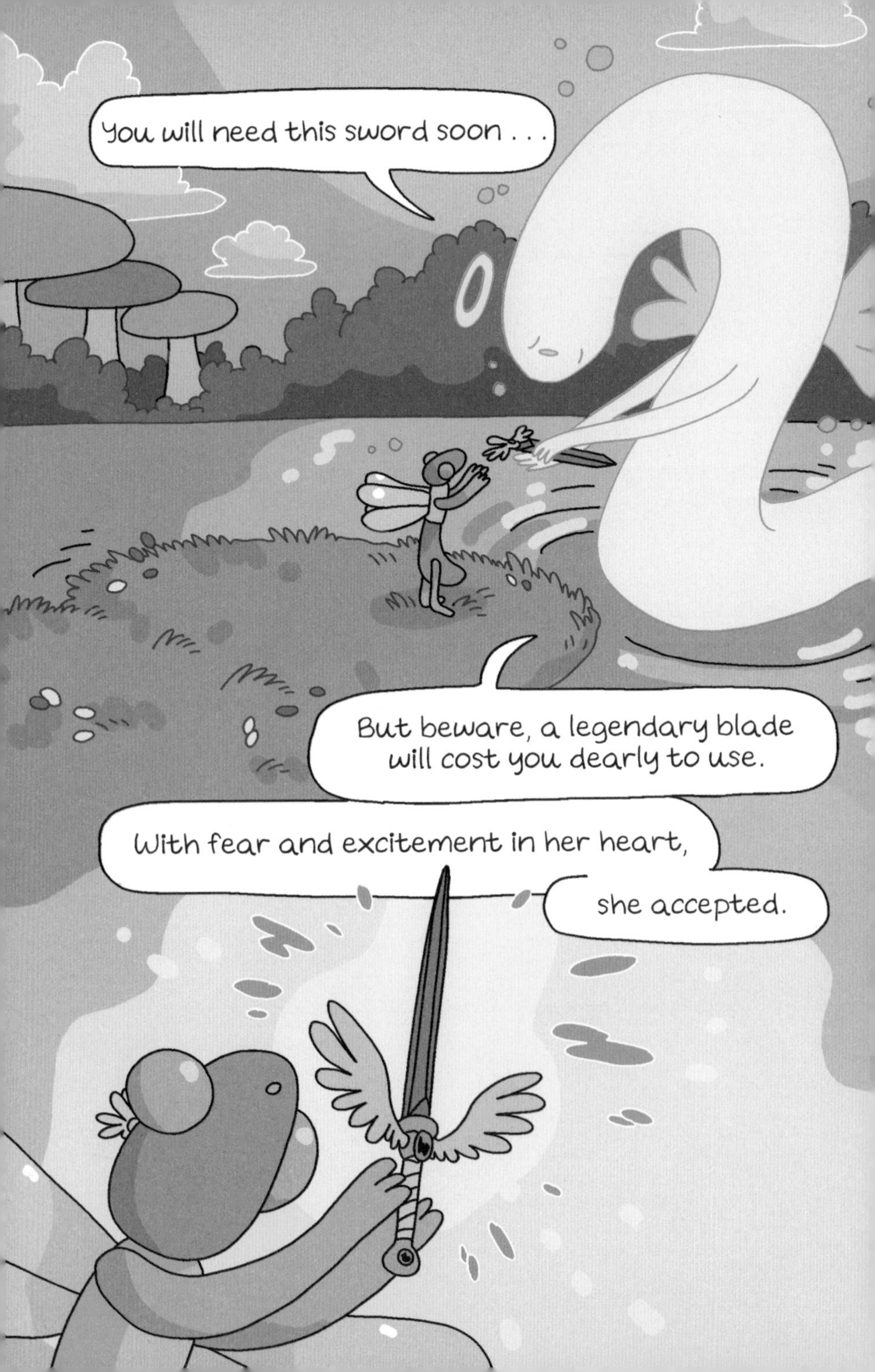
You will need this sword soon . . .
But beware, a legendary blade will cost you dearly to use.
With fear and excitement in her heart,
she accepted.

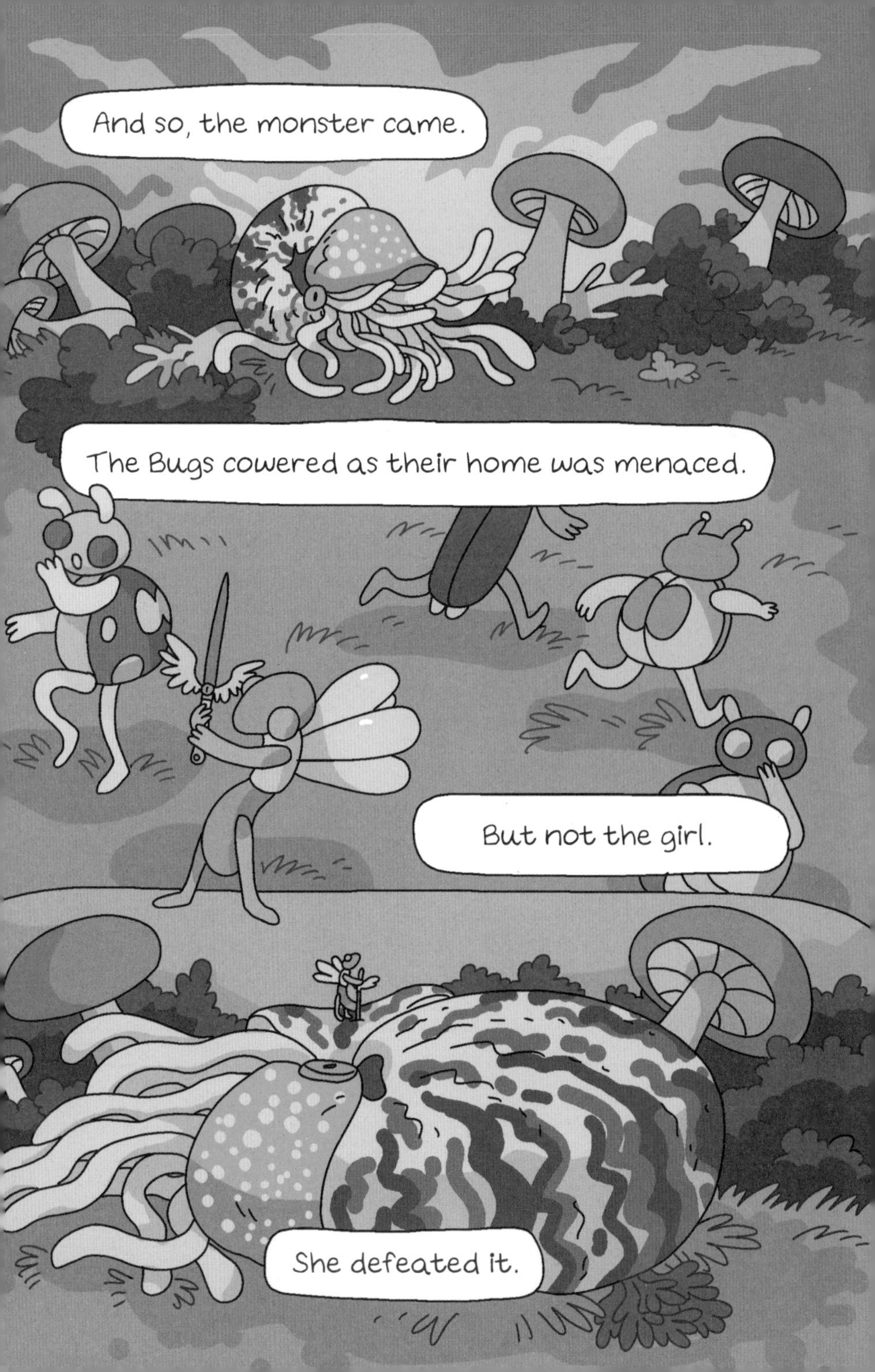
And so, the monster came.
The Bugs cowered as their home was menaced.
But not the girl.
She defeated it.

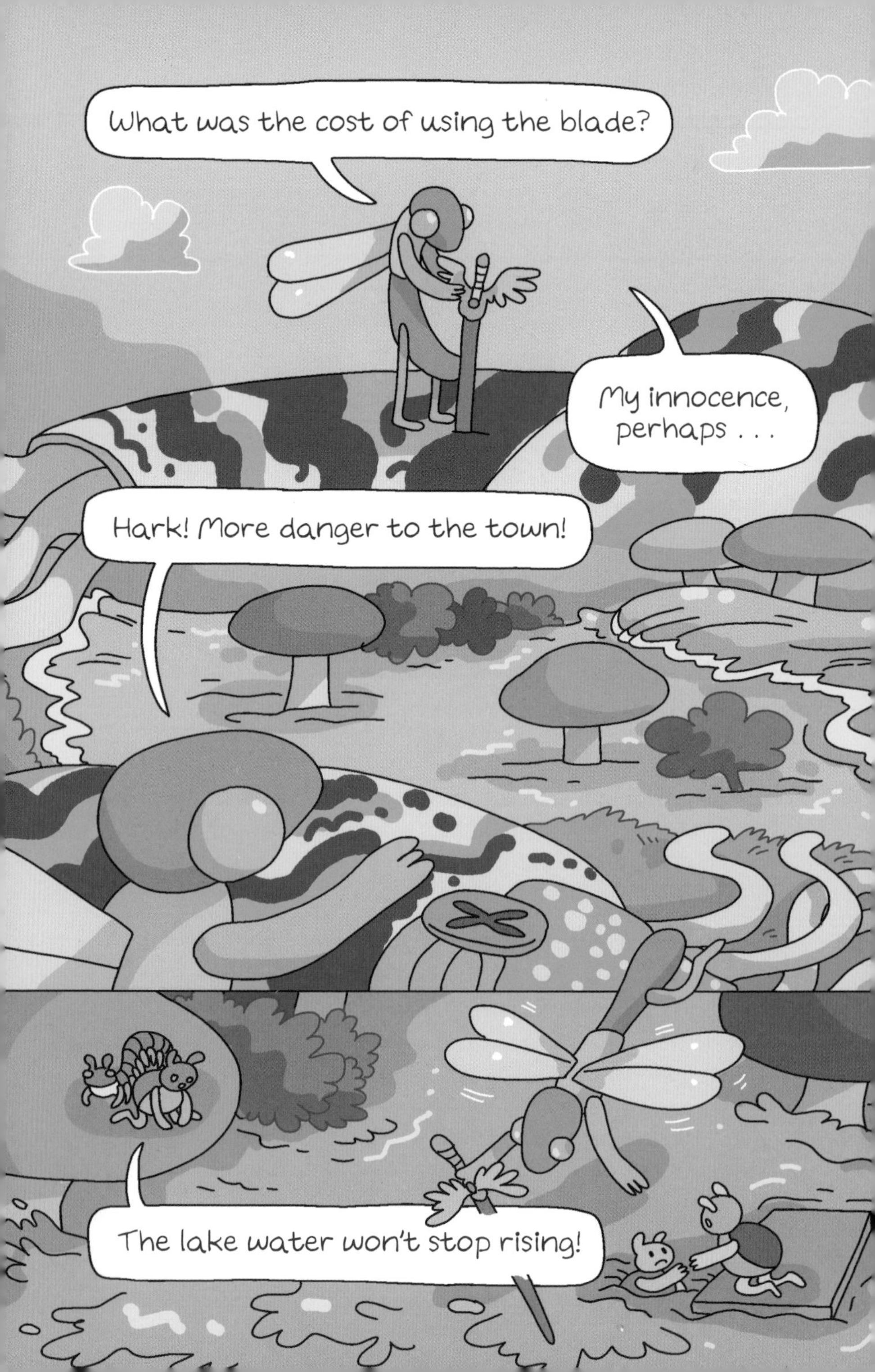
What was the cost of using the blade?
My innocence, perhaps . . .
Hark! More danger to the town!
The lake water won't stop rising!

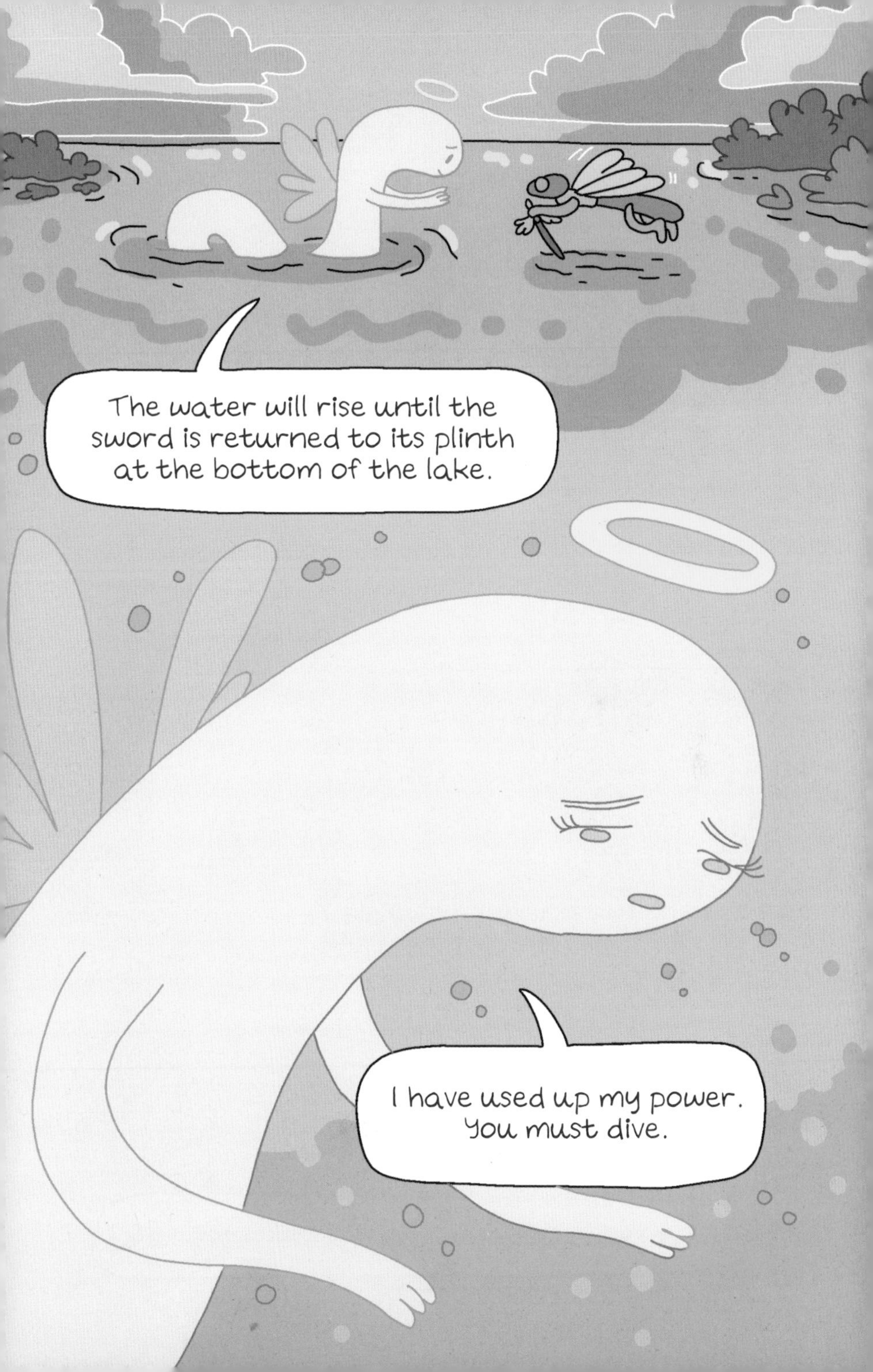
The water will rise until the sword is returned to its plinth at the bottom of the lake.
I have used up my power. You must dive.

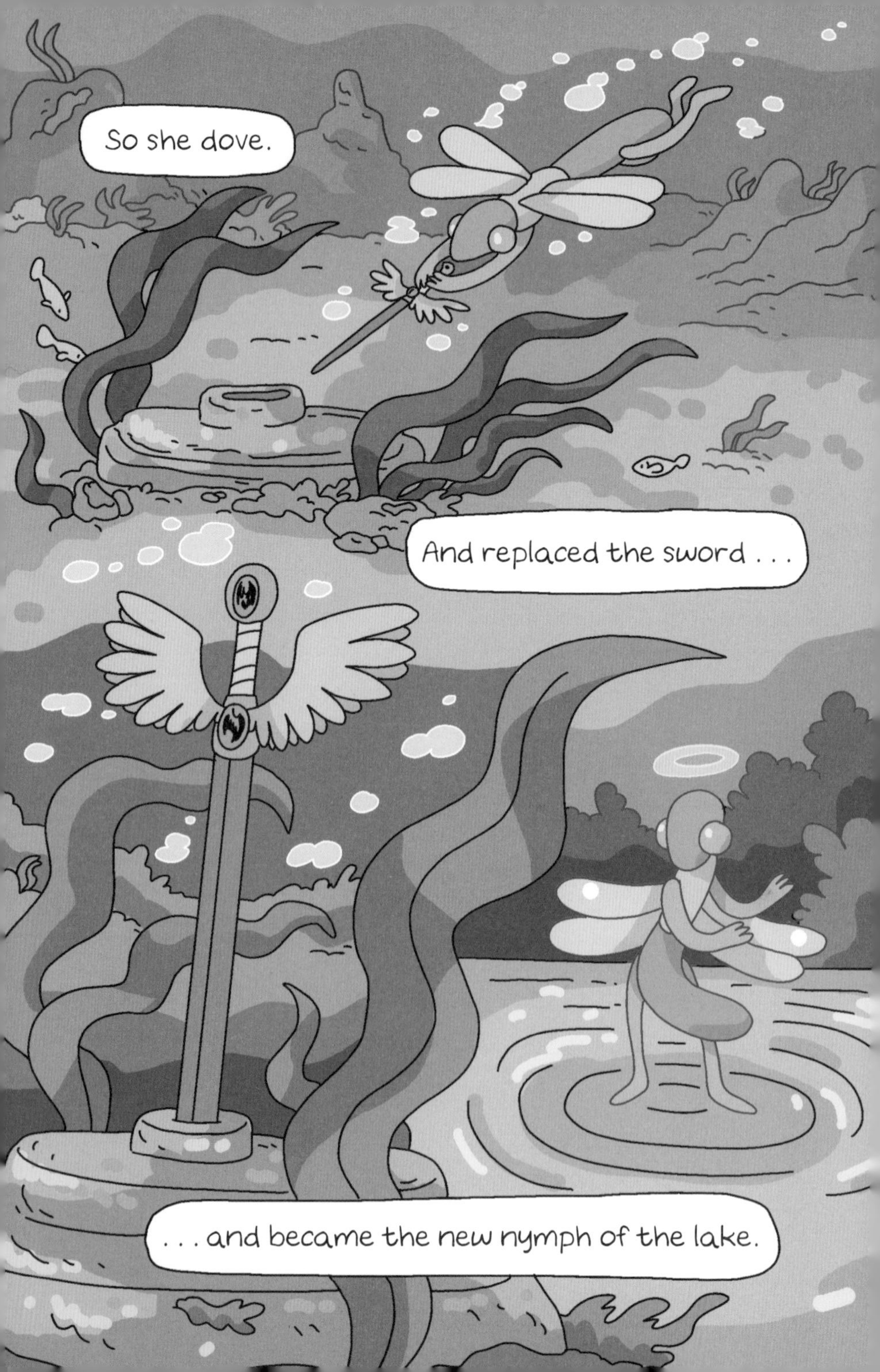
So she dove.
And replaced the sword . . .
. . . and became the new nymph of the lake.

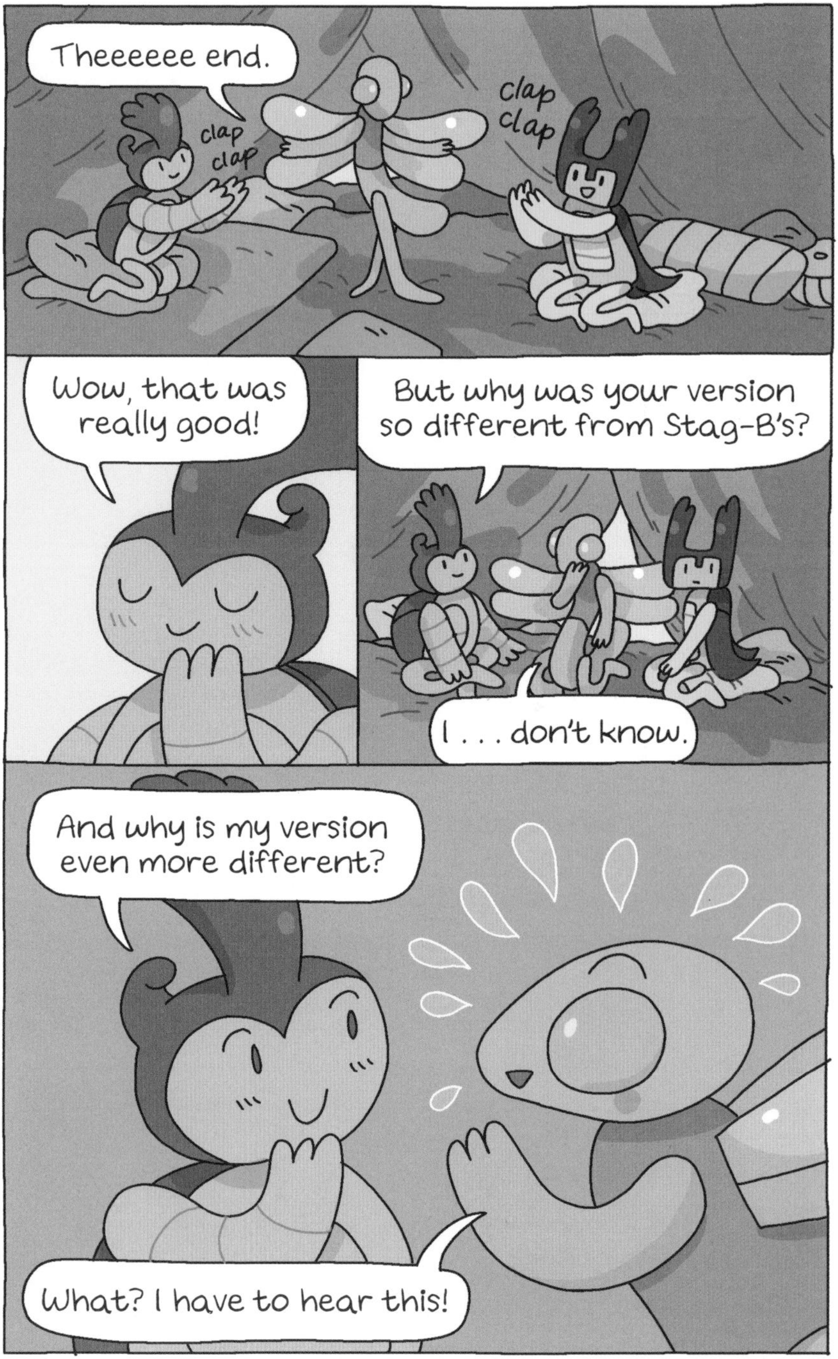
Theeeeee end.
clap clap
clap clap
Wow, that was really good!
But why was your version so different from Stag-B's?
I . . . don't know.
And why is my version even more different?
What? I have to hear this!

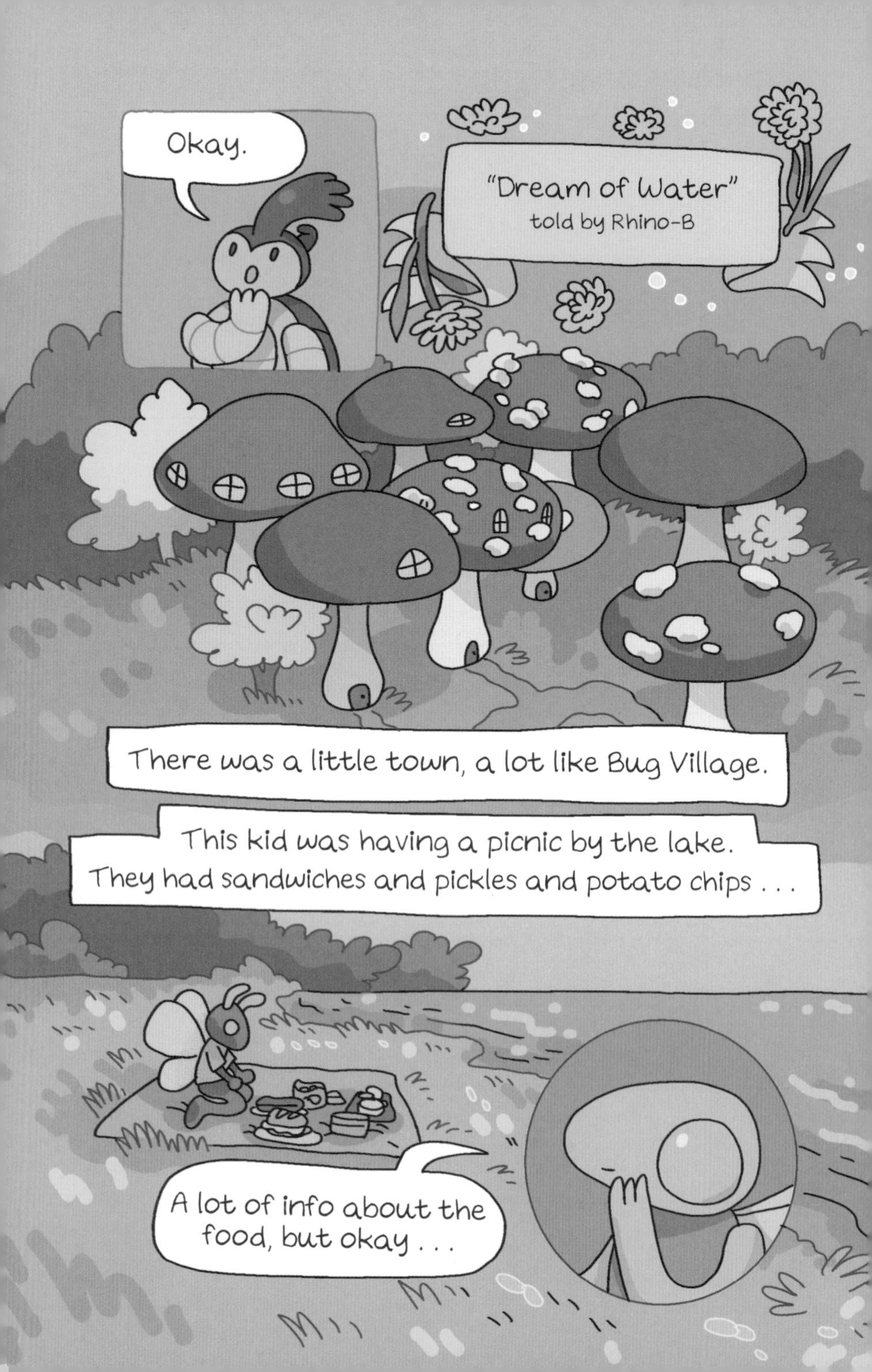
Okay.
"Dream of Water"
told by Rhino-B
There was a little town, a lot like Bug Village.
This kid was having a picnic by the lake.
They had sandwiches and pickles and potato chips . . .
A lot of info about the food, but okay . . .

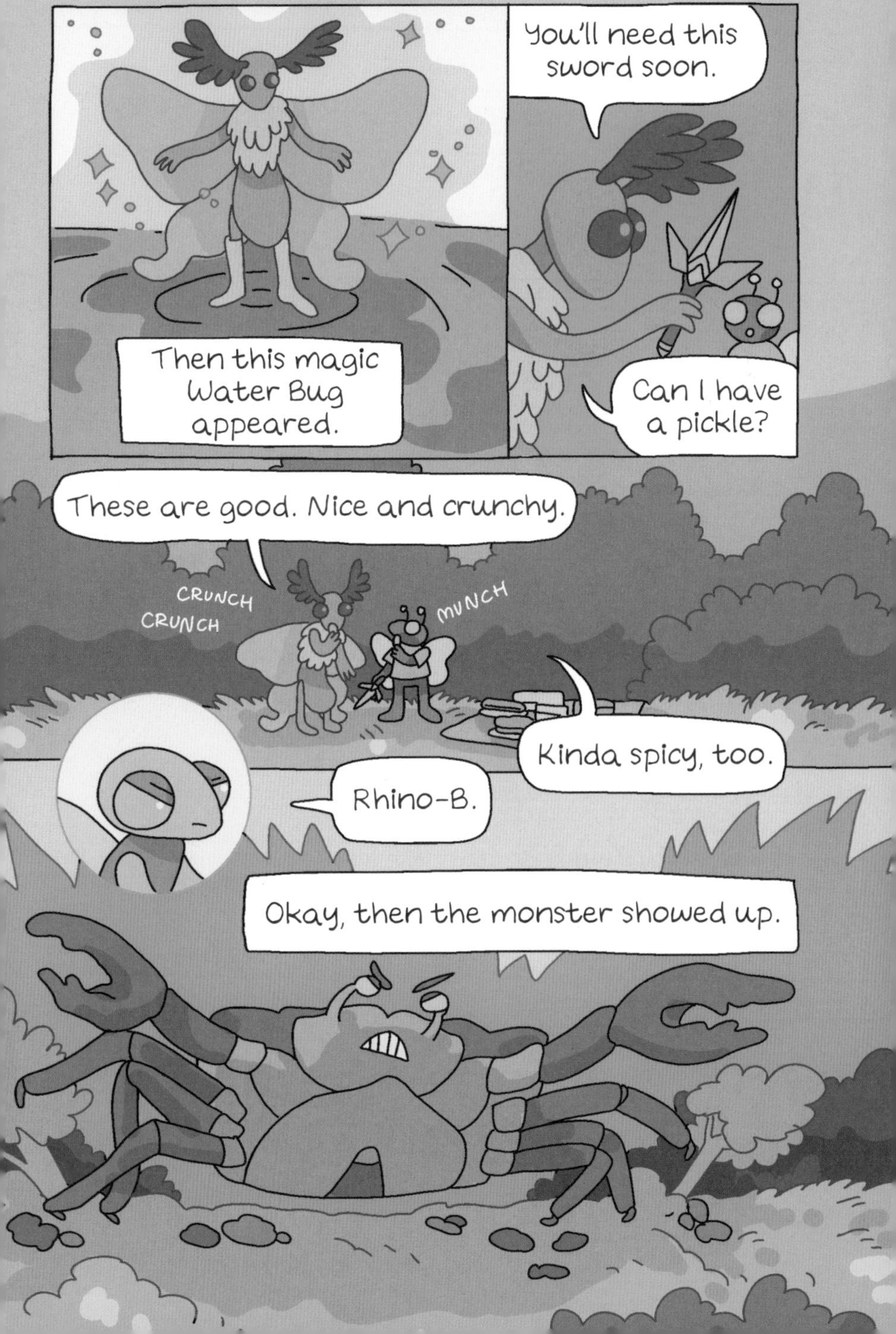
Then this magic Water Bug appeared.
You'll need this sword soon.
Can I have a pickle?
These are good. Nice and crunchy.
CRUNCH
CRUNCH
MUNCH
Kinda spicy, too.
Rhino-B.
Okay, then the monster showed up.

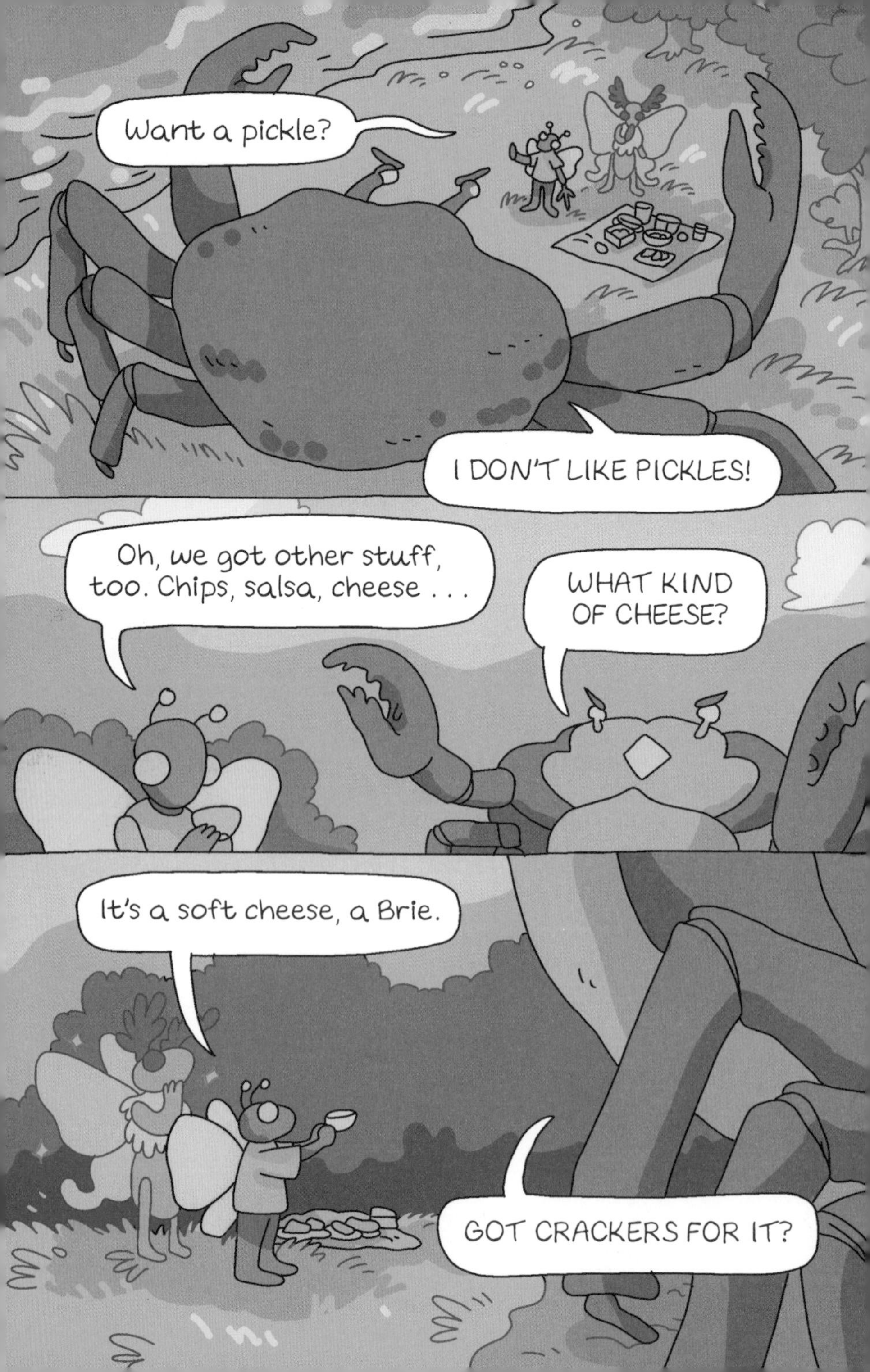
Want a pickle?
I DON'T LIKE PICKLES!
Oh, we got other stuff, too. Chips, salsa, cheese . . .
WHAT KIND OF CHEESE?
It's a soft cheese, a Brie.
GOT CRACKERS FOR IT?

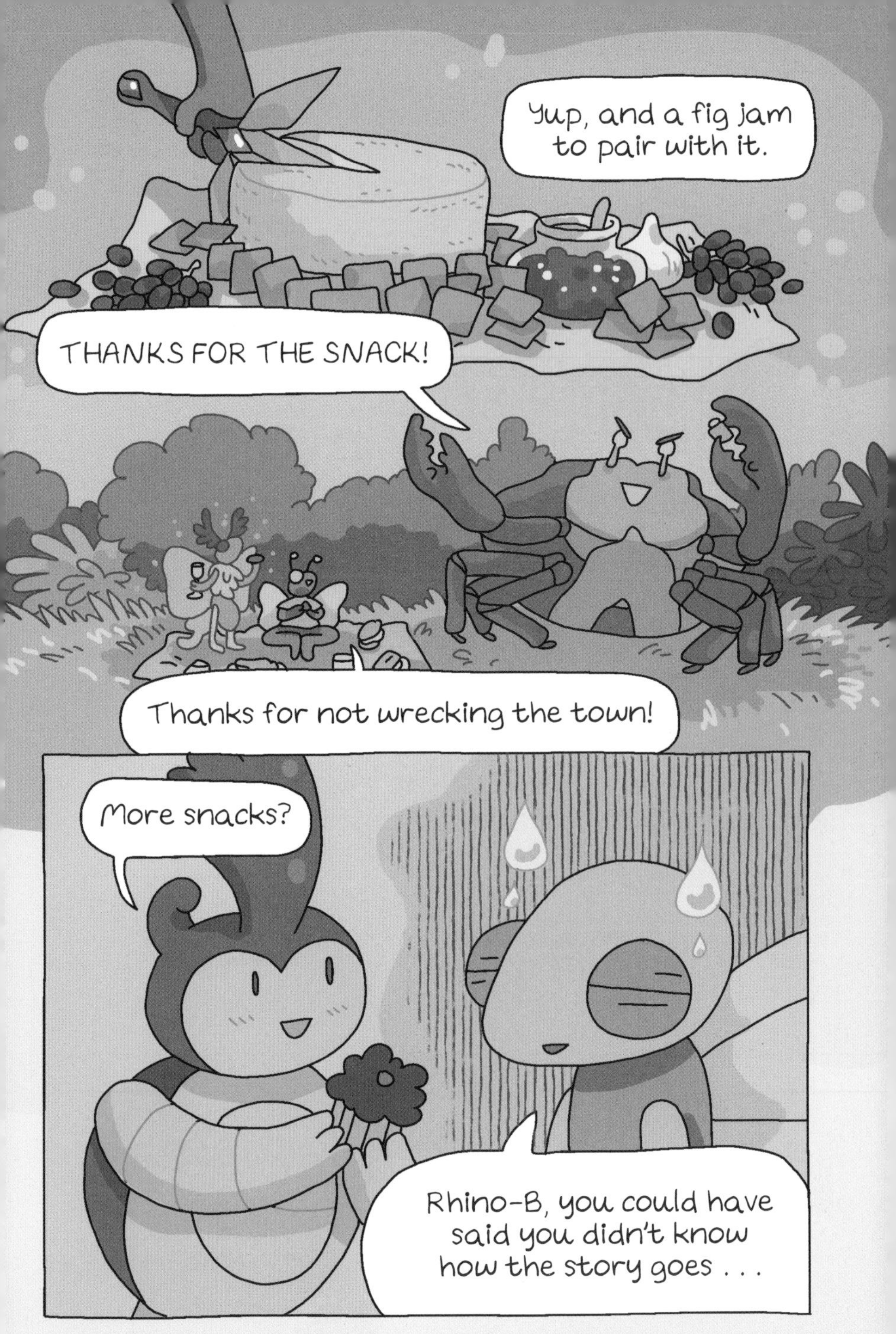

Yup, and a fig jam to pair with it.
THANKS FOR THE SNACK!
Thanks for not wrecking the town!
More snacks?
Rhino-B, you could have said you didn't know how the story goes . . .

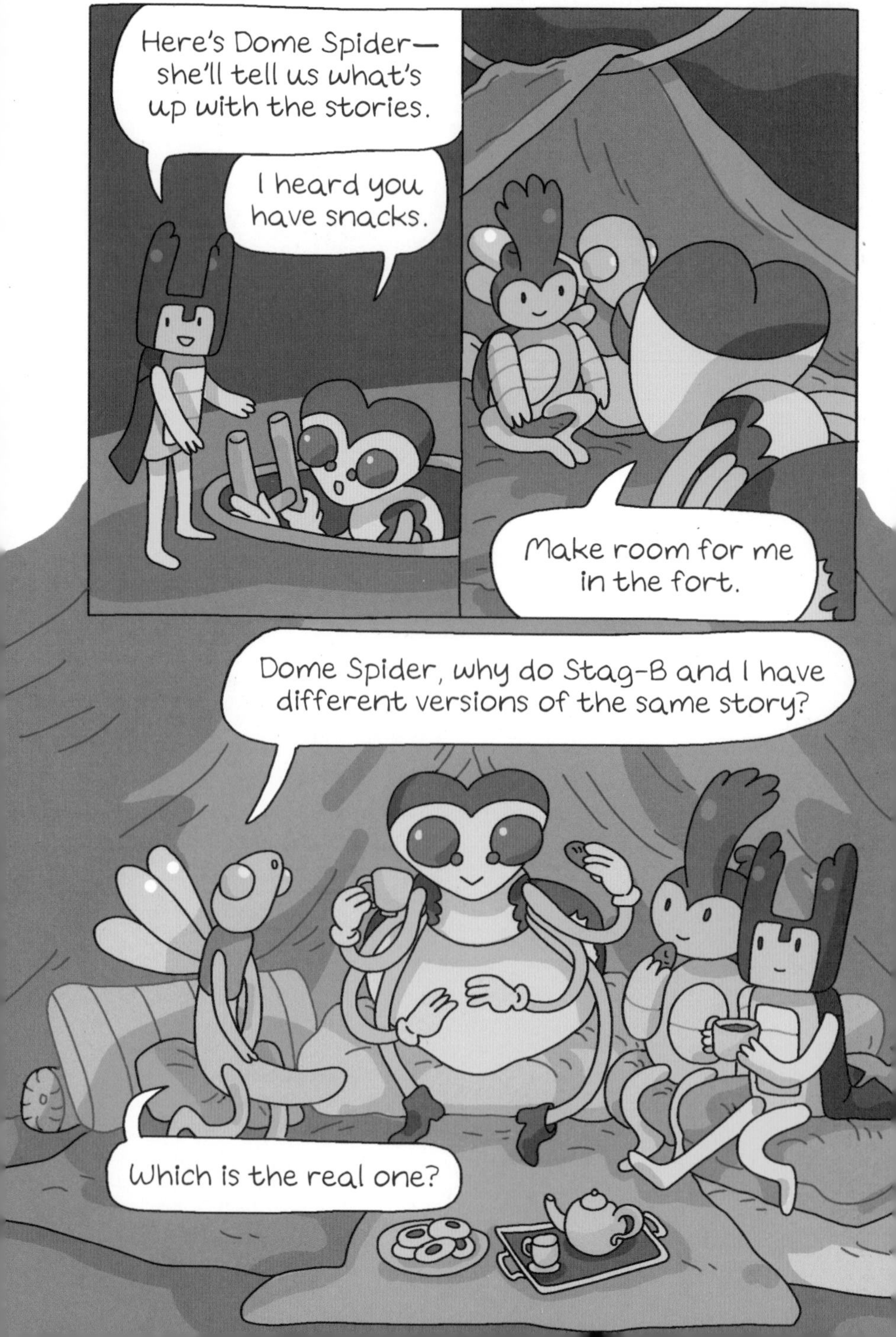
Here's Dome Spider—she'll tell us what's up with the stories.
I heard you have snacks.
Make room for me in the fort.
Dome Spider, why do Stag-B and I have different versions of the same story?
Which is the real one?

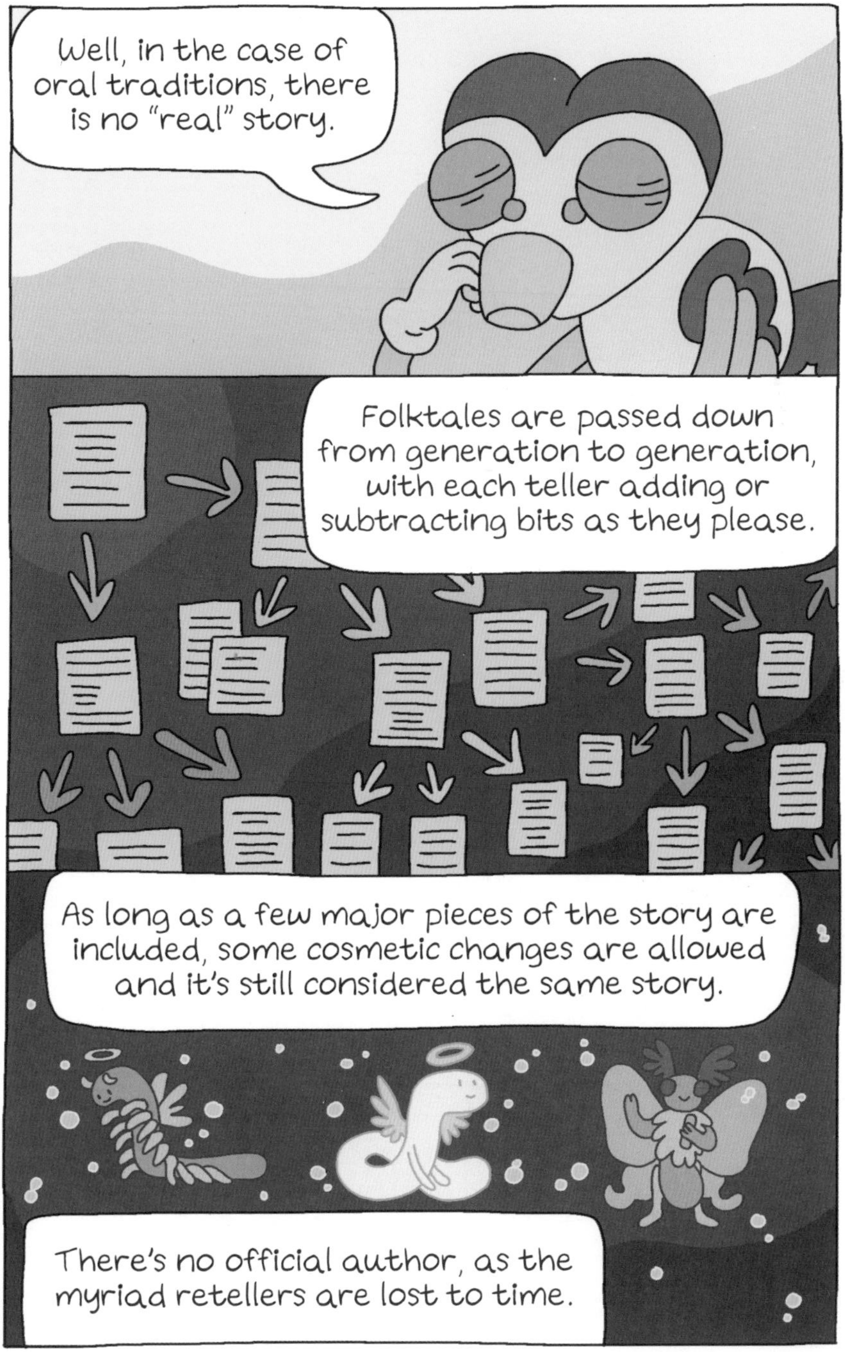
Well, in the case of oral traditions, there is no "real" story.
Folktales are passed down from generation to generation, with each teller adding or subtracting bits as they please.
As long as a few major pieces of the story are included, some cosmetic changes are allowed and it's still considered the same story.
There's no official author, as the myriad retellers are lost to time.

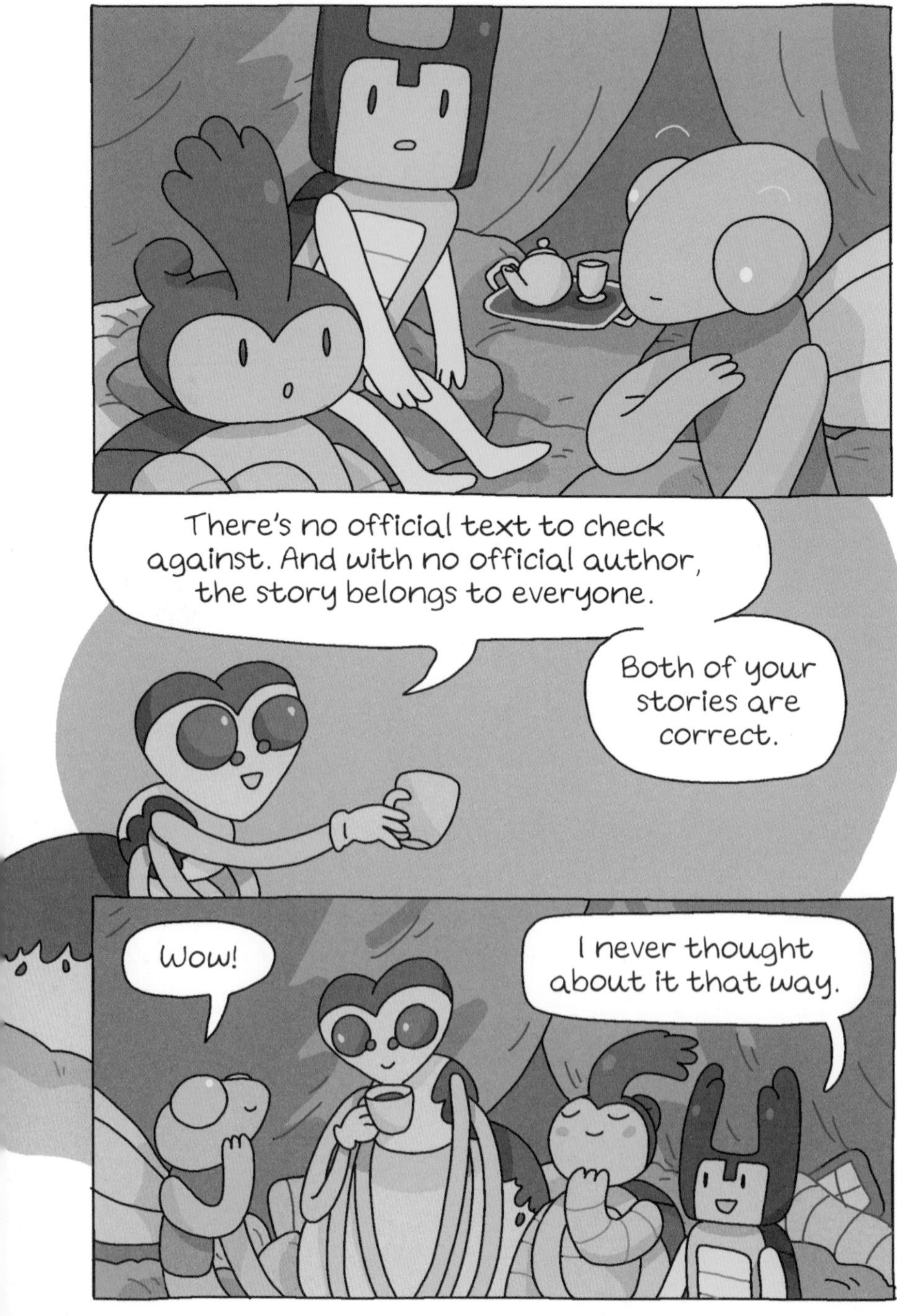
There's no official text to check against. And with no official author, the story belongs to everyone.
Both of your stories are correct.
Wow!
I never thought about it that way.

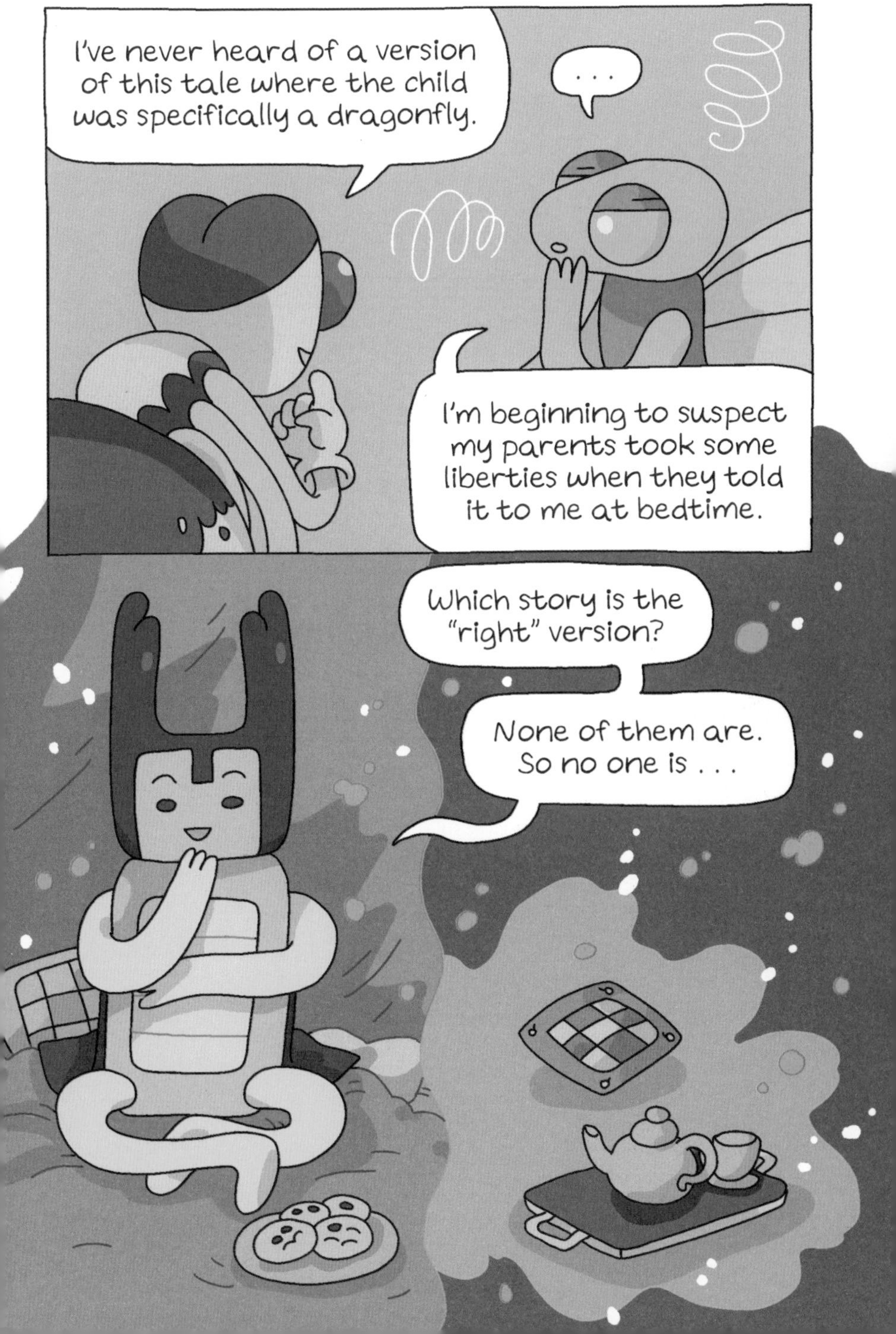
I've never heard of a version of this tale where the child was specifically a dragonfly.
. . .
I'm beginning to suspect my parents took some liberties when they told it to me at bedtime.
Which story is the "right" version?
None of them are. So no one is . . .

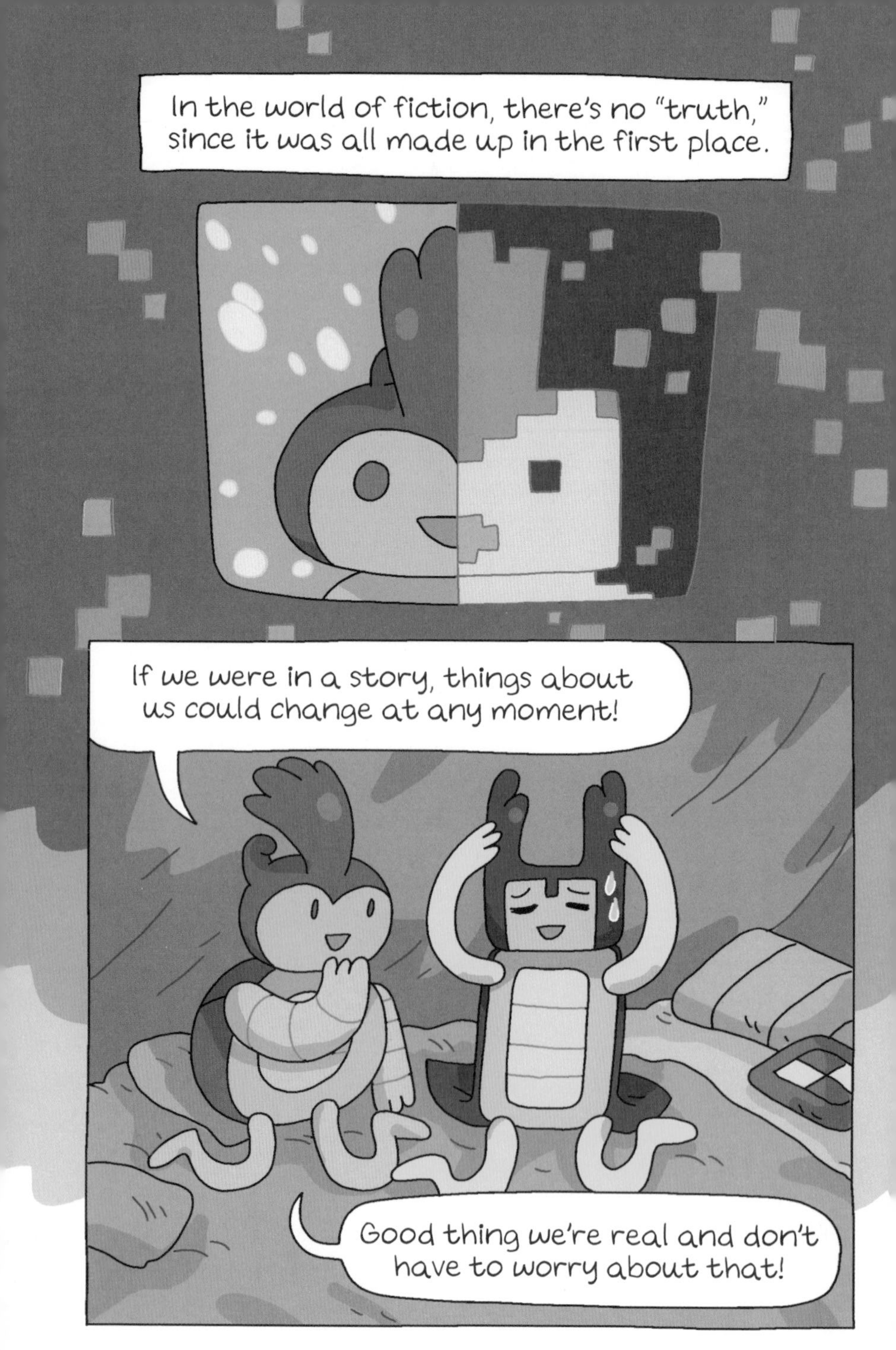
In the world of fiction, there's no "truth," since it was all made up in the first place.
If we were in a story, things about us could change at any moment!
Good thing we're real and don't have to worry about that!

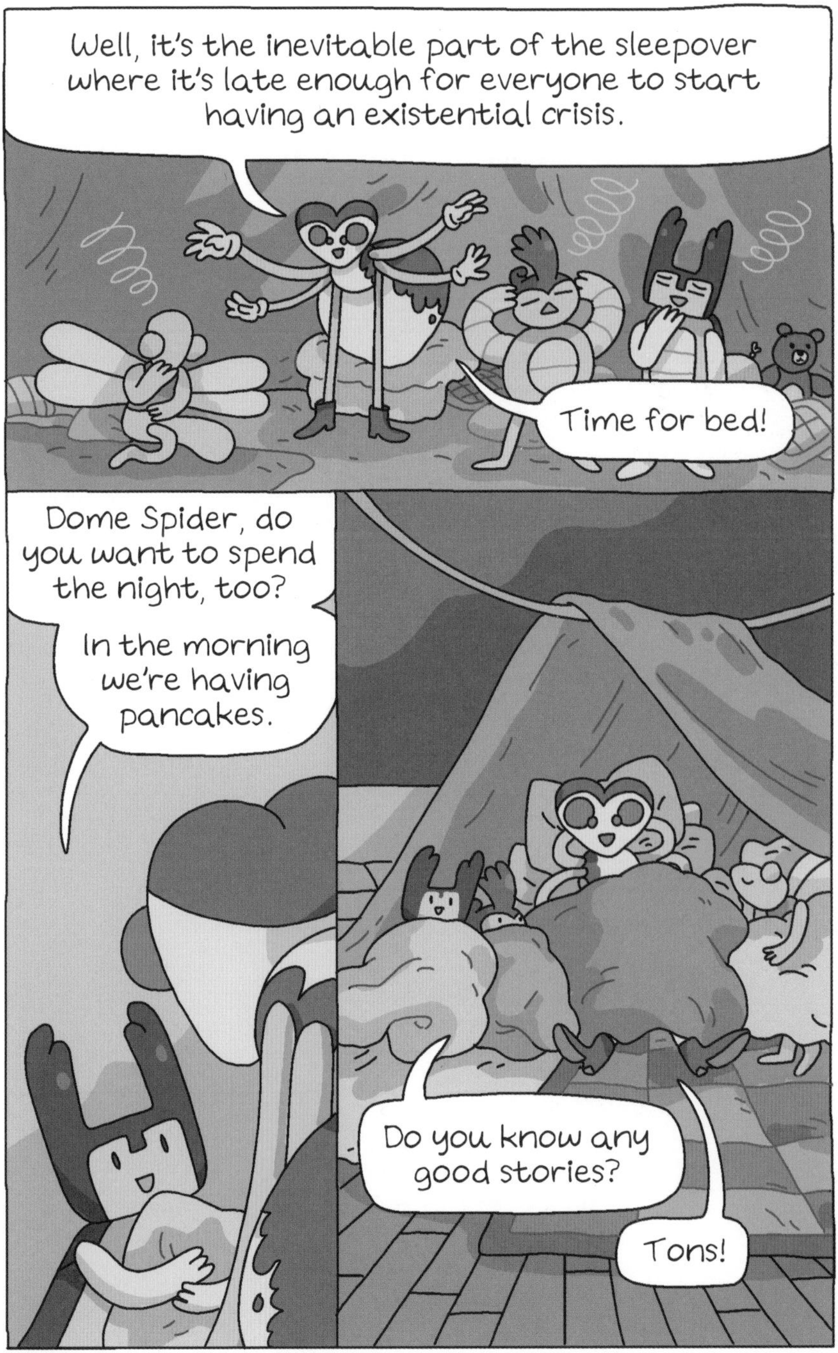
Well, it's the inevitable part of the sleepover where it's late enough for everyone to start having an existential crisis.
Time for bed!
Dome Spider, do you want to spend the night, too?
In the morning we're having pancakes.
Do you know any good stories?
Tons!

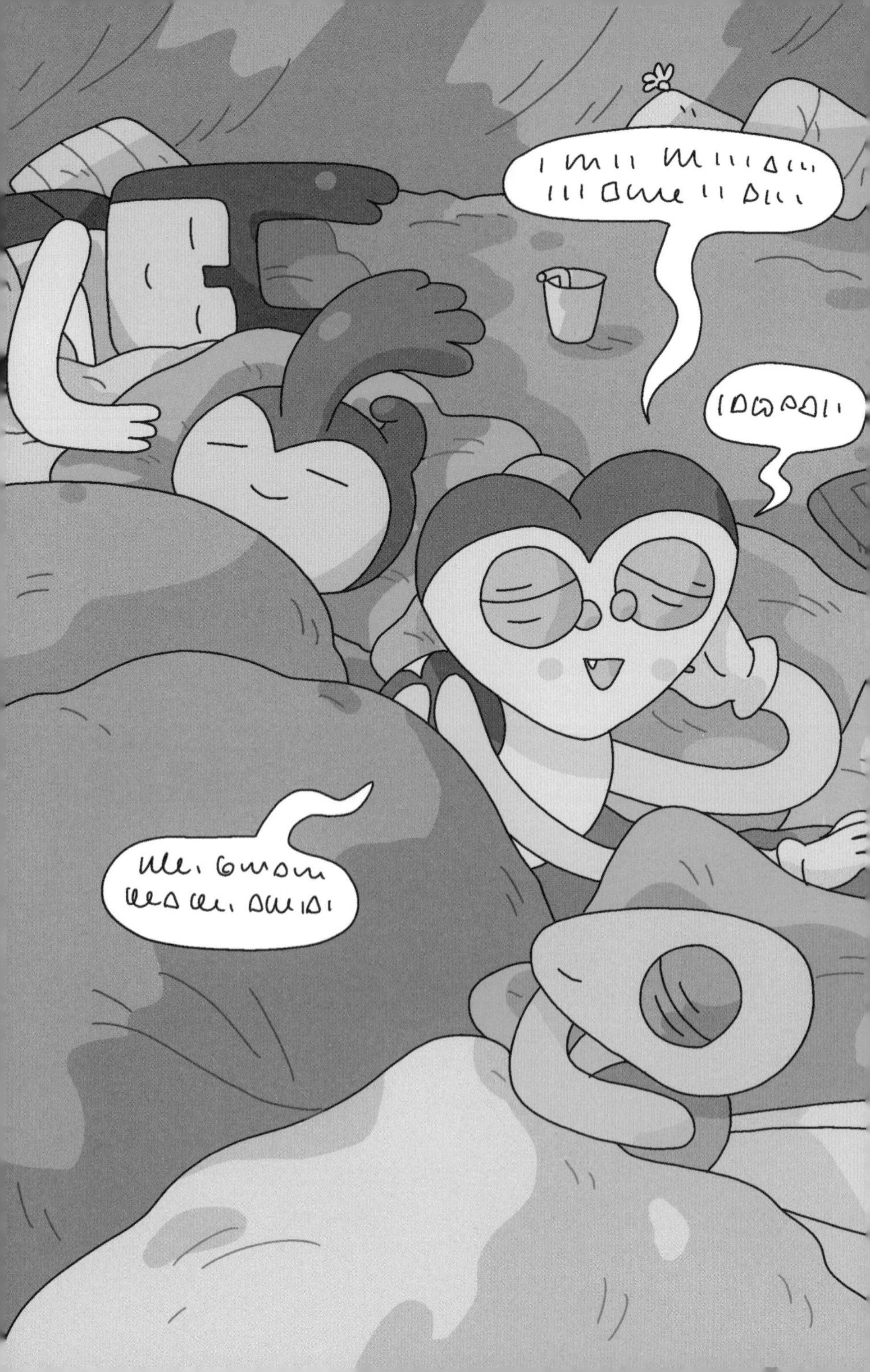

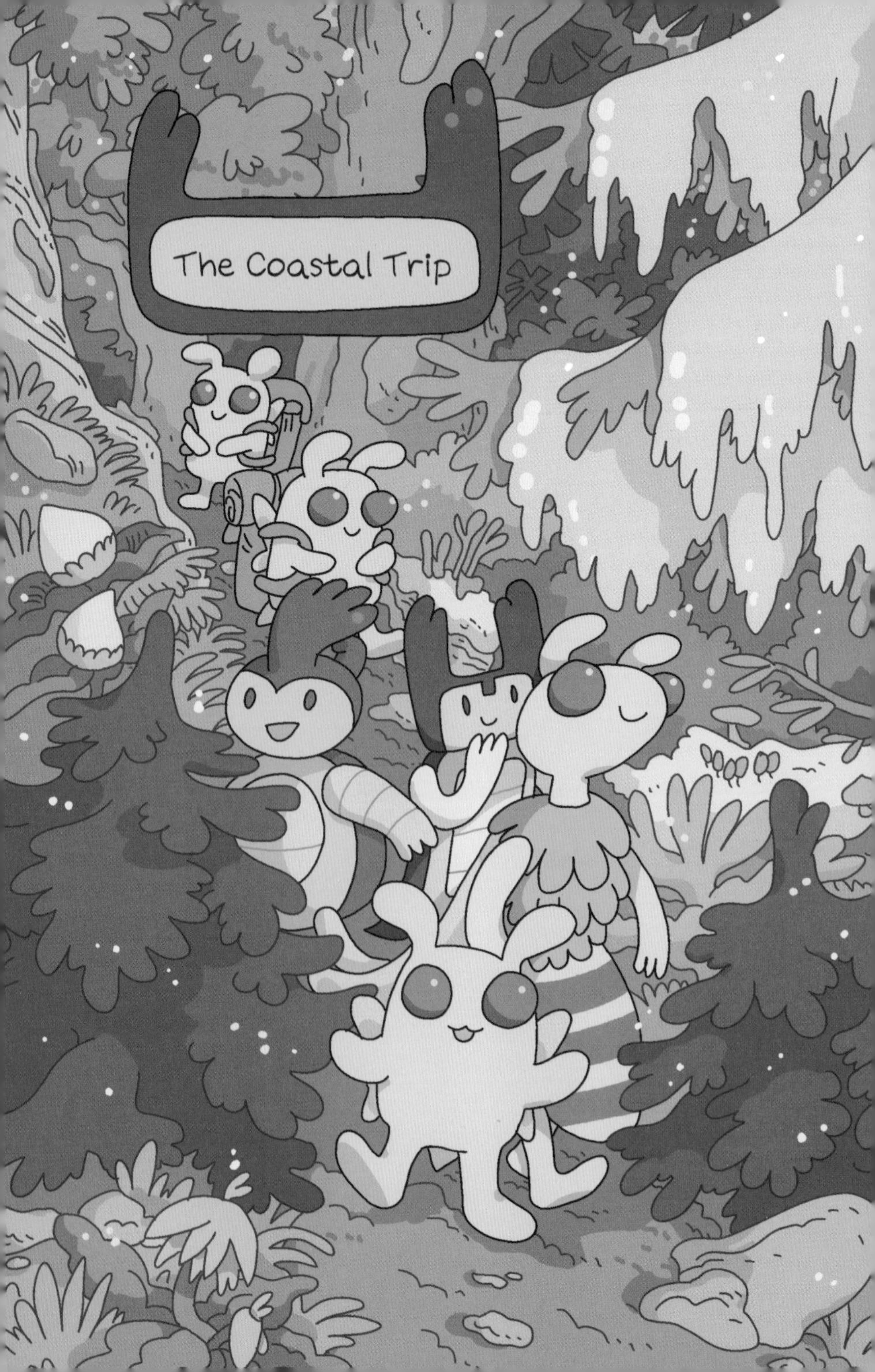
The Coastal Trip

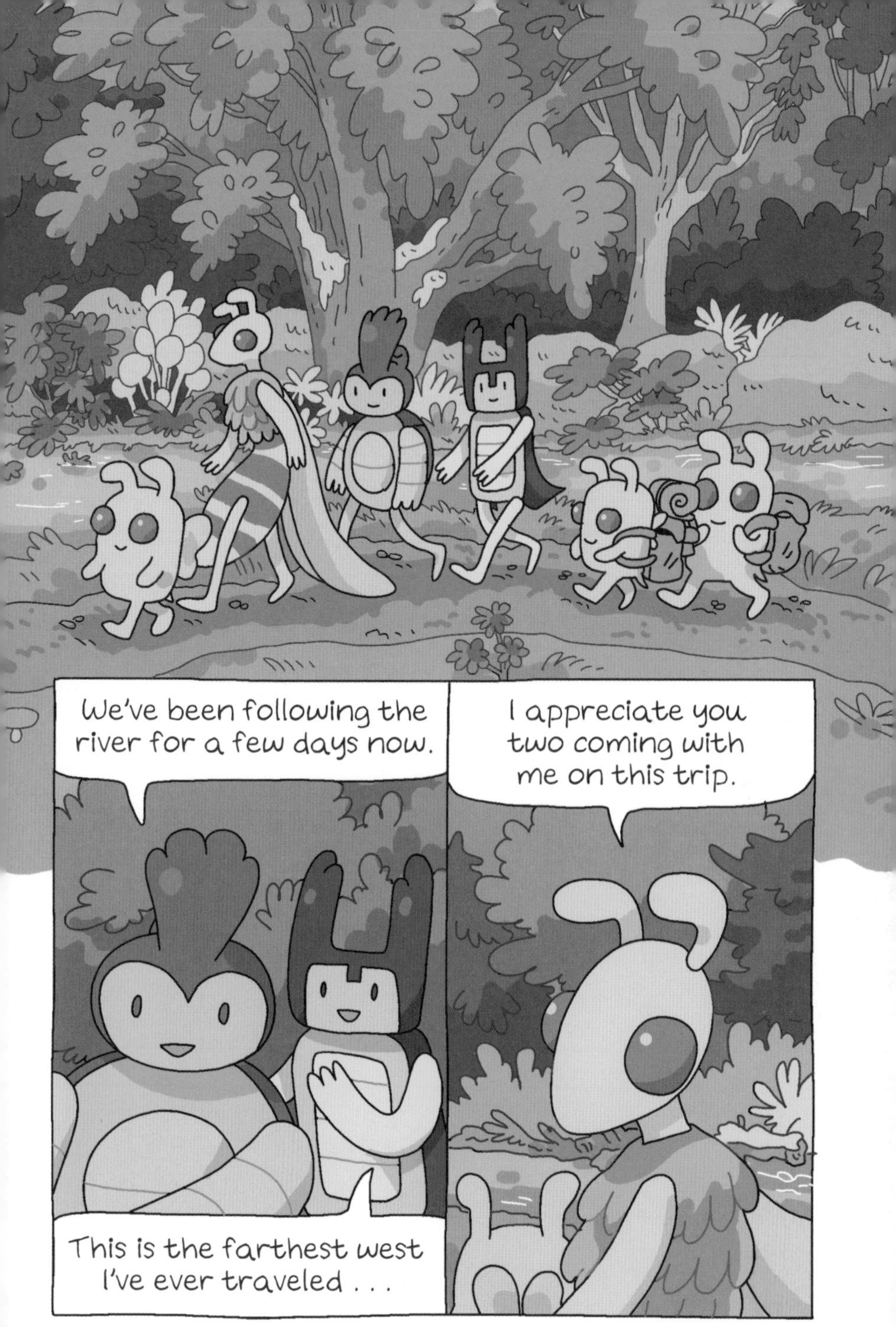
We've been following the river for a few days now.
I appreciate you two coming with me on this trip.
This is the farthest west I've ever traveled . . .

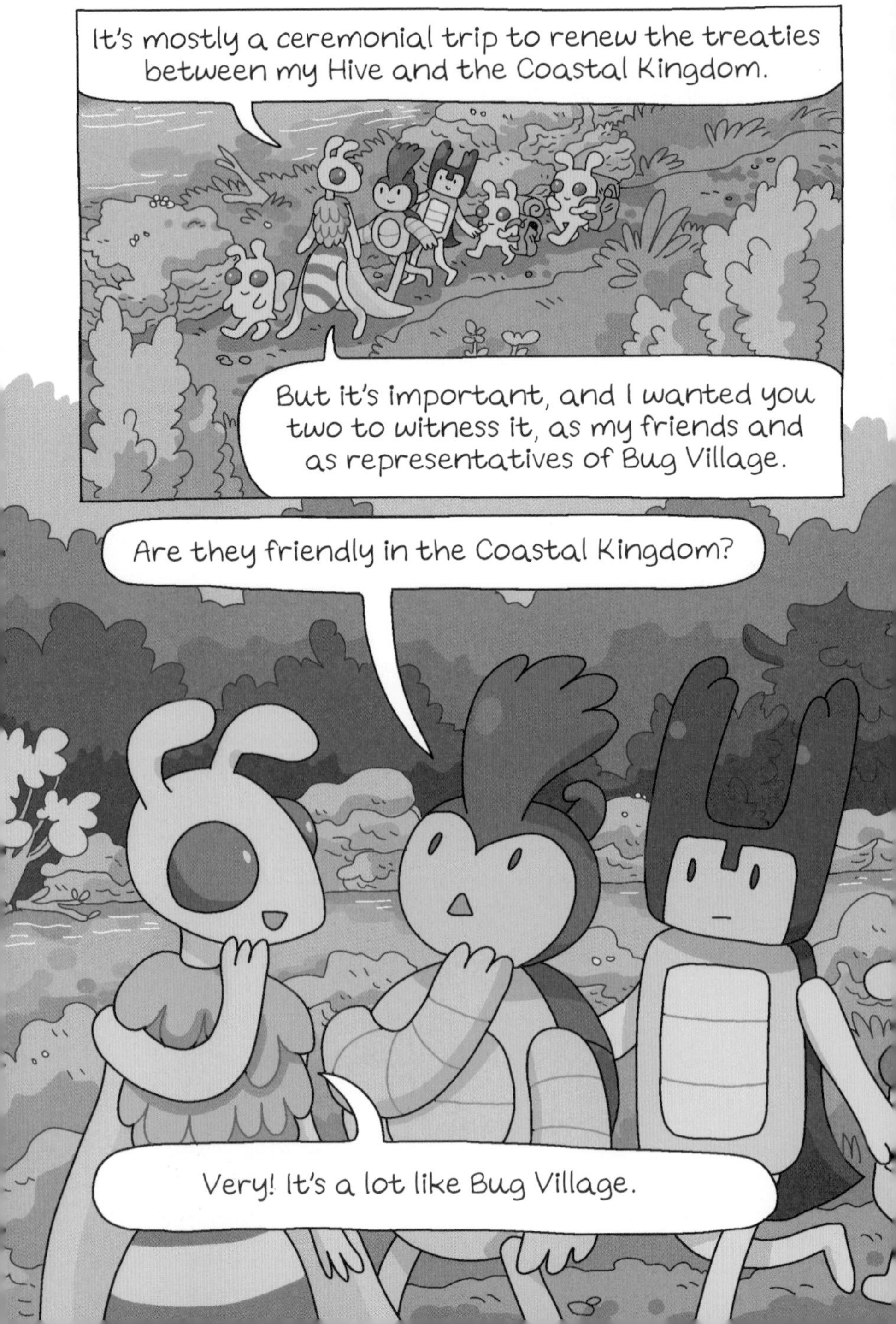
It's mostly a ceremonial trip to renew the treaties between my Hive and the Coastal Kingdom.
But it's important, and I wanted you two to witness it, as my friends and as representatives of Bug Village.
Are they friendly in the Coastal Kingdom?
Very! It's a lot like Bug Village.

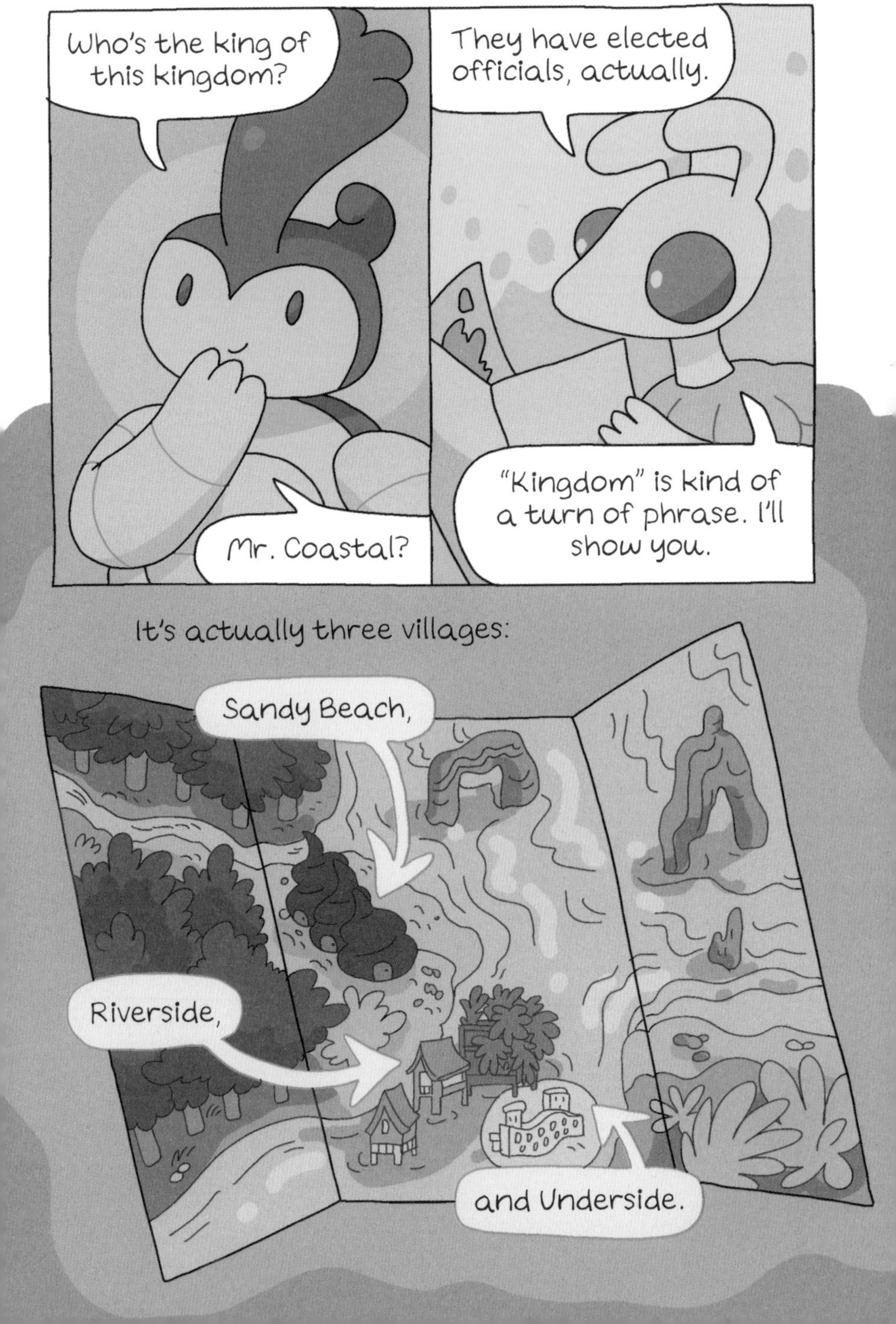
Who's the king of this kingdom?
Mr. Coastal?
They have elected officials, actually.
"Kingdom" is kind of a turn of phrase. I'll show you.
It's actually three villages:
Sandy Beach,
Riverside,
and Underside.

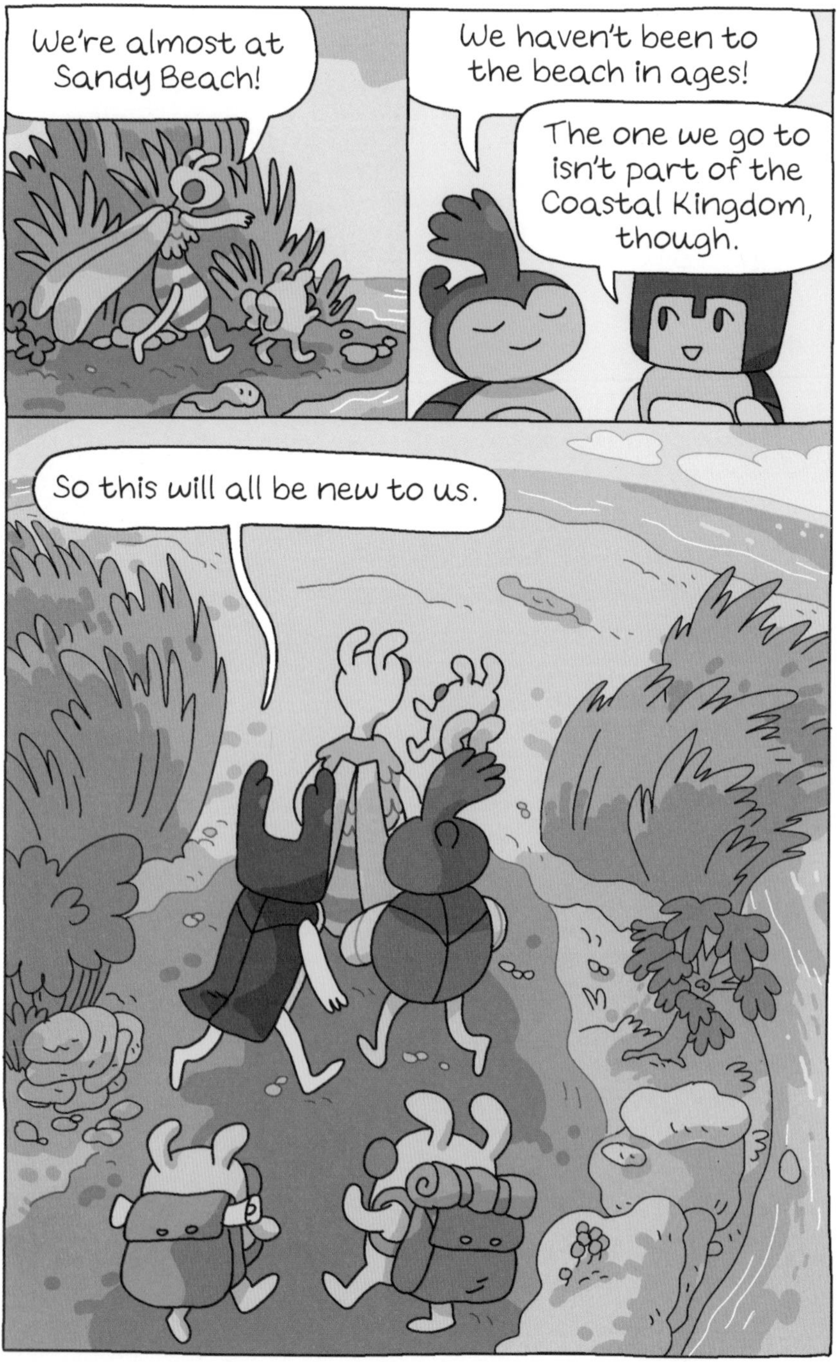
We're almost at Sandy Beach!
We haven't been to the beach in ages!
The one we go to isn't part of the Coastal Kingdom, though.
So this will all be new to us.

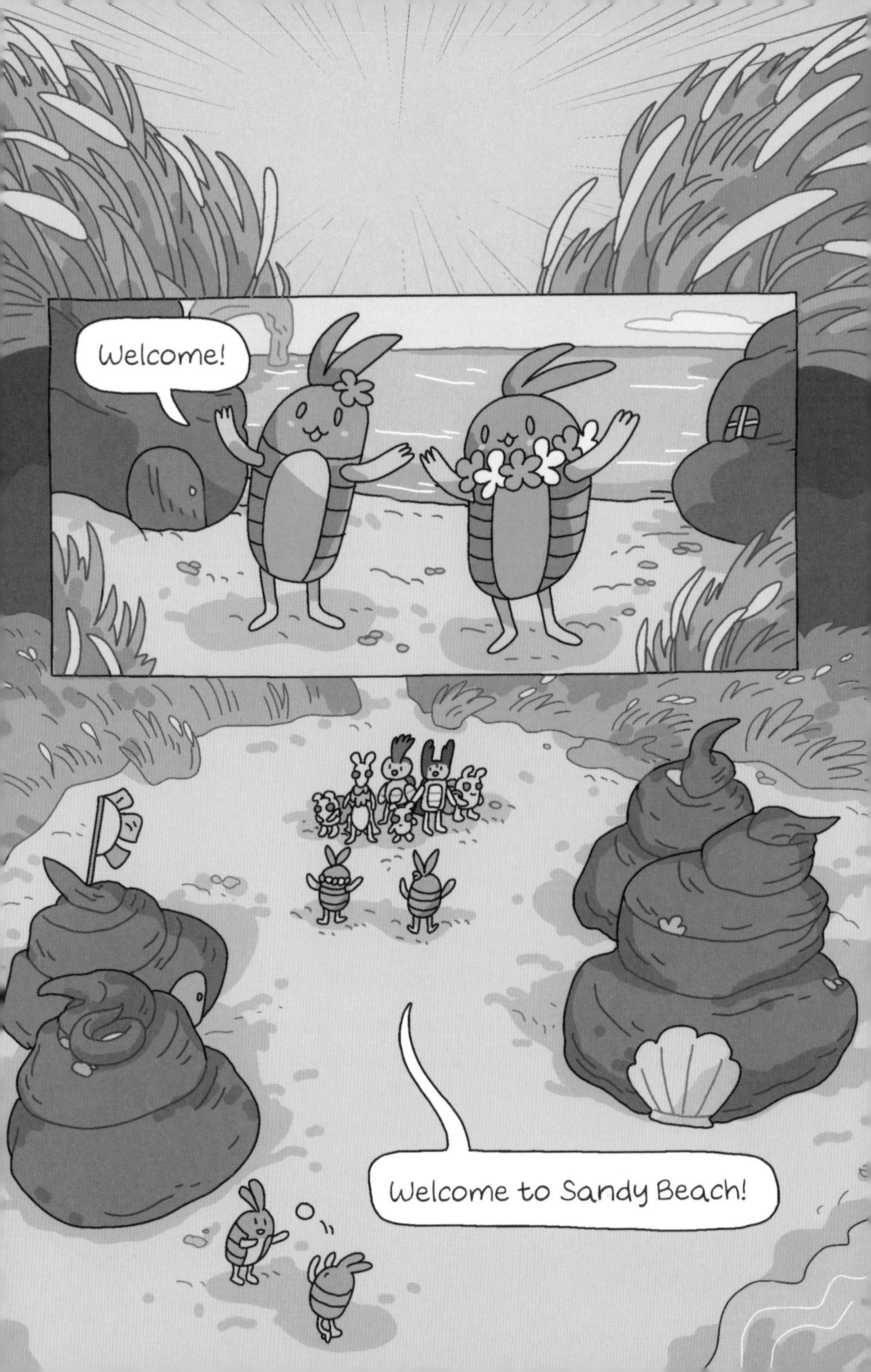
Welcome!
Welcome to Sandy Beach!

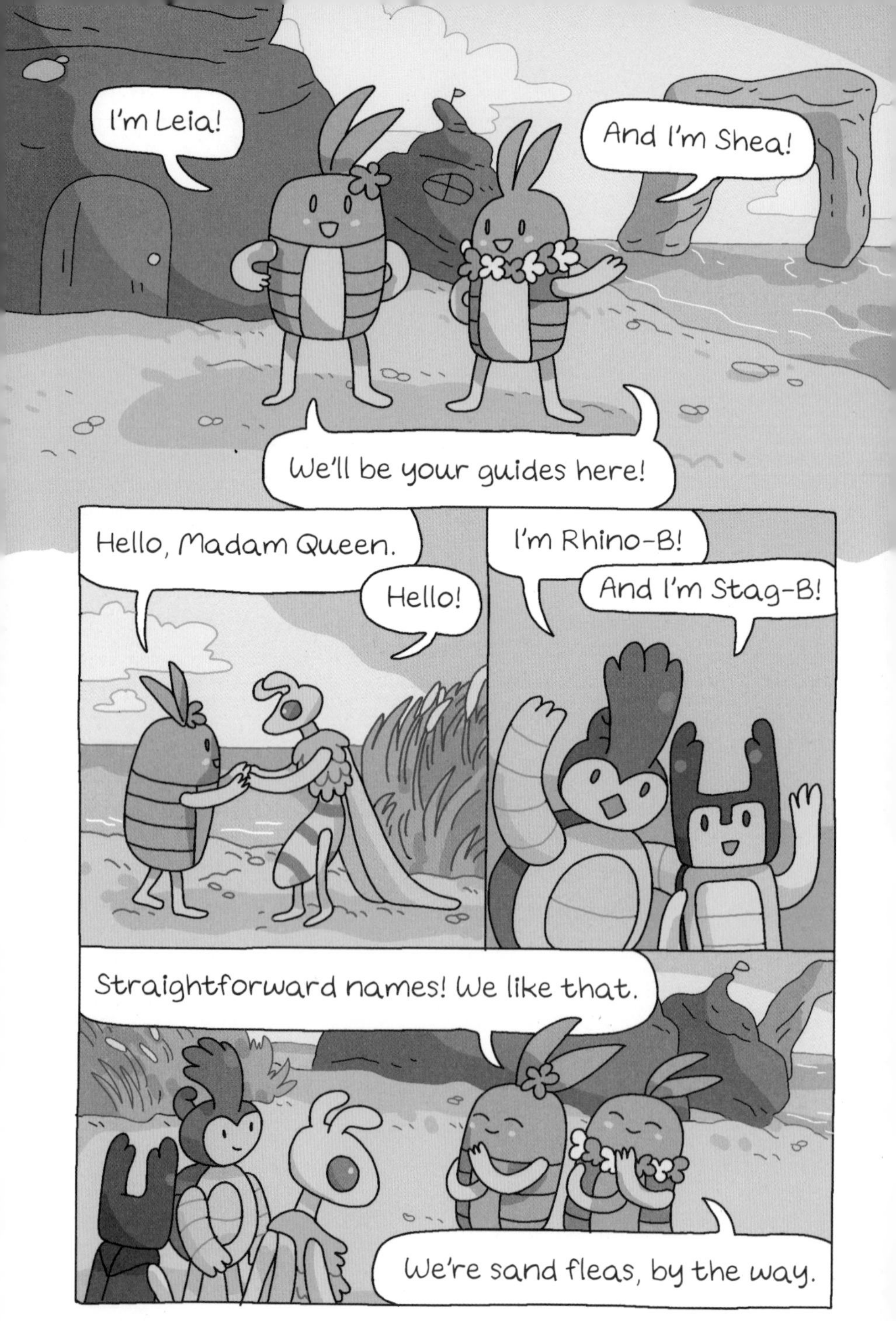
I'm Leia!
And I'm Shea!
We'll be your guides here!
Hello, Madam Queen.
Hello!
I'm Rhino-B!
And I'm Stag-B!
Straightforward names! We like that.
We're sand fleas, by the way.

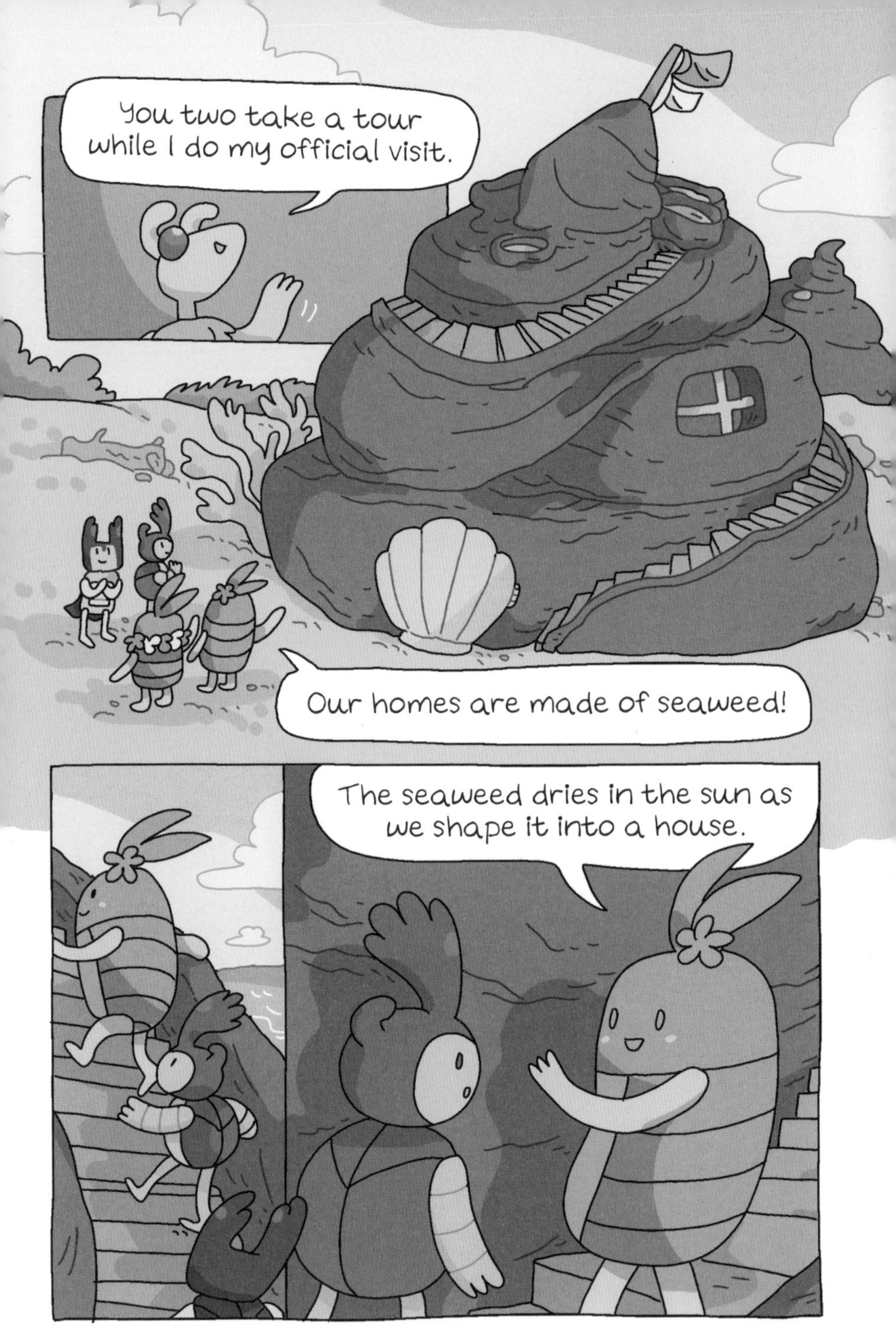
You two take a tour while I do my official visit.
Our homes are made of seaweed!
The seaweed dries in the sun as we shape it into a house.

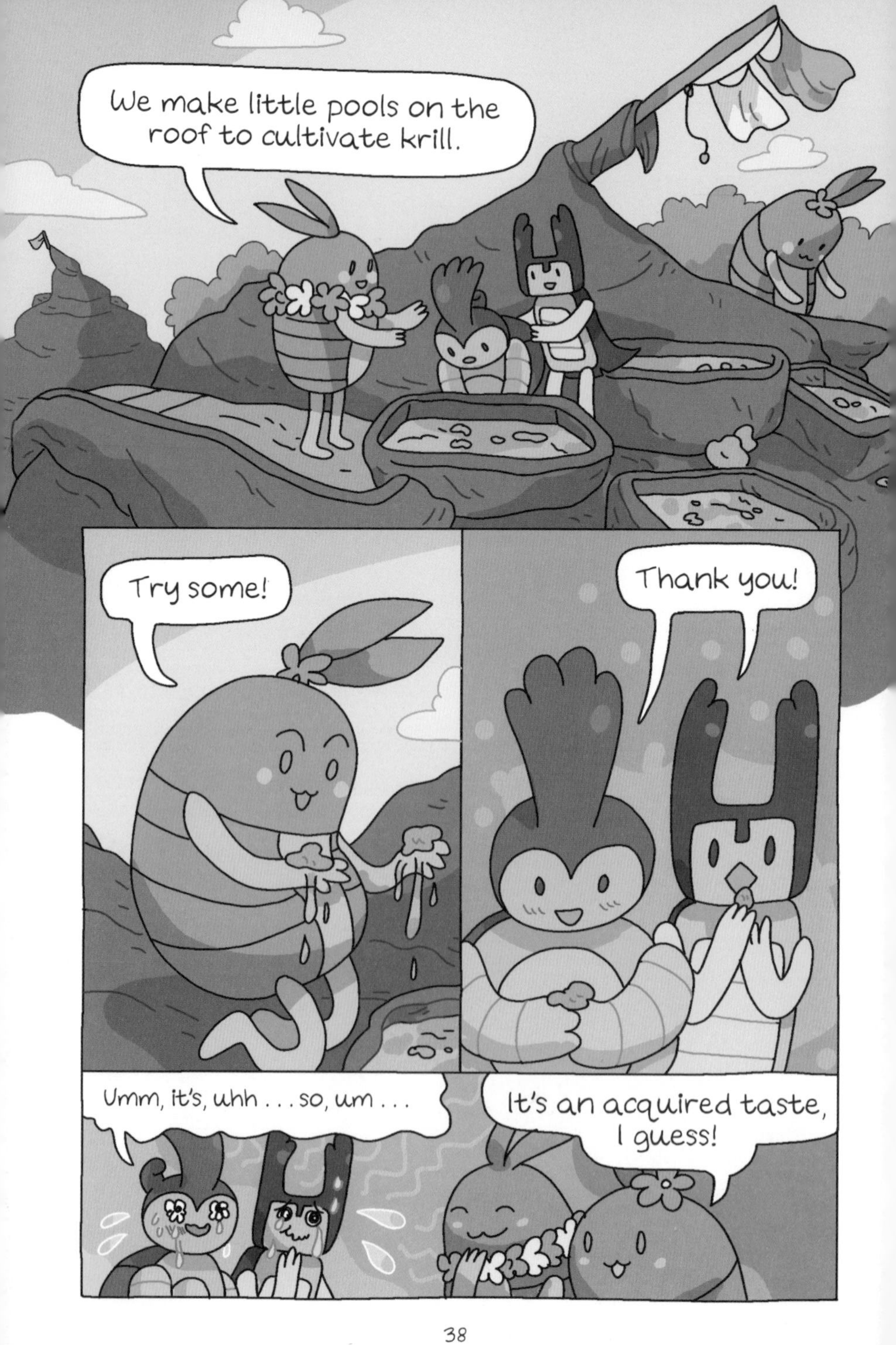
We make little pools on the roof to cultivate krill.
Try some!
Thank you!
Umm, it's, uhh . . . so, um . . .
It's an acquired taste, I guess!

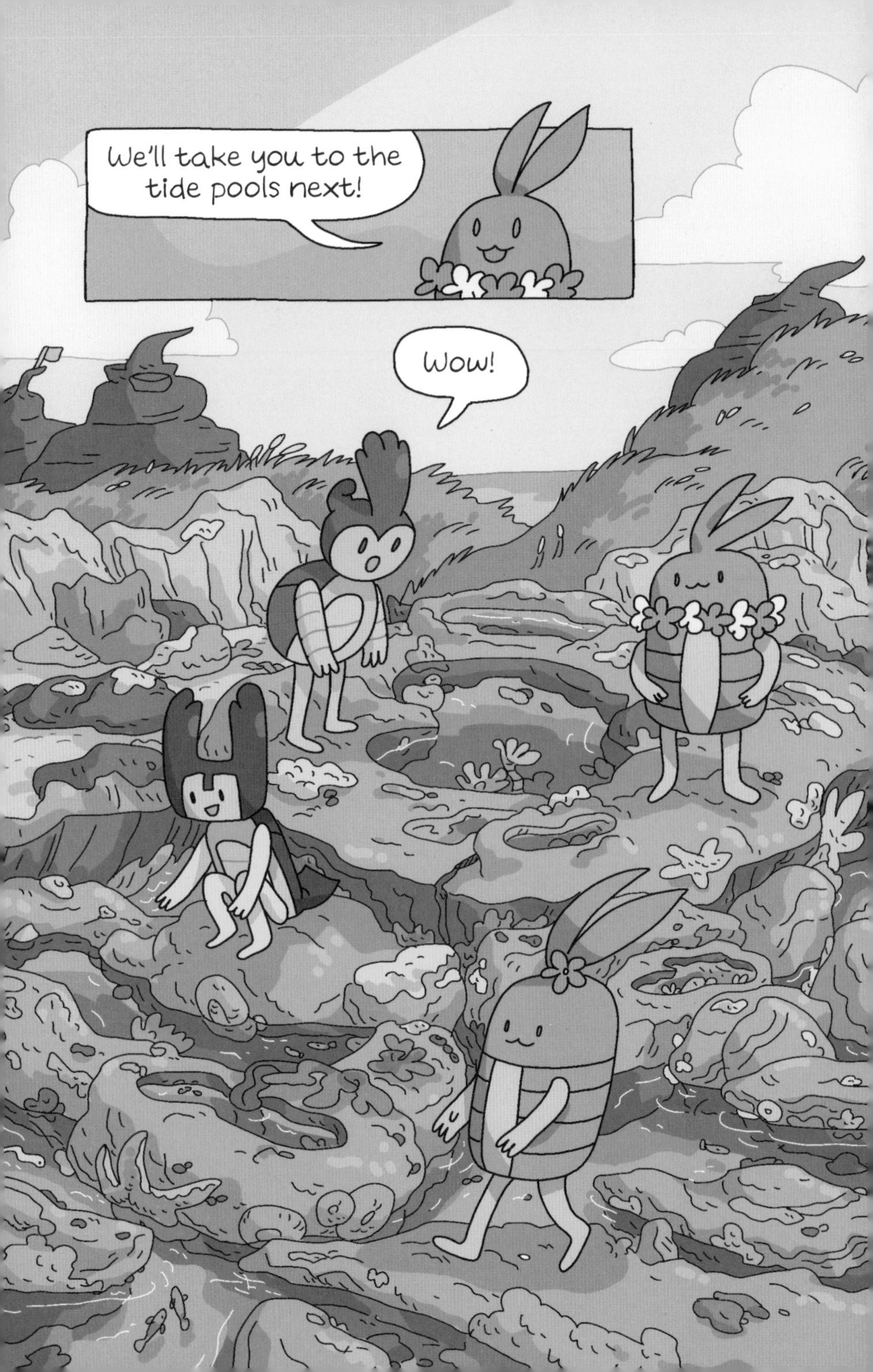
We'll take you to the tide pools next!
Wow!

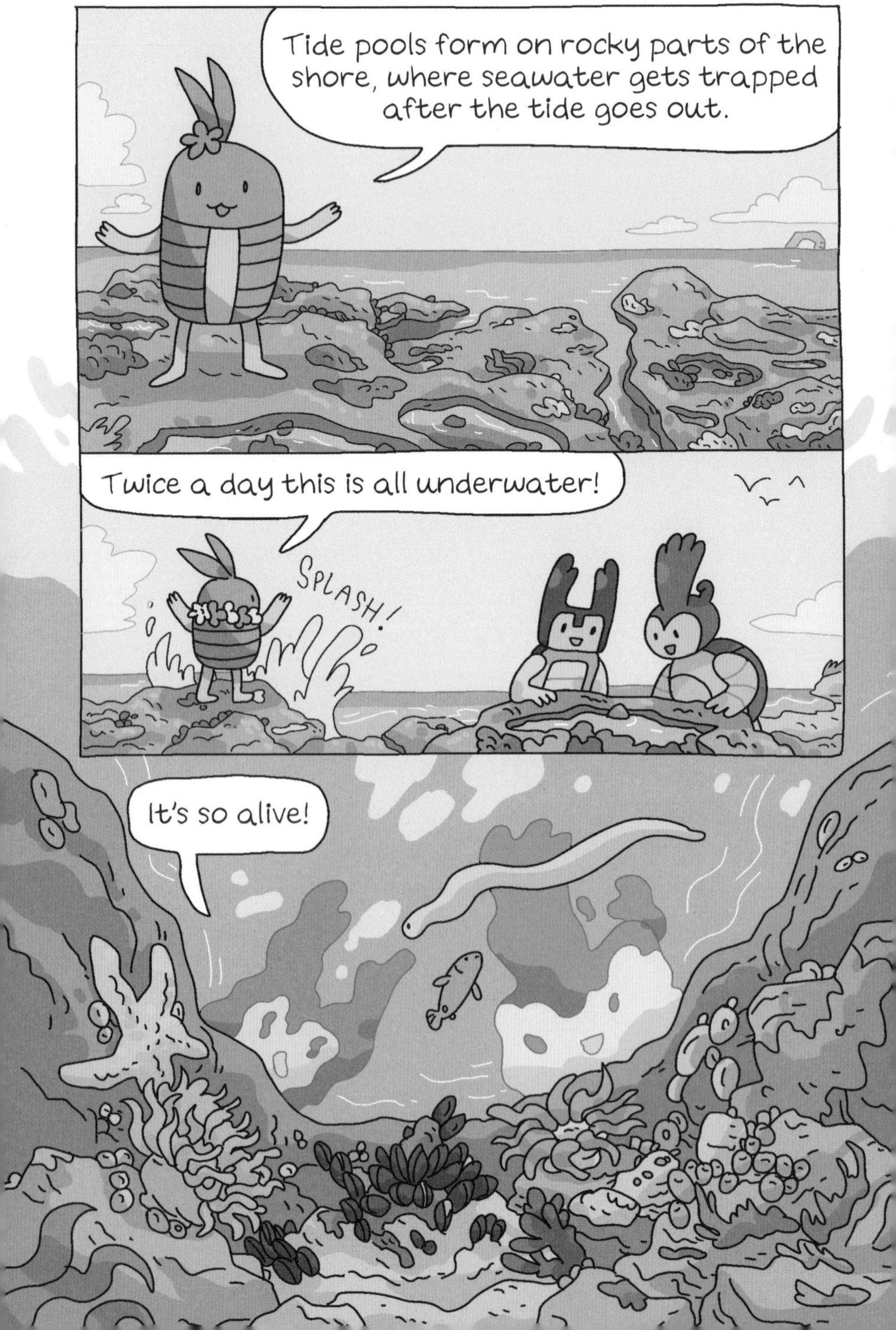
Tide pools form on rocky parts of the shore, where seawater gets trapped after the tide goes out.
Twice a day this is all underwater!
SPLASH!
It's so alive!

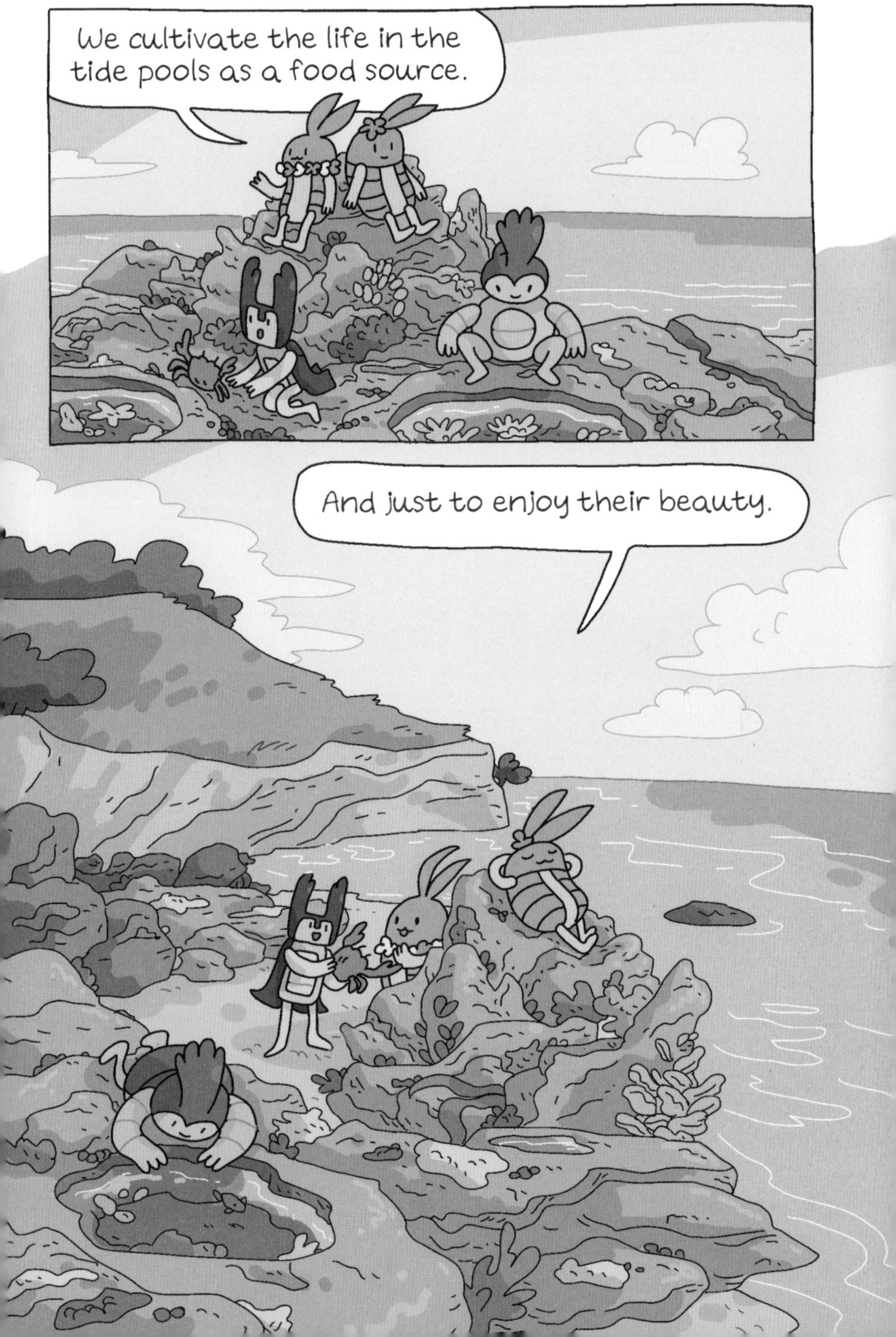
We cultivate the life in the tide pools as a food source.
And just to enjoy their beauty.

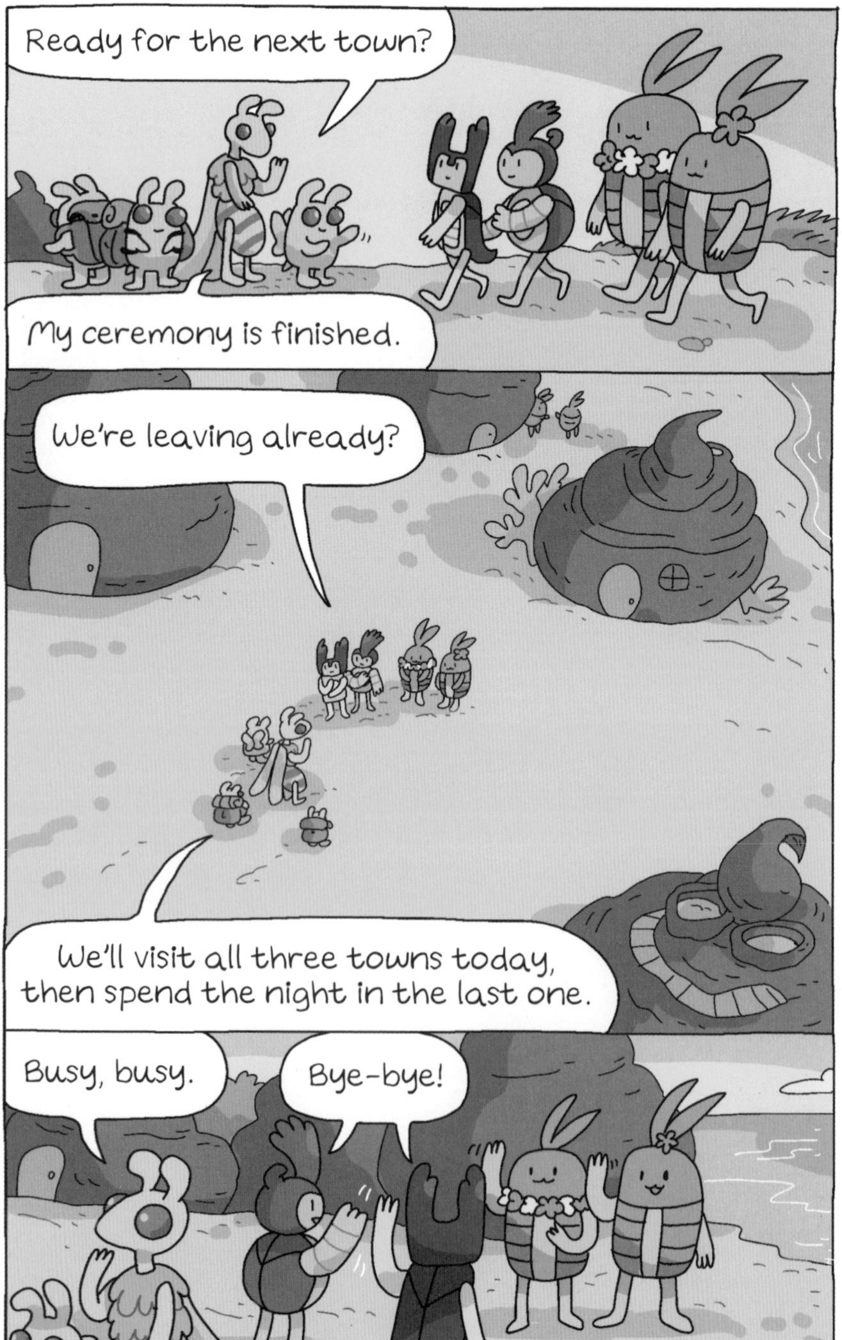
Ready for the next town?
My ceremony is finished.
We're leaving already?
We'll visit all three towns today, then spend the night in the last one.
Busy, busy.
Bye-bye!

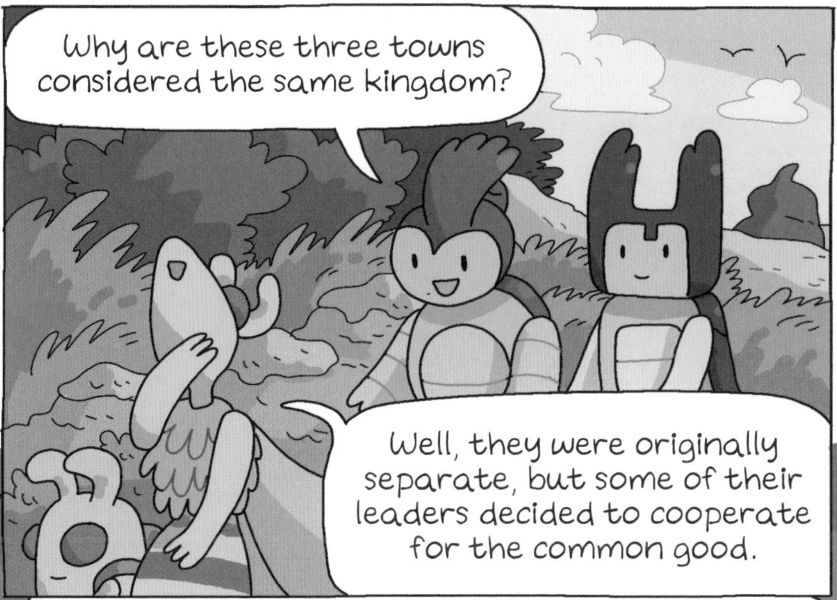
Why are these three towns considered the same kingdom?
Well, they were originally separate, but some of their leaders decided to cooperate for the common good.

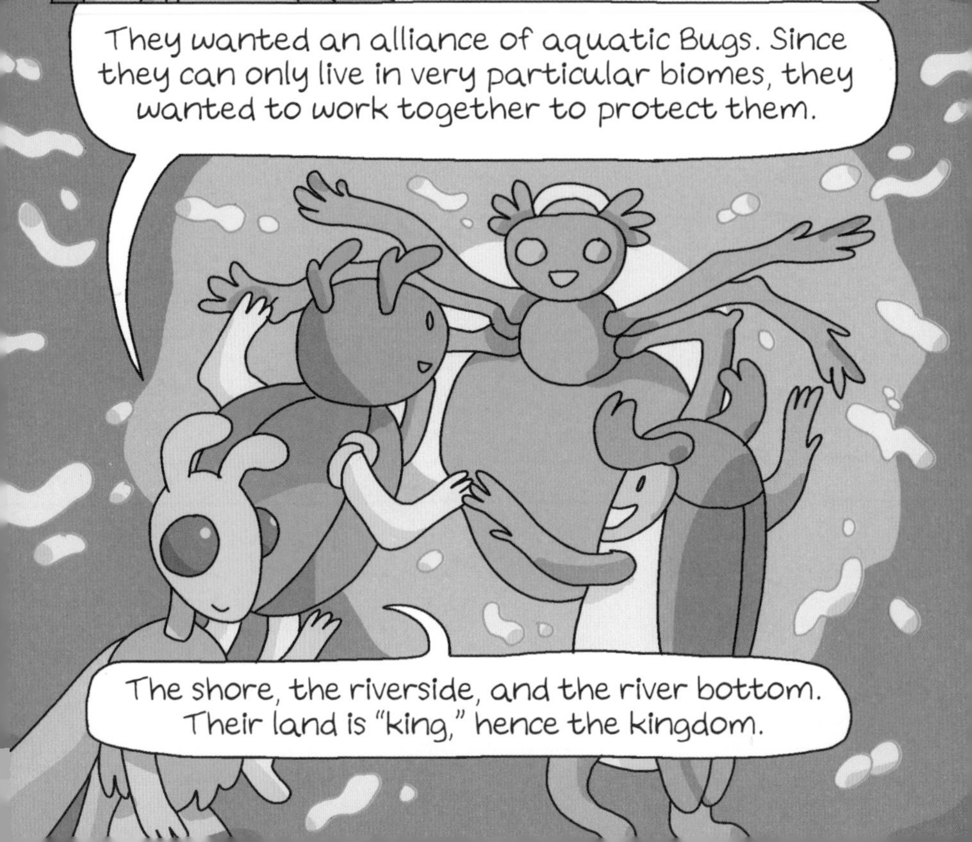
They wanted an alliance of aquatic Bugs. Since they can only live in very particular biomes, they wanted to work together to protect them.
The shore, the riverside, and the river bottom. Their land is "king," hence the kingdom.

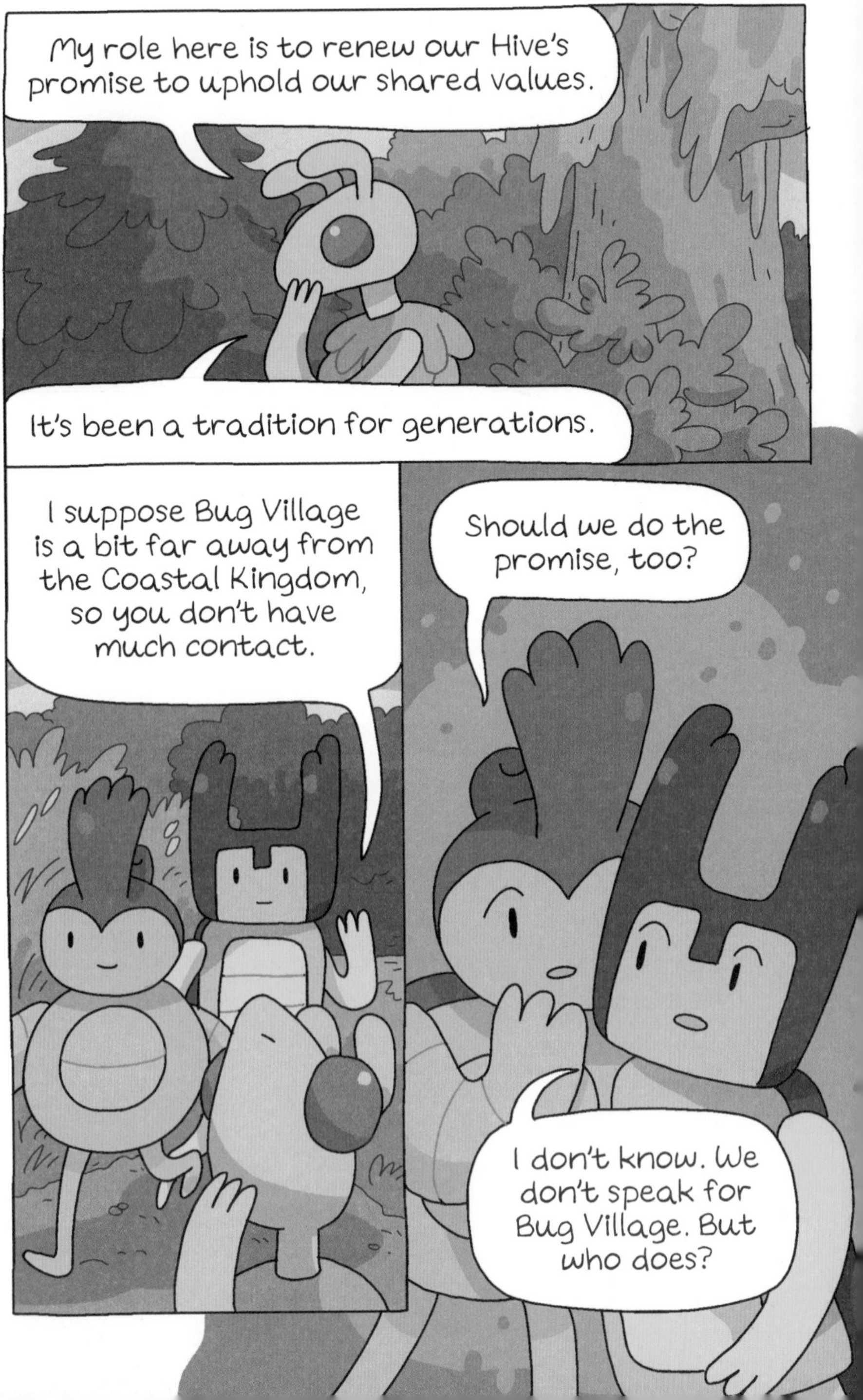
My role here is to renew our Hive's promise to uphold our shared values.
It's been a tradition for generations.
I suppose Bug Village is a bit far away from the Coastal Kingdom, so you don't have much contact.
Should we do the promise, too?
I don't know. We don't speak for Bug Village. But who does?

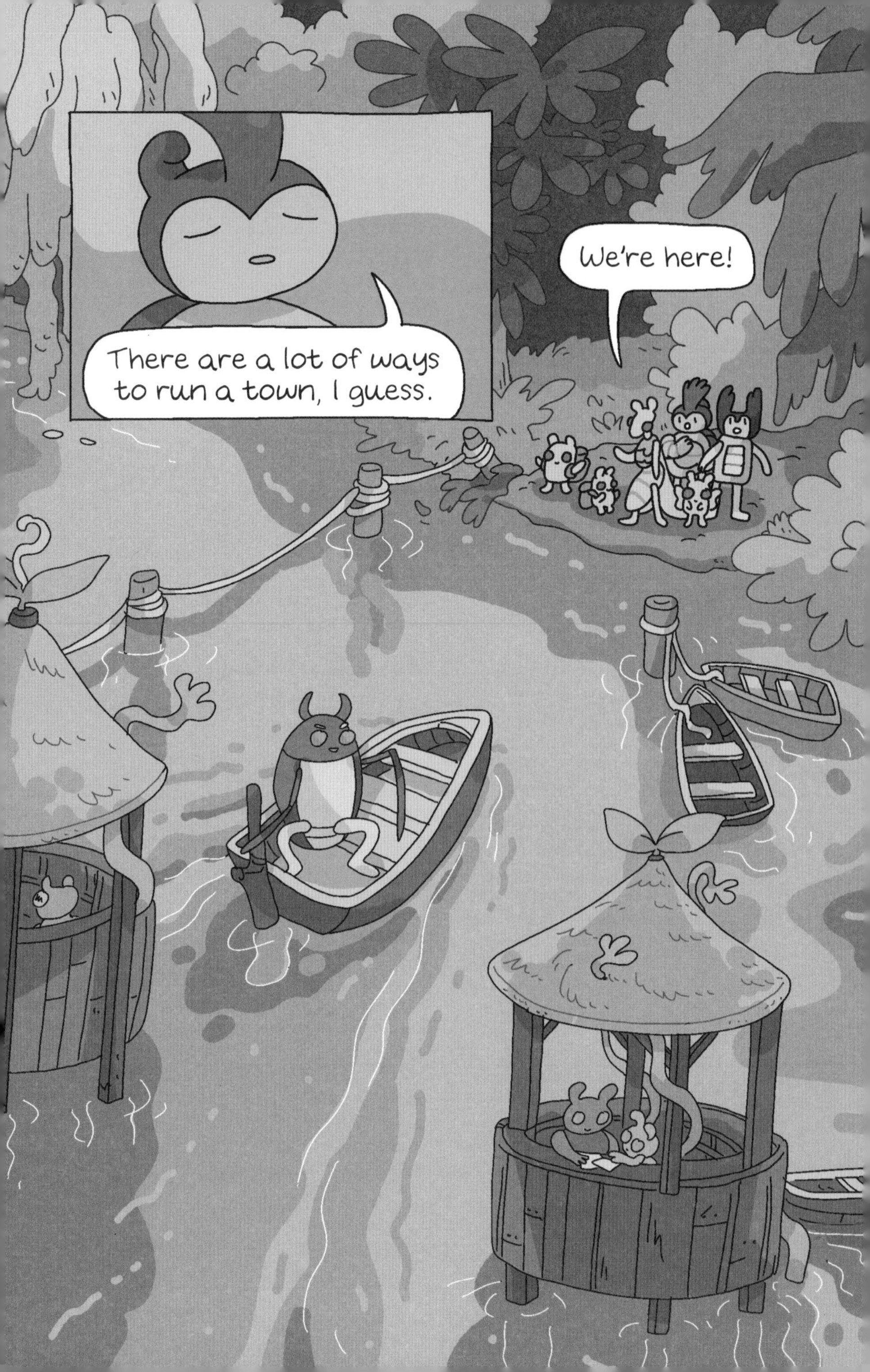
There are a lot of ways to run a town, I guess.
We're here!

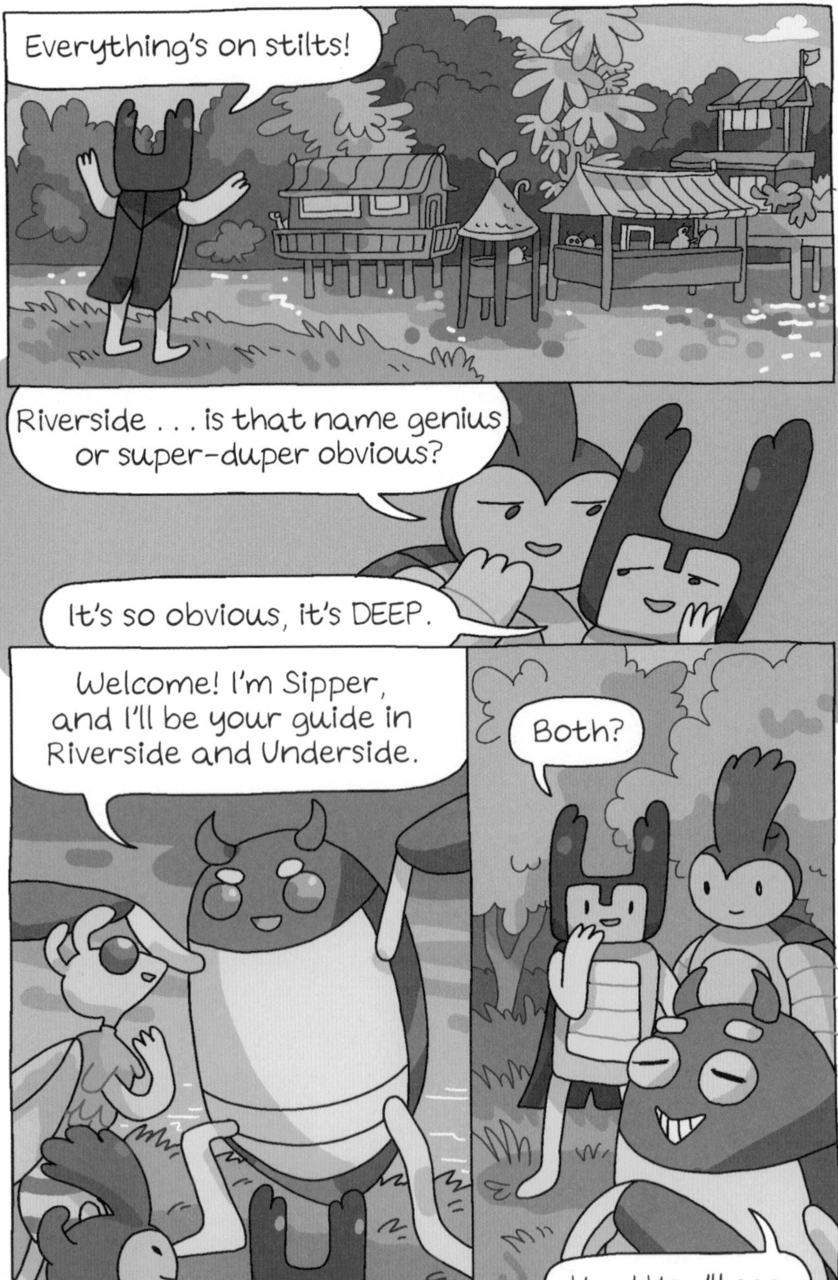
Everything's on stilts!
Riverside . . . is that name genius or super-duper obvious?
It's so obvious, it's DEEP.
Welcome! I'm Sipper, and I'll be your guide in Riverside and Underside.
Both?
Yup! You'll see.

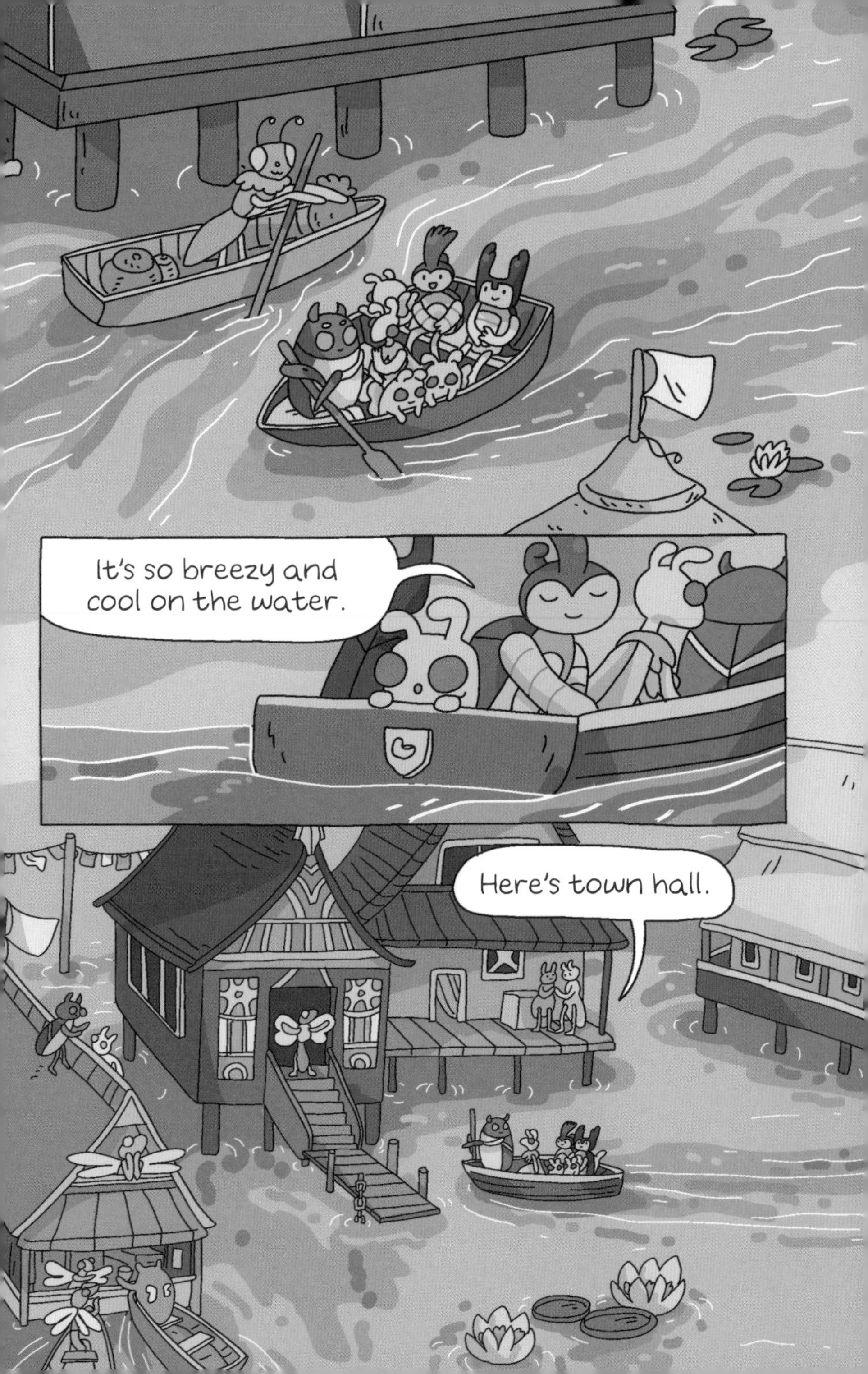
It's so breezy and cool on the water.
Here's town hall.

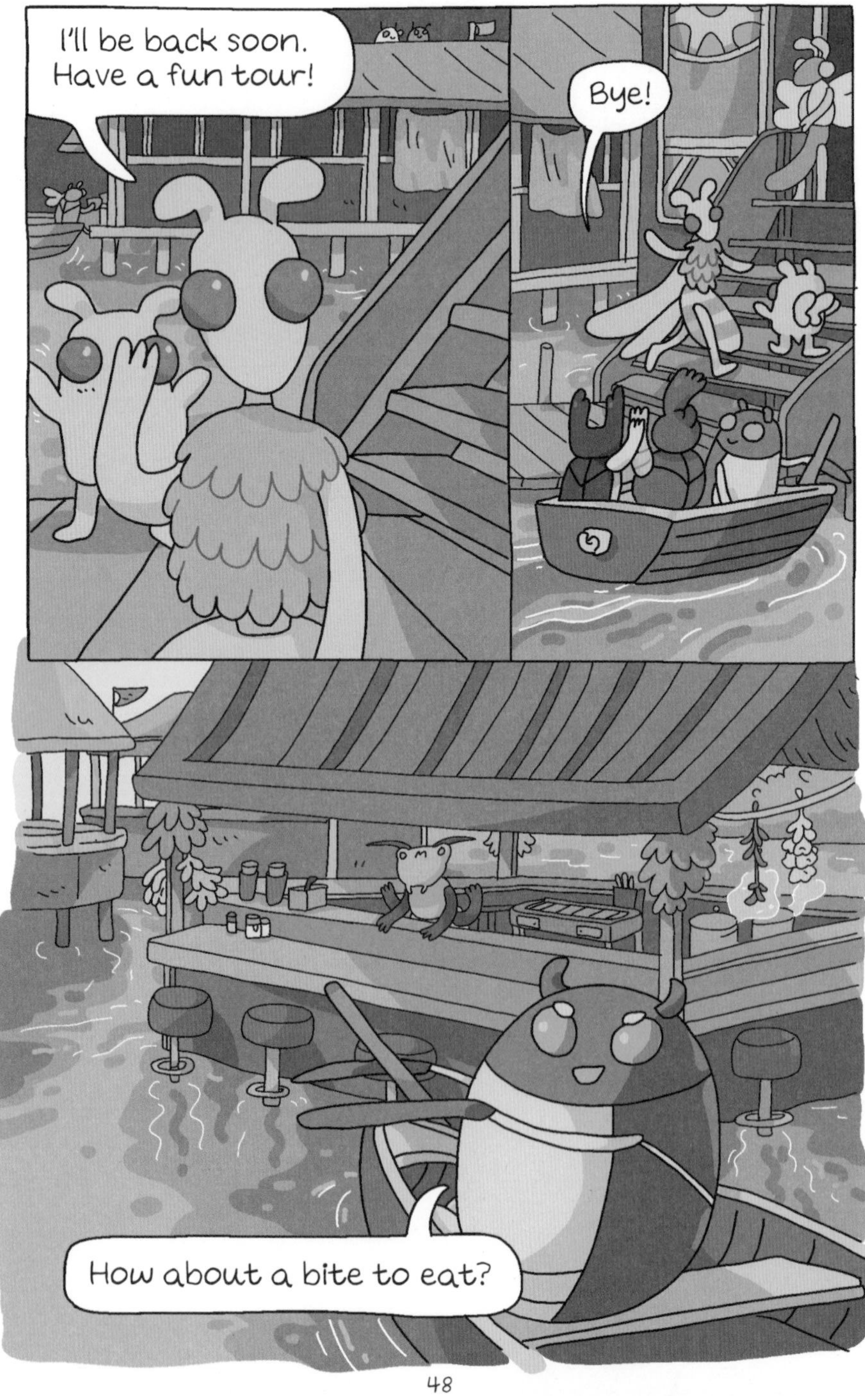
I'll be back soon. Have a fun tour!
Bye!
How about a bite to eat?

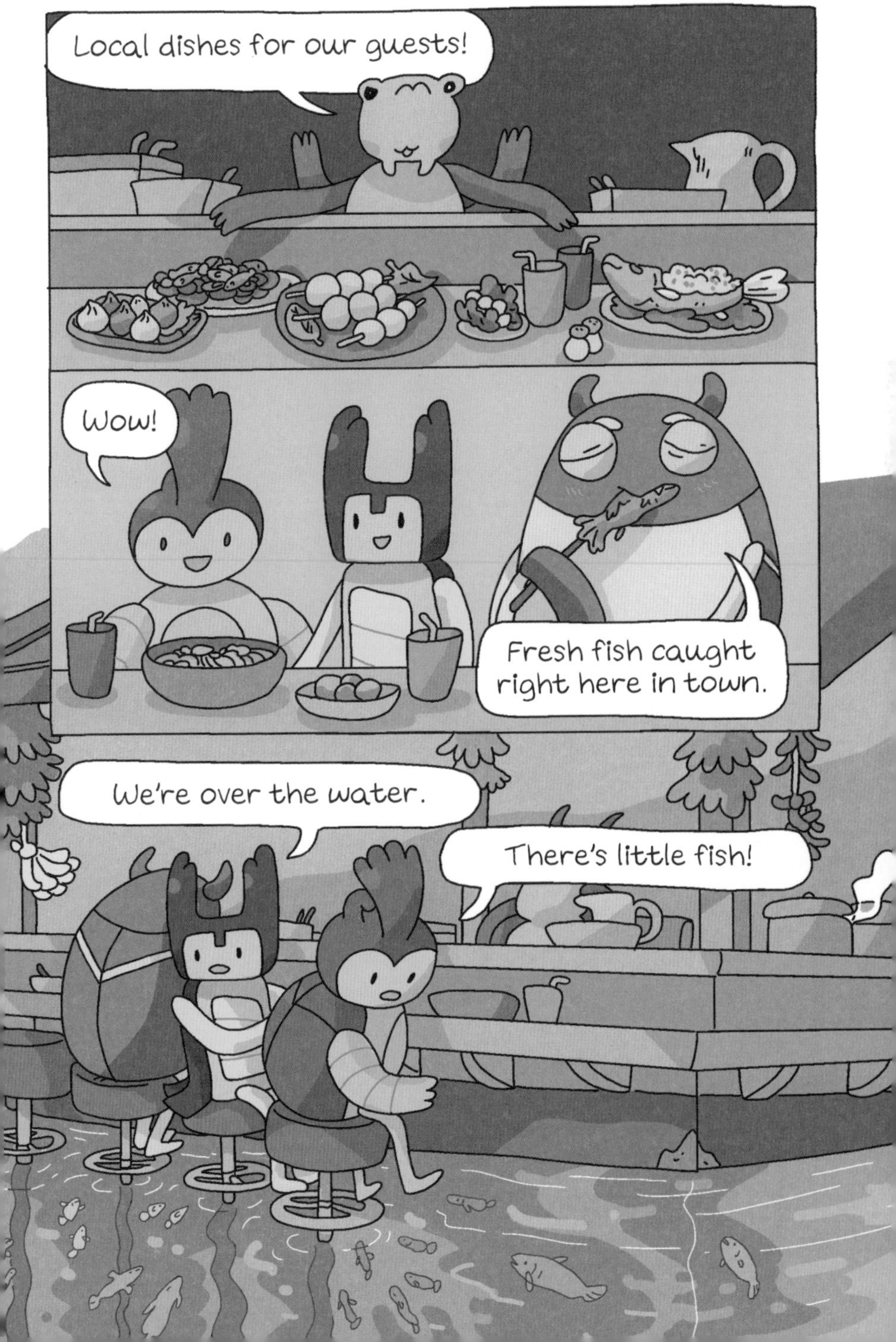
Local dishes for our guests!
Wow!
Fresh fish caught right here in town.
We're over the water.
There's little fish!

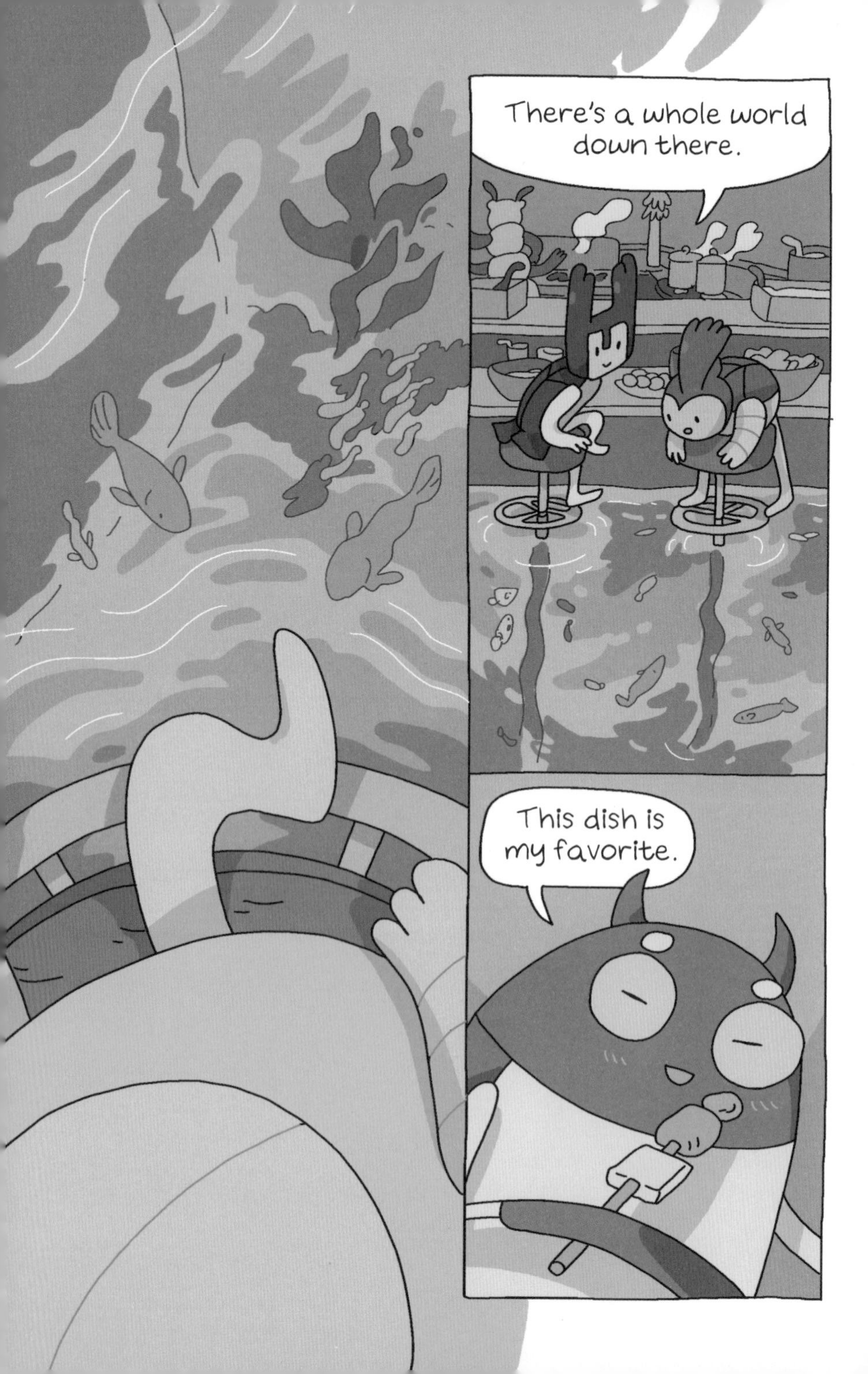
There's a whole world down there.
This dish is my favorite.

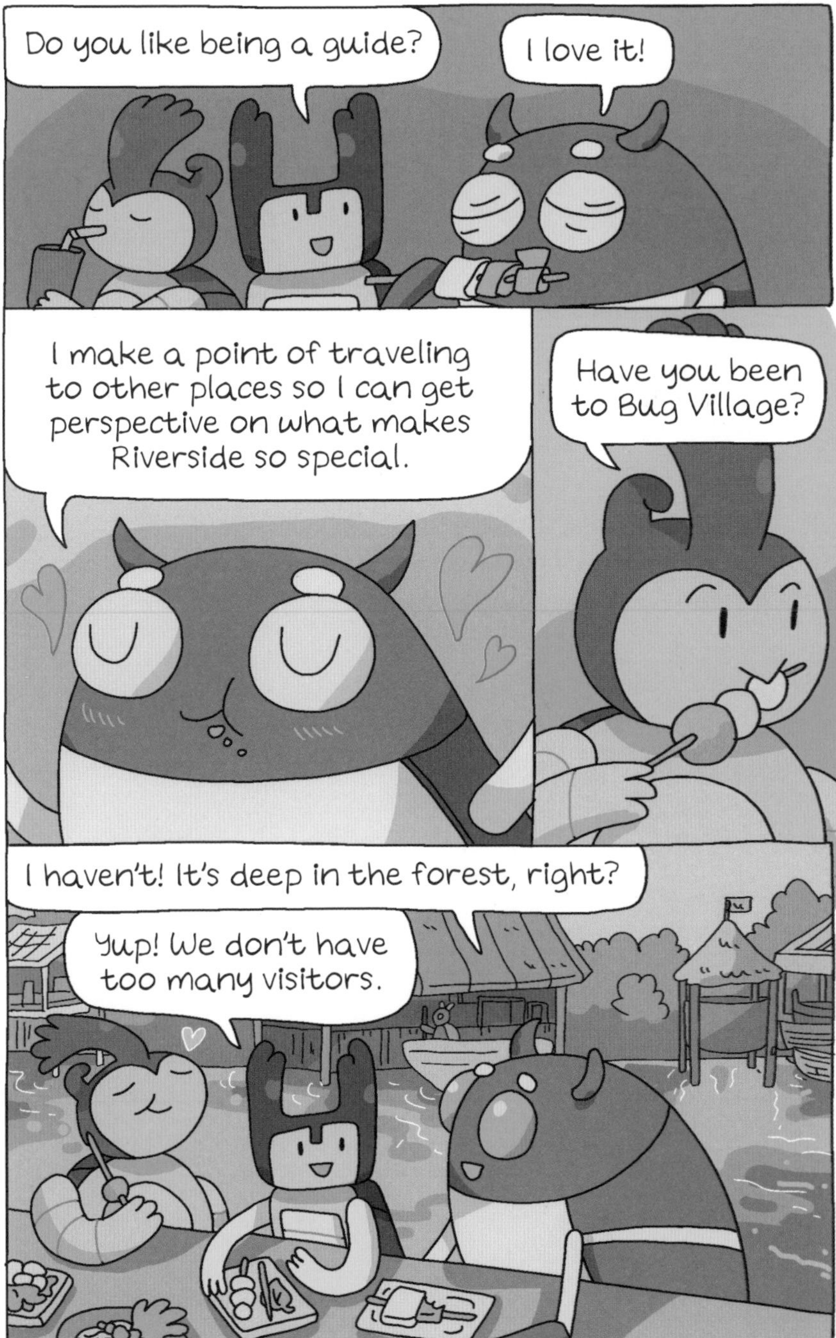
Do you like being a guide?
I love it!
I make a point of traveling to other places so I can get perspective on what makes Riverside so special.
Have you been to Bug Village?
I haven't! It's deep in the forest, right?
Yup! We don't have too many visitors.

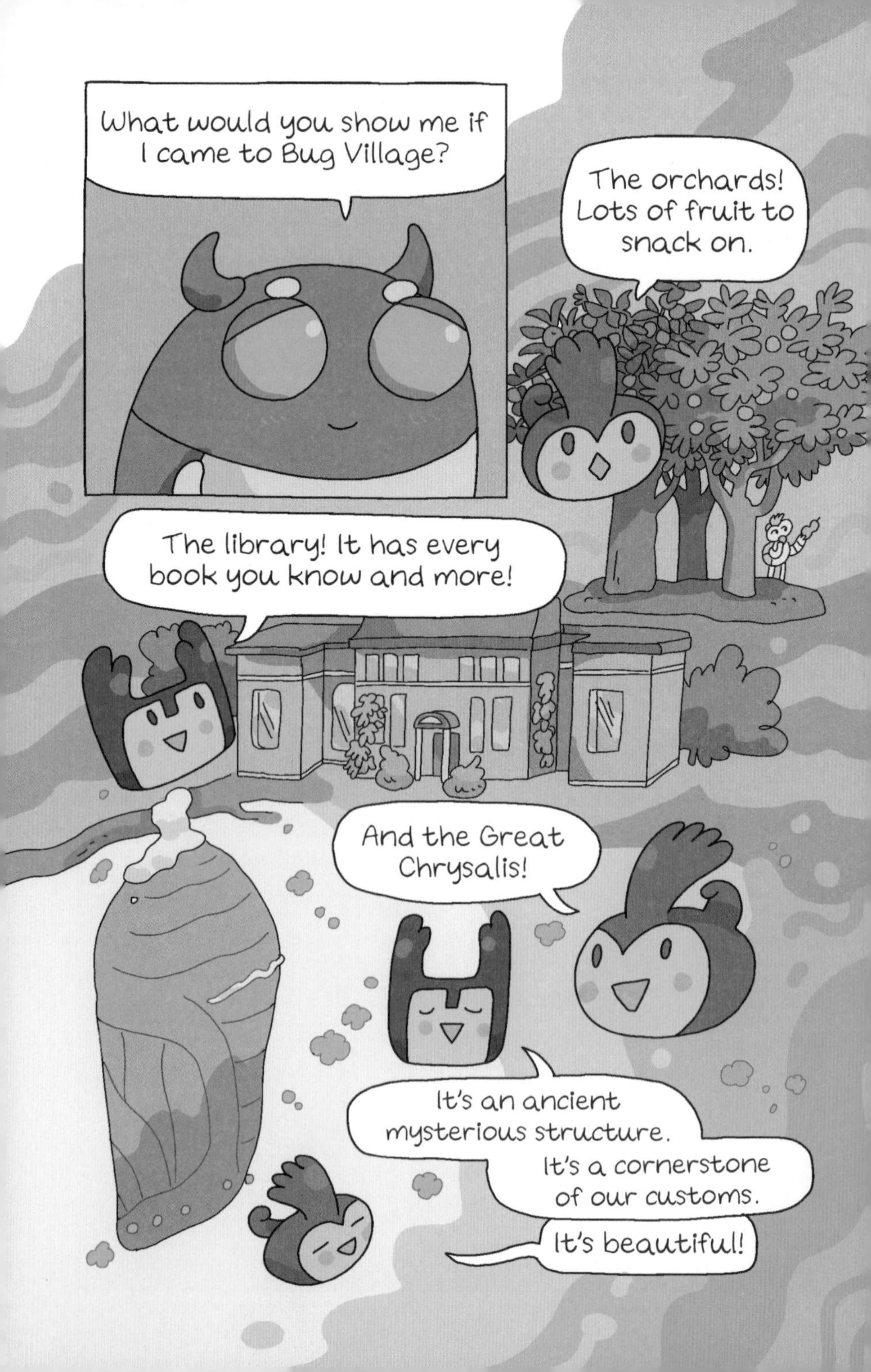
What would you show me if I came to Bug Village?
The orchards! Lots of fruit to snack on.
The library! It has every book you know and more!
And the Great Chrysalis!
It's an ancient mysterious structure.
It's a cornerstone of our customs.
It's beautiful!

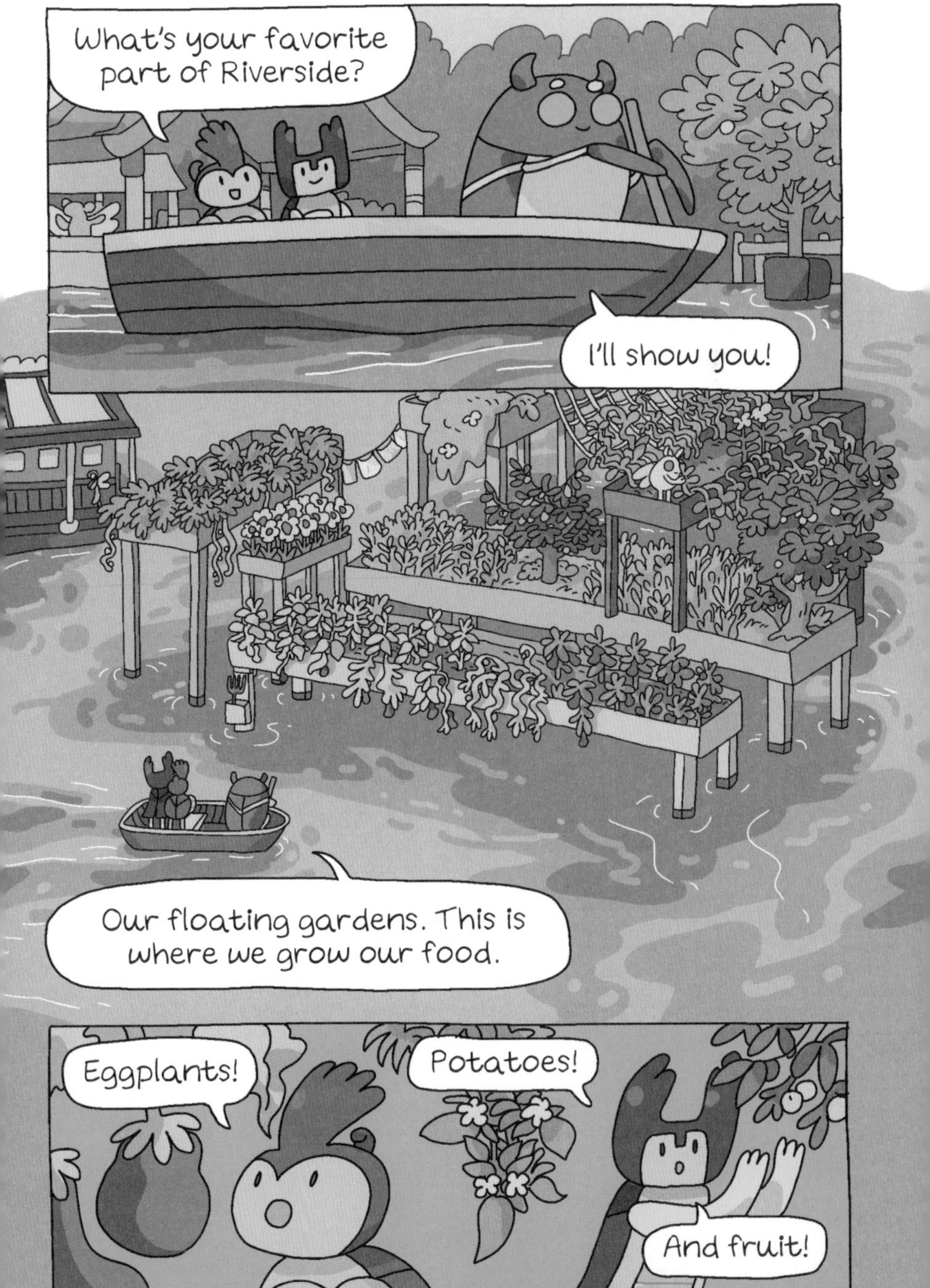
What's your favorite part of Riverside?
I'll show you!
Our floating gardens. This is where we grow our food.
Eggplants!
Potatoes!
And fruit!

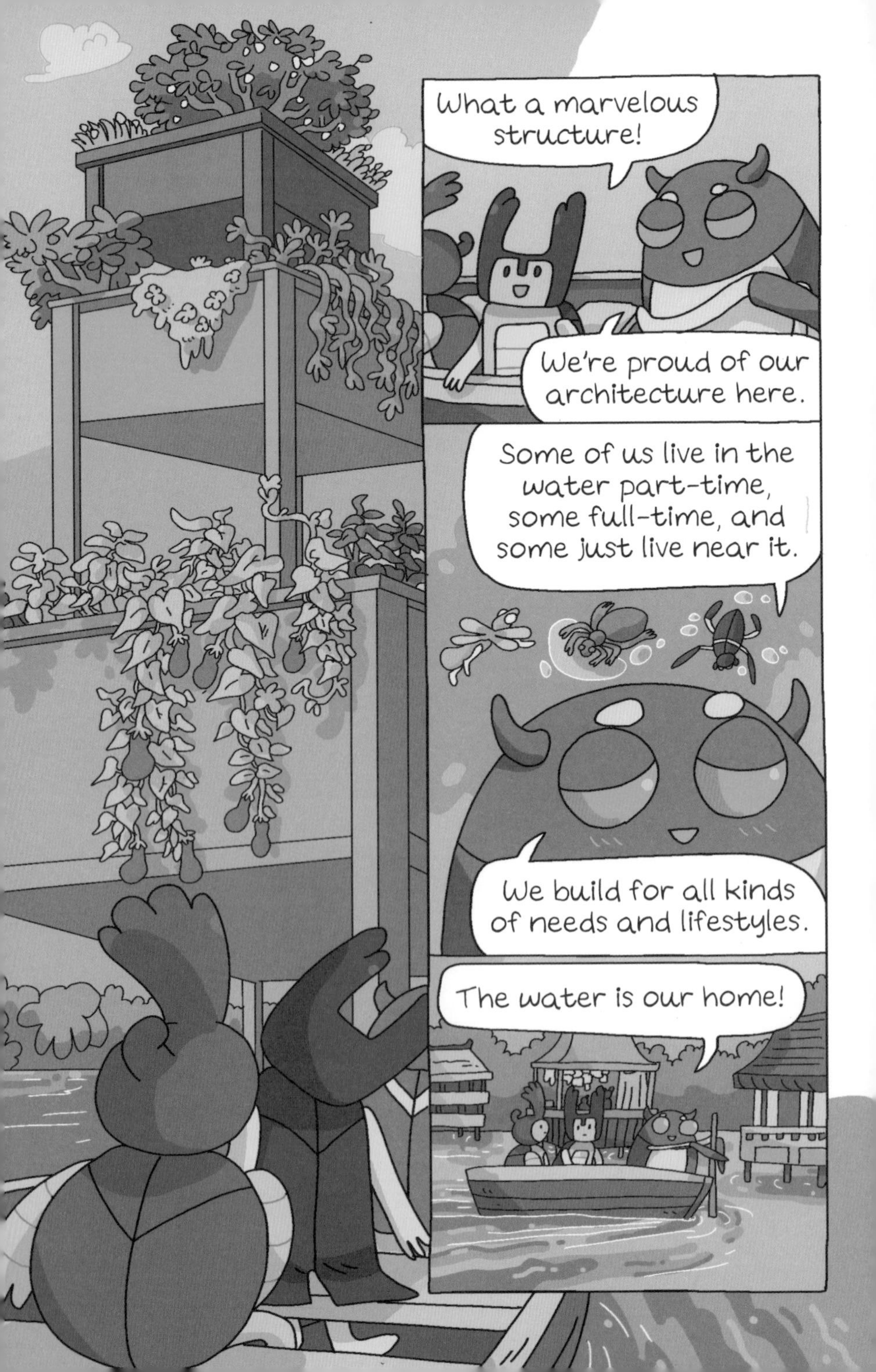
What a marvelous structure!
We're proud of our architecture here.
Some of us live in the water part-time, some full-time, and some just live near it.
We build for all kinds of needs and lifestyles.
The water is our home!

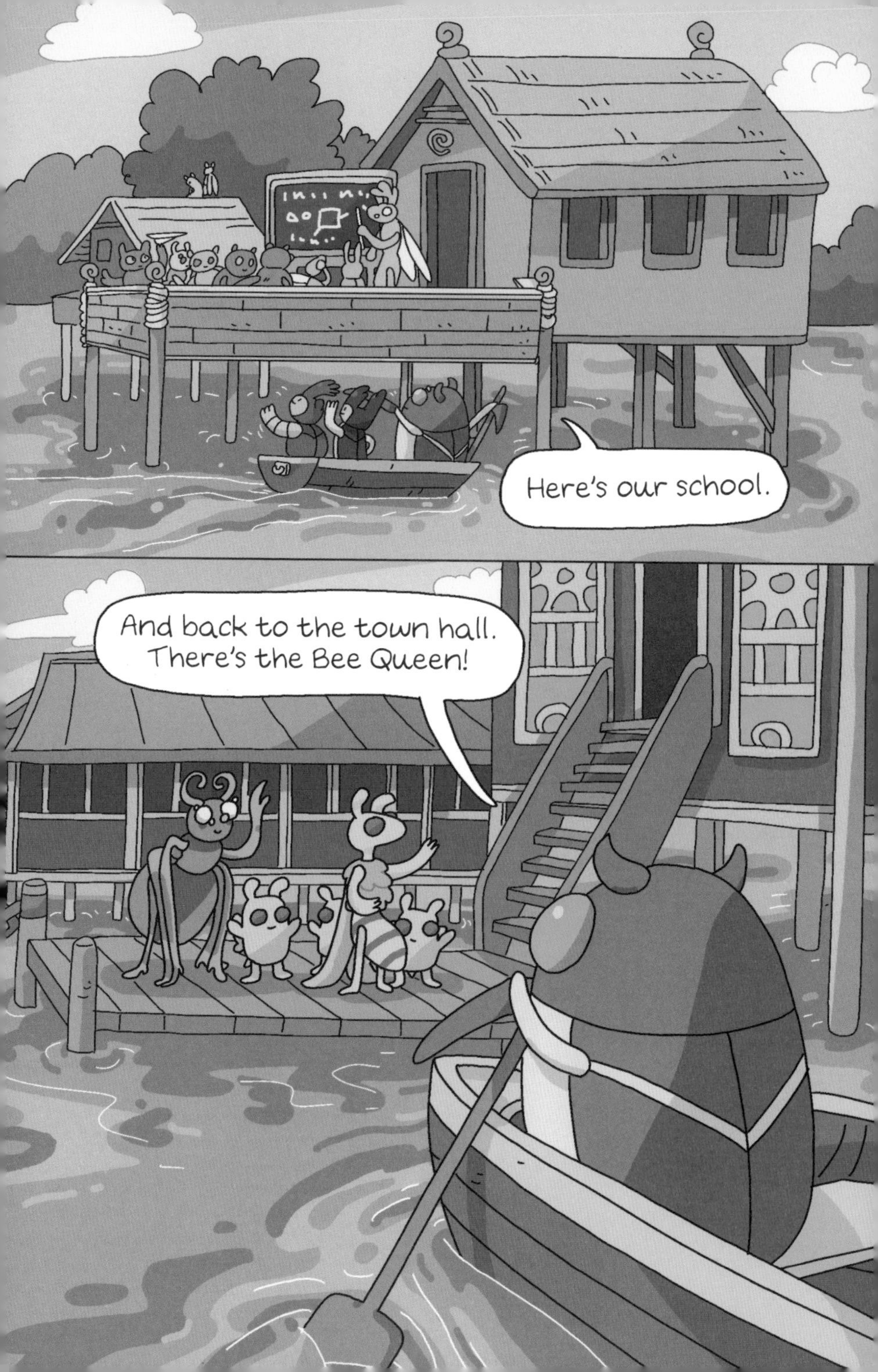
Here's our school.
And back to the town hall. There's the Bee Queen!

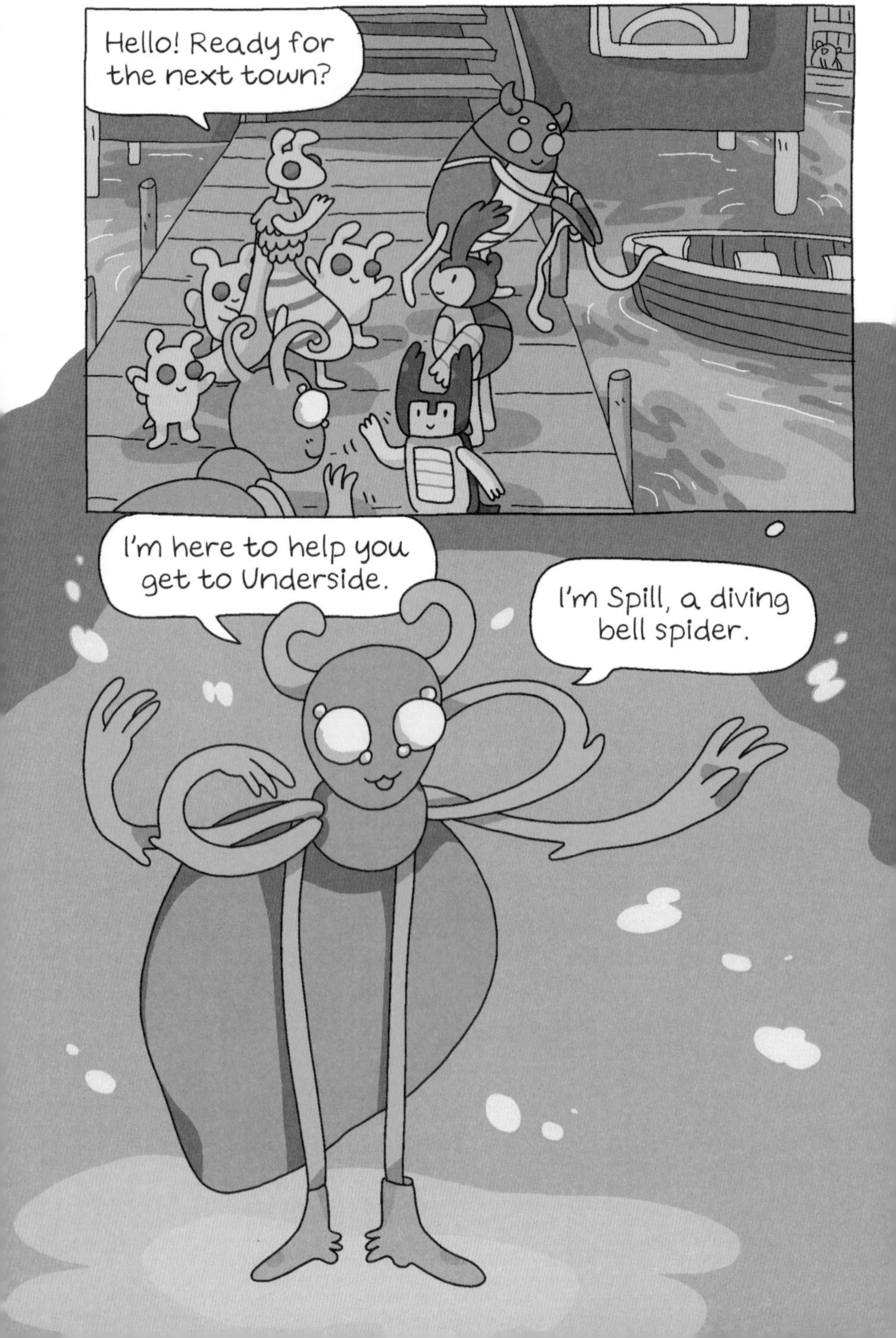
Hello! Ready for the next town?
I'm here to help you get to Underside.
I'm Spill, a diving bell spider.

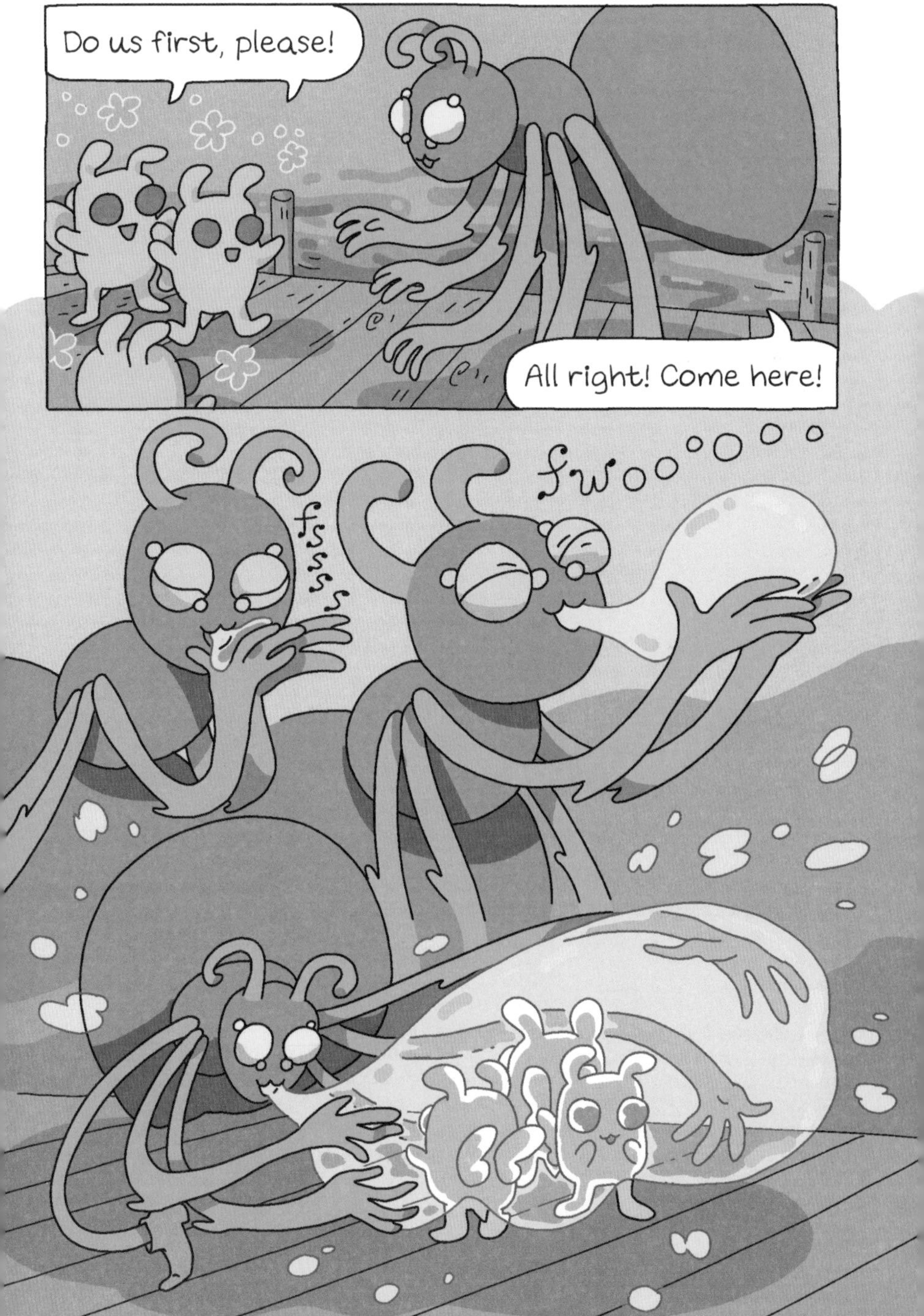
Do us first, please!
All right! Come here!
fssss
fwoooooo

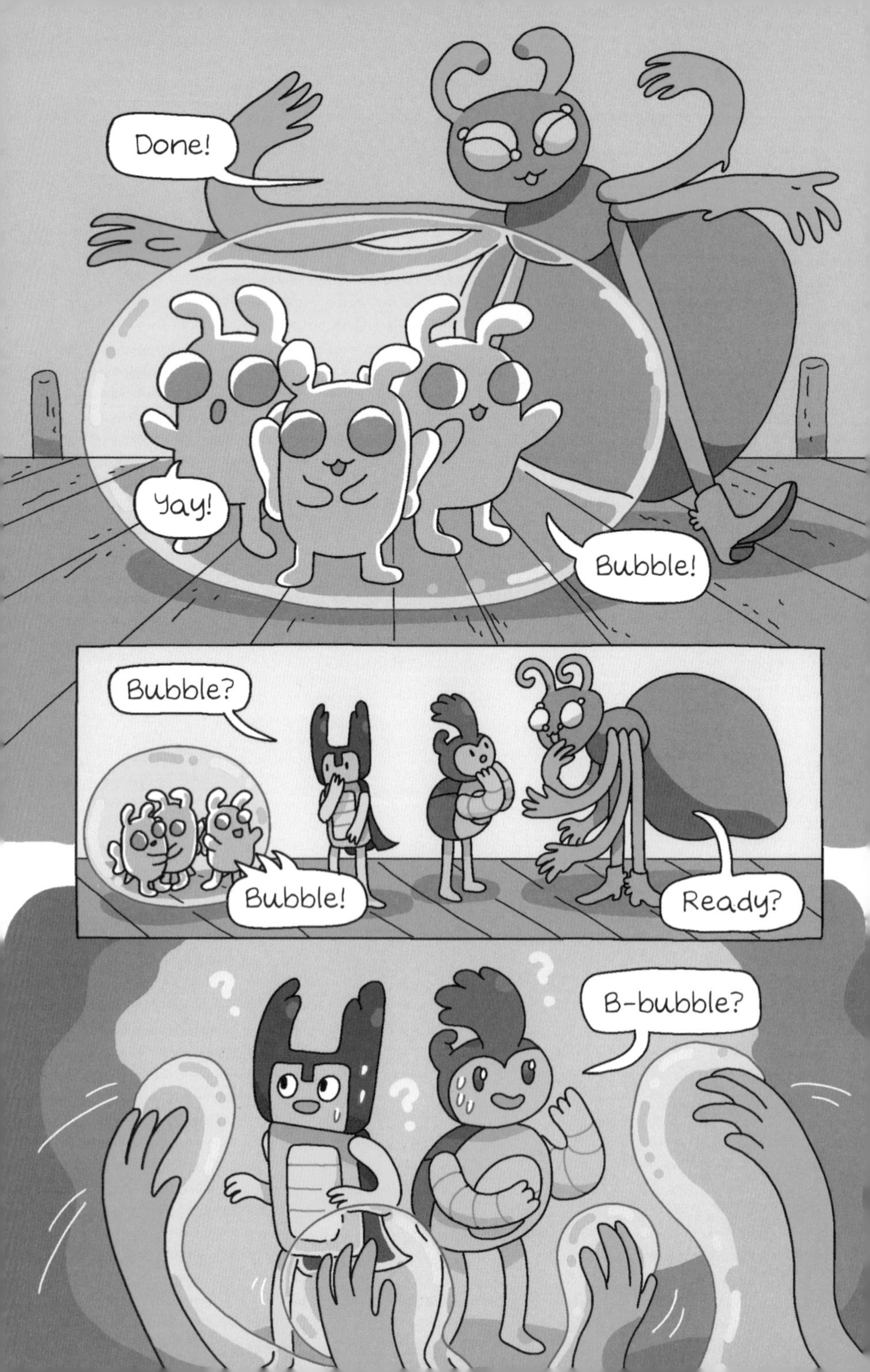
Done!
Yay!
Bubble!
Bubble?
Bubble!
Ready?
B-bubble?

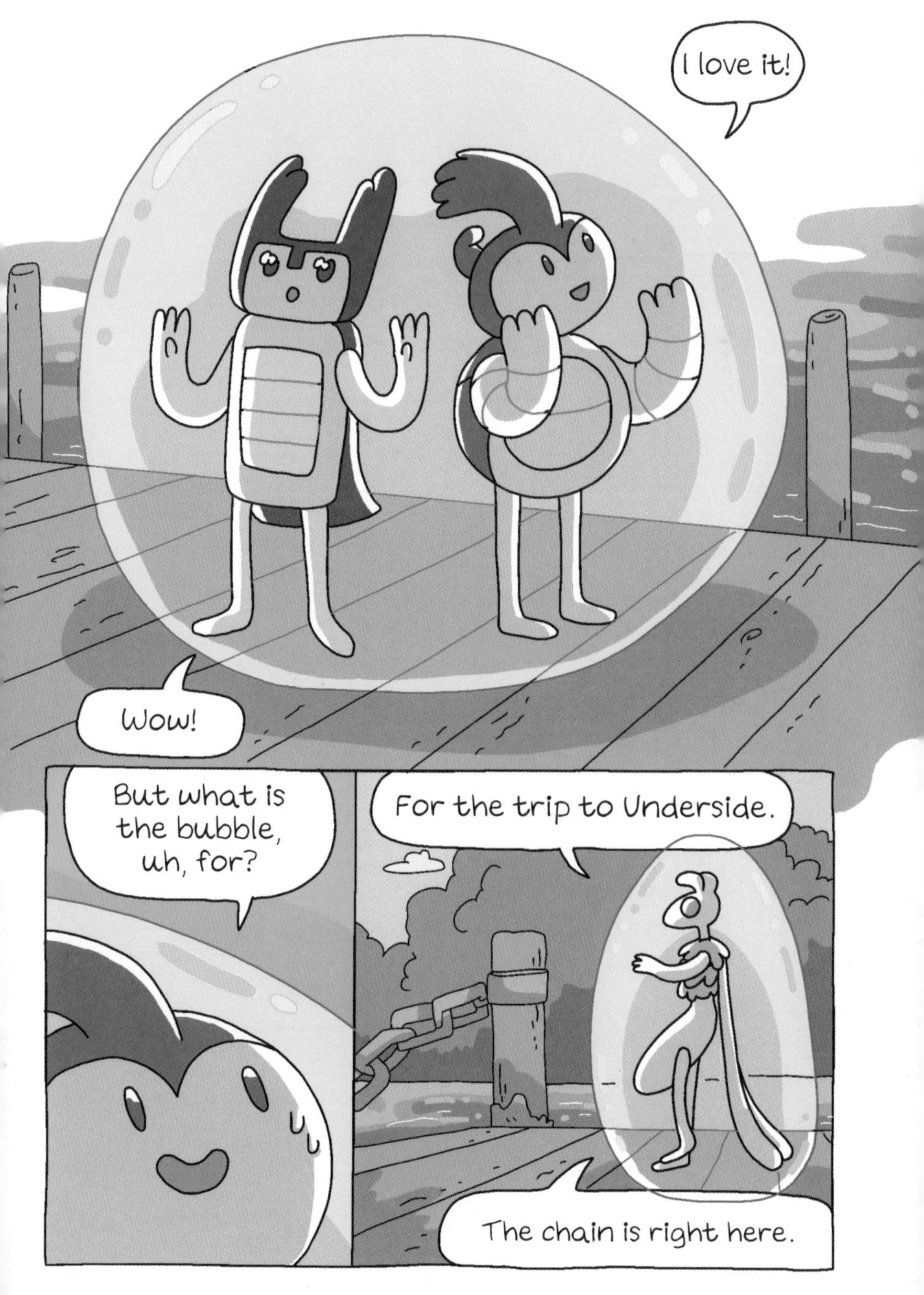
I love it!
Wow!
But what is the bubble, uh, for?
For the trip to Underside.
The chain is right here.

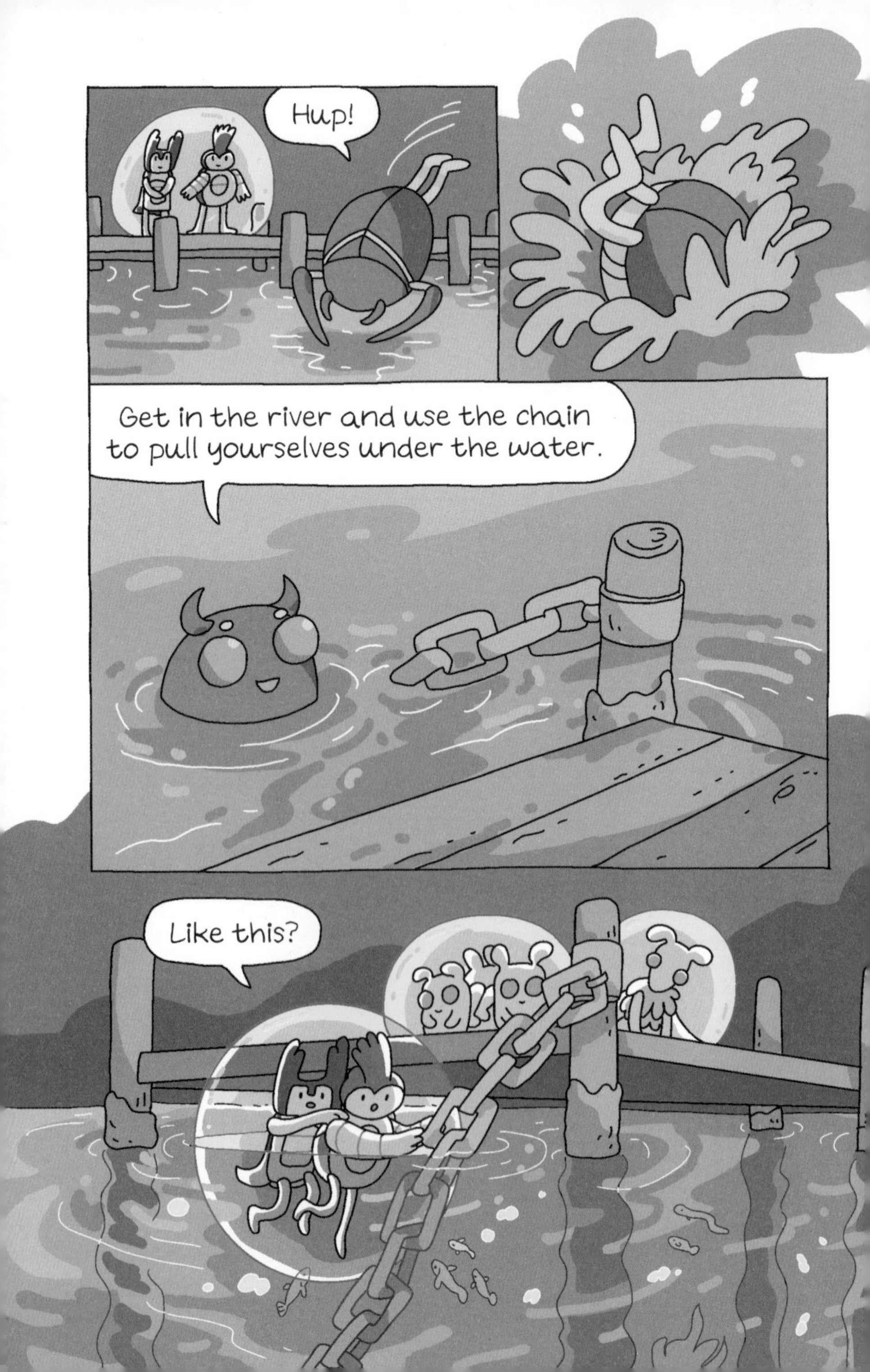
Hup!
Get in the river and use the chain to pull yourselves under the water.
Like this?

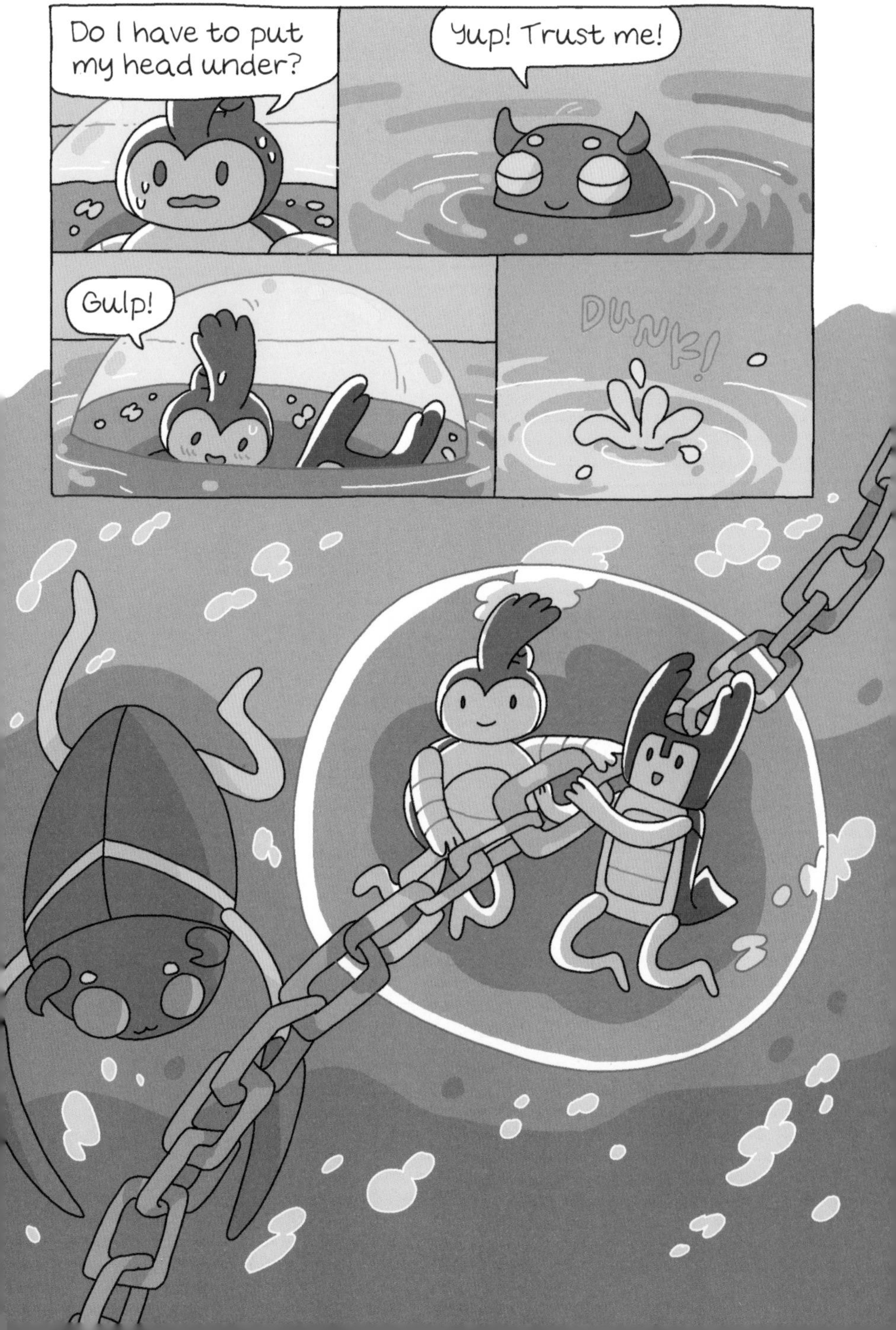
Do I have to put my head under?
Yup! Trust me!
Gulp!
DUNK!

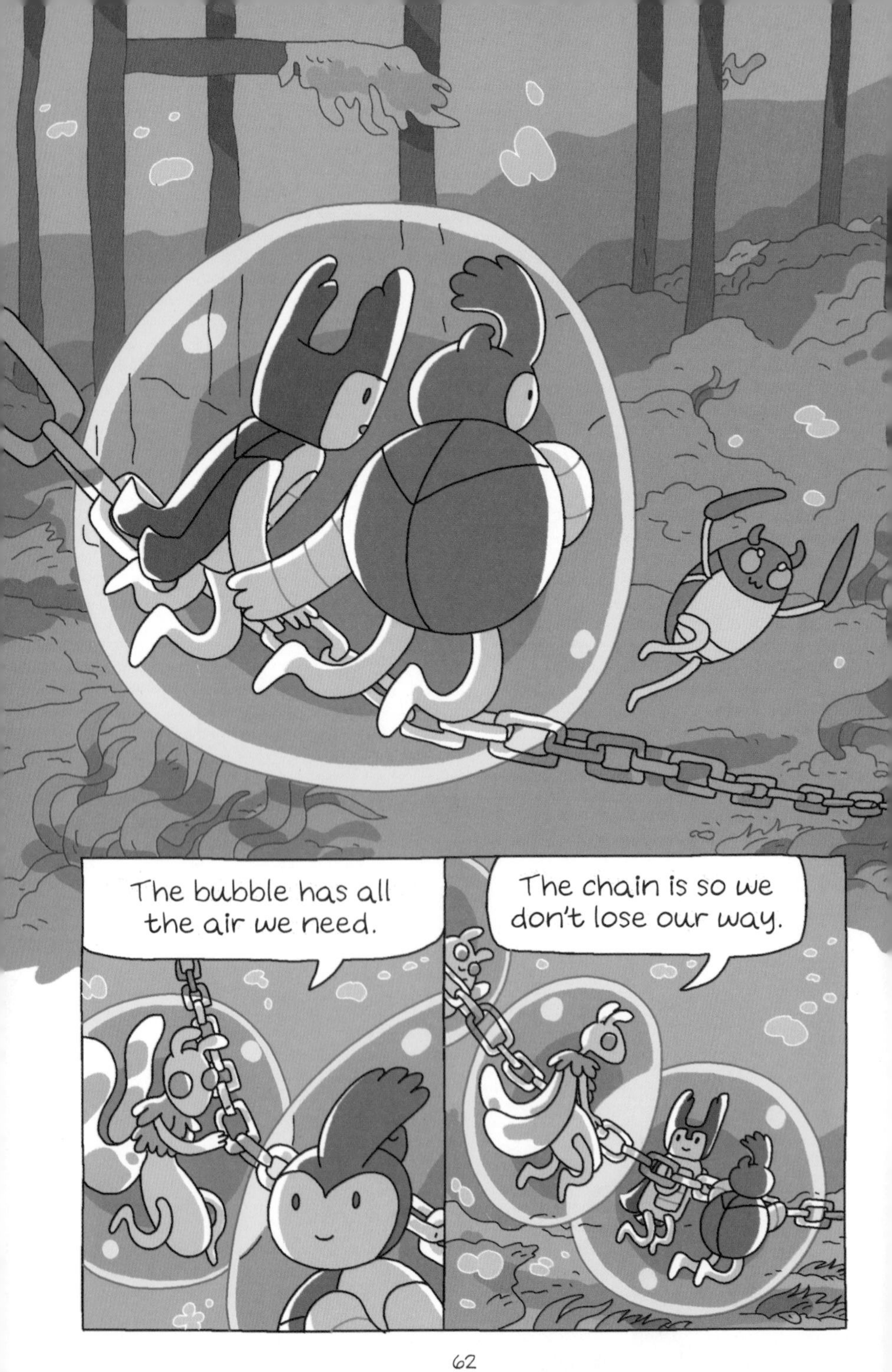
The bubble has all the air we need.
The chain is so we don't lose our way.

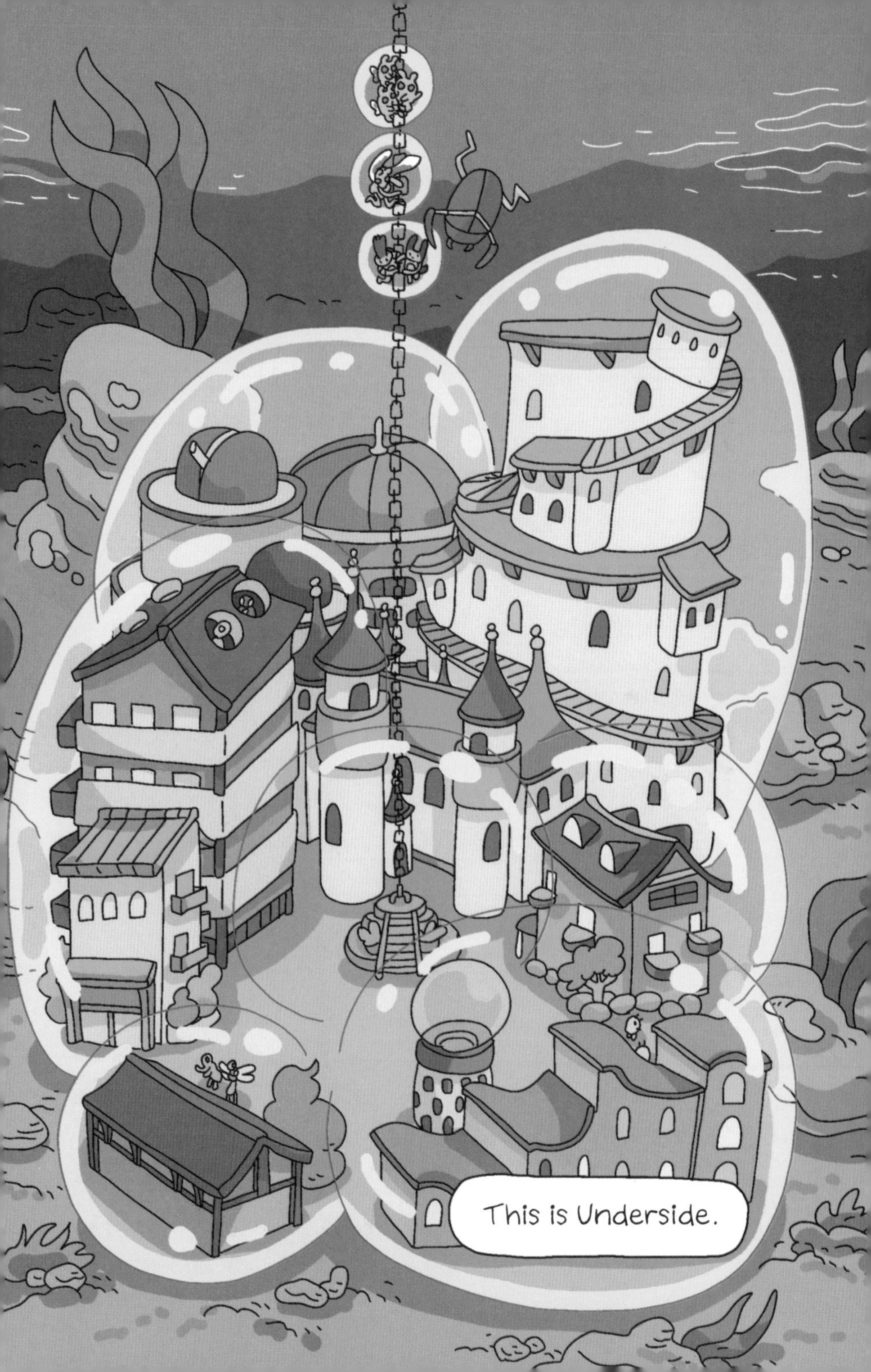
This is Underside.

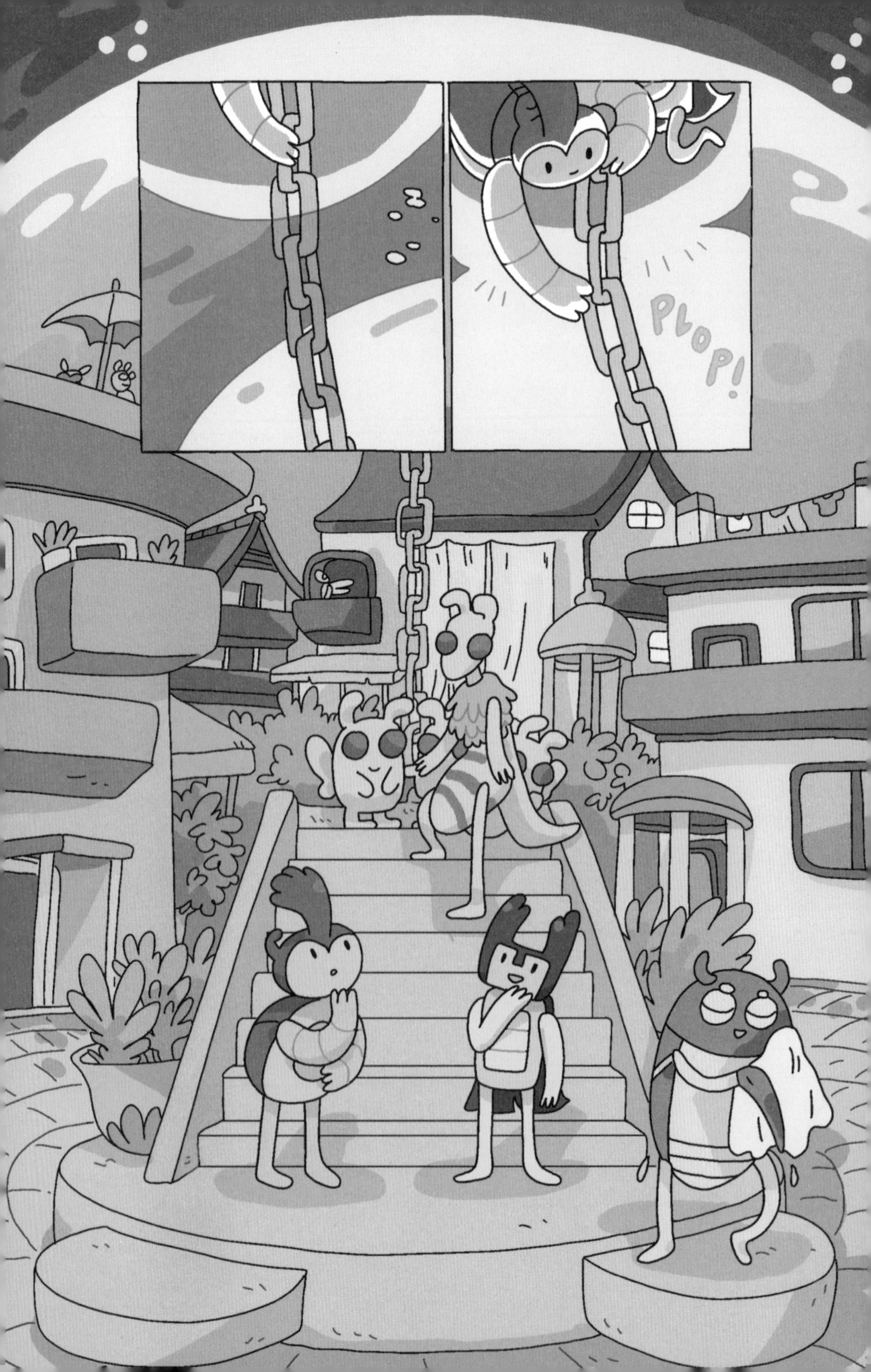
PLOP!

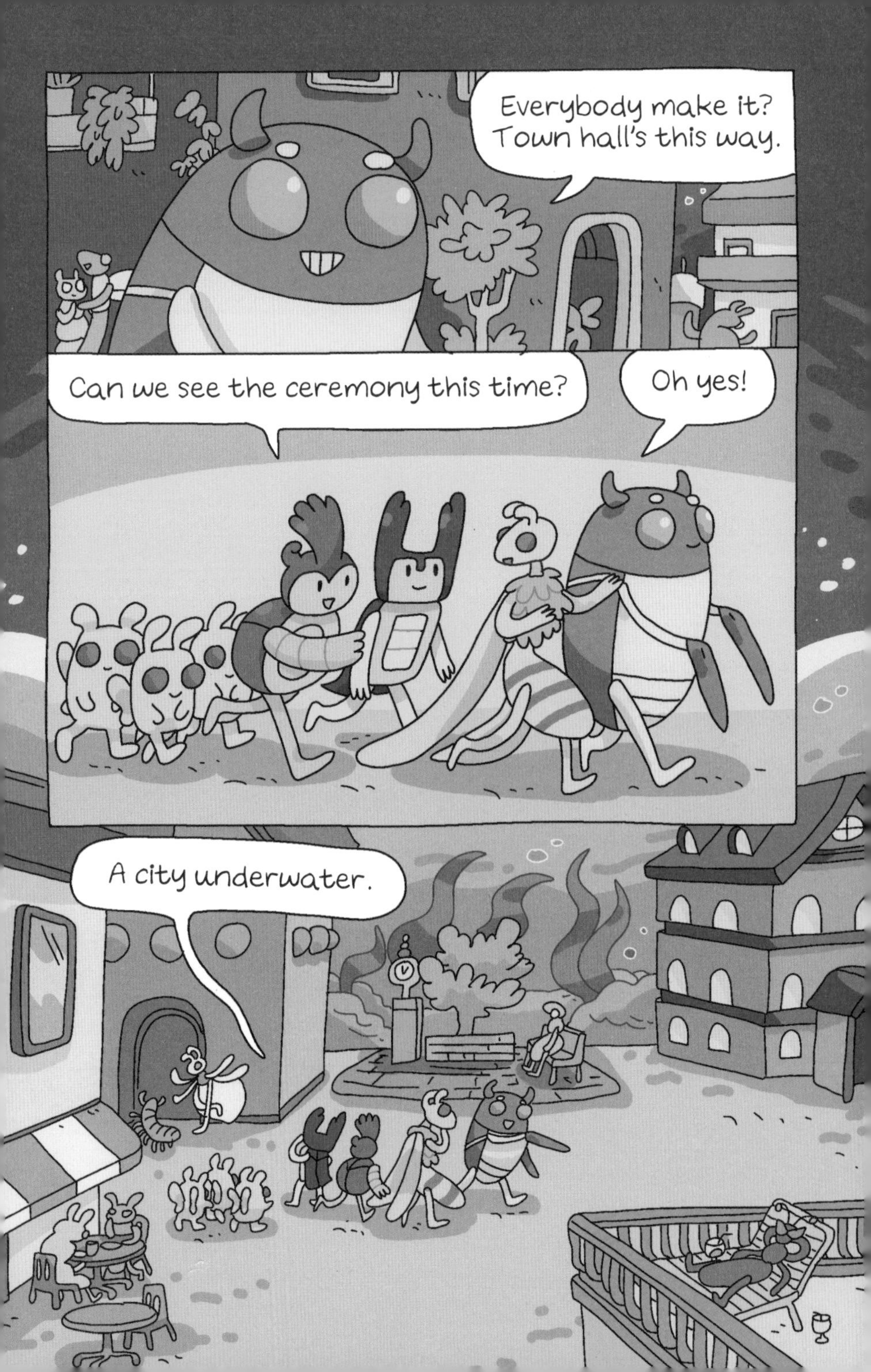
Everybody make it? Town hall's this way.
Can we see the ceremony this time?
Oh yes!
A city underwater.

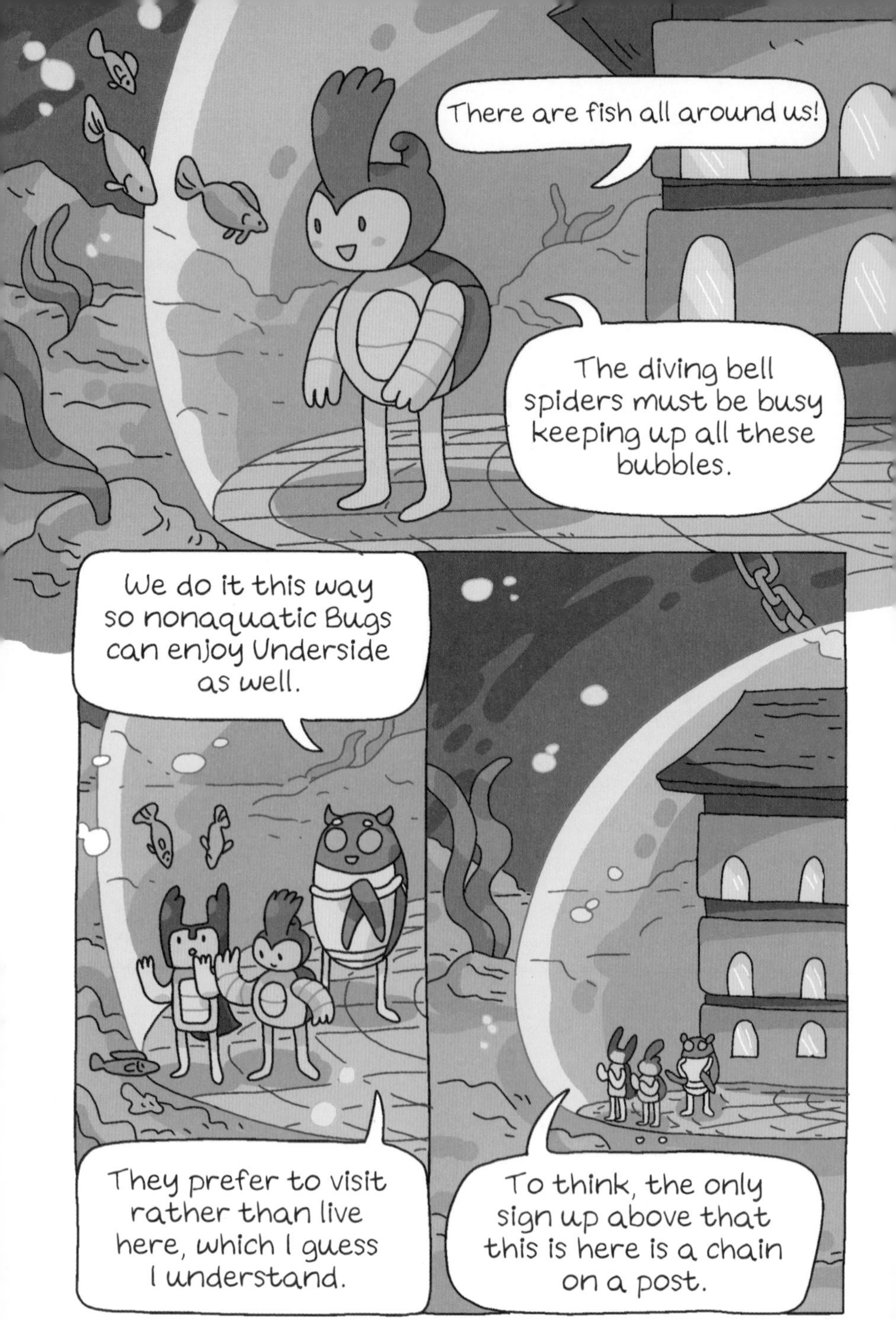
There are fish all around us!
The diving bell spiders must be busy keeping up all these bubbles.
We do it this way so nonaquatic Bugs can enjoy Underside as well.
They prefer to visit rather than live here, which I guess I understand.
To think, the only sign up above that this is here is a chain on a post.

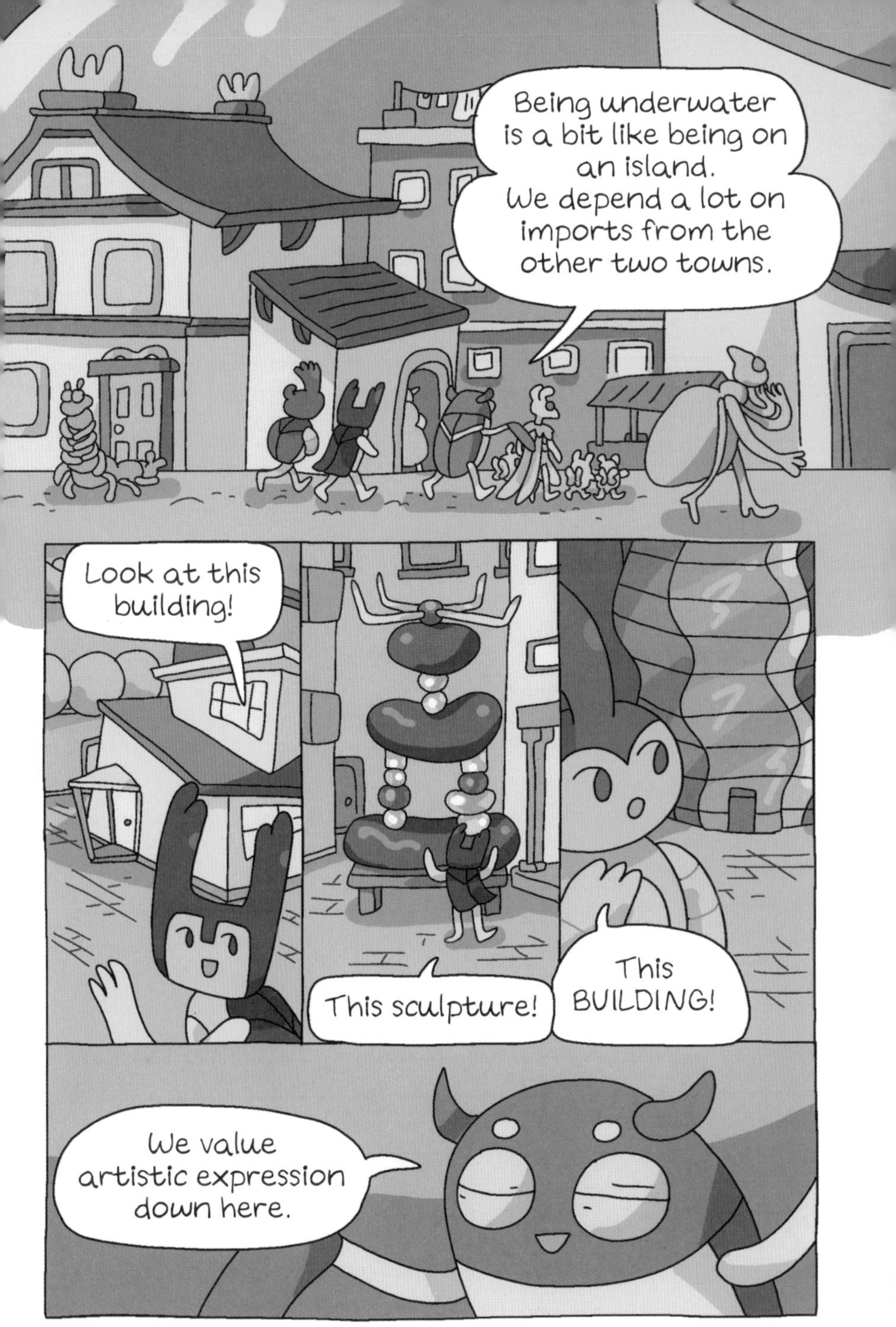
Being underwater is a bit like being on an island.
We depend a lot on imports from the other two towns.
Look at this building!
This sculpture!
This BUILDING!
We value artistic expression down here.

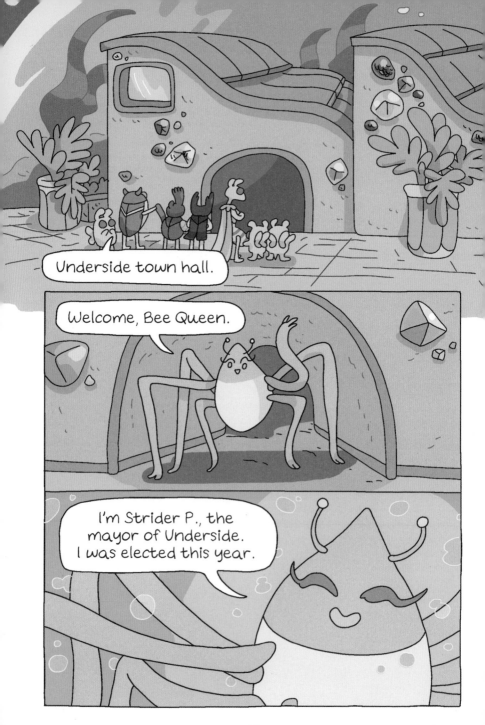

Underside town hall.

Welcome, Bee Queen.

I'm Strider P., the mayor of Underside. I was elected this year.

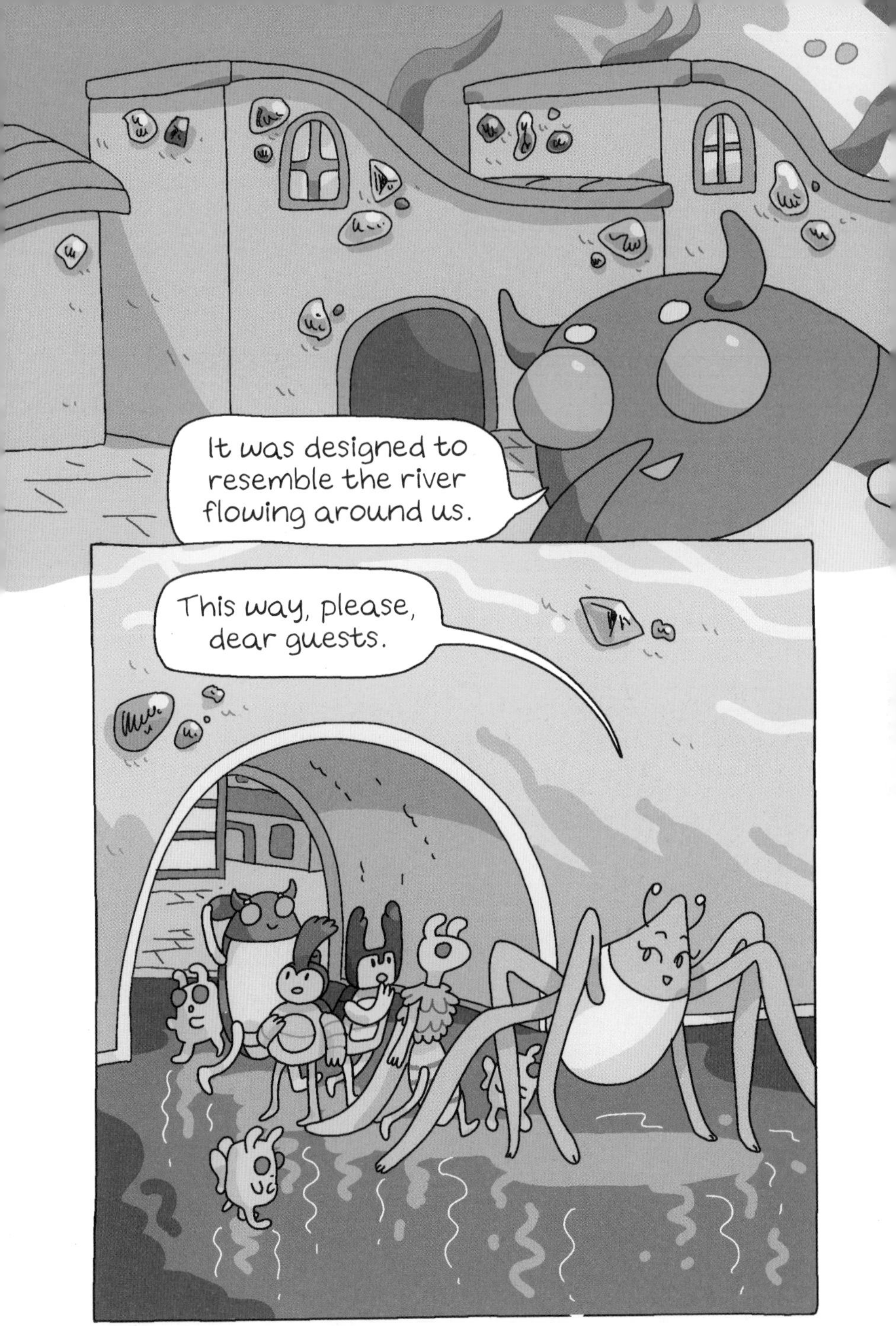
It was designed to resemble the river flowing around us.
This way, please, dear guests.

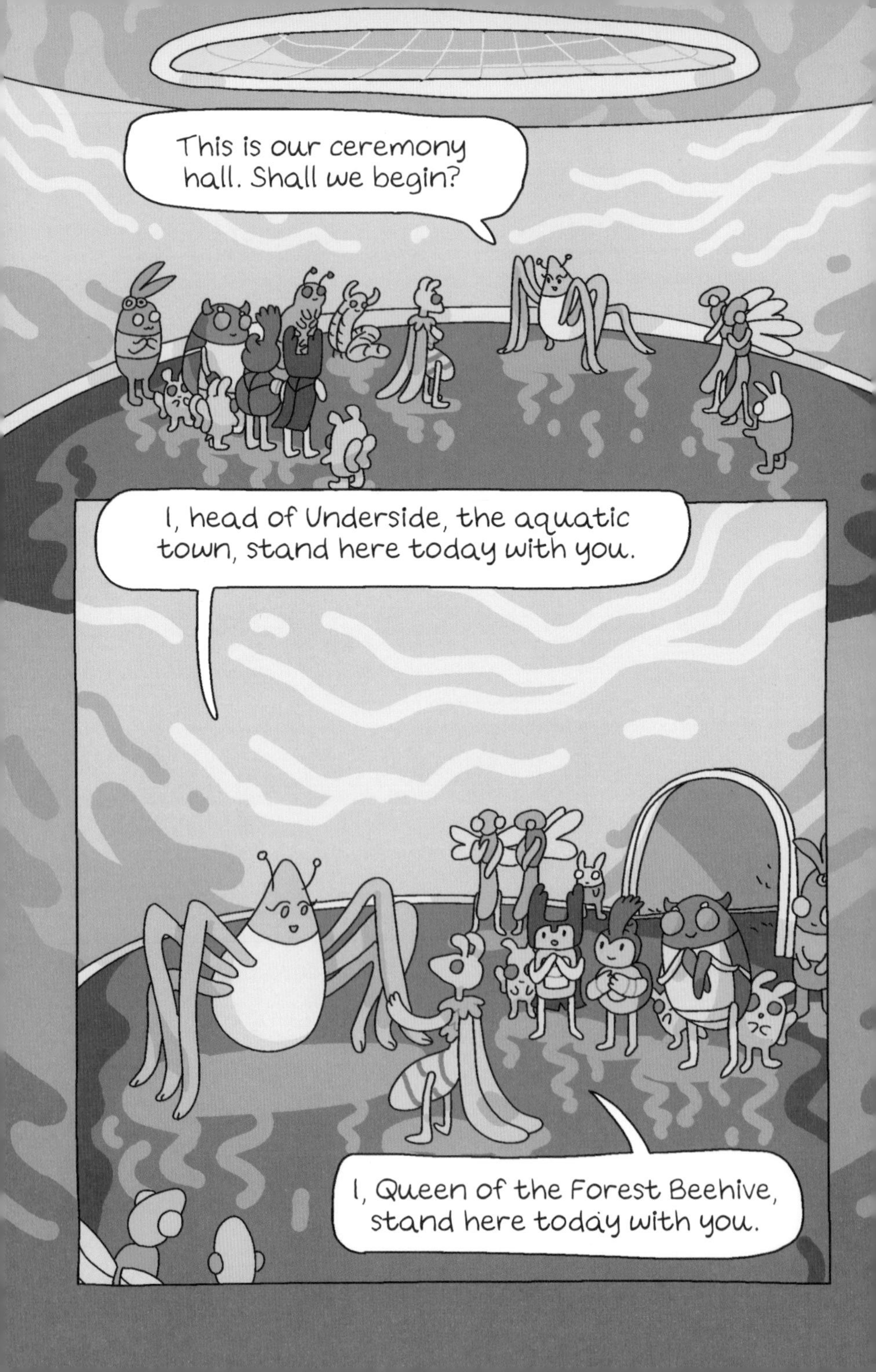
This is our ceremony hall. Shall we begin?
I, head of Underside, the aquatic town, stand here today with you.
I, Queen of the Forest Beehive, stand here today with you.

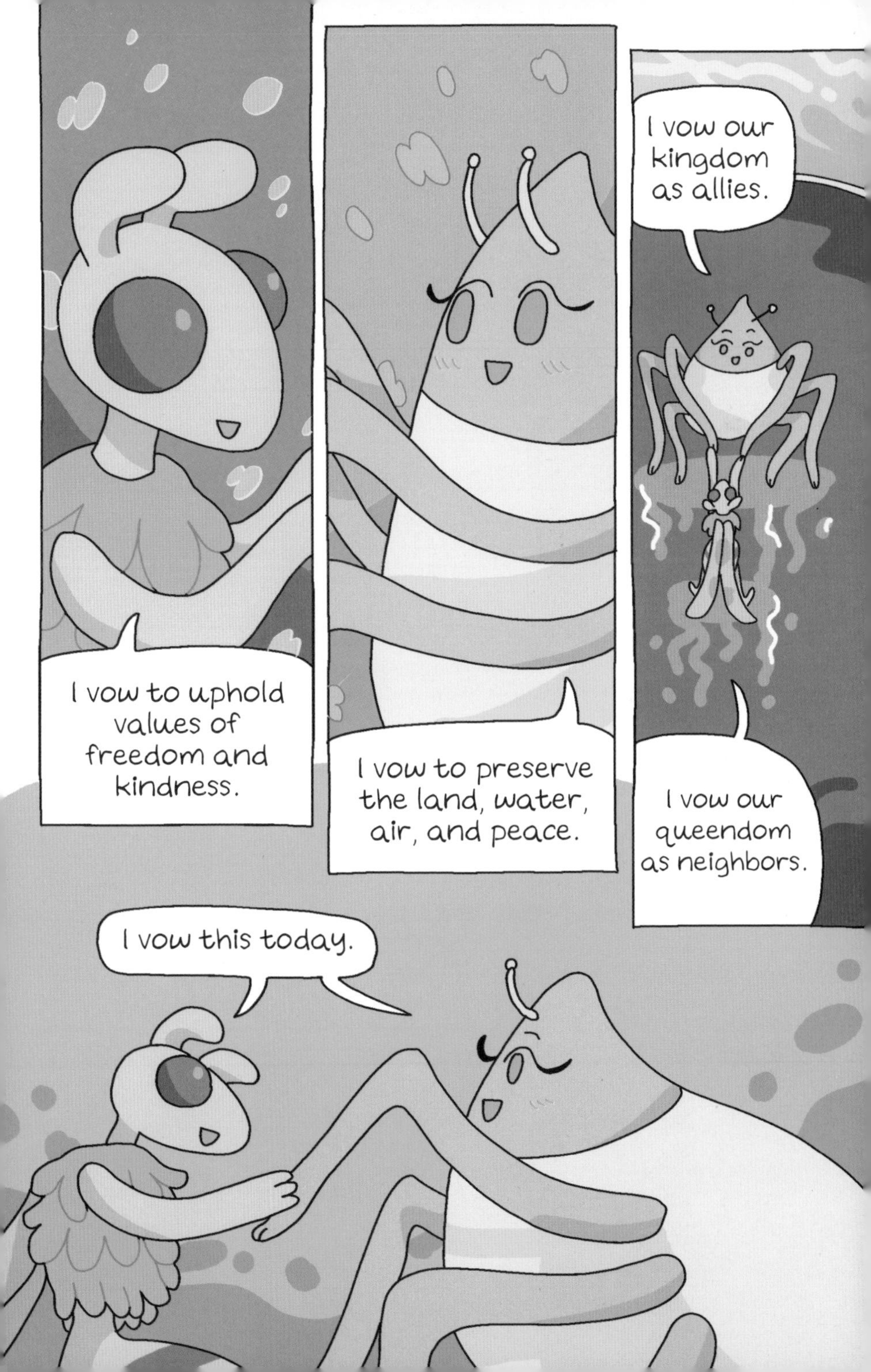
I vow to uphold values of freedom and kindness.
I vow to preserve the land, water, air, and peace.
I vow our kingdom as allies.
I vow our queendom as neighbors.
I vow this today.

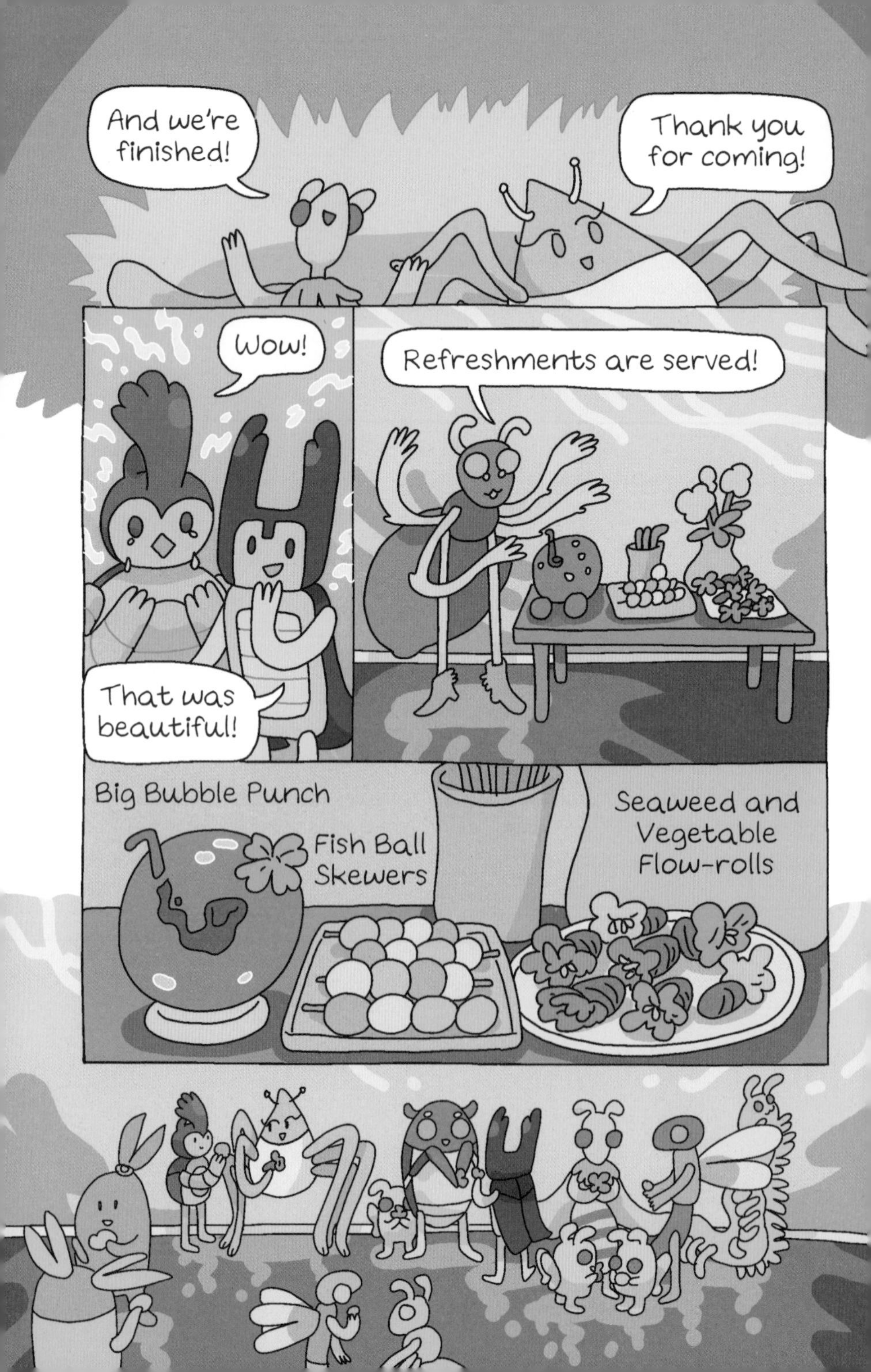
And we're finished!
Thank you for coming!
Wow!
That was beautiful!
Refreshments are served!
Big Bubble Punch
Fish Ball Skewers
Seaweed and Vegetable Flow-rolls

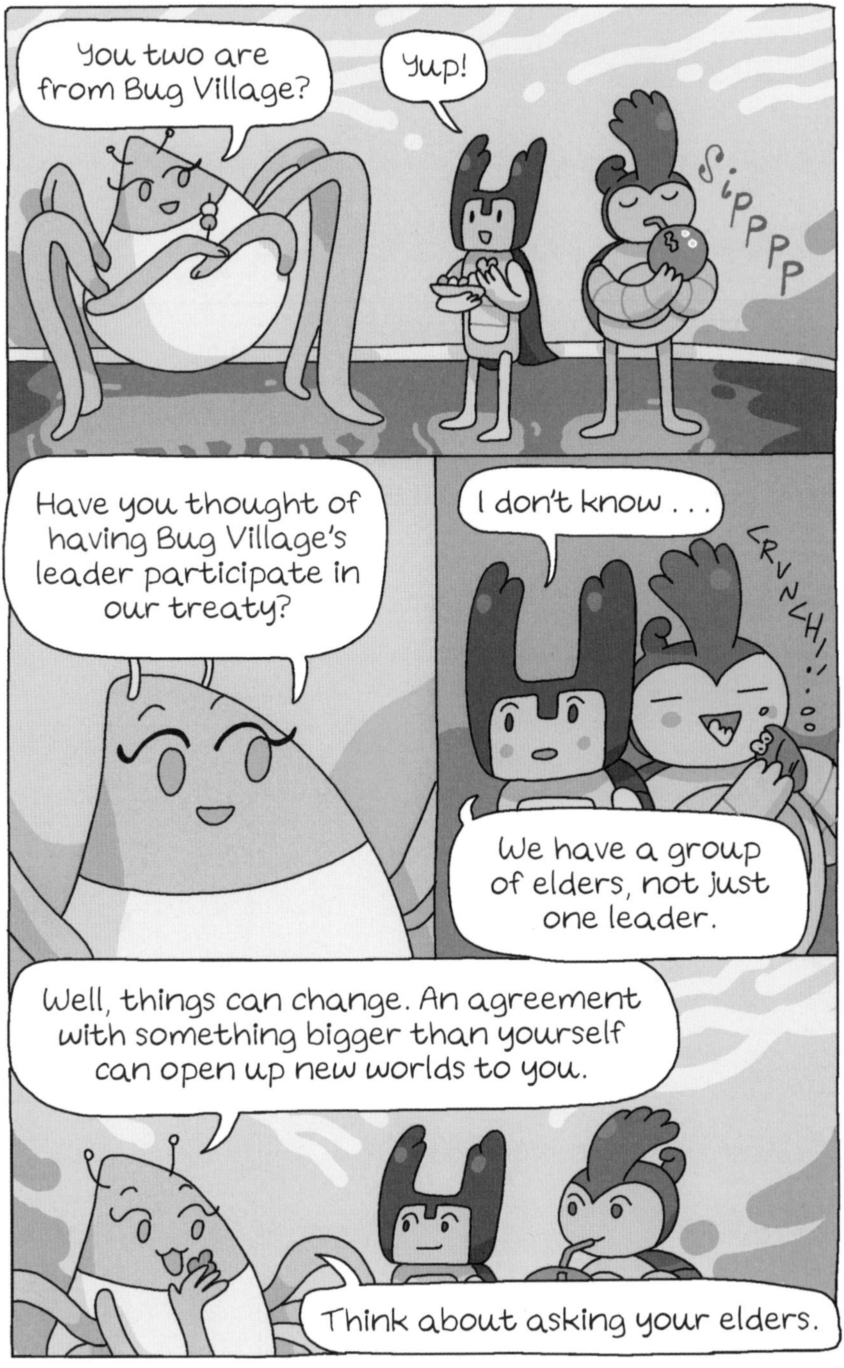
You two are from Bug Village?
Yup!
SiPPPP
Have you thought of having Bug Village's leader participate in our treaty?
I don't know . . .
CRVNCH!!
We have a group of elders, not just one leader.
Well, things can change. An agreement with something bigger than yourself can open up new worlds to you.
Think about asking your elders.

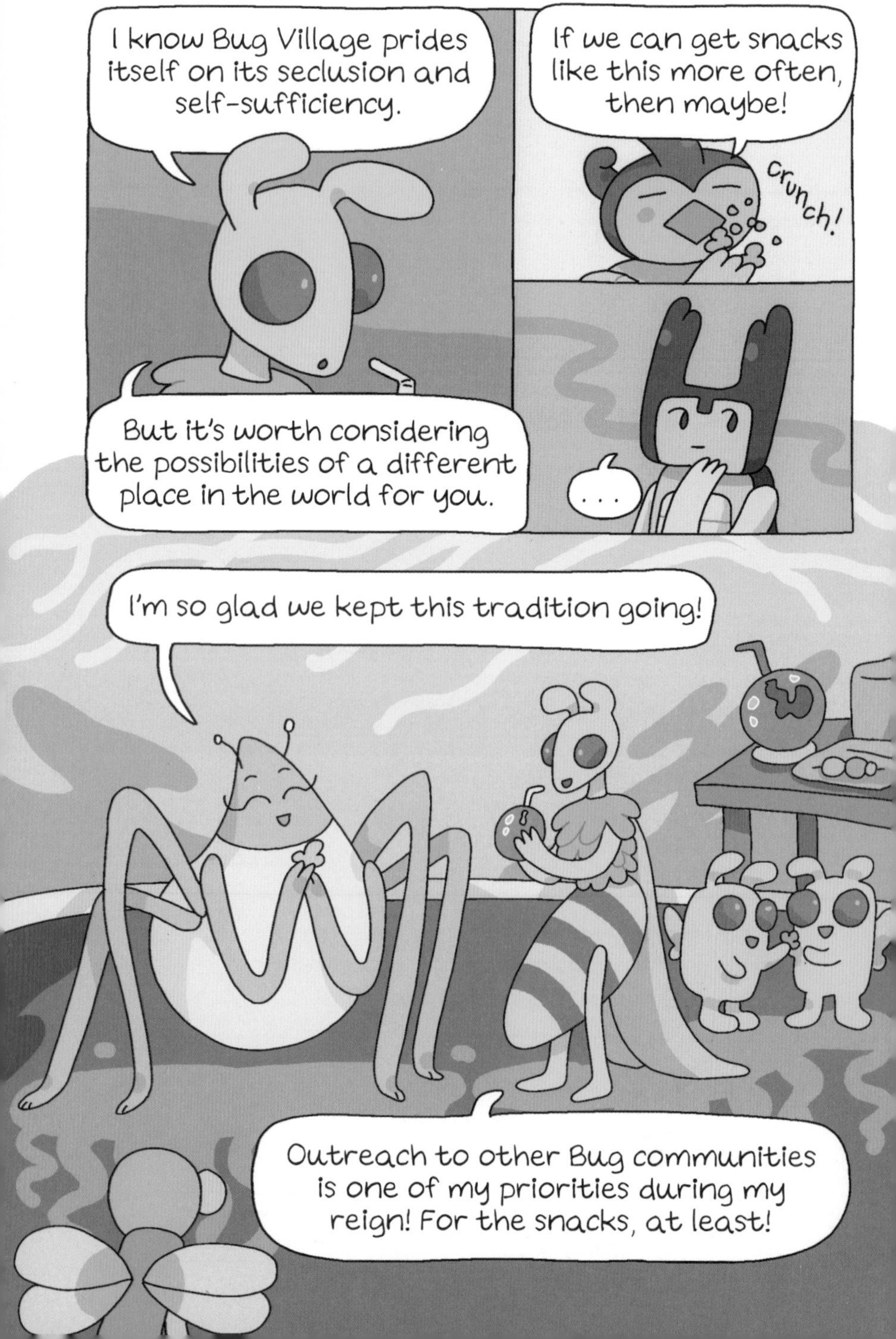
I know Bug Village prides itself on its seclusion and self-sufficiency.
If we can get snacks like this more often, then maybe!
Crunch!
But it's worth considering the possibilities of a different place in the world for you.
...
I'm so glad we kept this tradition going!
Outreach to other Bug communities is one of my priorities during my reign! For the snacks, at least!

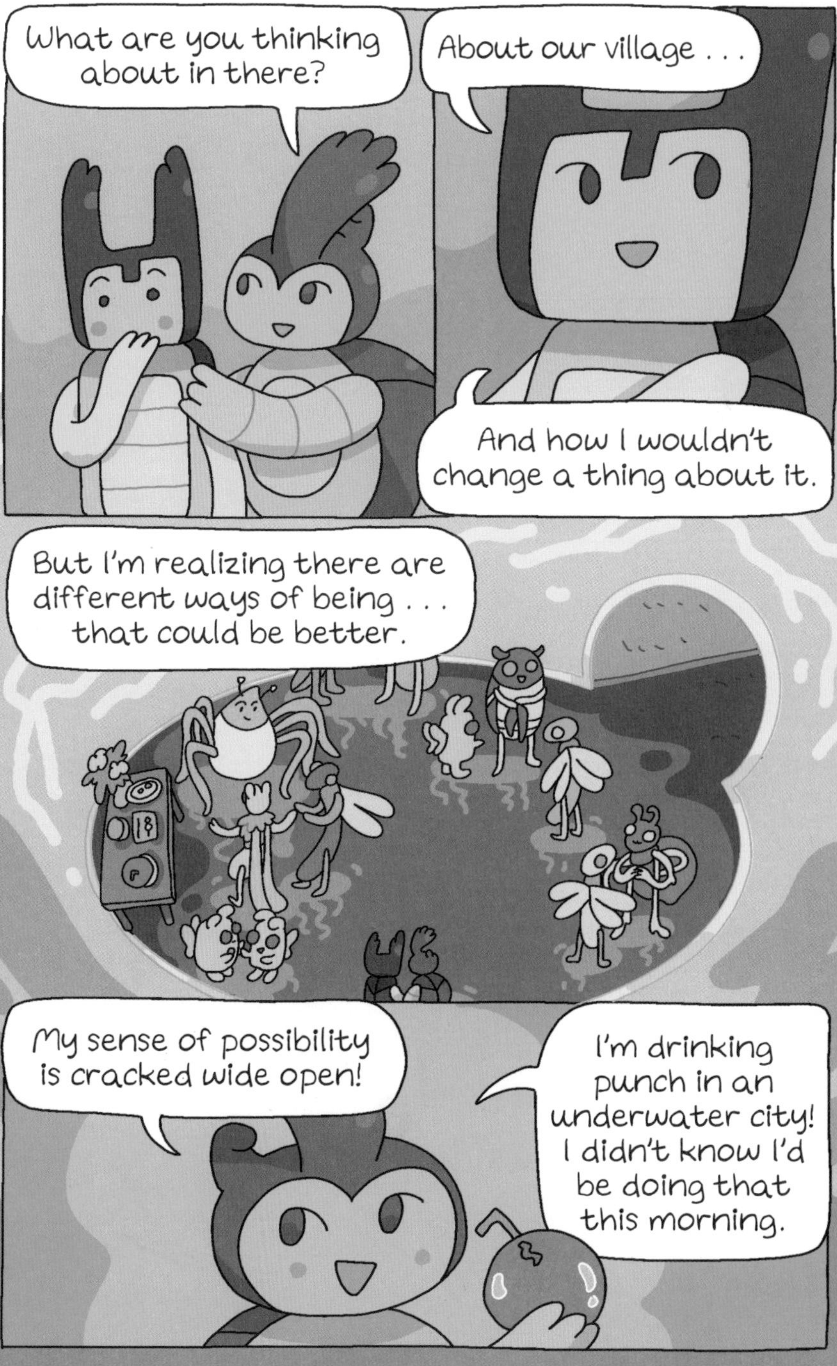
What are you thinking about in there?
About our village . . .
And how I wouldn't change a thing about it.
But I'm realizing there are different ways of being . . . that could be better.
My sense of possibility is cracked wide open!
I'm drinking punch in an underwater city! I didn't know I'd be doing that this morning.

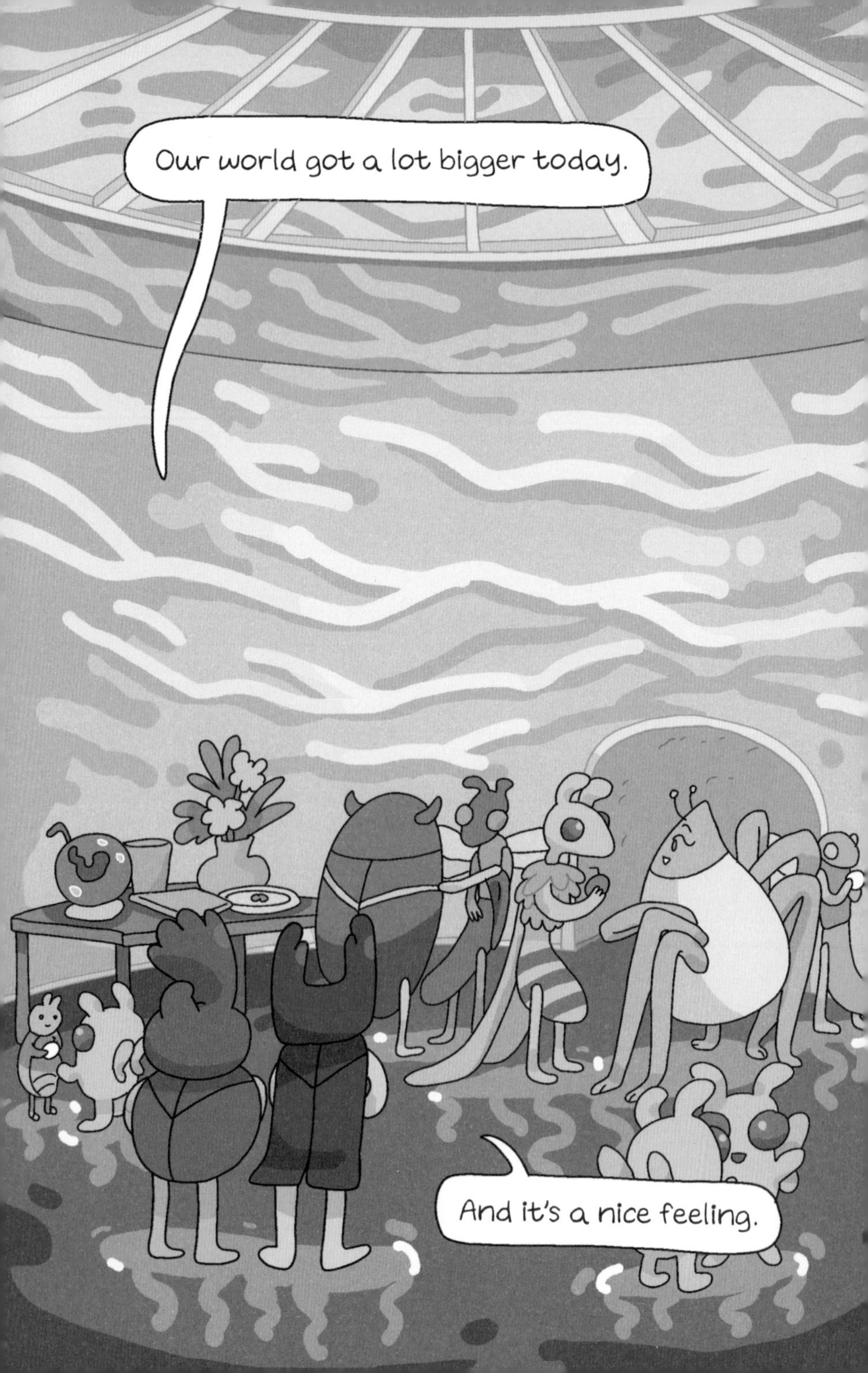
Our world got a lot bigger today.
And it's a nice feeling.

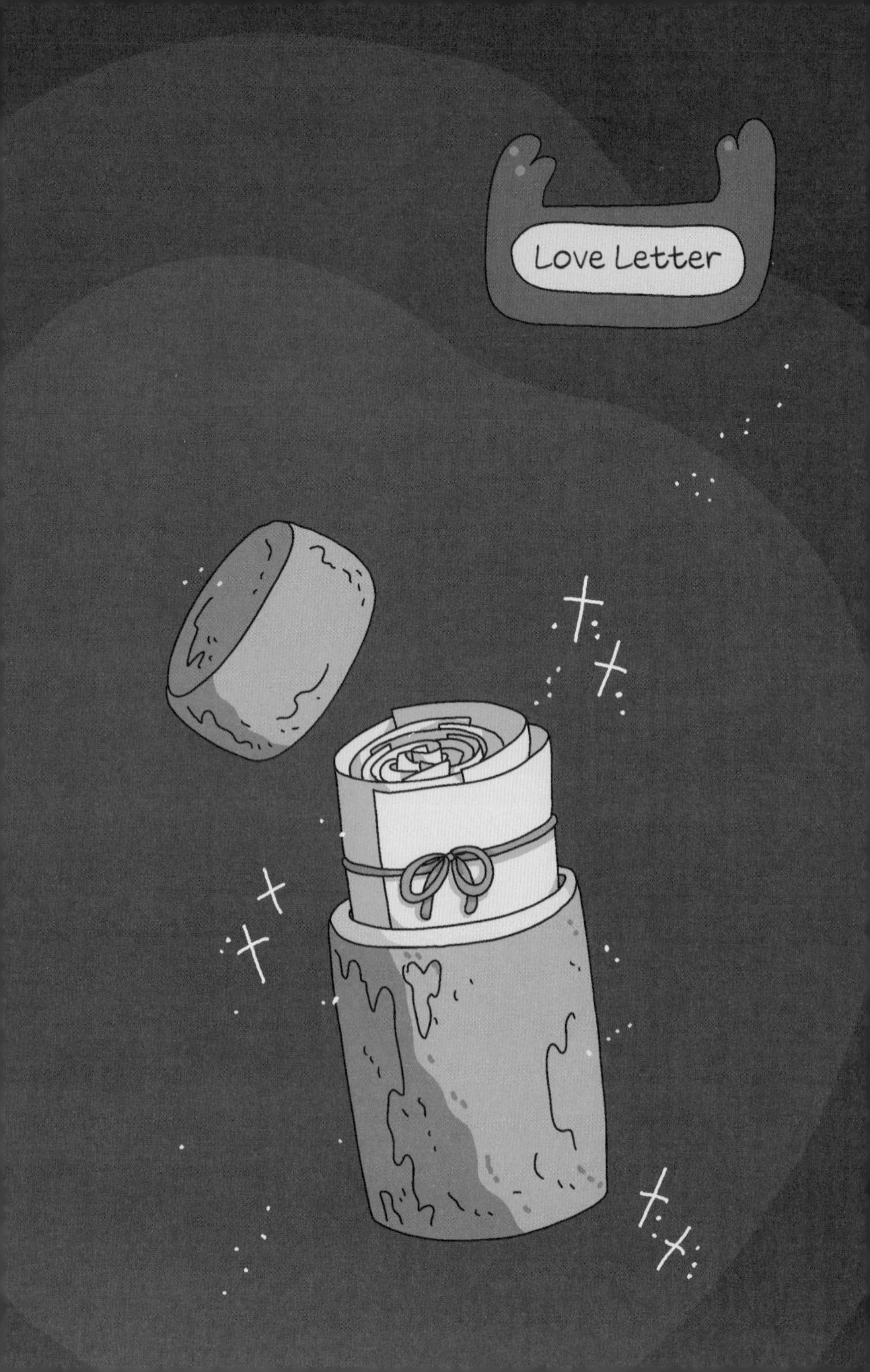
Love Letter

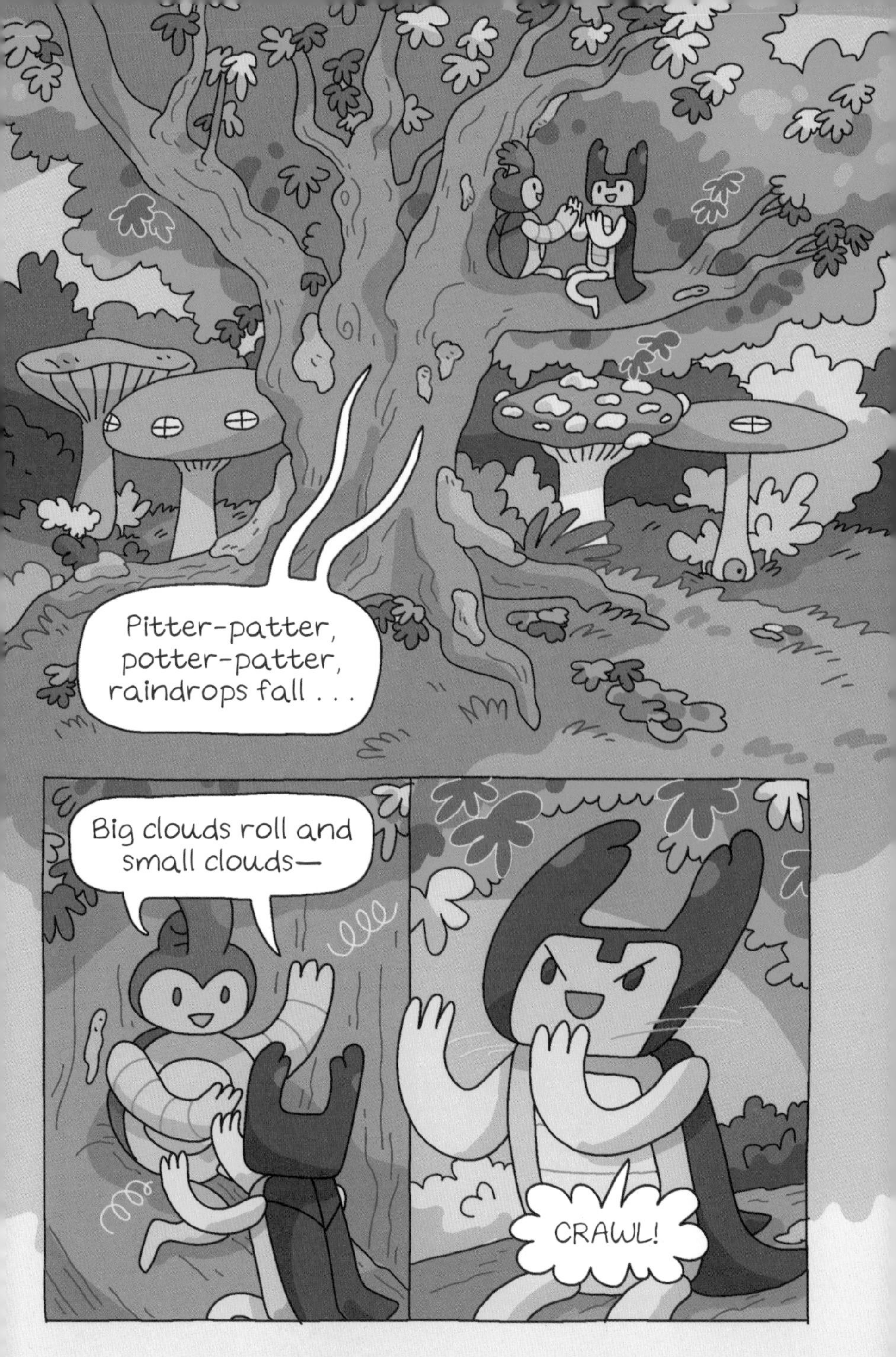
Pitter-patter, potter-patter, raindrops fall . . .
Big clouds roll and small clouds—
CRAWL!

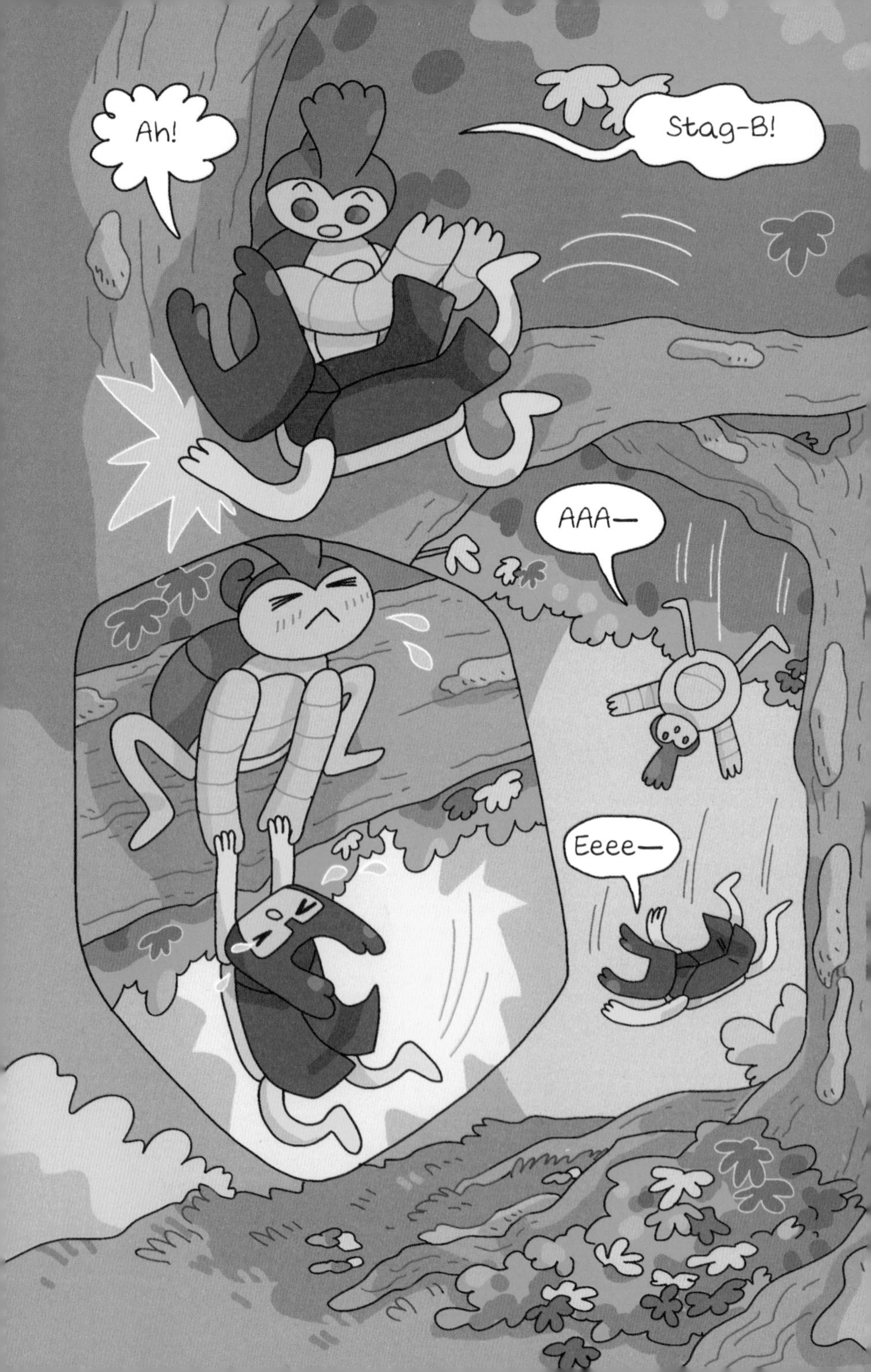
Ah!
Stag-B!
AAA—
Eeee—

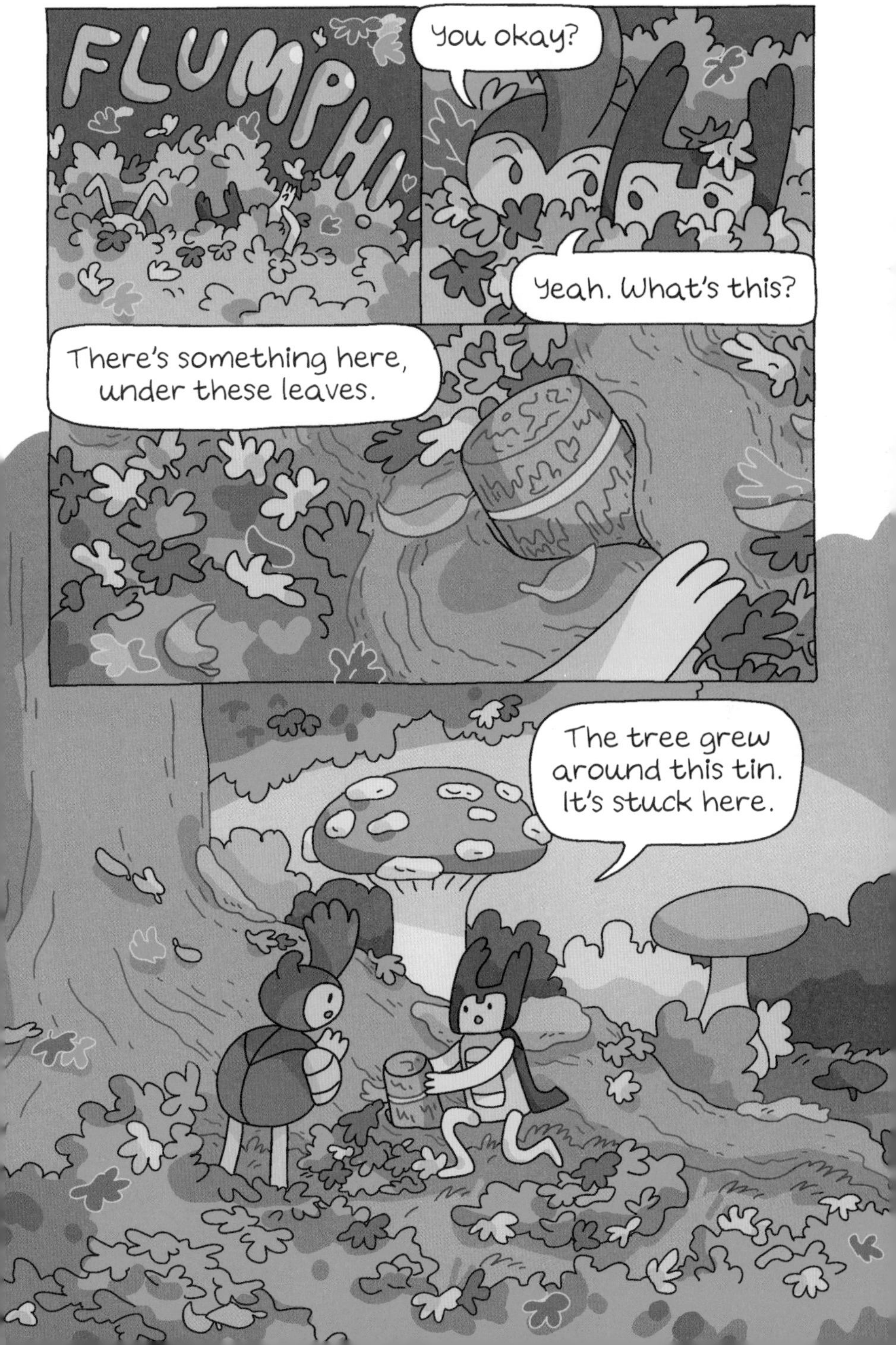
FLUMPH!
You okay?
Yeah. What's this?
There's something here, under these leaves.
The tree grew around this tin. It's stuck here.

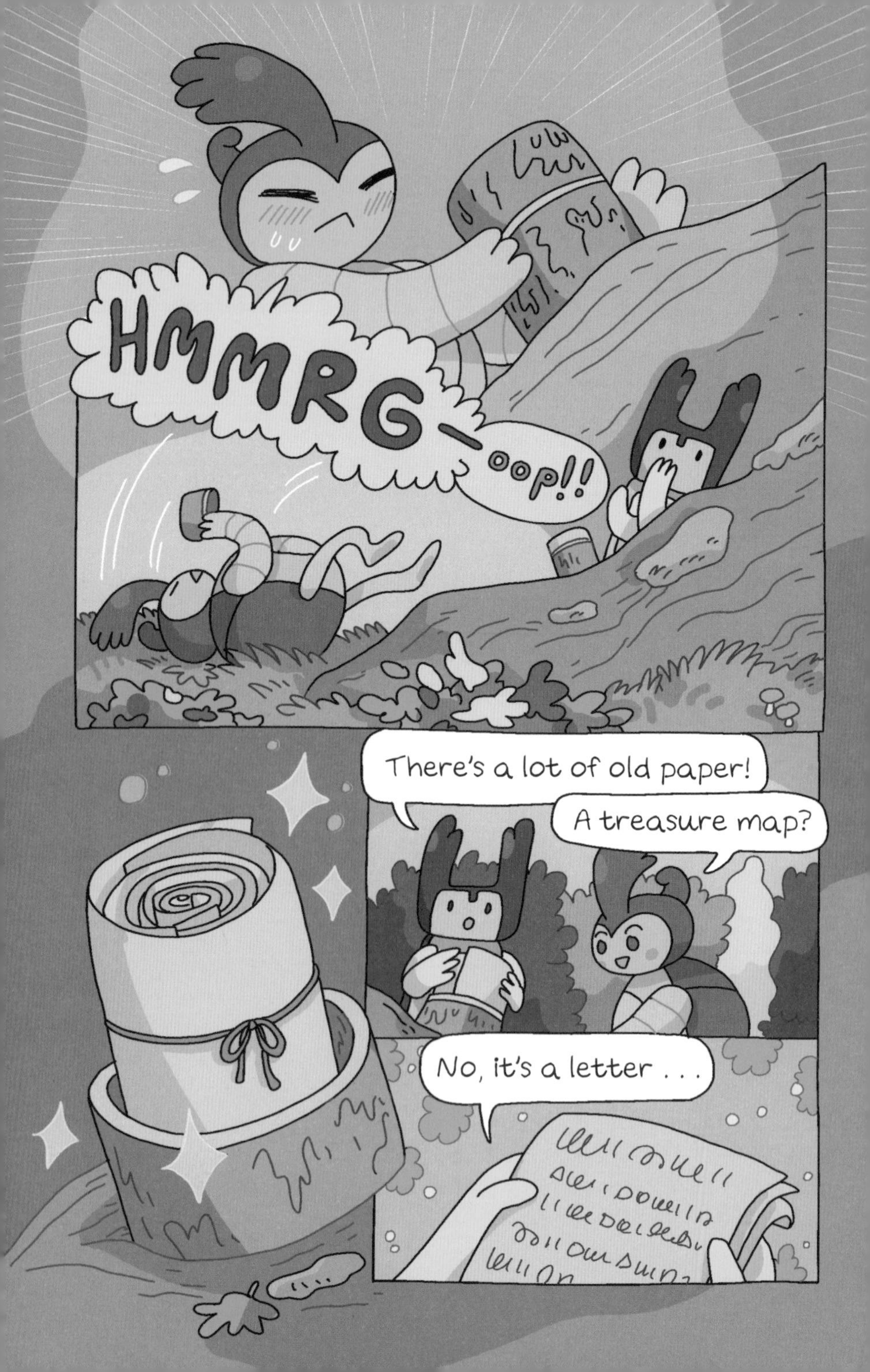
HMMRG—
oop!!
There's a lot of old paper!
A treasure map?
No, it's a letter . . .

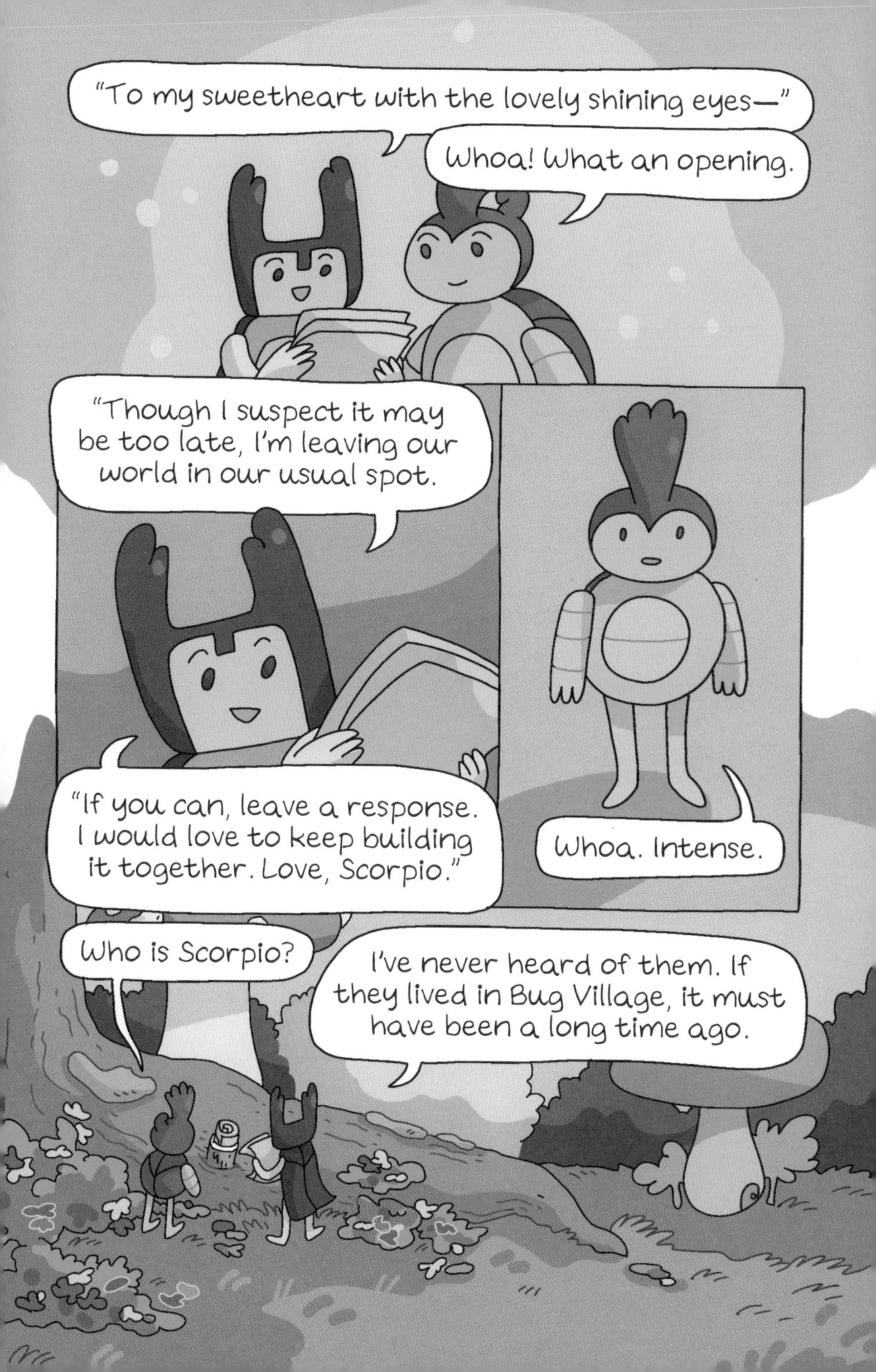
"To my sweetheart with the lovely shining eyes—"
Whoa! What an opening.
"Though I suspect it may be too late, I'm leaving our world in our usual spot.
"If you can, leave a response. I would love to keep building it together. Love, Scorpio."
Whoa. Intense.
Who is Scorpio?
I've never heard of them. If they lived in Bug Village, it must have been a long time ago.

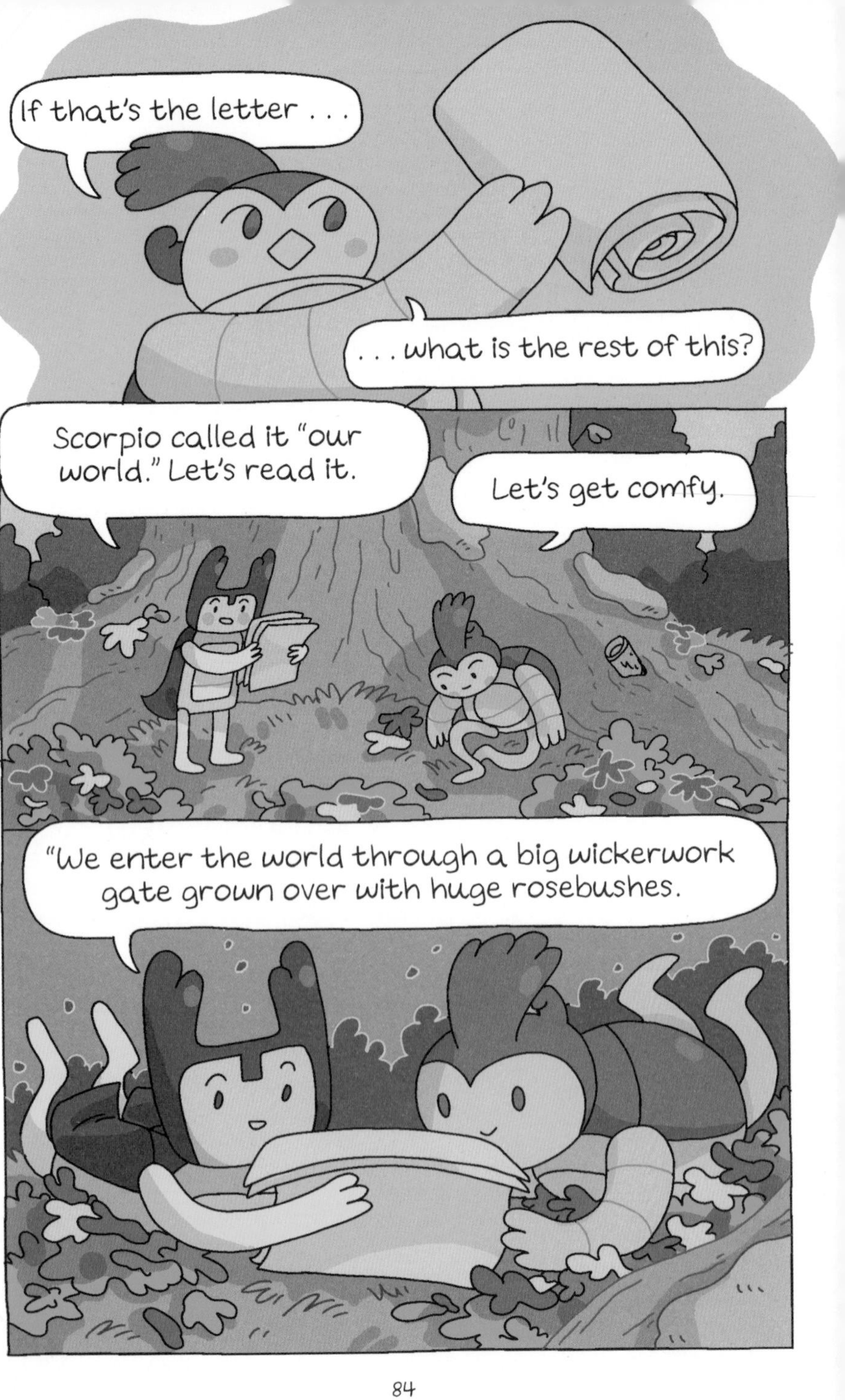
If that's the letter . . .
. . . what is the rest of this?
Scorpio called it "our world." Let's read it.
Let's get comfy.
"We enter the world through a big wickerwork gate grown over with huge rosebushes.

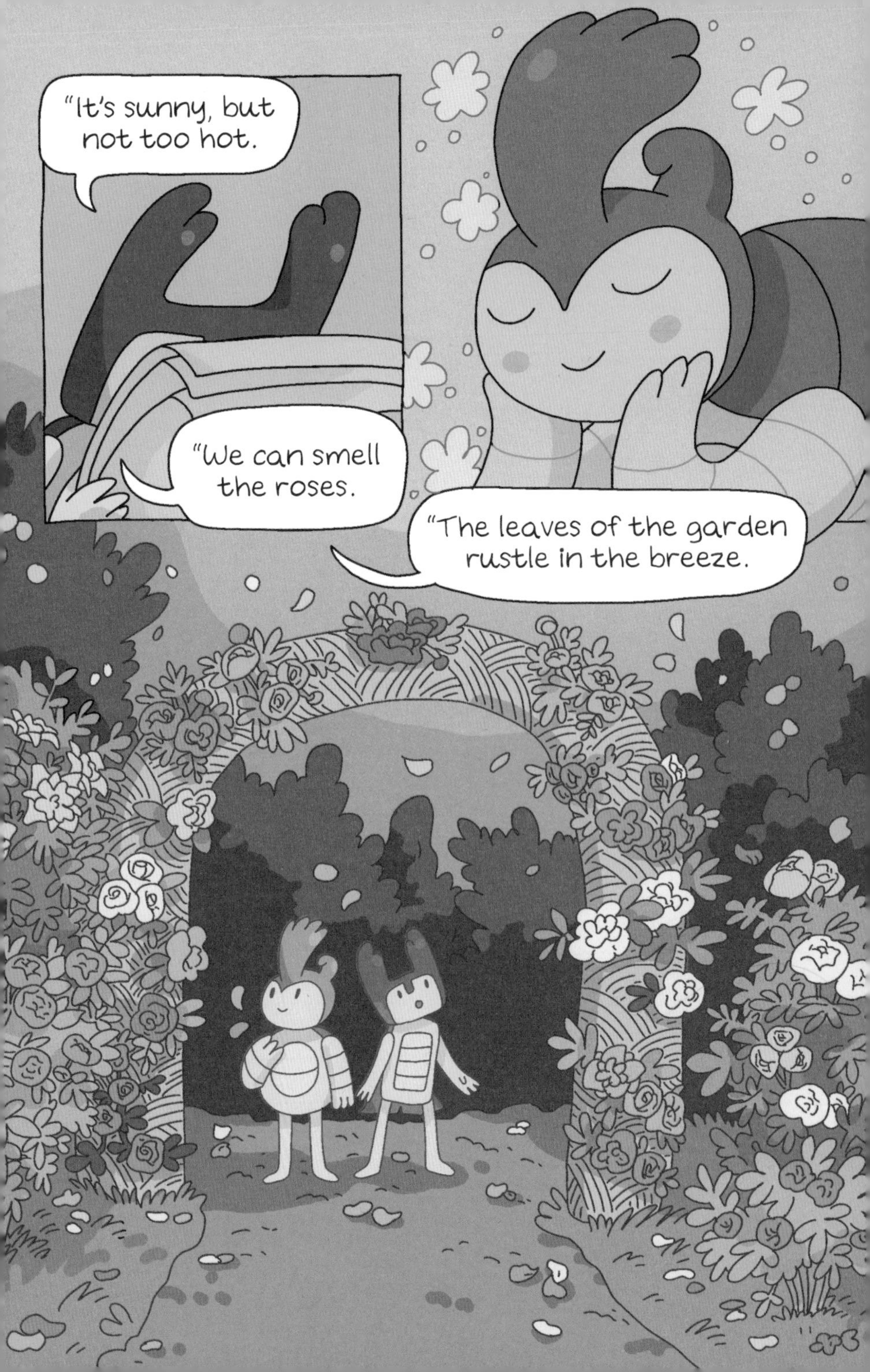
"It's sunny, but not too hot.
"We can smell the roses.
"The leaves of the garden rustle in the breeze.

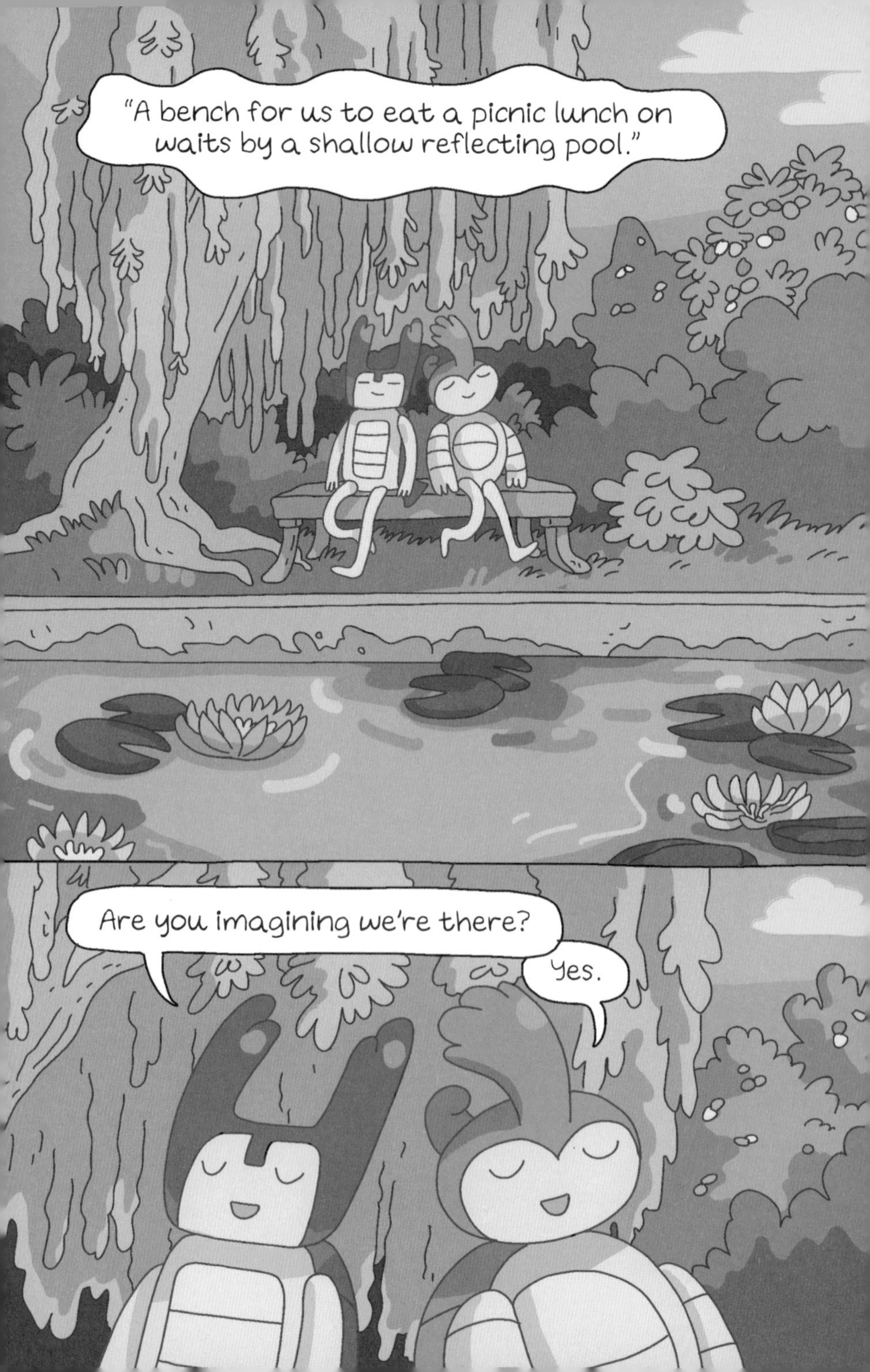
"A bench for us to eat a picnic lunch on waits by a shallow reflecting pool."
Are you imagining we're there?
Yes.

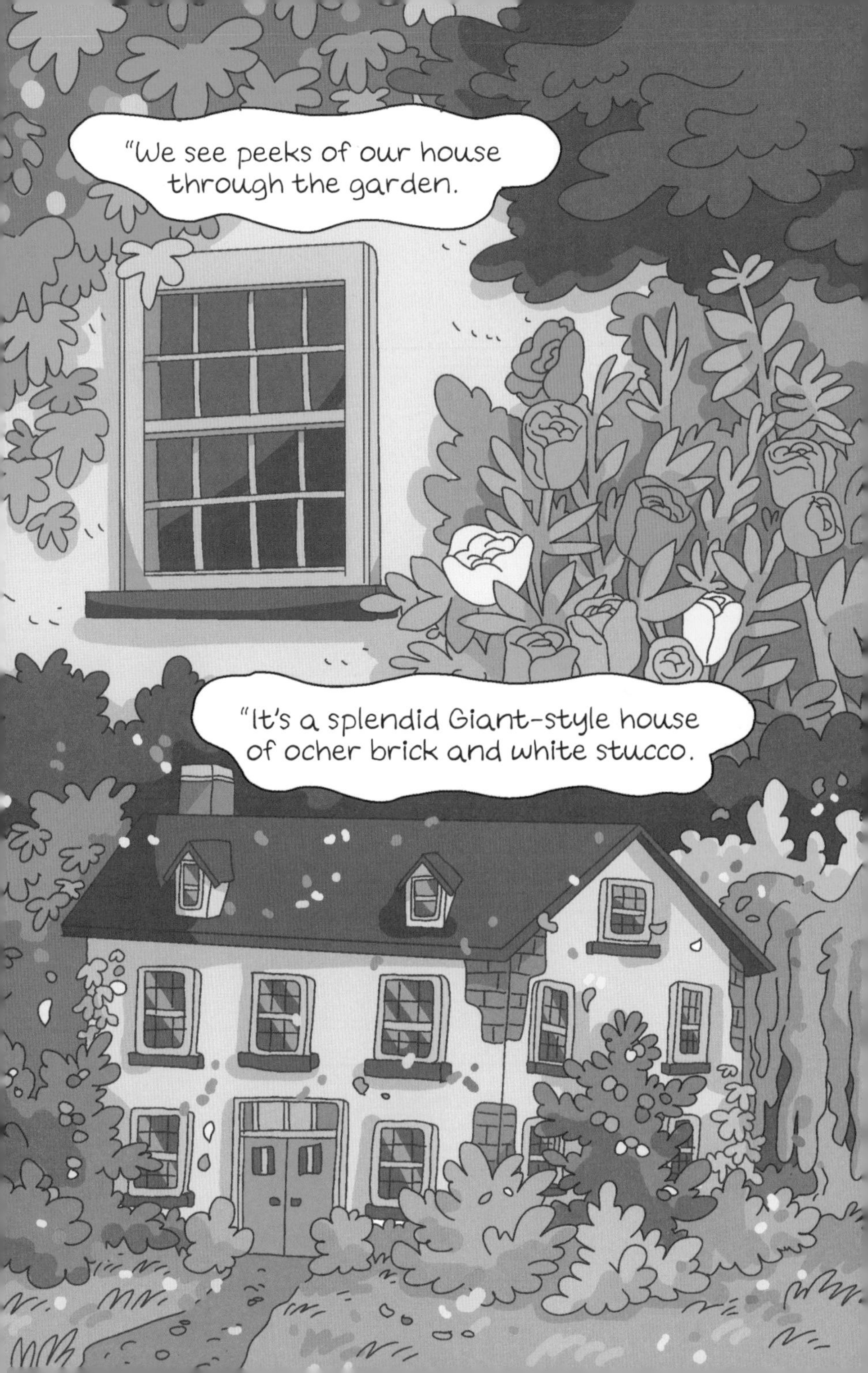
"We see peeks of our house through the garden.
"It's a splendid Giant-style house of ocher brick and white stucco.

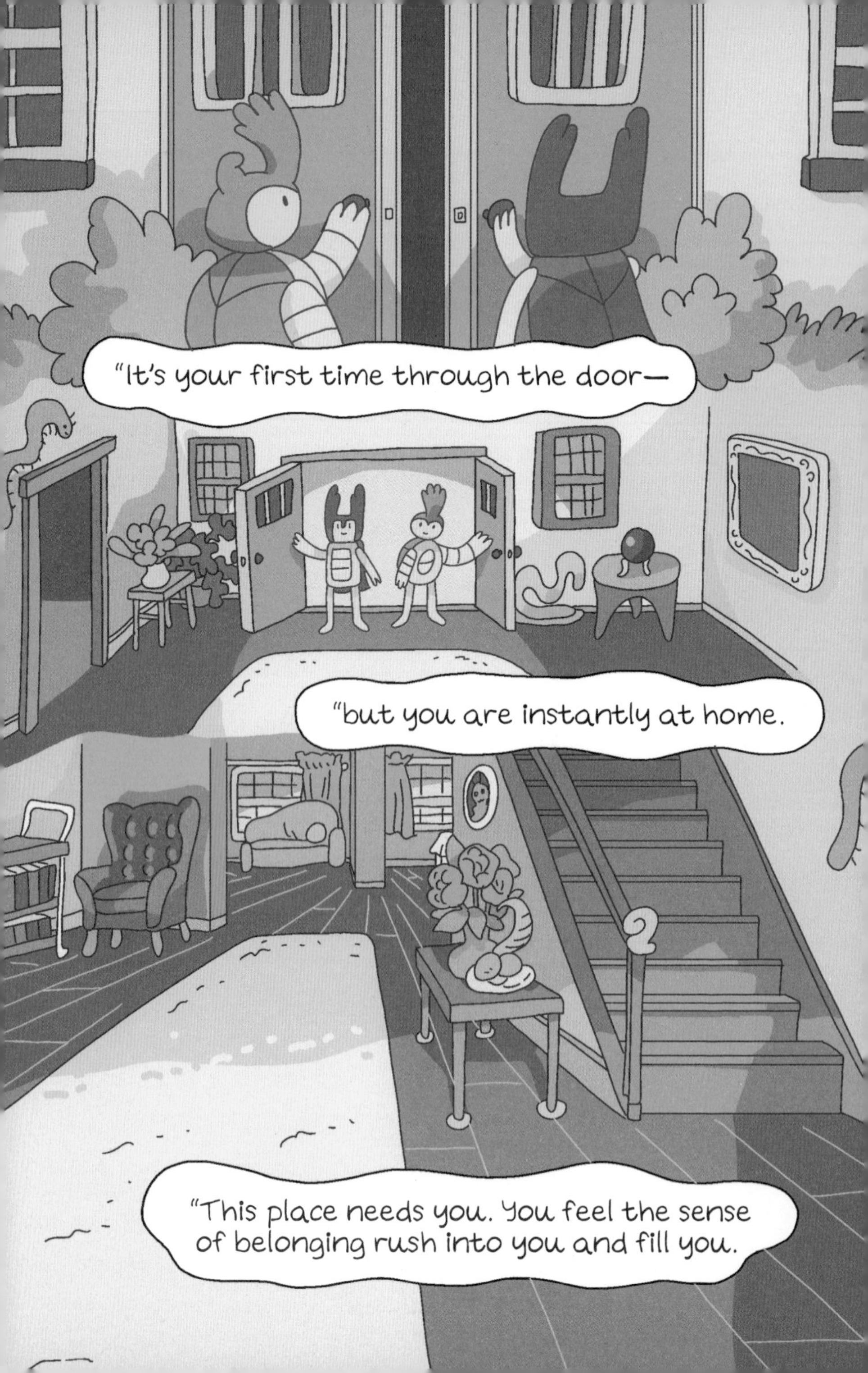
"It's your first time through the door—
"but you are instantly at home.
"This place needs you. You feel the sense of belonging rush into you and fill you.

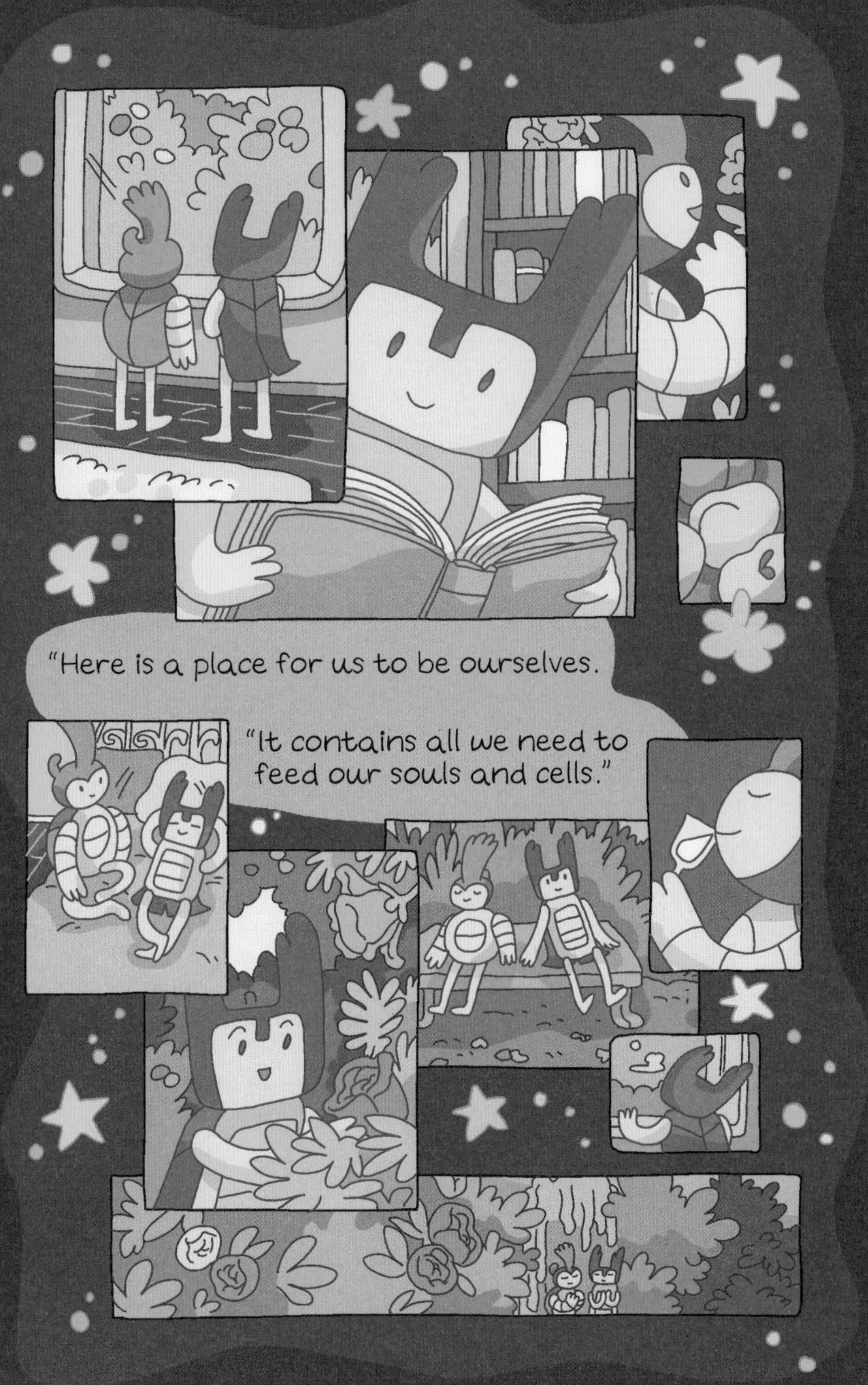
"Here is a place for us to be ourselves.
"It contains all we need to feed our souls and cells."

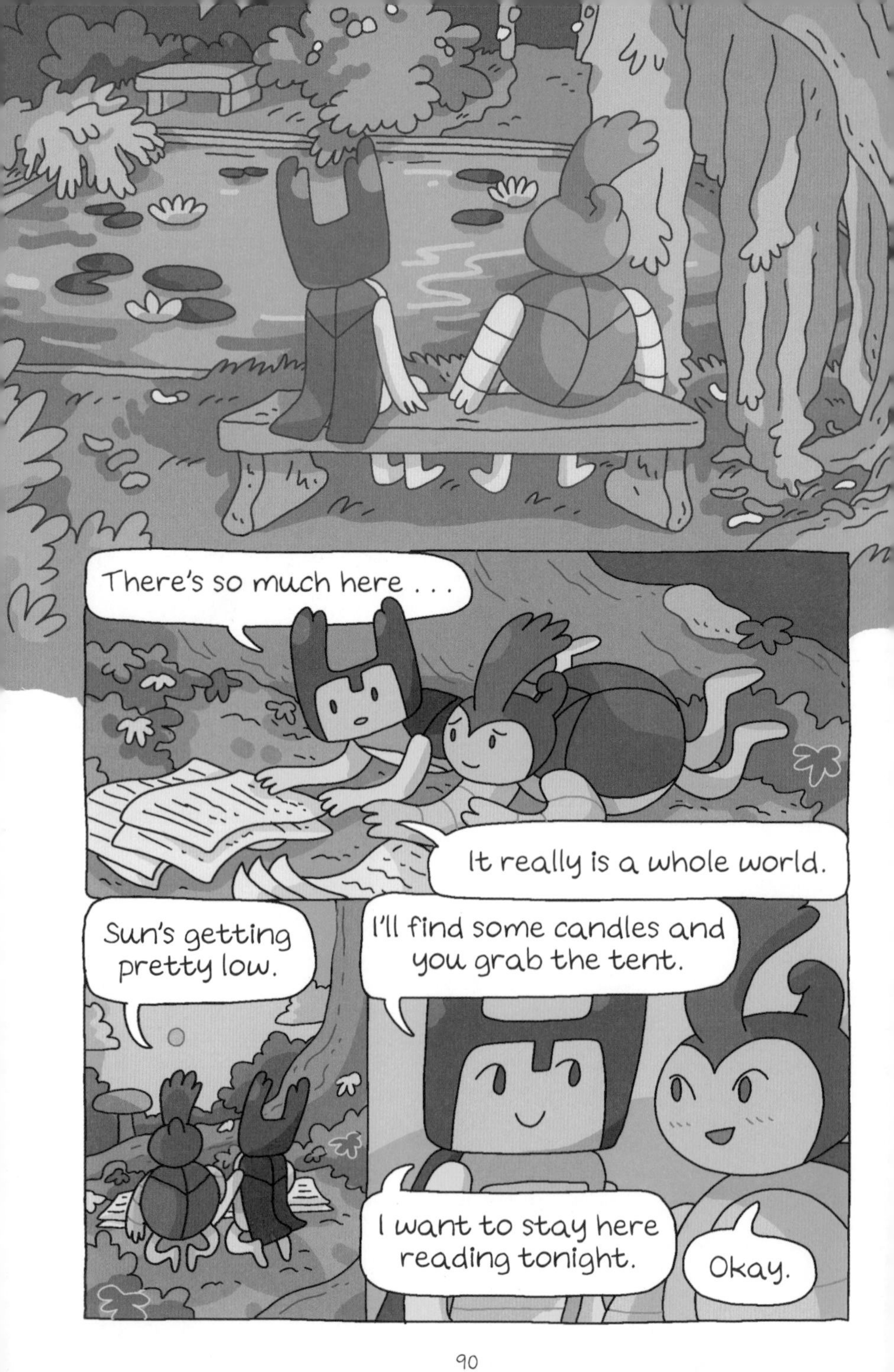
There's so much here . . .
It really is a whole world.
Sun's getting pretty low.
I'll find some candles and you grab the tent.
I want to stay here reading tonight.
Okay.

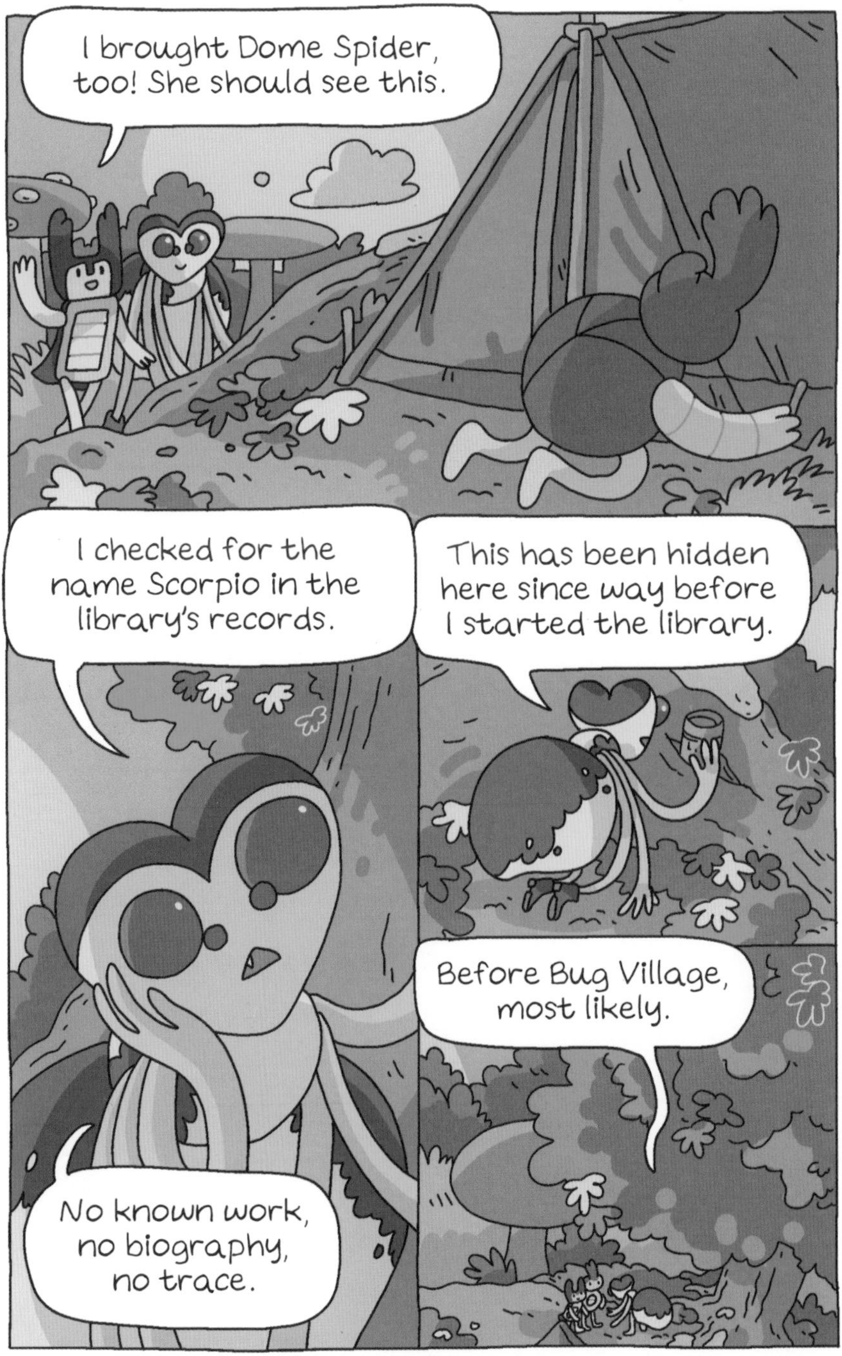
I brought Dome Spider, too! She should see this.
I checked for the name Scorpio in the library's records.
This has been hidden here since way before I started the library.
No known work, no biography, no trace.
Before Bug Village, most likely.

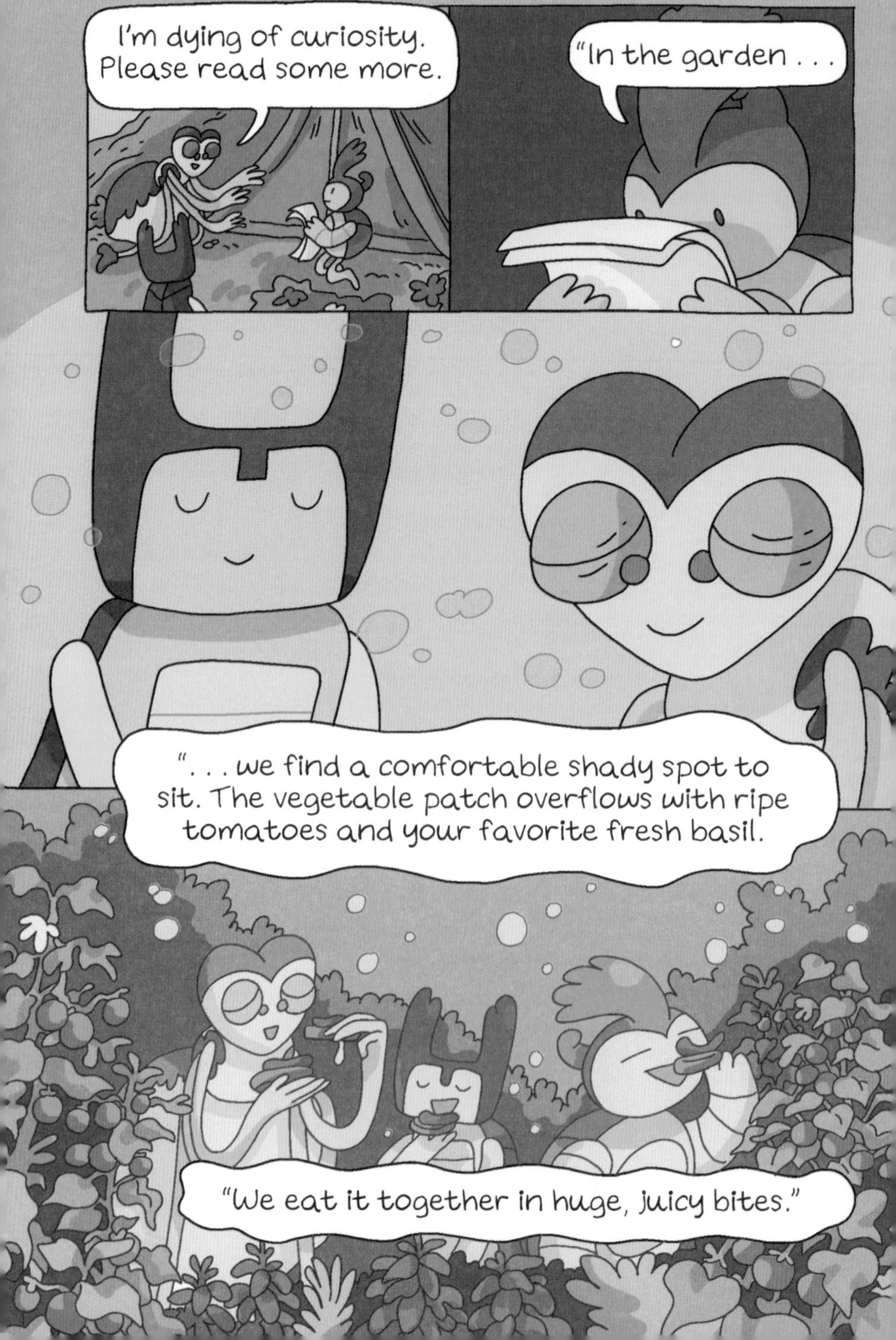
I'm dying of curiosity. Please read some more.
"In the garden . . .
". . . we find a comfortable shady spot to sit. The vegetable patch overflows with ripe tomatoes and your favorite fresh basil.
"We eat it together in huge, juicy bites."

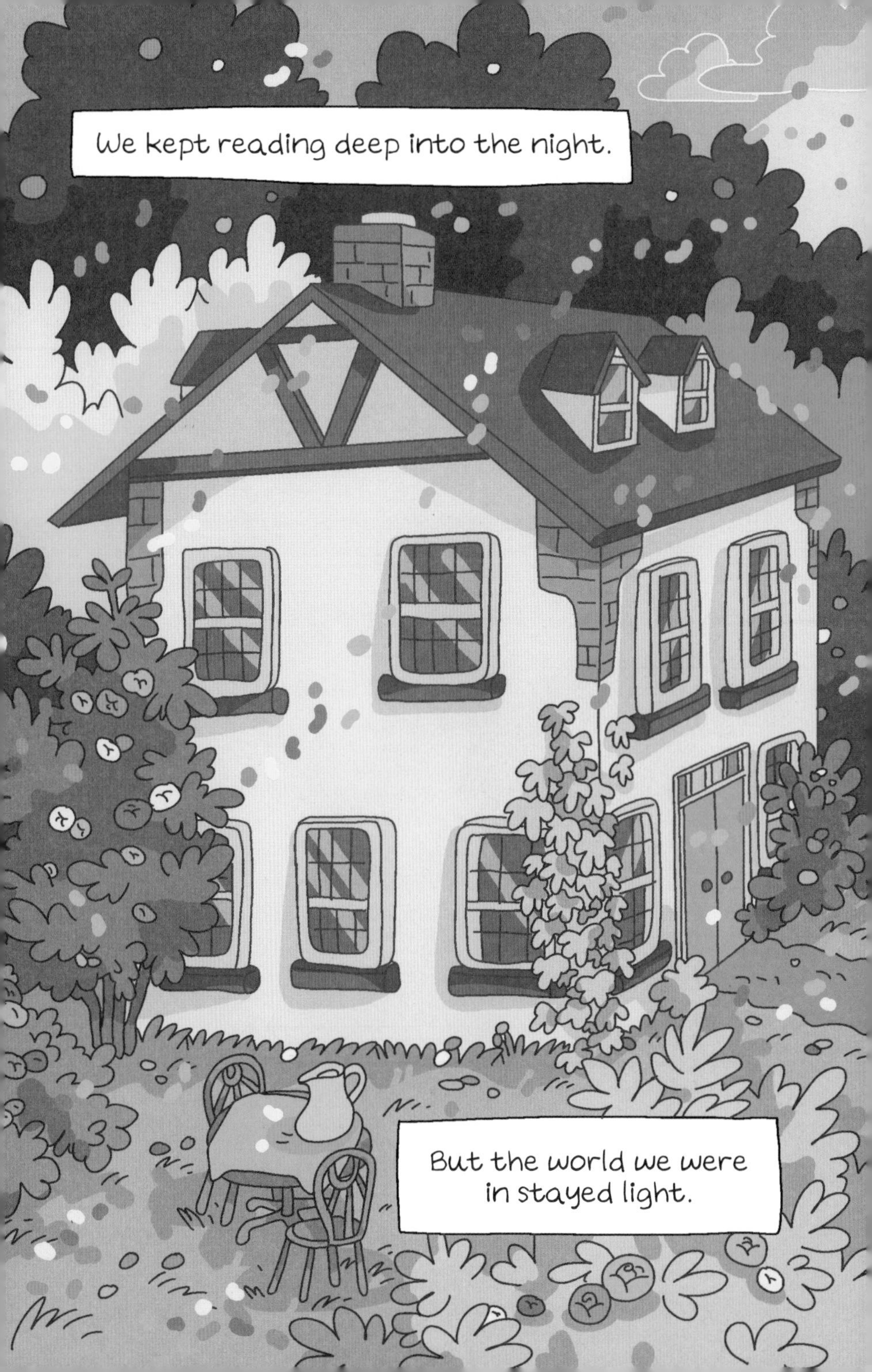
We kept reading deep into the night.
But the world we were in stayed light.

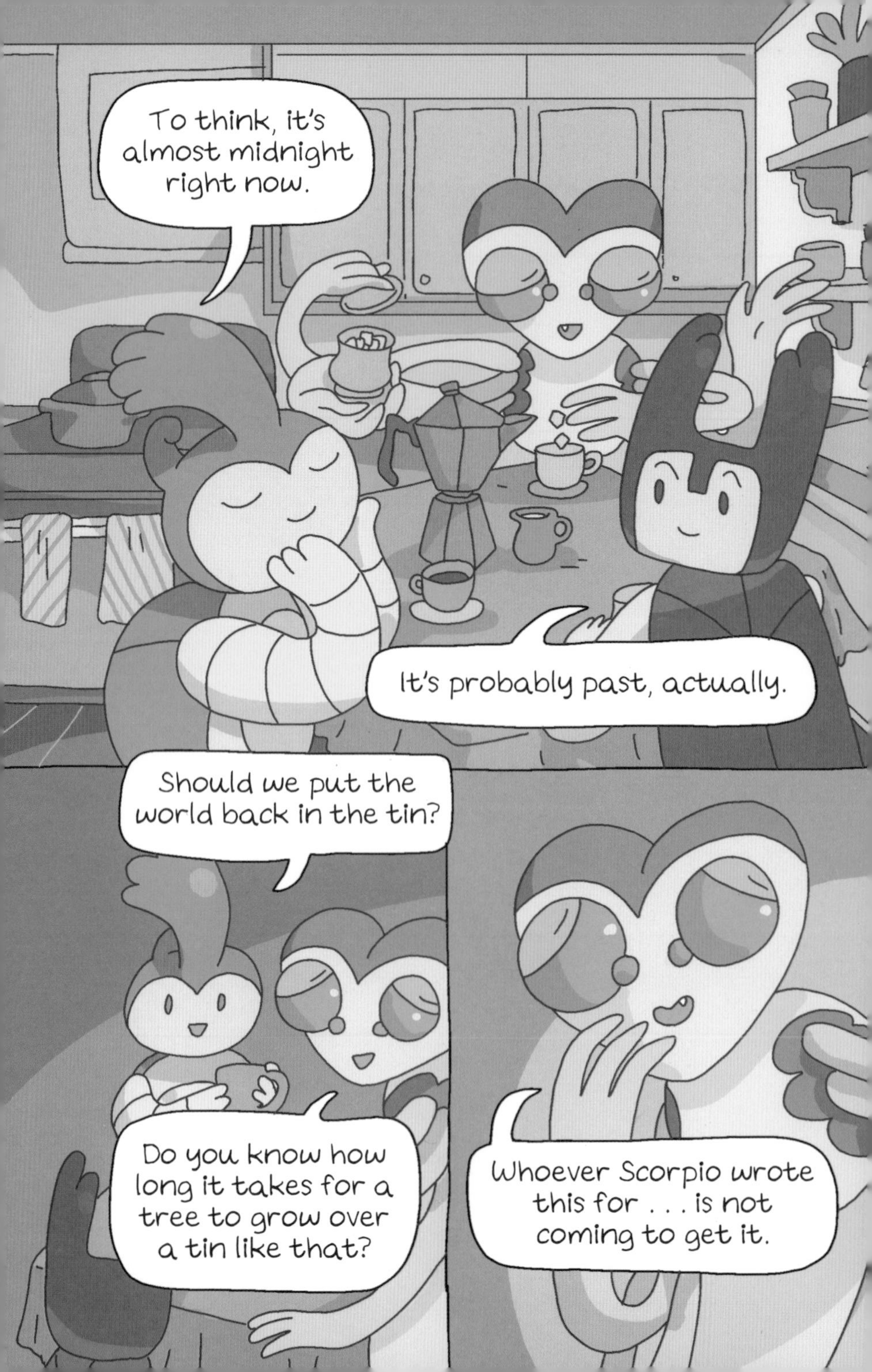
To think, it's almost midnight right now.
It's probably past, actually.
Should we put the world back in the tin?
Do you know how long it takes for a tree to grow over a tin like that?
Whoever Scorpio wrote this for . . . is not coming to get it.

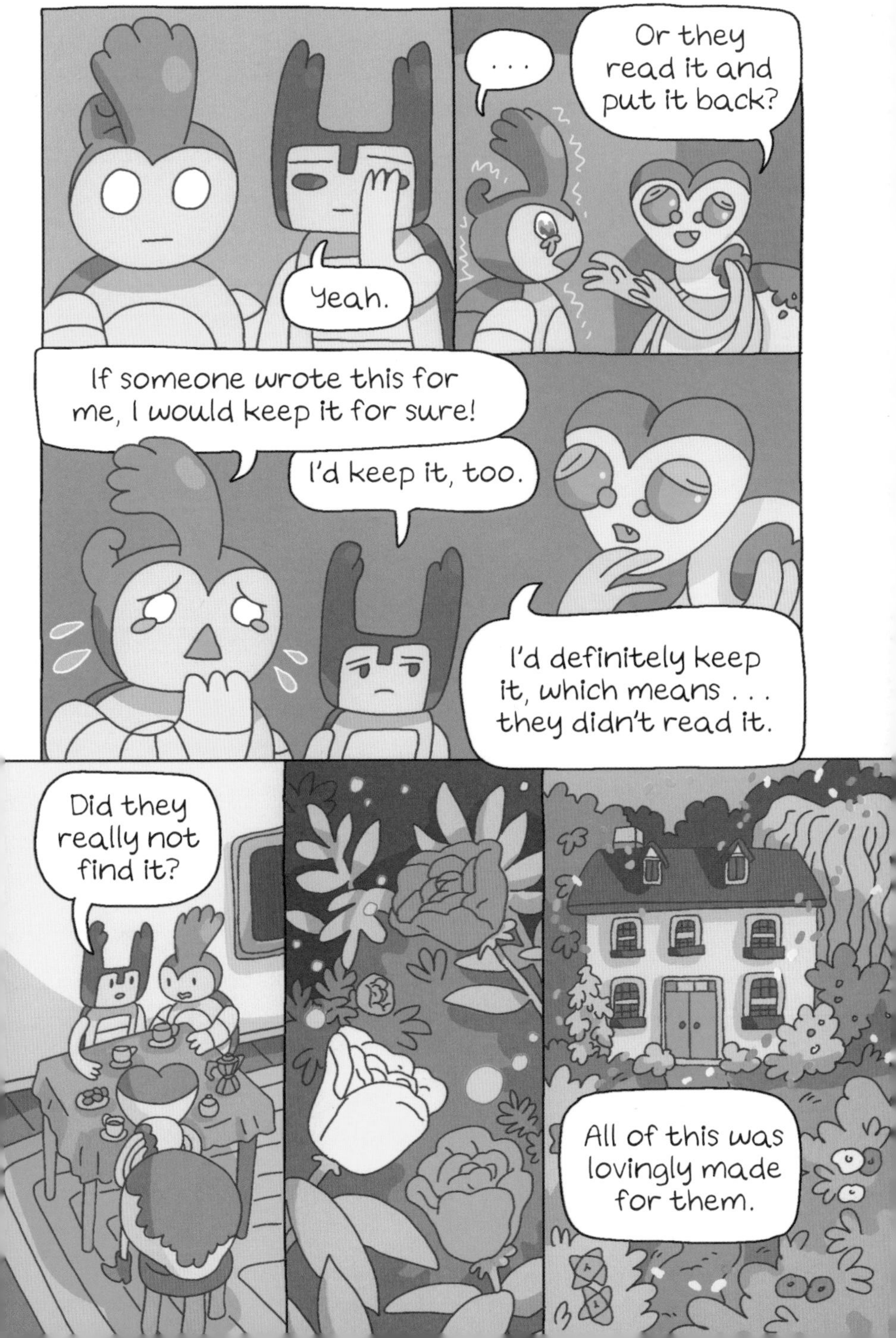

Yeah.
. . .
Or they read it and put it back?
If someone wrote this for me, I would keep it for sure!
I'd keep it, too.
I'd definitely keep it, which means . . . they didn't read it.
Did they really not find it?
All of this was lovingly made for them.

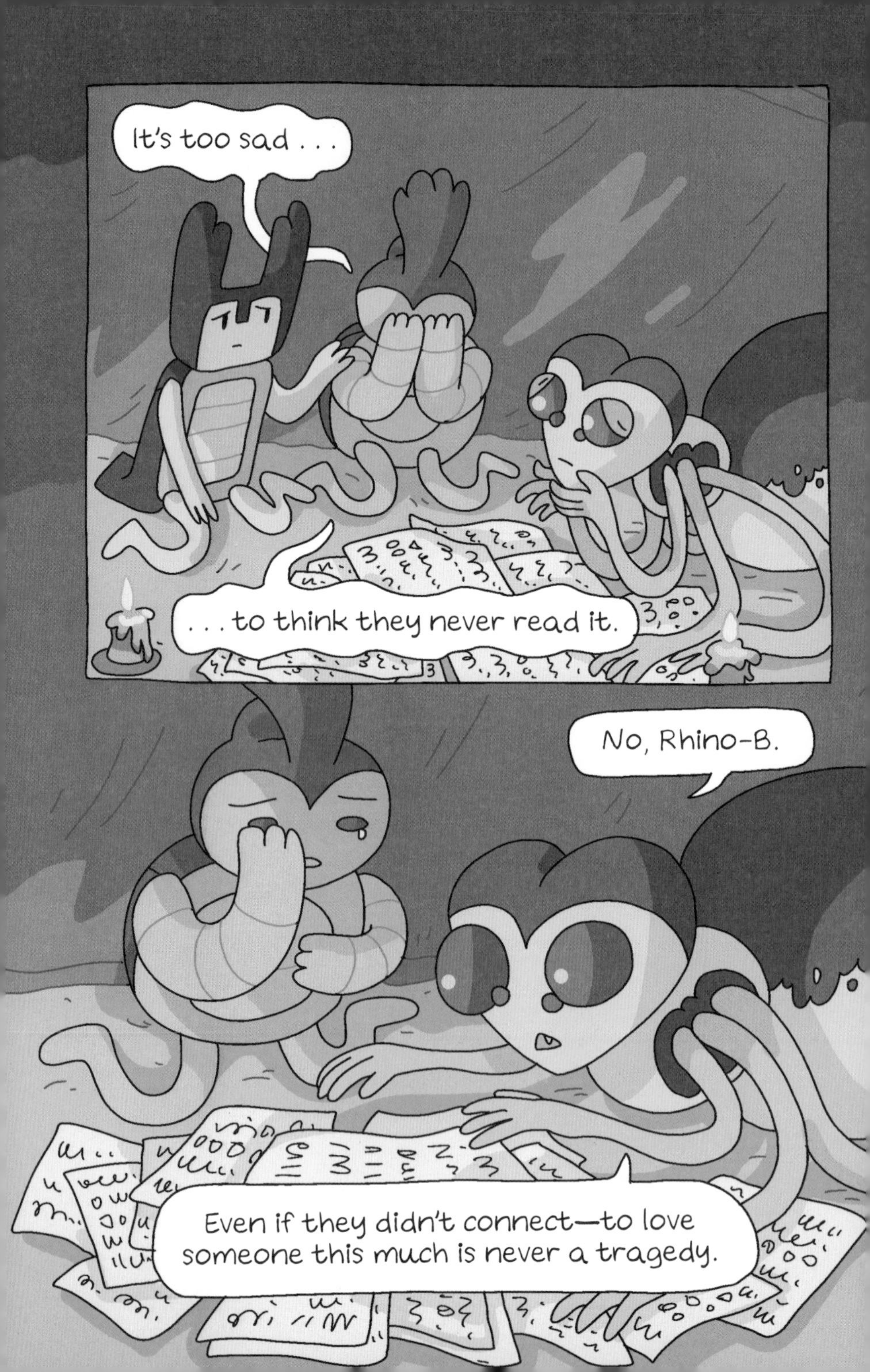
It's too sad . . .
. . . to think they never read it.
No, Rhino-B.
Even if they didn't connect—to love someone this much is never a tragedy.

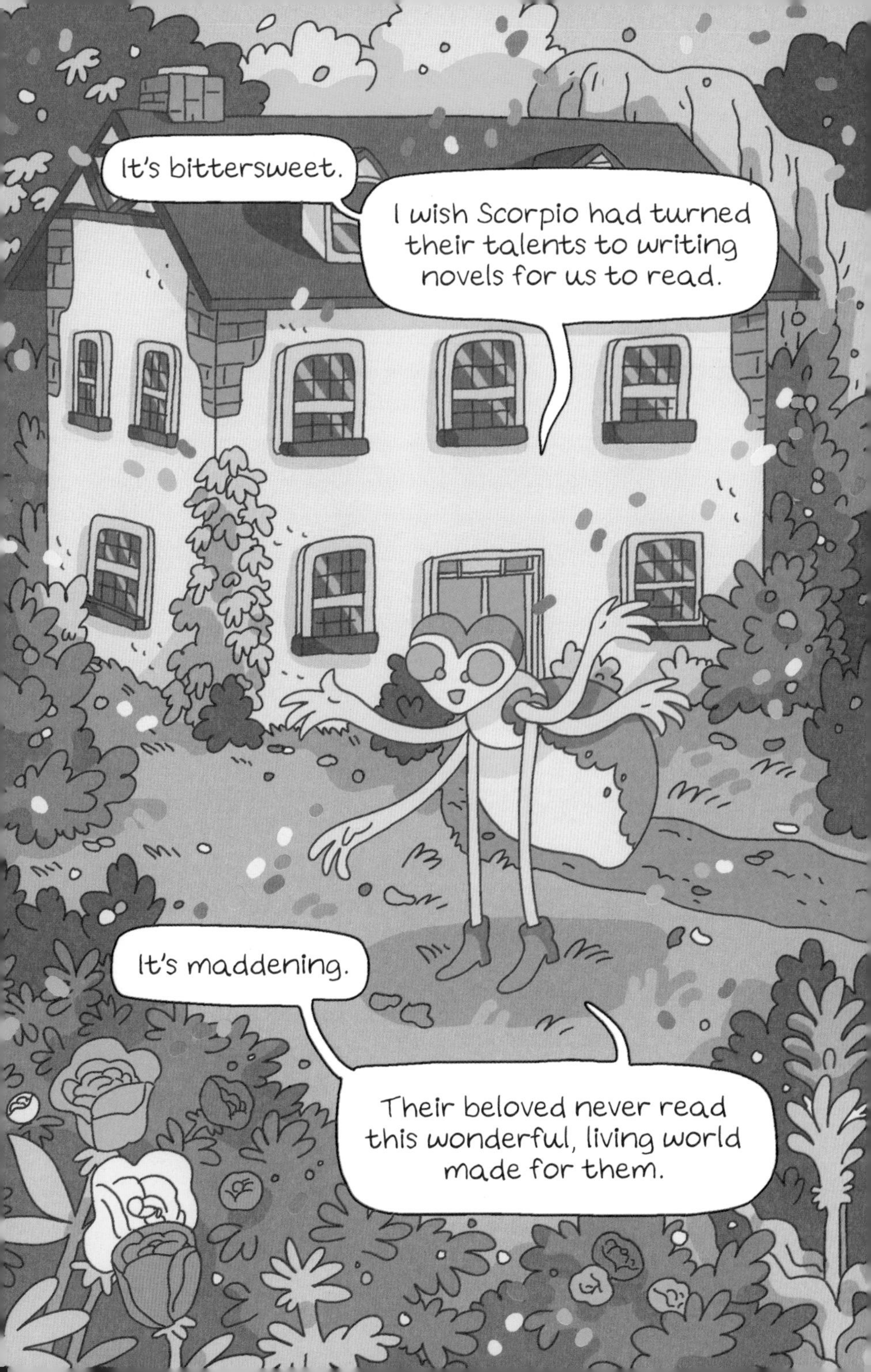
It's bittersweet.
I wish Scorpio had turned their talents to writing novels for us to read.
It's maddening.
Their beloved never read this wonderful, living world made for them.

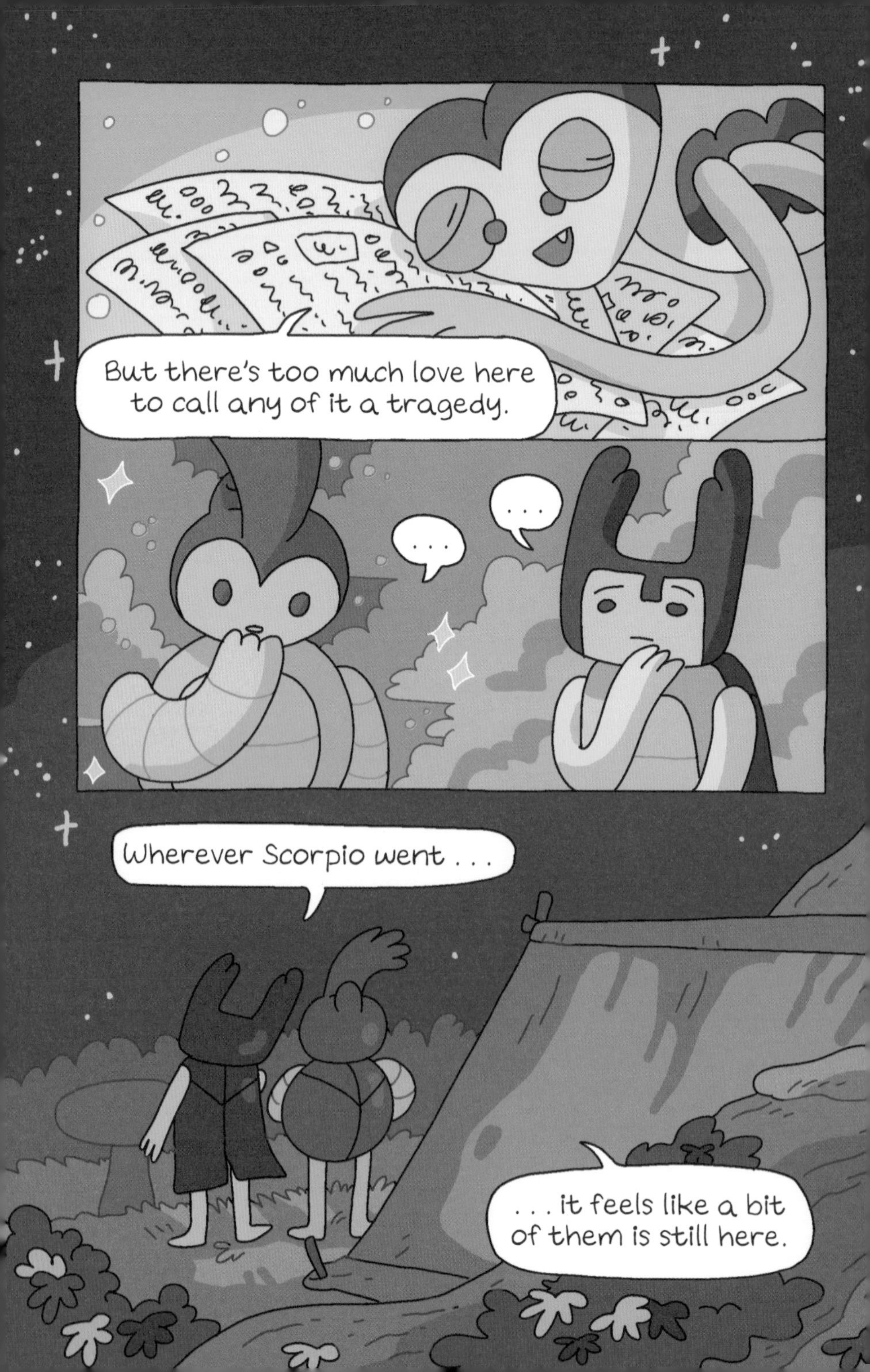
But there's too much love here to call any of it a tragedy.
. . .
. . .
Wherever Scorpio went . . .
. . . it feels like a bit of them is still here.

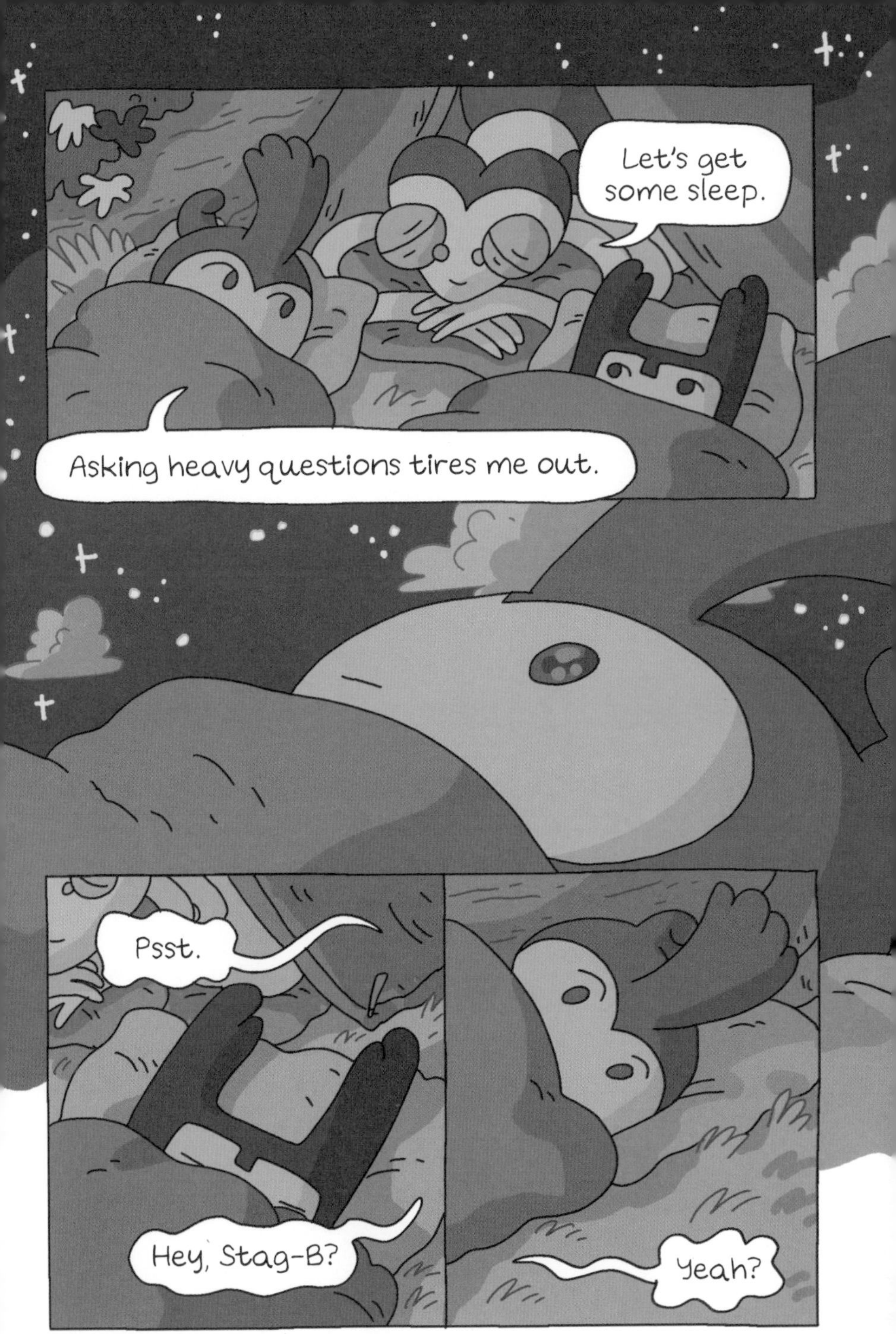
Let's get some sleep.
Asking heavy questions tires me out.
Psst.
Hey, Stag-B?
Yeah?

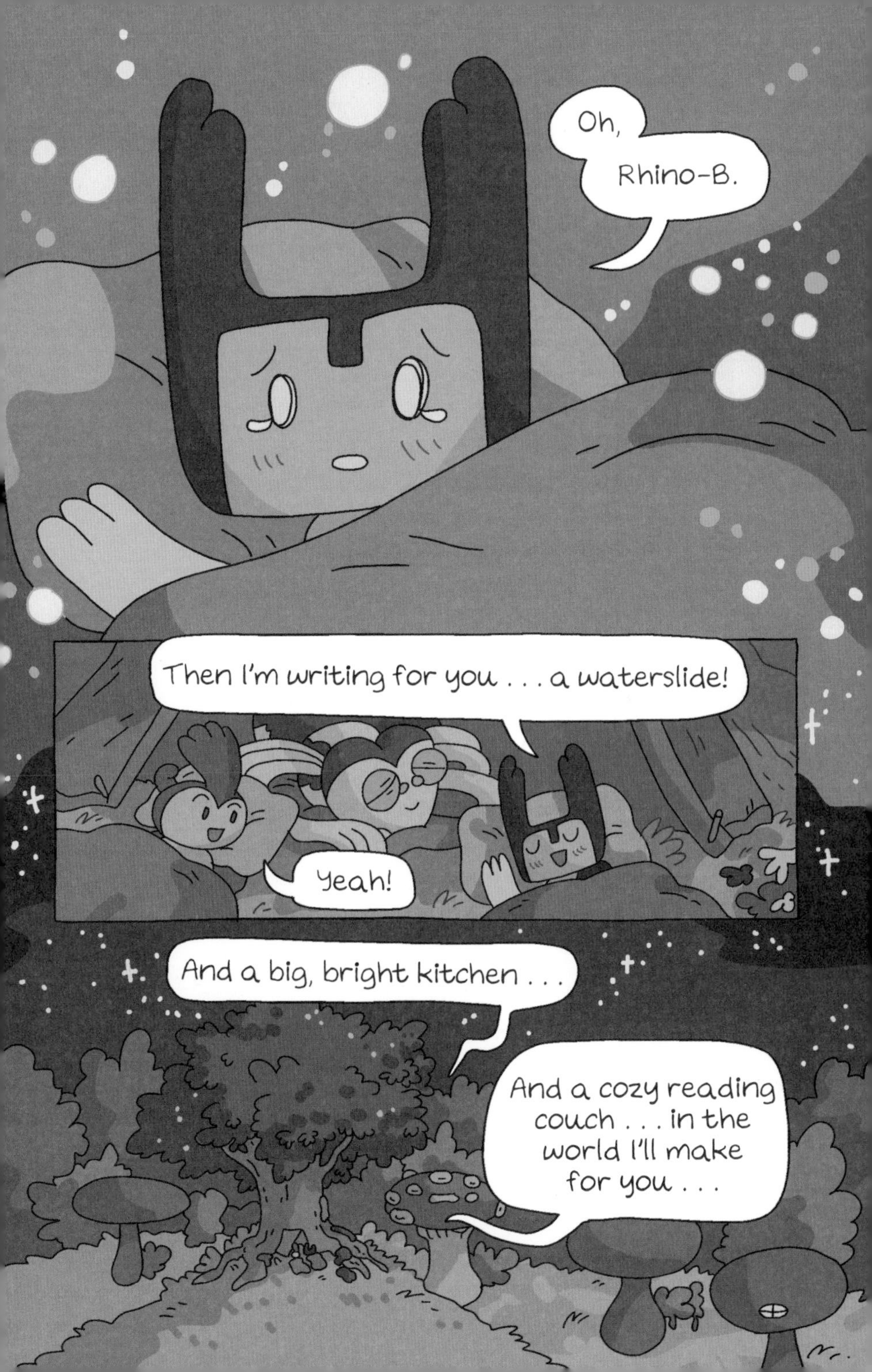
Oh,
Rhino-B.
Then I'm writing for you . . . a waterslide!
Yeah!
And a big, bright kitchen . . .
And a cozy reading couch . . . in the world I'll make for you . . .

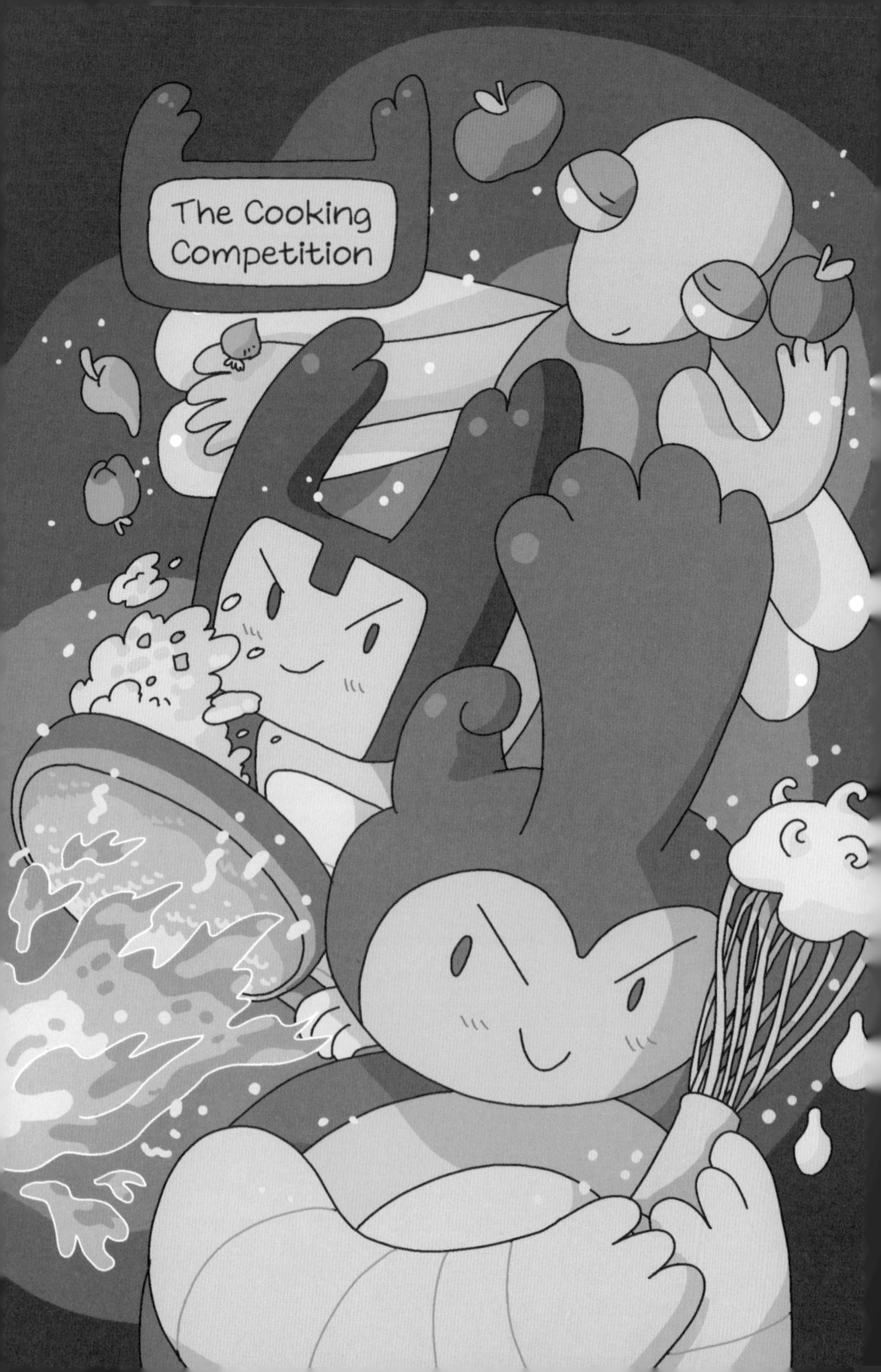
The Cooking
Competition

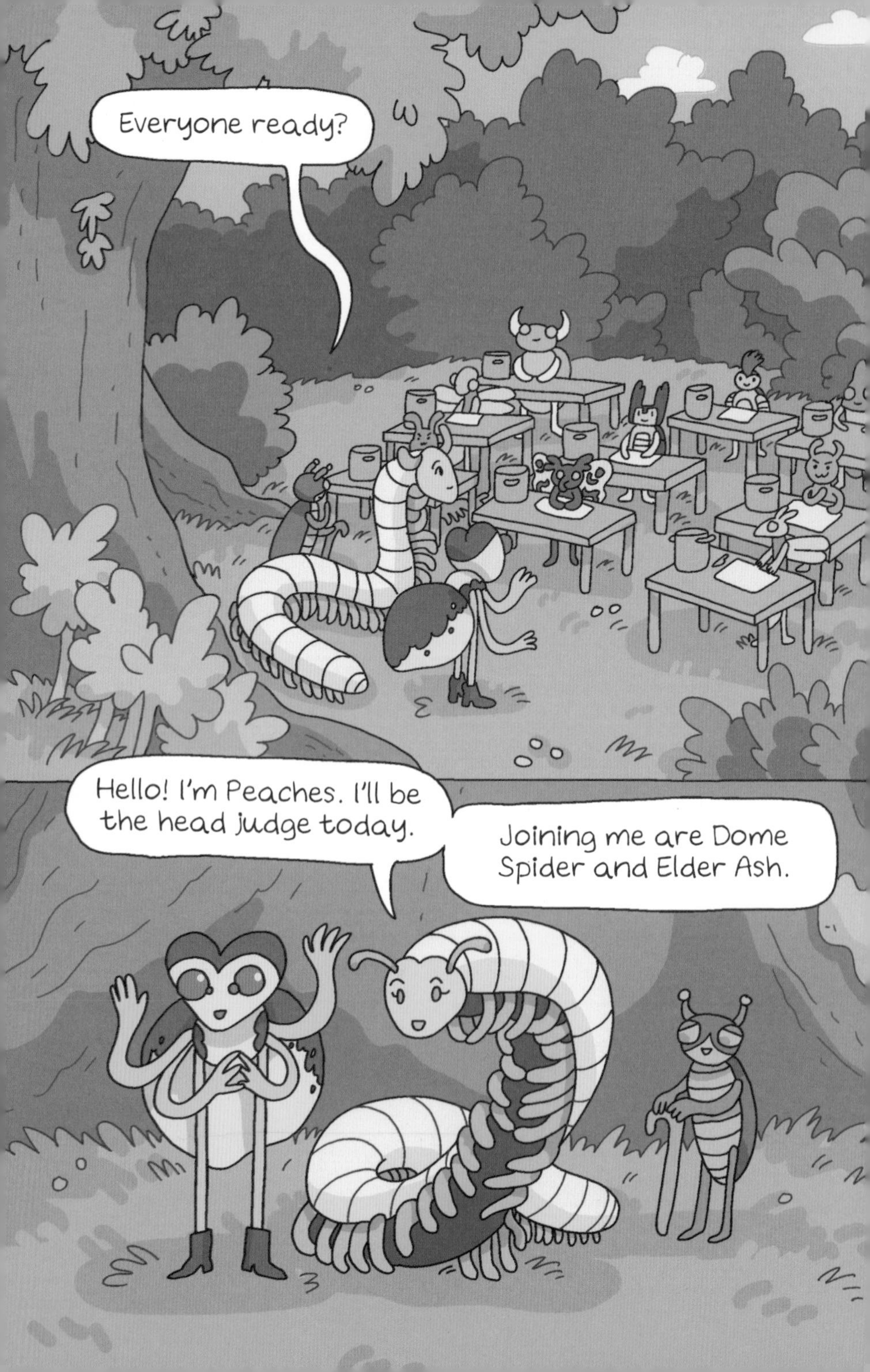
Everyone ready?
Hello! I'm Peaches. I'll be the head judge today.
Joining me are Dome Spider and Elder Ash.

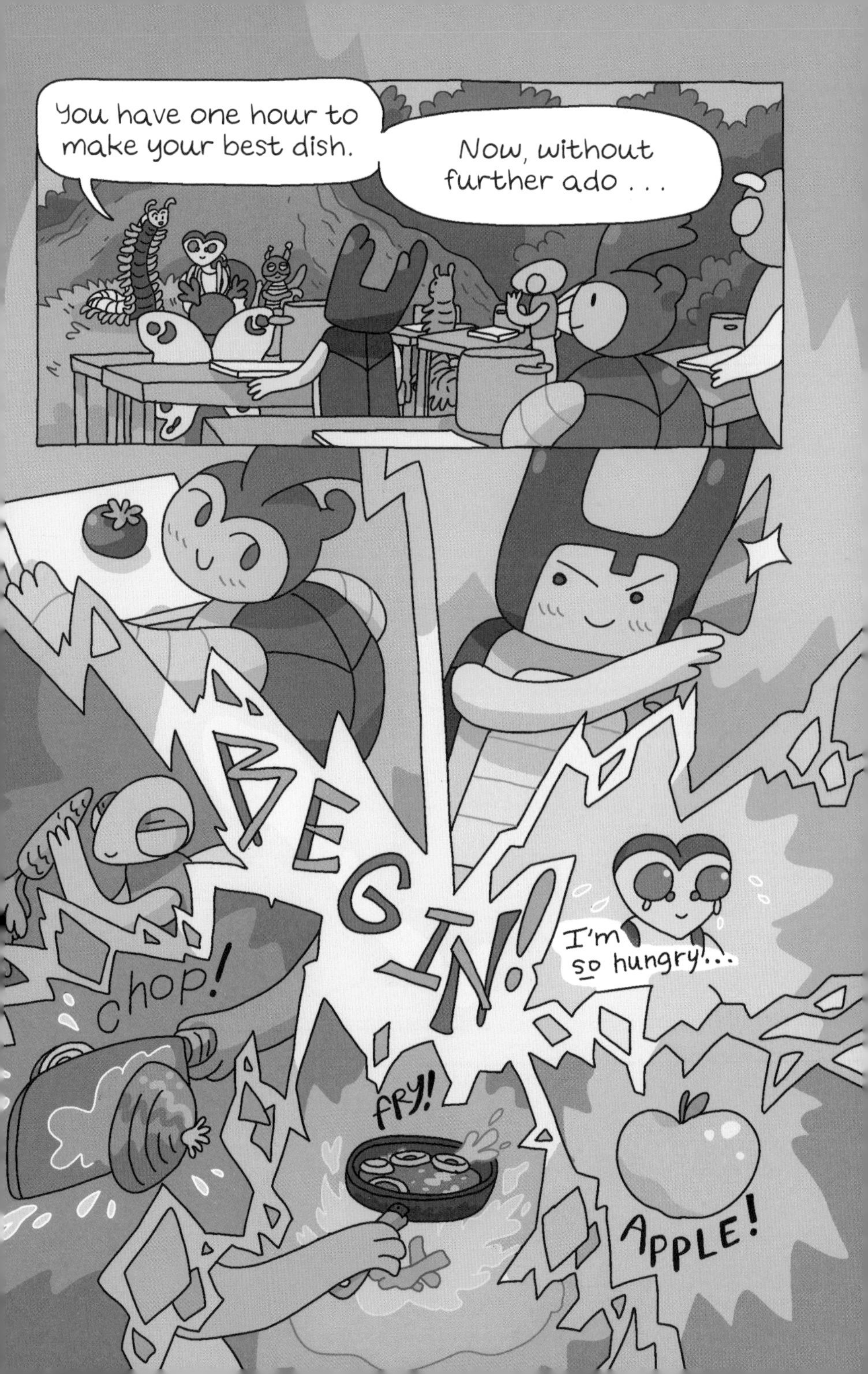
You have one hour to make your best dish.
Now, without further ado . . .
BEGIN!
I'm so hungry! . . .
chop!
FRY!
APPLE!

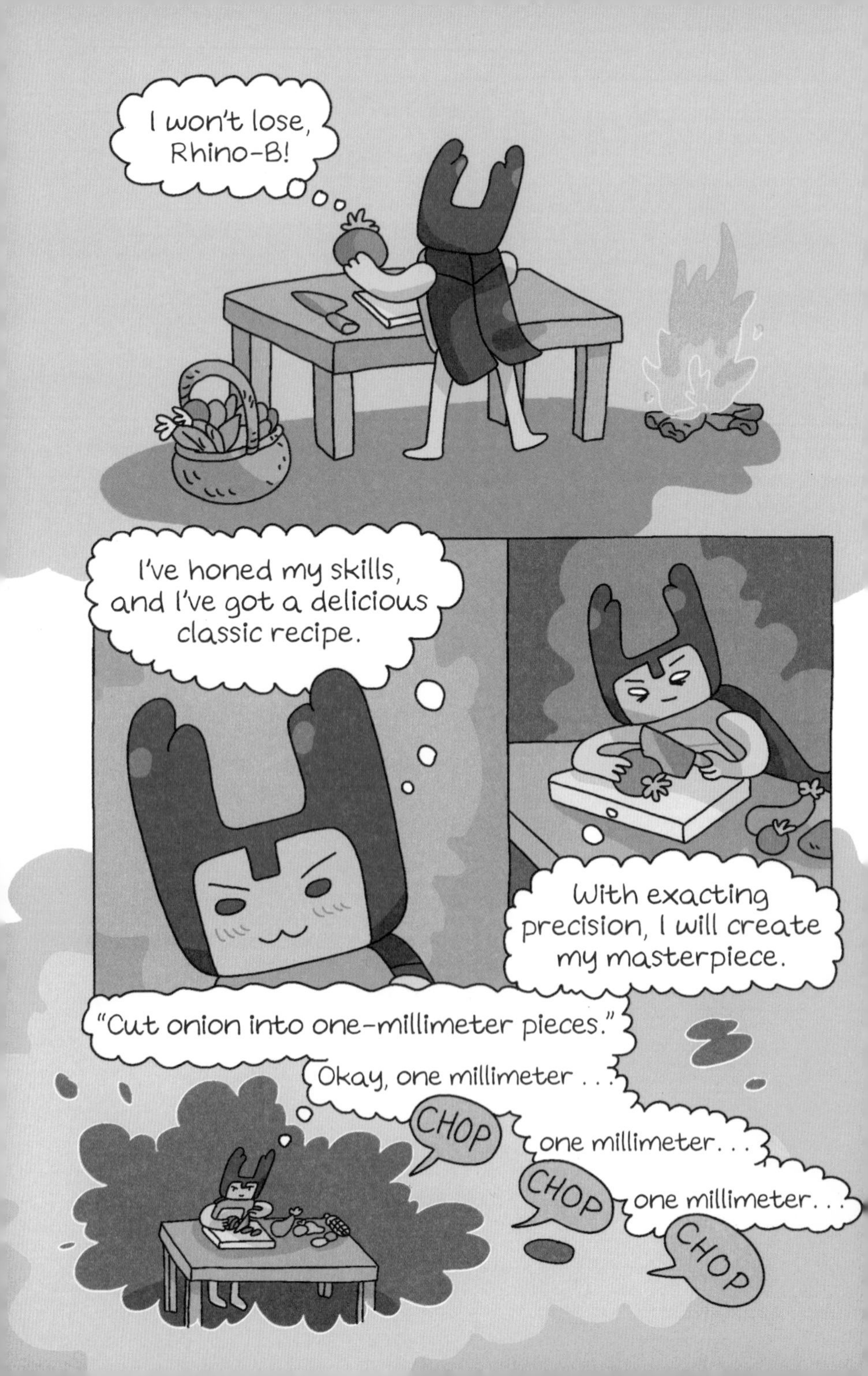
I won't lose, Rhino-B!
I've honed my skills, and I've got a delicious classic recipe.
With exacting precision, I will create my masterpiece.
"Cut onion into one-millimeter pieces."
Okay, one millimeter . . .
CHOP
one millimeter. . .
CHOP
one millimeter. . .
CHOP

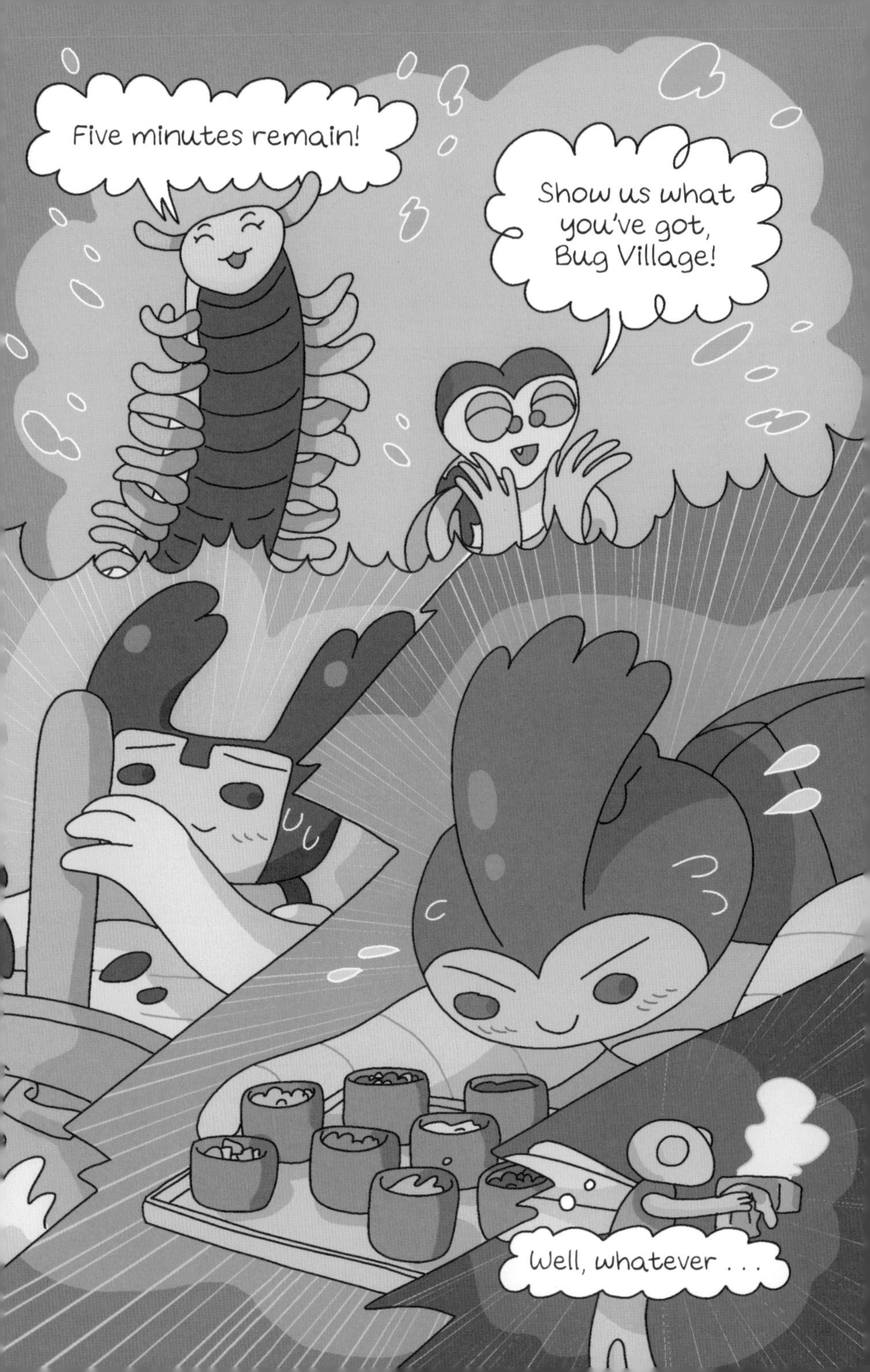
Five minutes remain!
Show us what you've got, Bug Village!
Well, whatever . . .

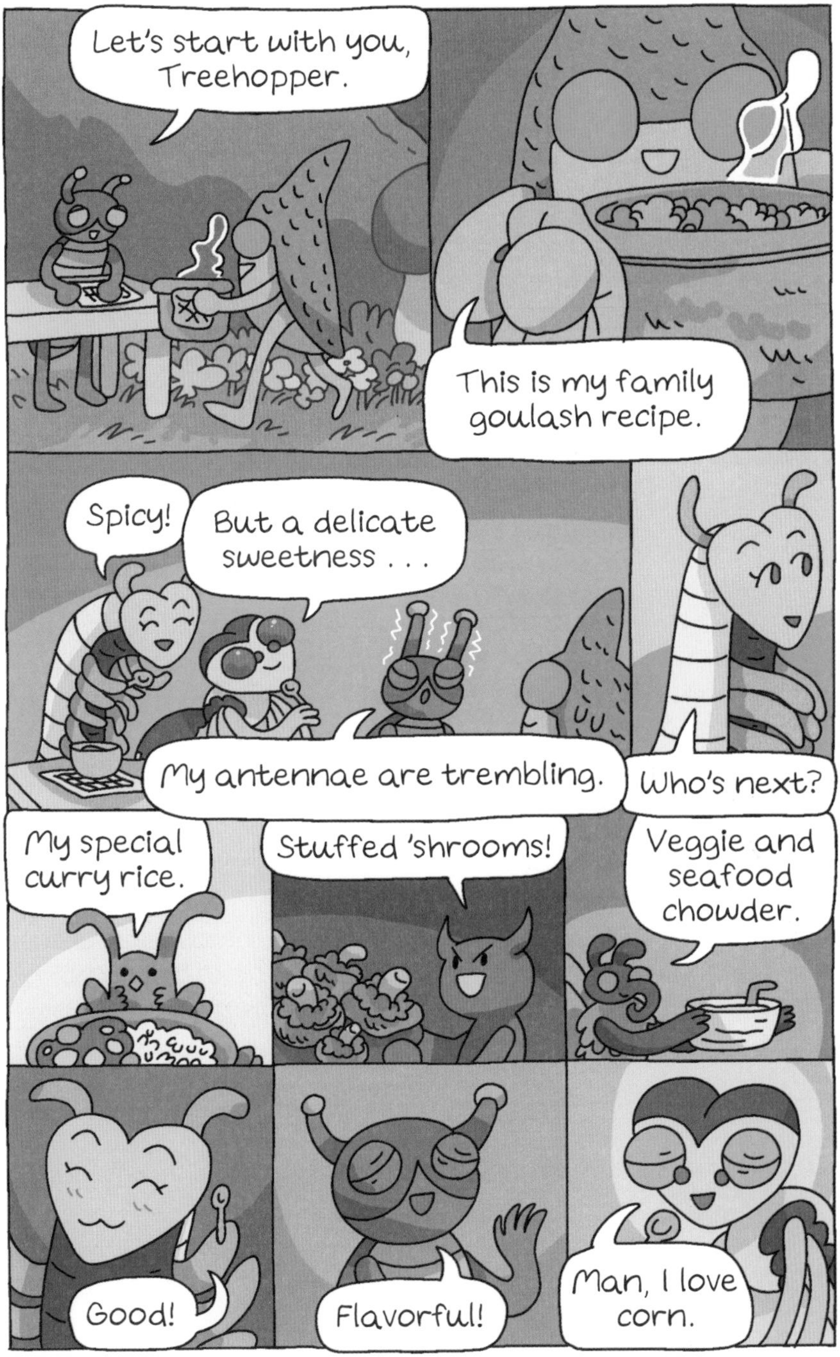
Let's start with you, Treehopper.
This is my family goulash recipe.
Spicy!
But a delicate sweetness . . .
My antennae are trembling.
Who's next?
My special curry rice.
Stuffed 'shrooms!
Veggie and seafood chowder.
Good!
Flavorful!
Man, I love corn.

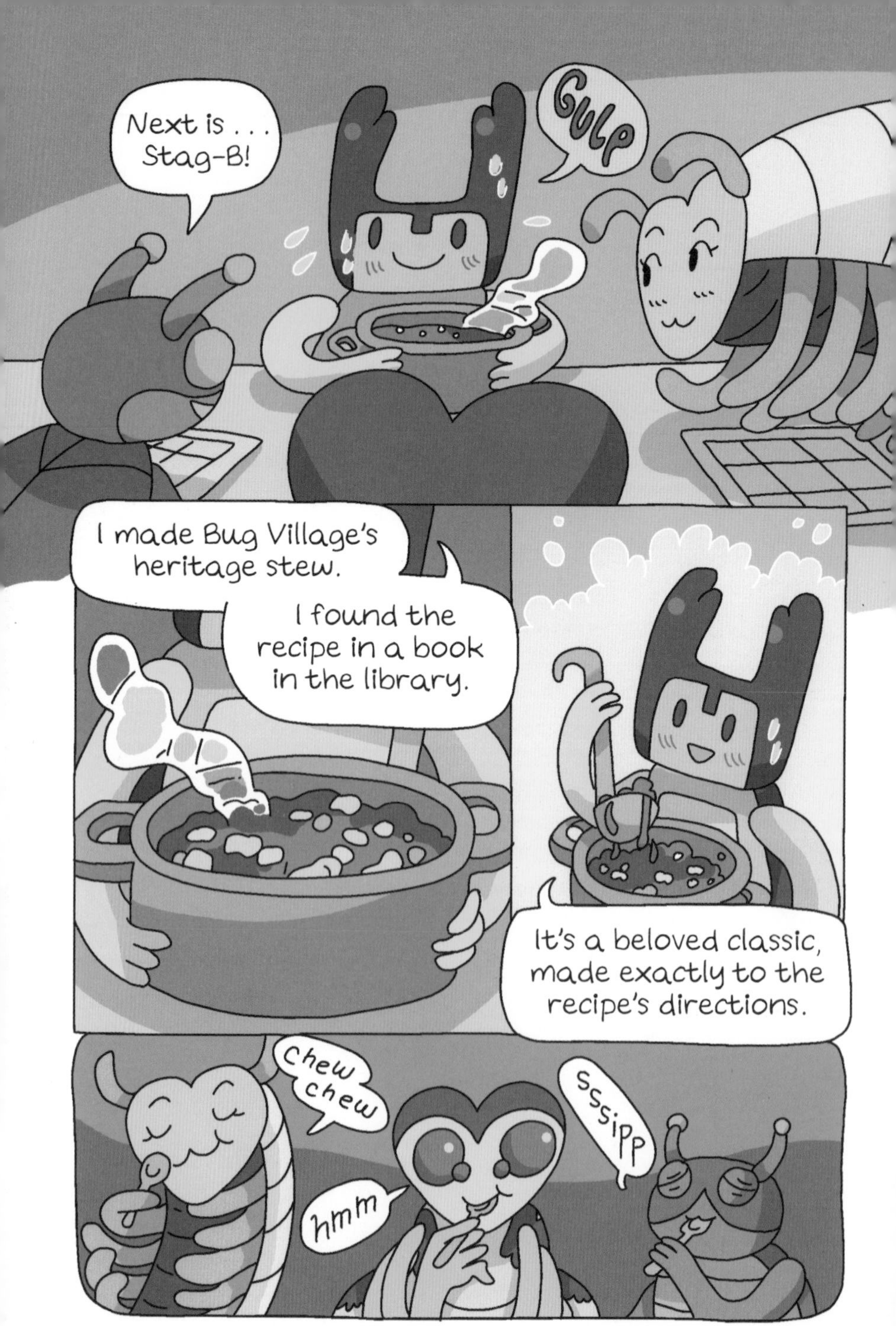
Next is . . . Stag-B!
GULP
I made Bug Village's heritage stew.
I found the recipe in a book in the library.
It's a beloved classic, made exactly to the recipe's directions.
Chew chew
Sssipp
hmm

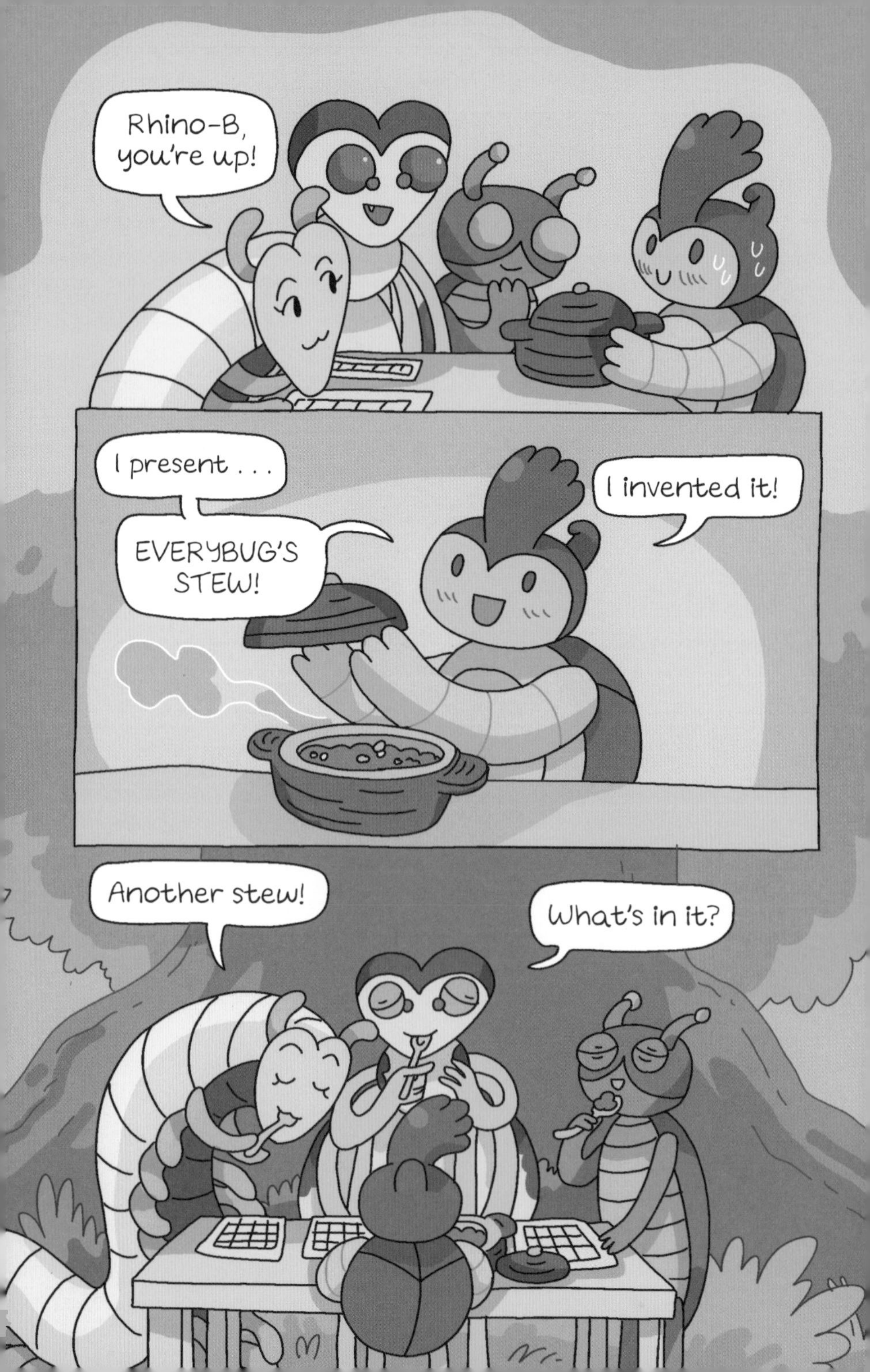

Rhino-B, you're up!
I present . . .
EVERYBUG'S STEW!
I invented it!
Another stew!
What's in it?

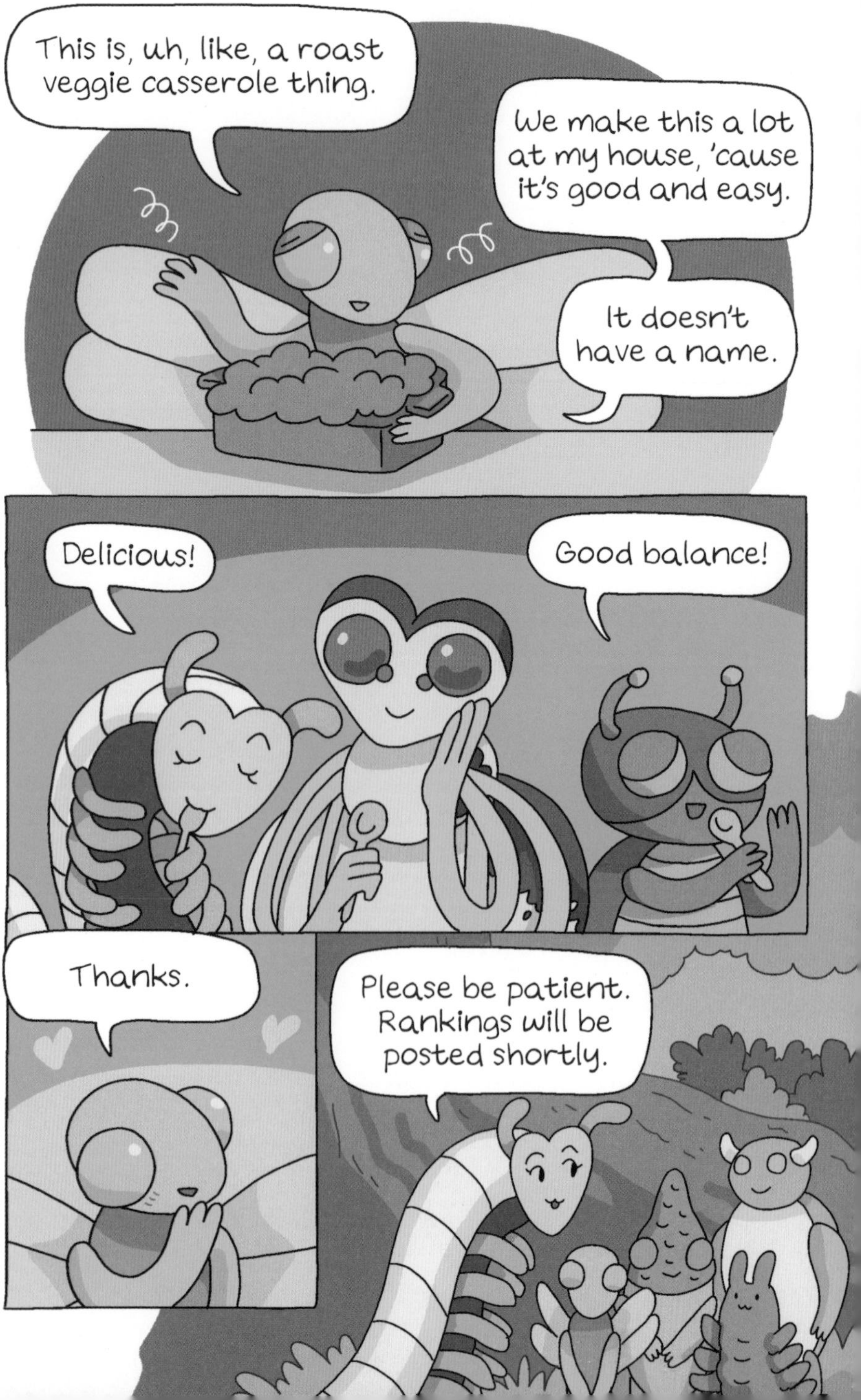
This is, uh, like, a roast veggie casserole thing.
We make this a lot at my house, 'cause it's good and easy.
It doesn't have a name.
Delicious!
Good balance!
Thanks.
Please be patient. Rankings will be posted shortly.

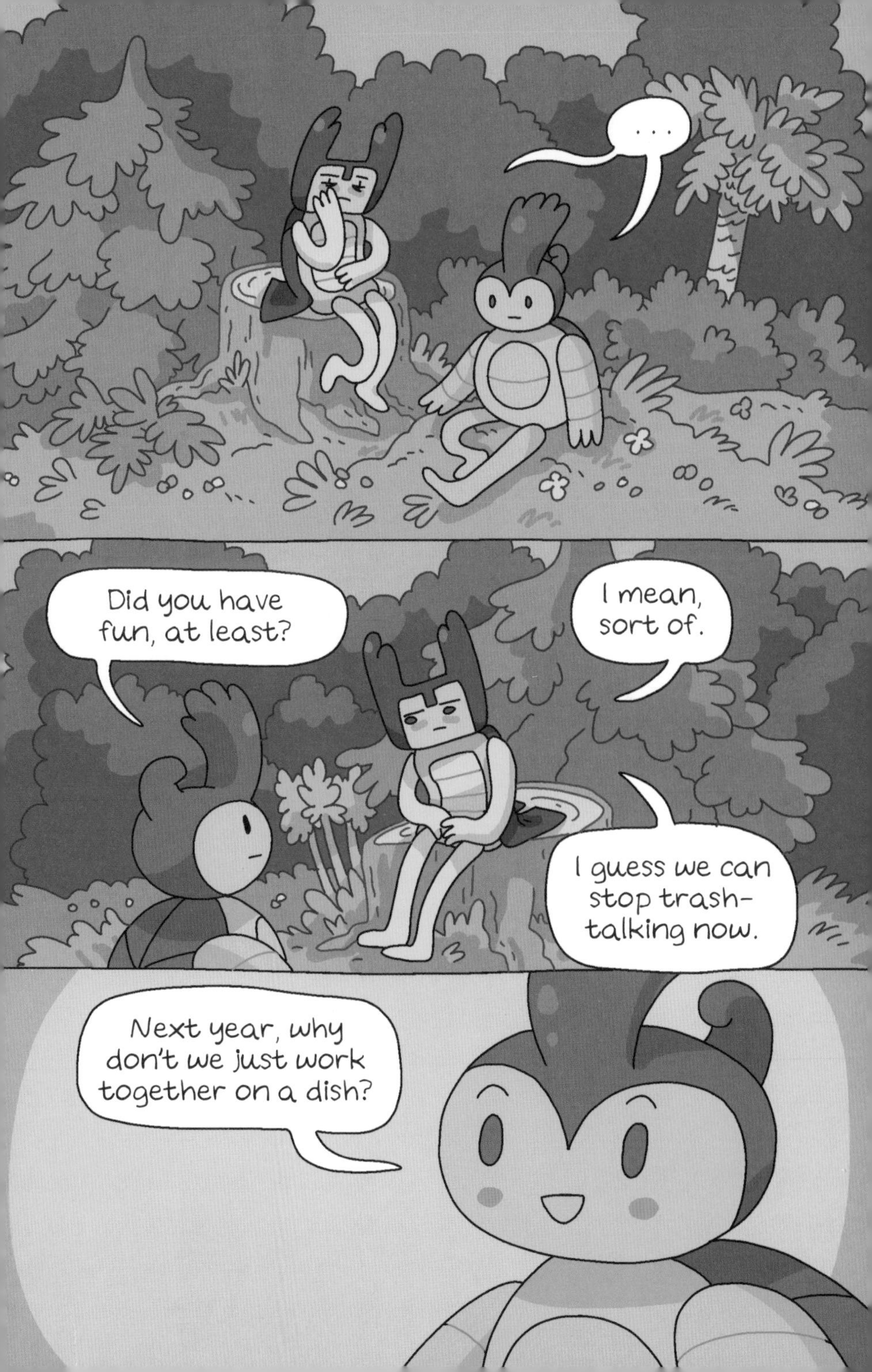
. . .
Did you have fun, at least?
I mean, sort of.
I guess we can stop trash-talking now.
Next year, why don't we just work together on a dish?

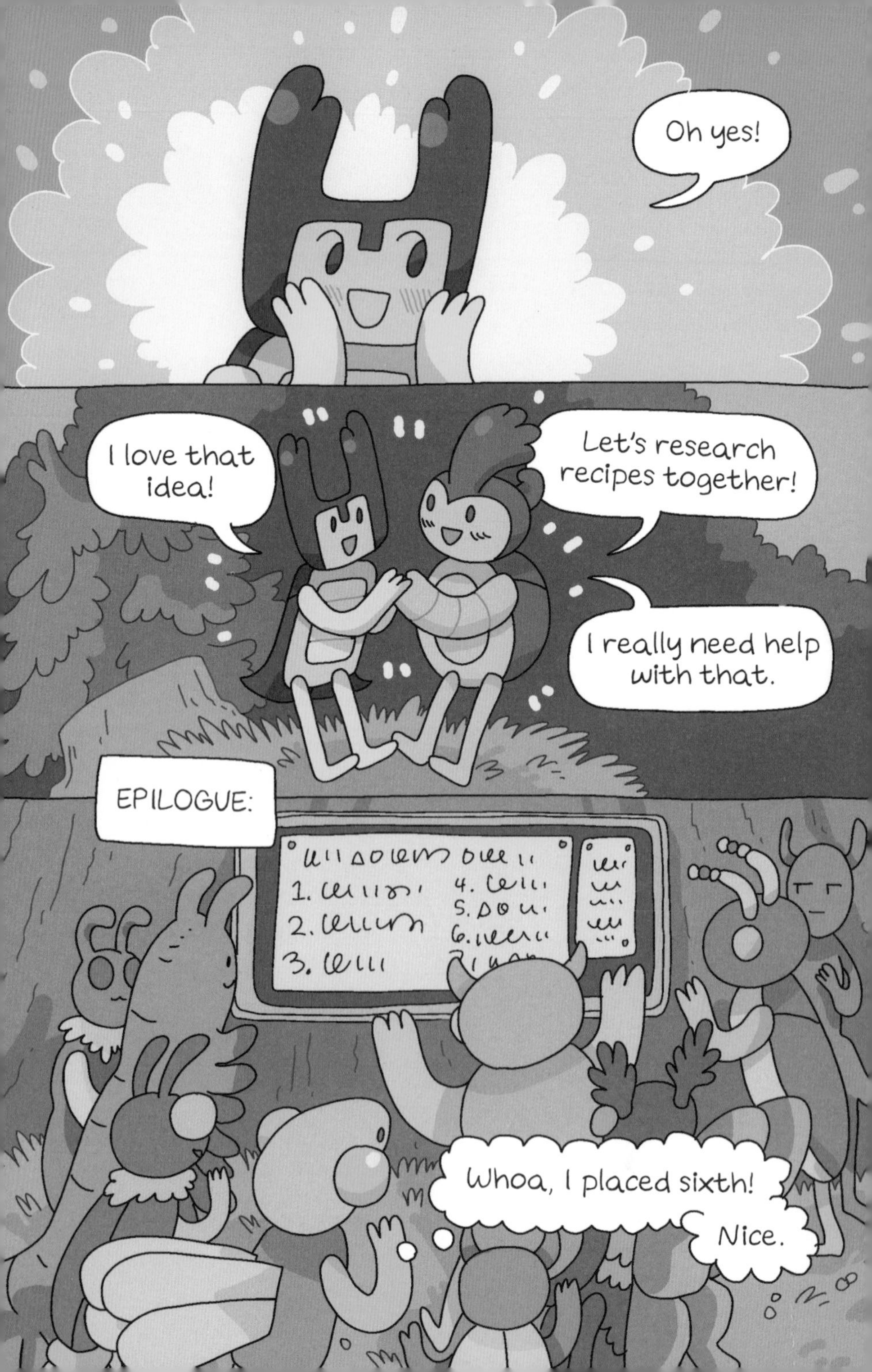
Oh yes!
I love that idea!
Let's research recipes together!
I really need help with that.
EPILOGUE:
Whoa, I placed sixth!
Nice.

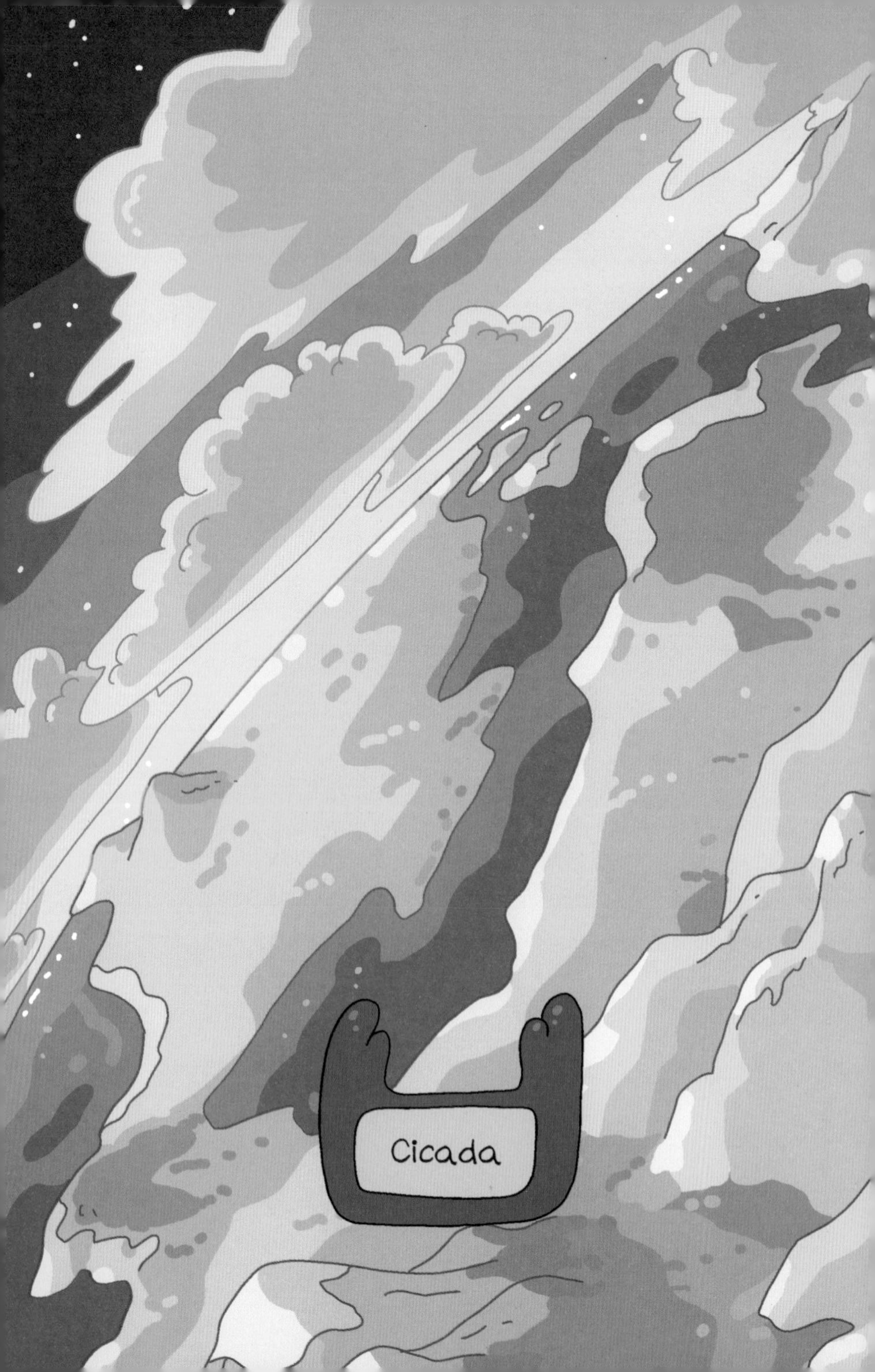
Cicada

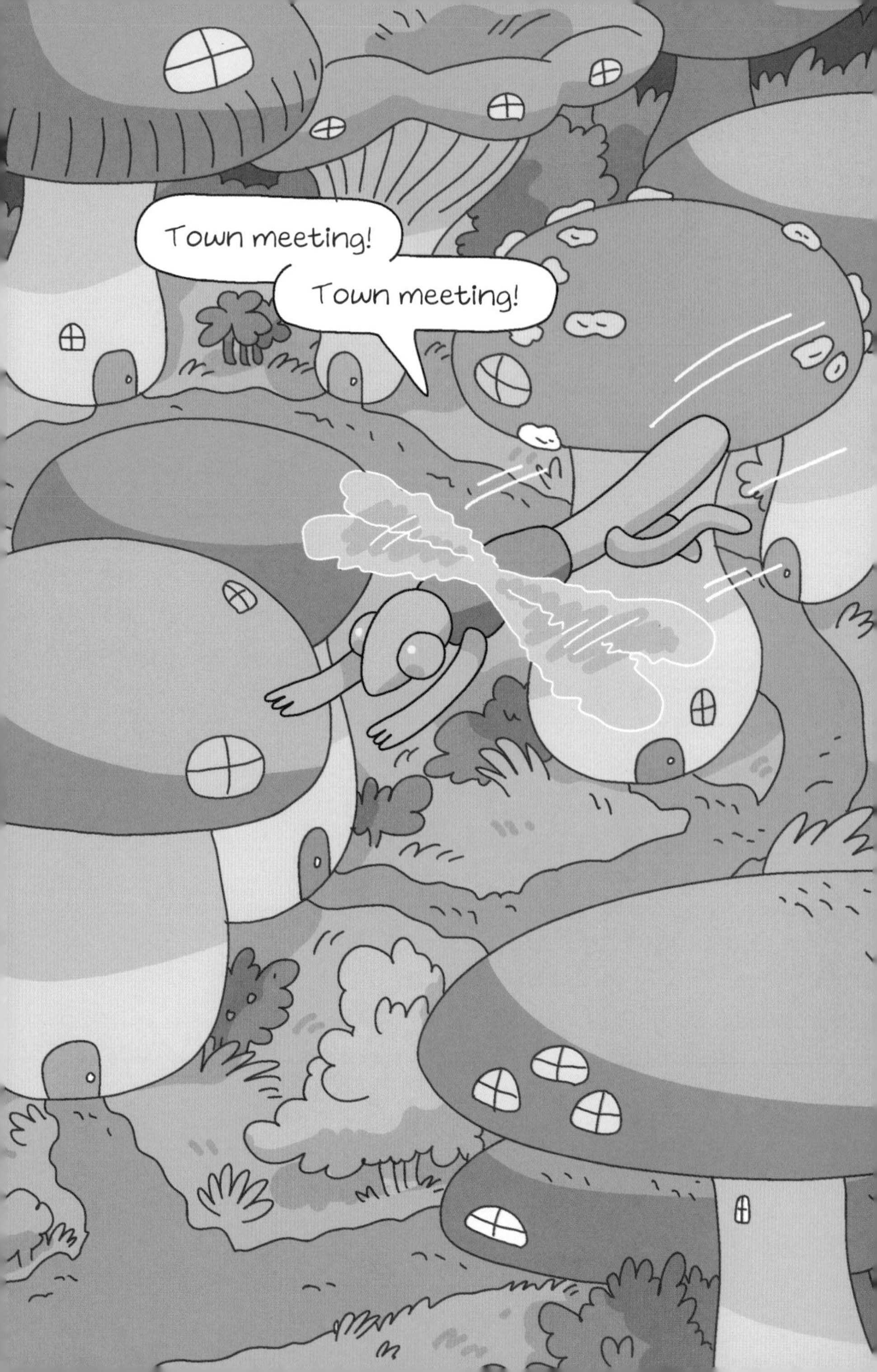
Town meeting!
Town meeting!

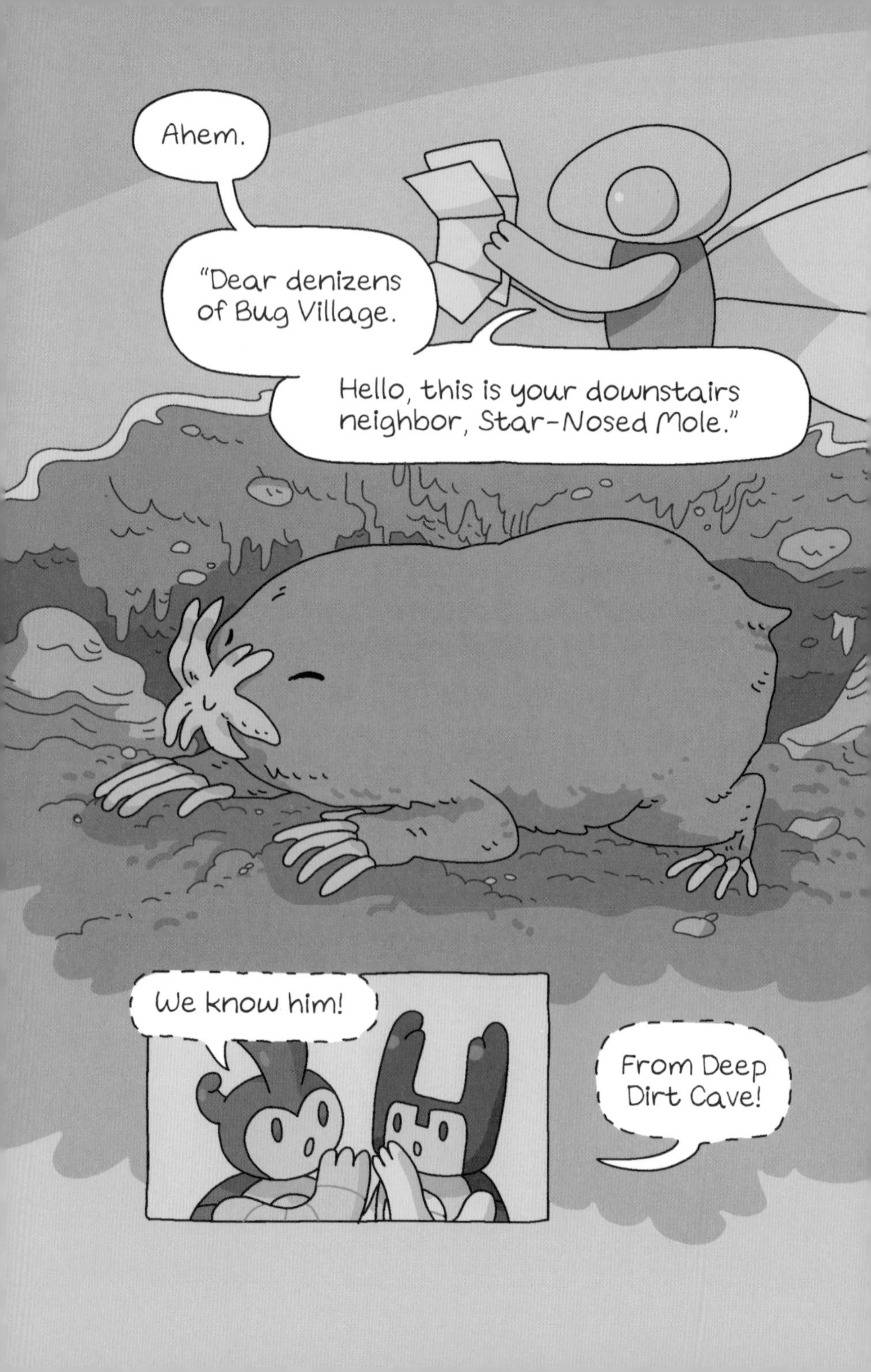
Ahem.
"Dear denizens of Bug Village.
Hello, this is your downstairs neighbor, Star-Nosed Mole."
We know him!
From Deep Dirt Cave!

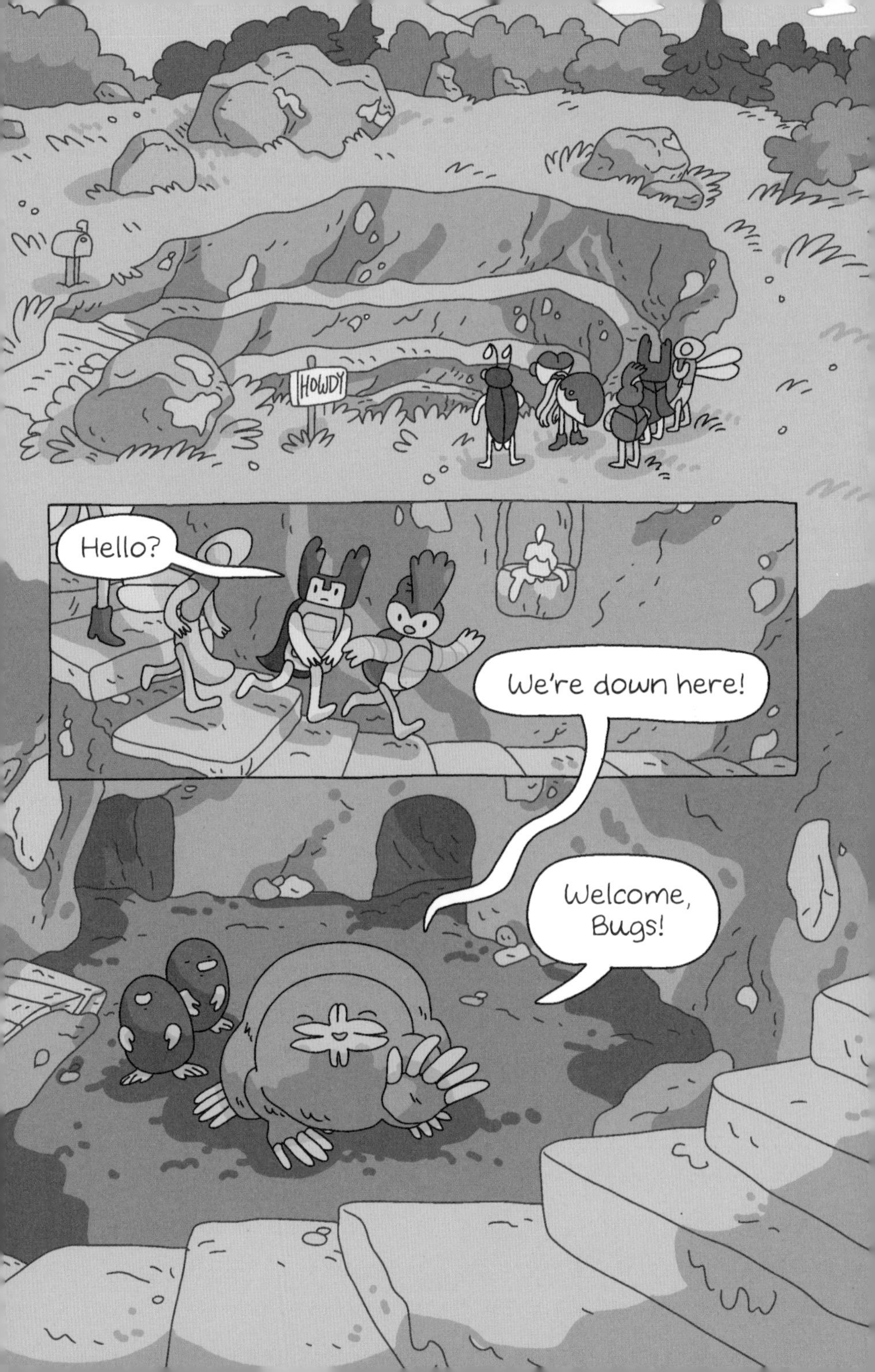
HOWDY
Hello?
We're down here!
Welcome, Bugs!

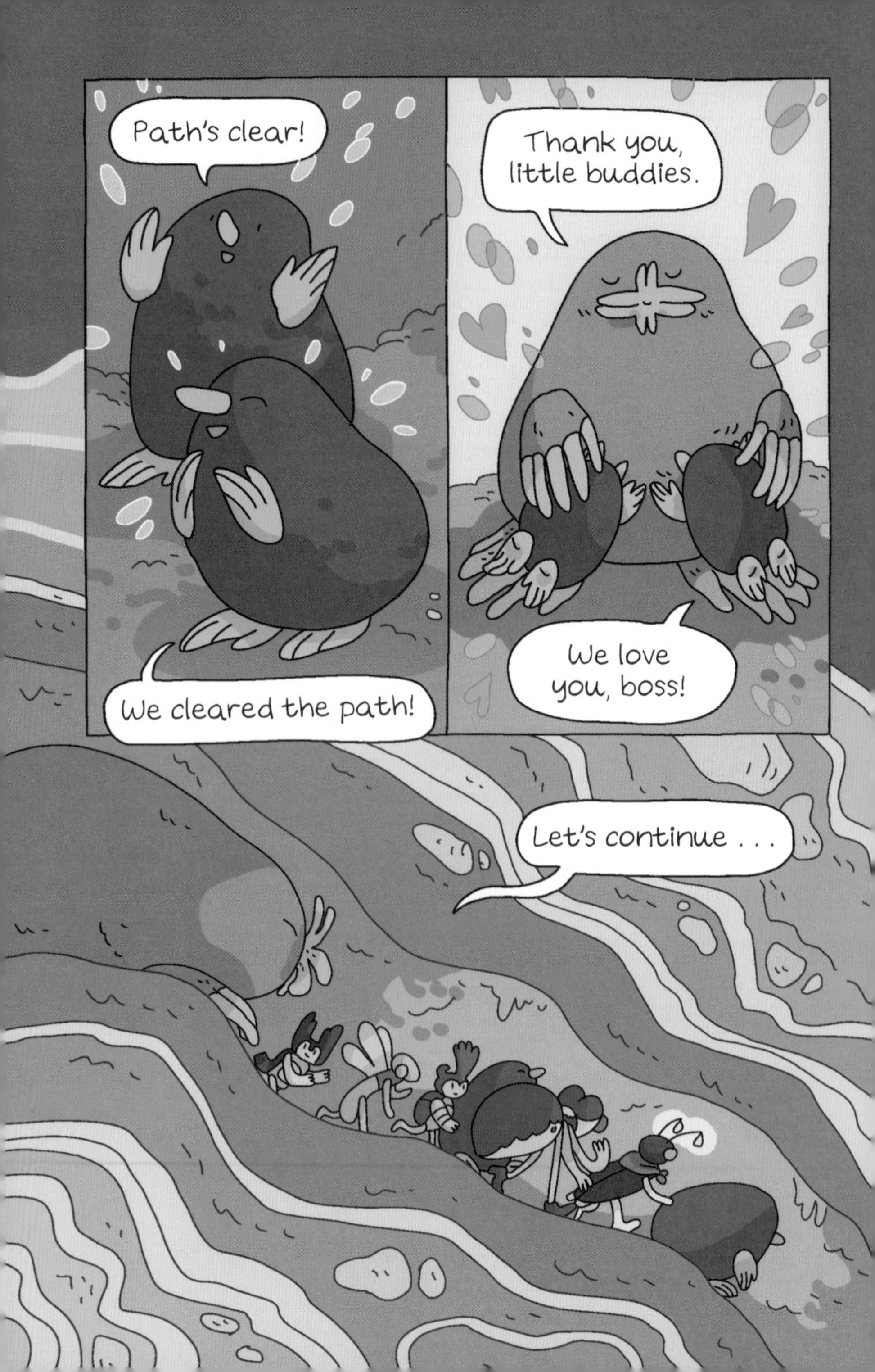
Path's clear!
We cleared the path!
Thank you, little buddies.
We love you, boss!
Let's continue . . .

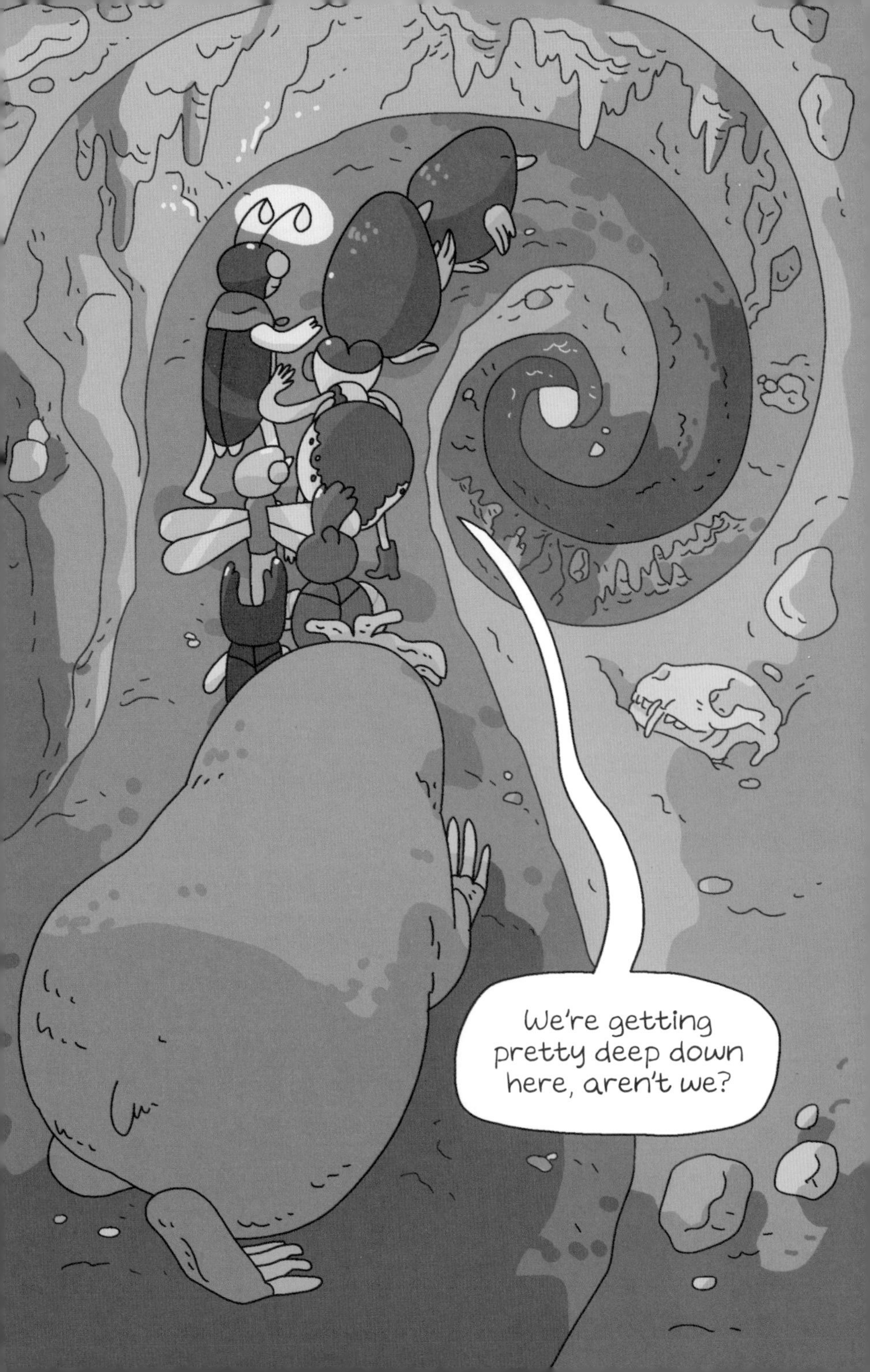
We're getting pretty deep down here, aren't we?

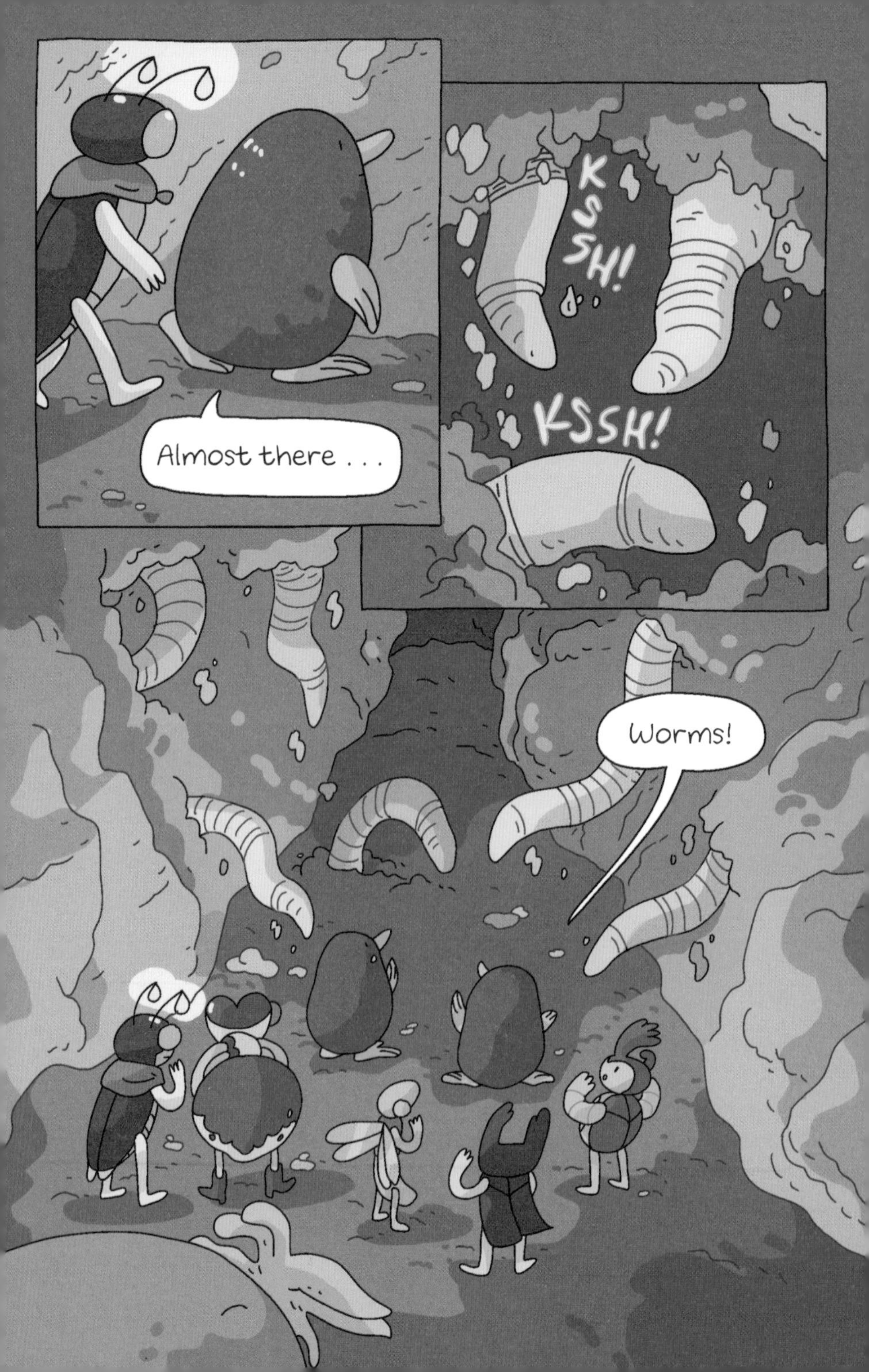
Almost there . . .
KSSH!
KSSH!
Worms!

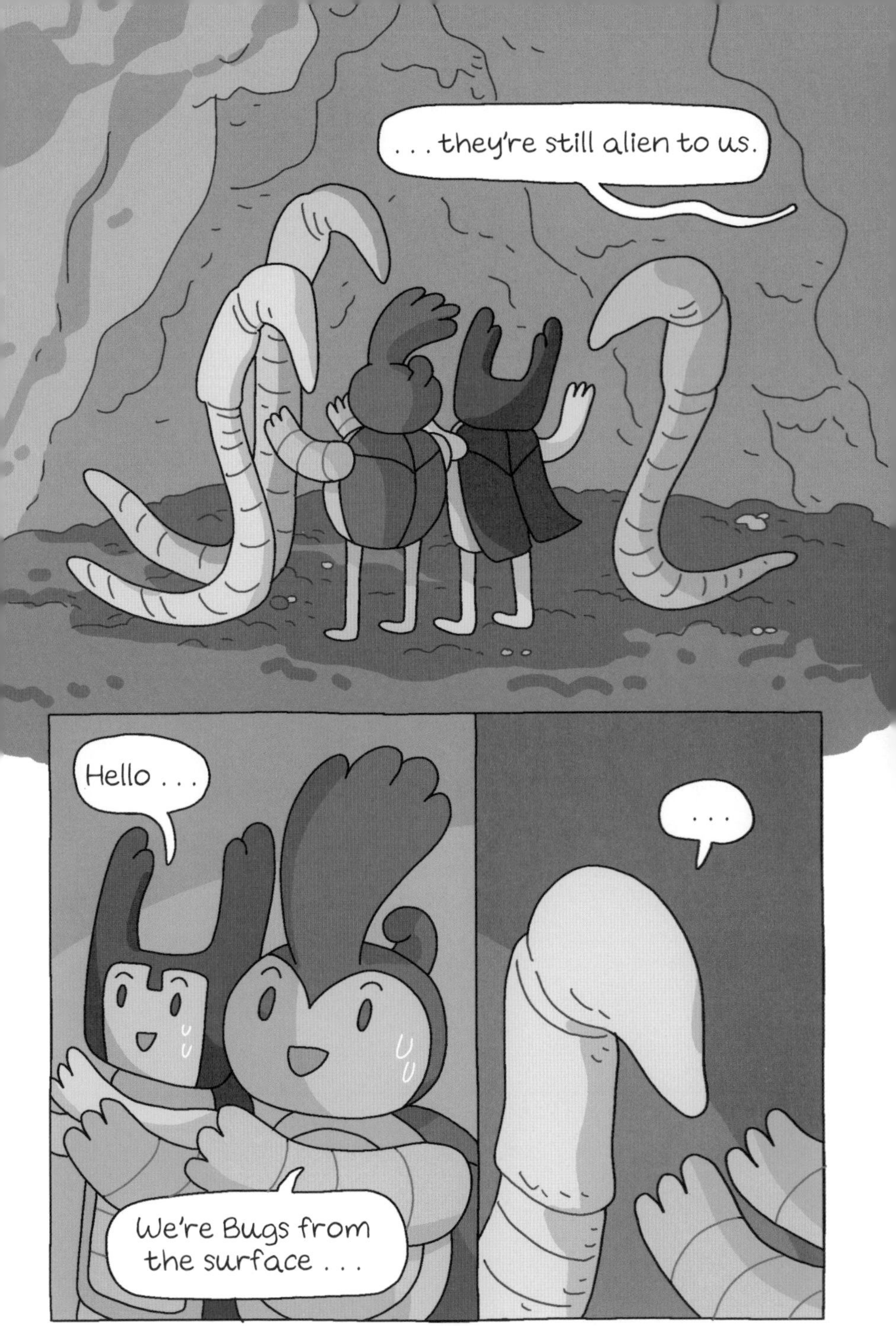
. . . they're still alien to us.
Hello . . .
We're Bugs from the surface . . .
. . .

150

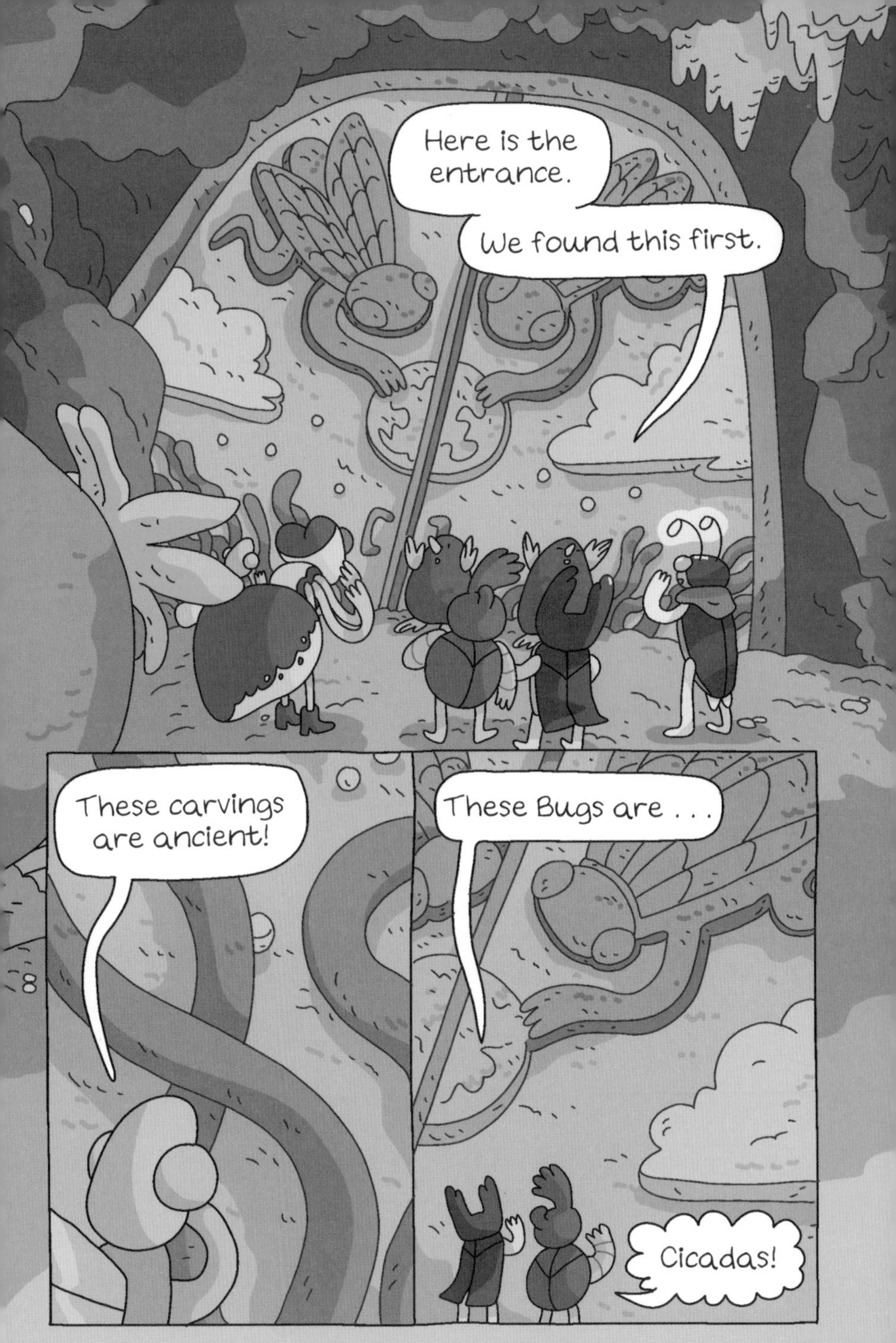
Here is the entrance.
We found this first.
These carvings are ancient!
These Bugs are . . .
Cicadas!

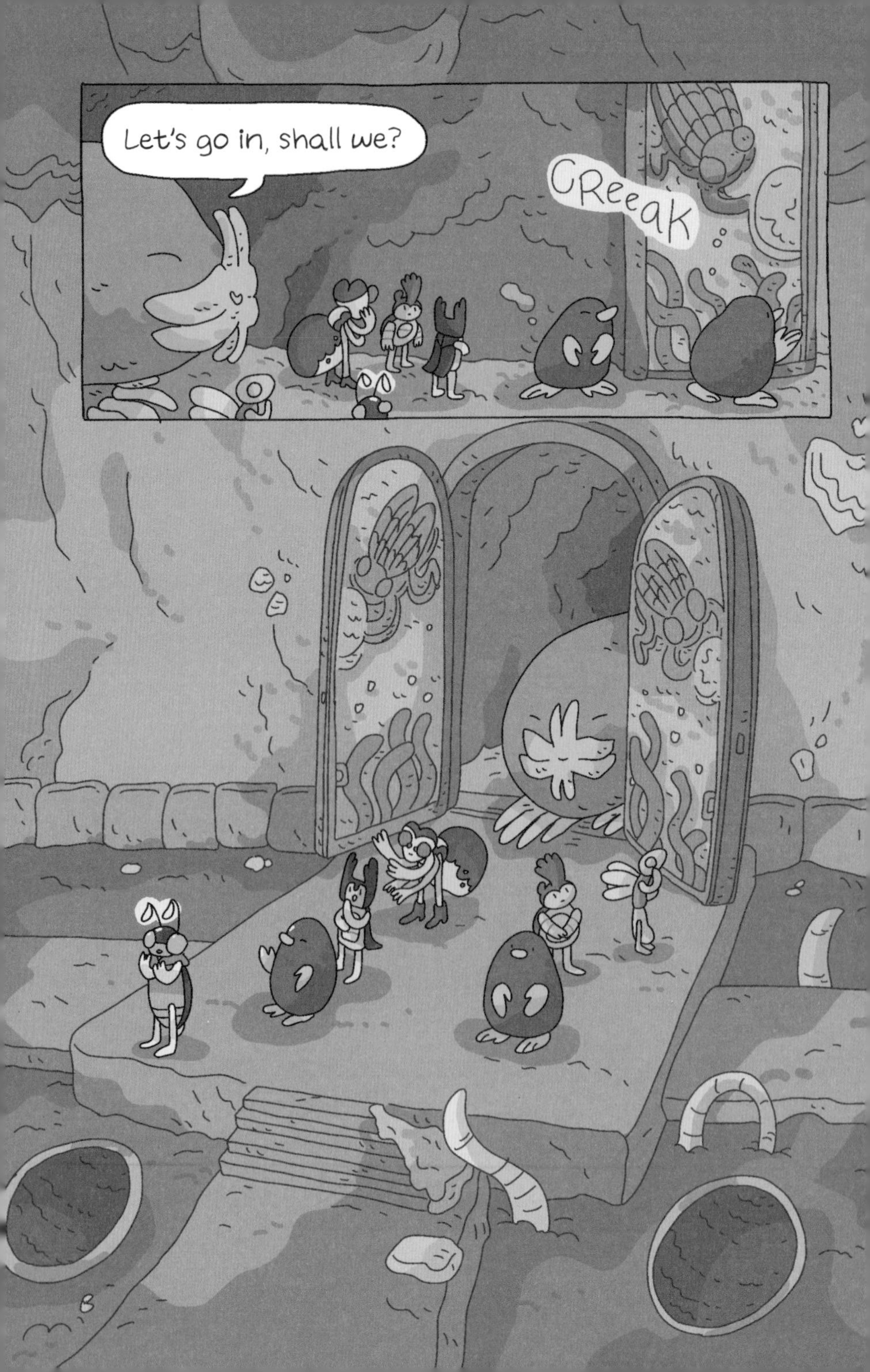
Let's go in, shall we?
CReeaK

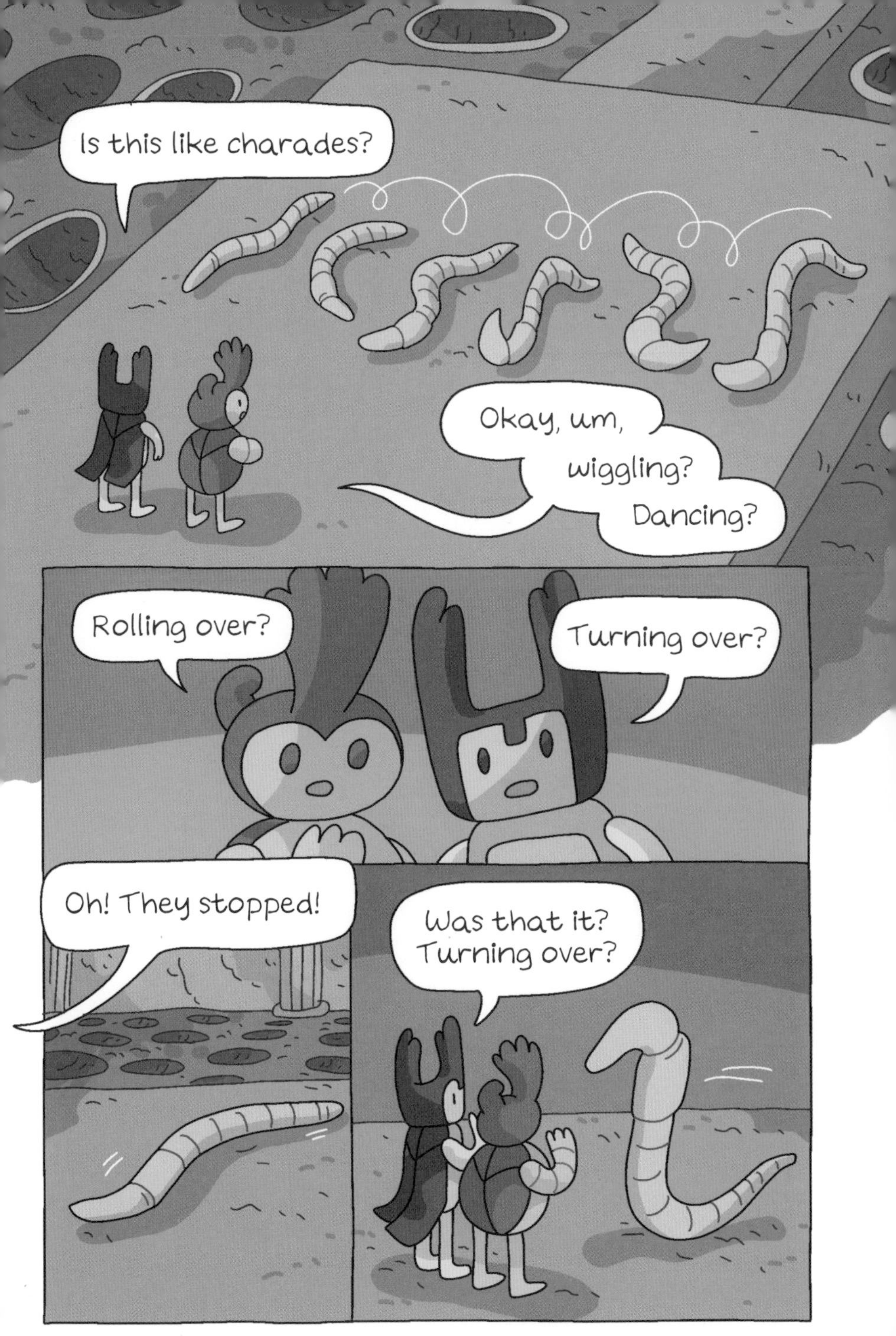
Is this like charades?
Okay, um,
wiggling?
Dancing?
Rolling over?
Turning over?
Oh! They stopped!
Was that it? Turning over?

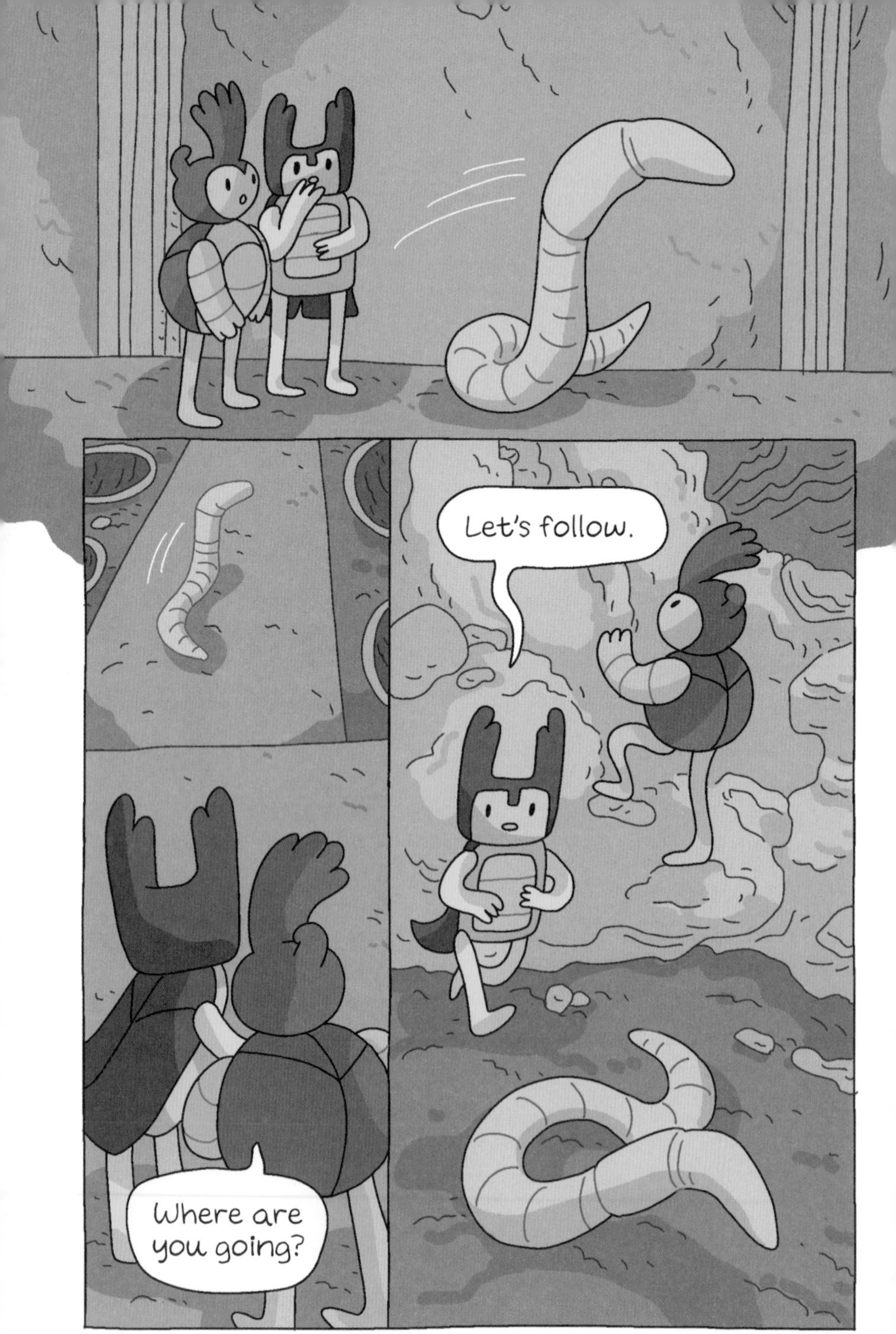
Let's follow.
Where are you going?

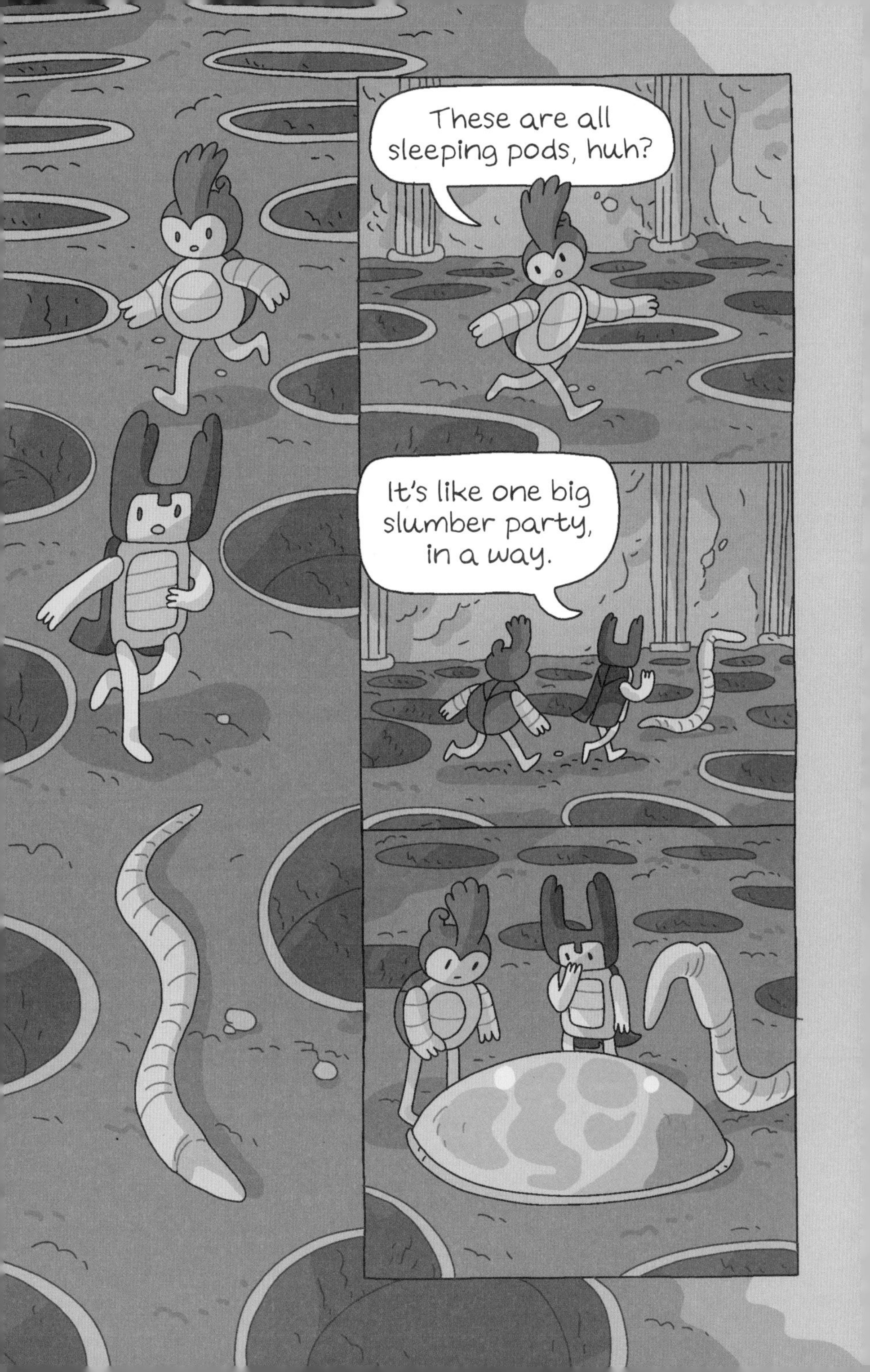
These are all sleeping pods, huh?
It's like one big slumber party, in a way.

162

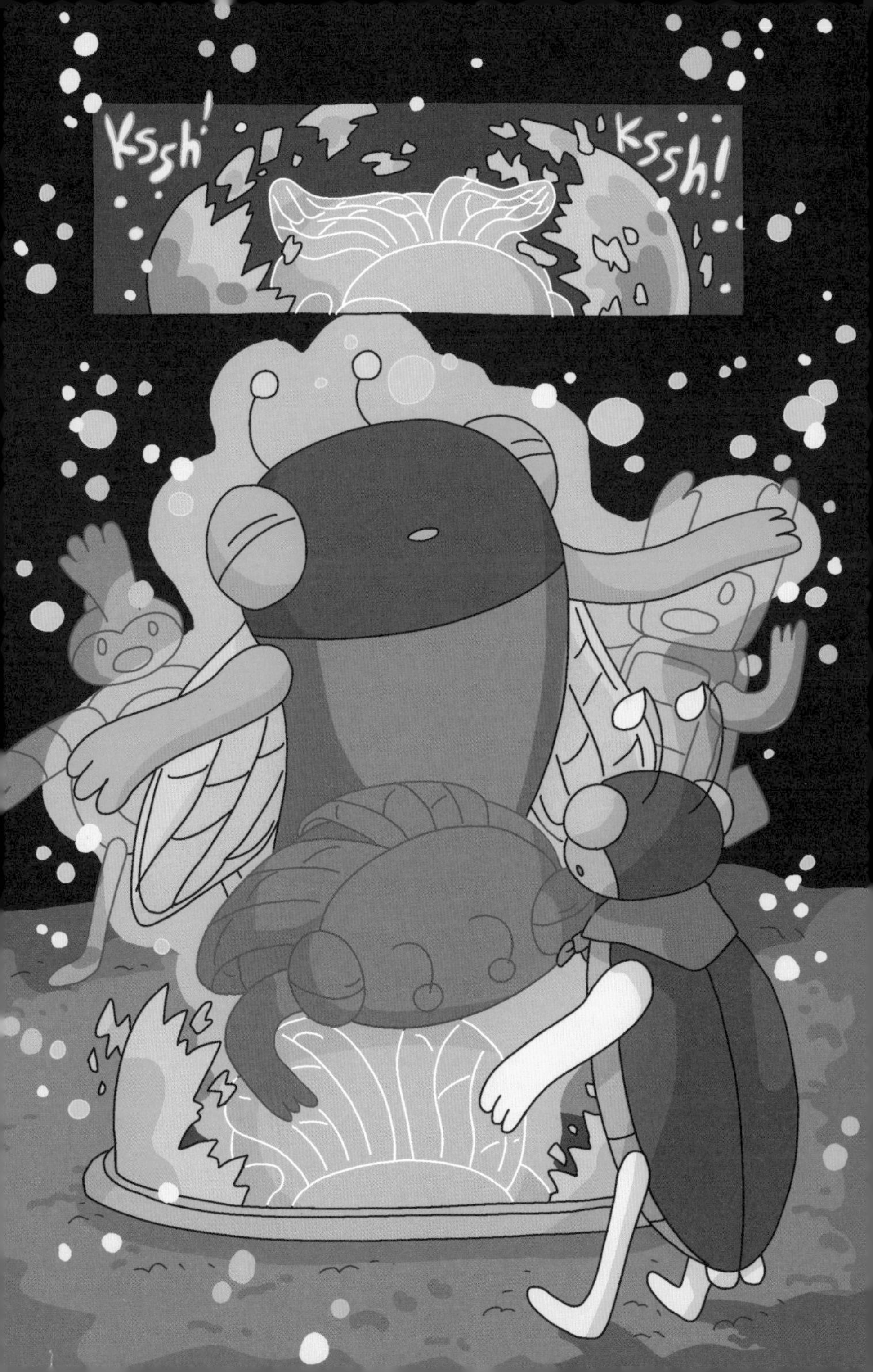
Kssh!
Kssh!

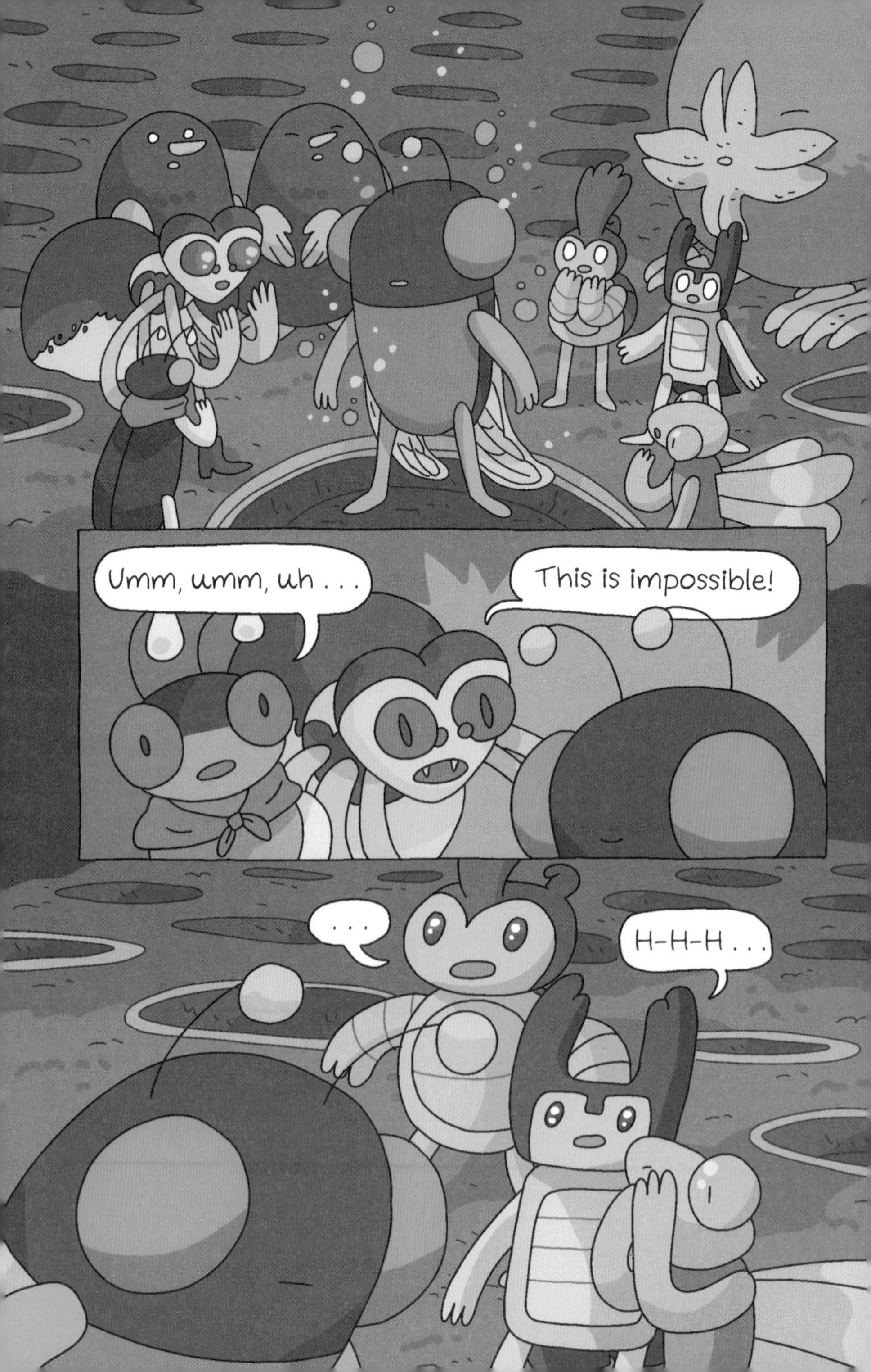
Umm, umm, uh . . .
This is impossible!
. . .
H-H-H . . .

165

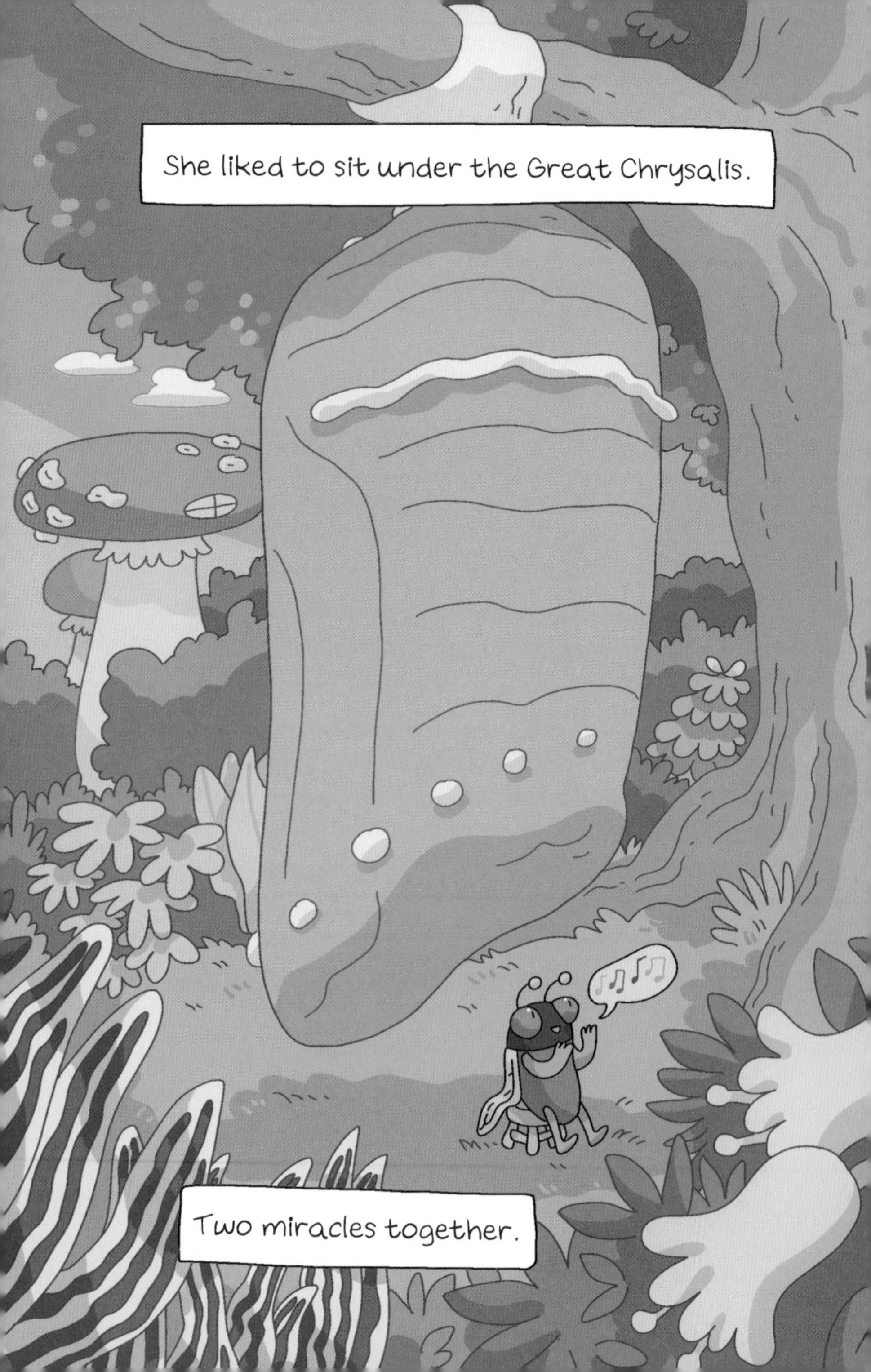
She liked to sit under the Great Chrysalis.
Two miracles together.

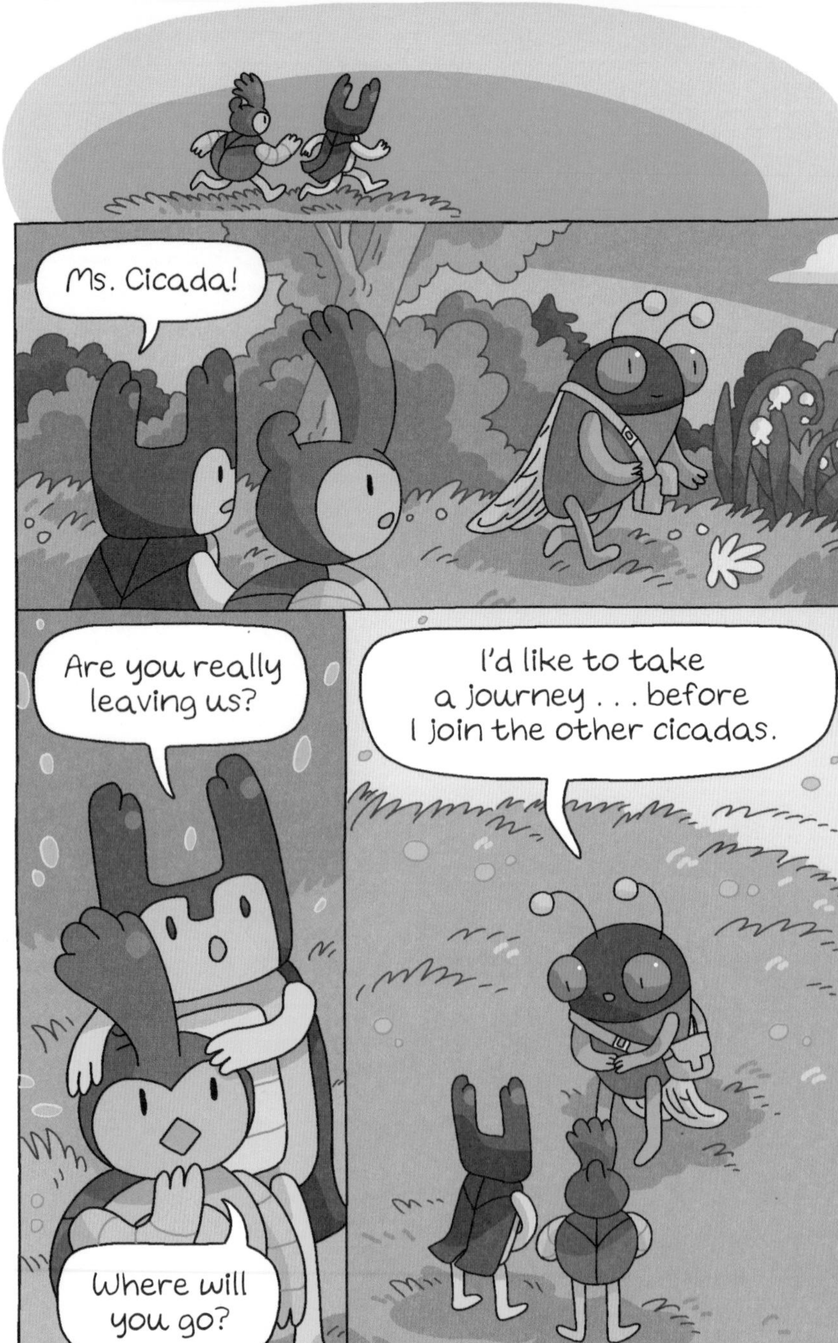
Ms. Cicada!
Are you really leaving us?
Where will you go?
I'd like to take a journey . . . before I join the other cicadas.

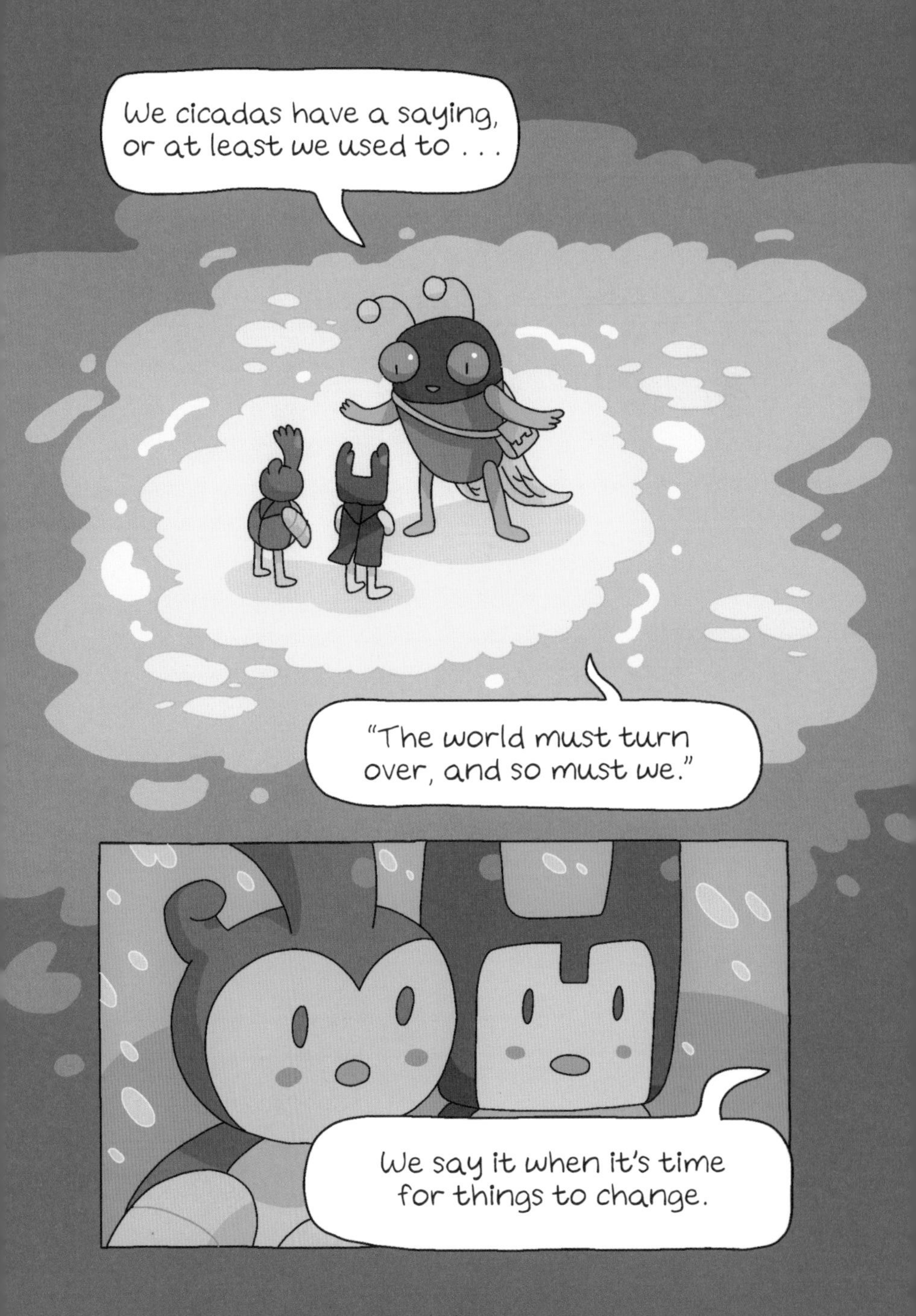
We cicadas have a saying, or at least we used to . . .
"The world must turn over, and so must we."
We say it when it's time for things to change.

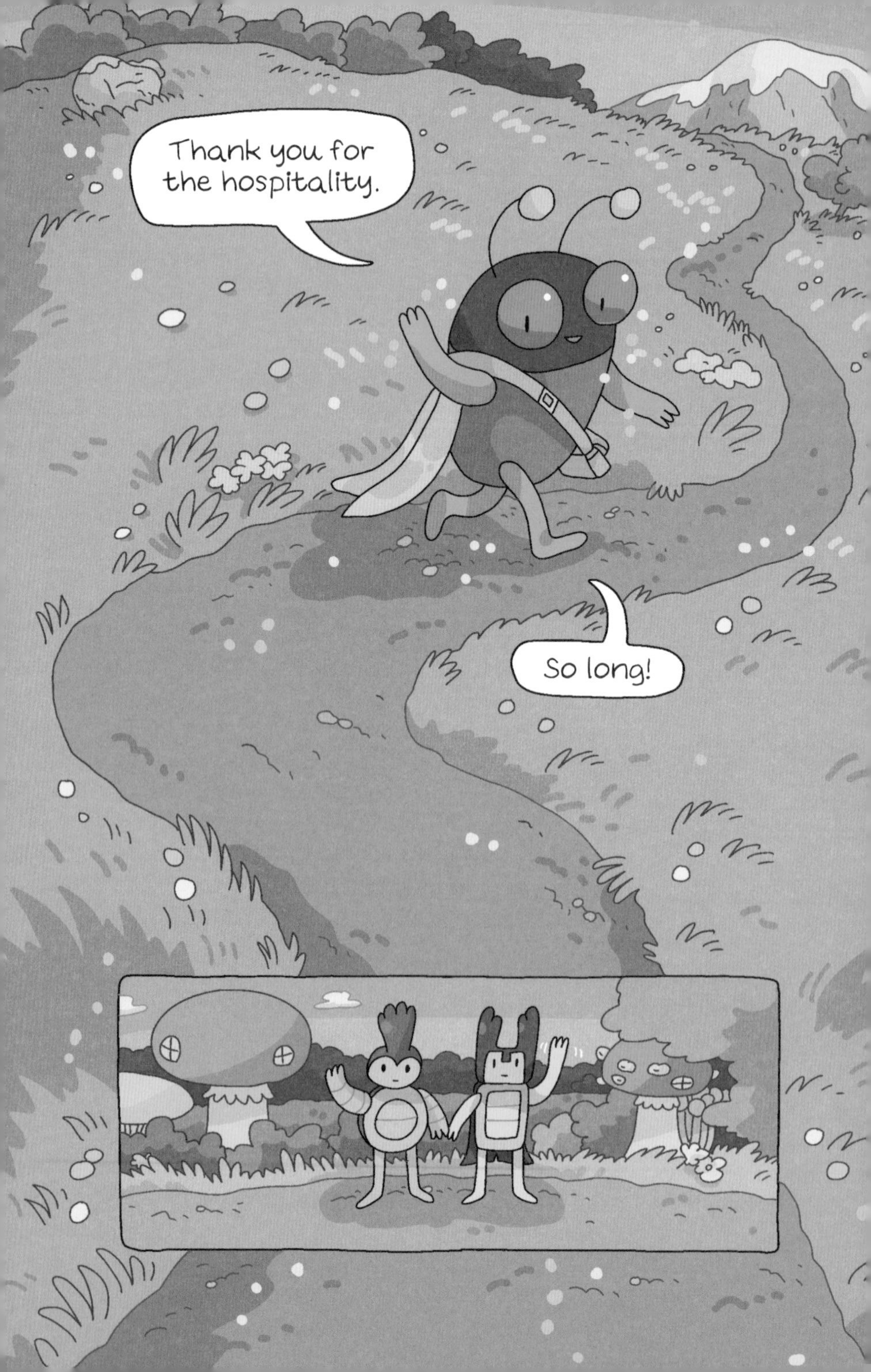
Thank you for the hospitality.
So long!

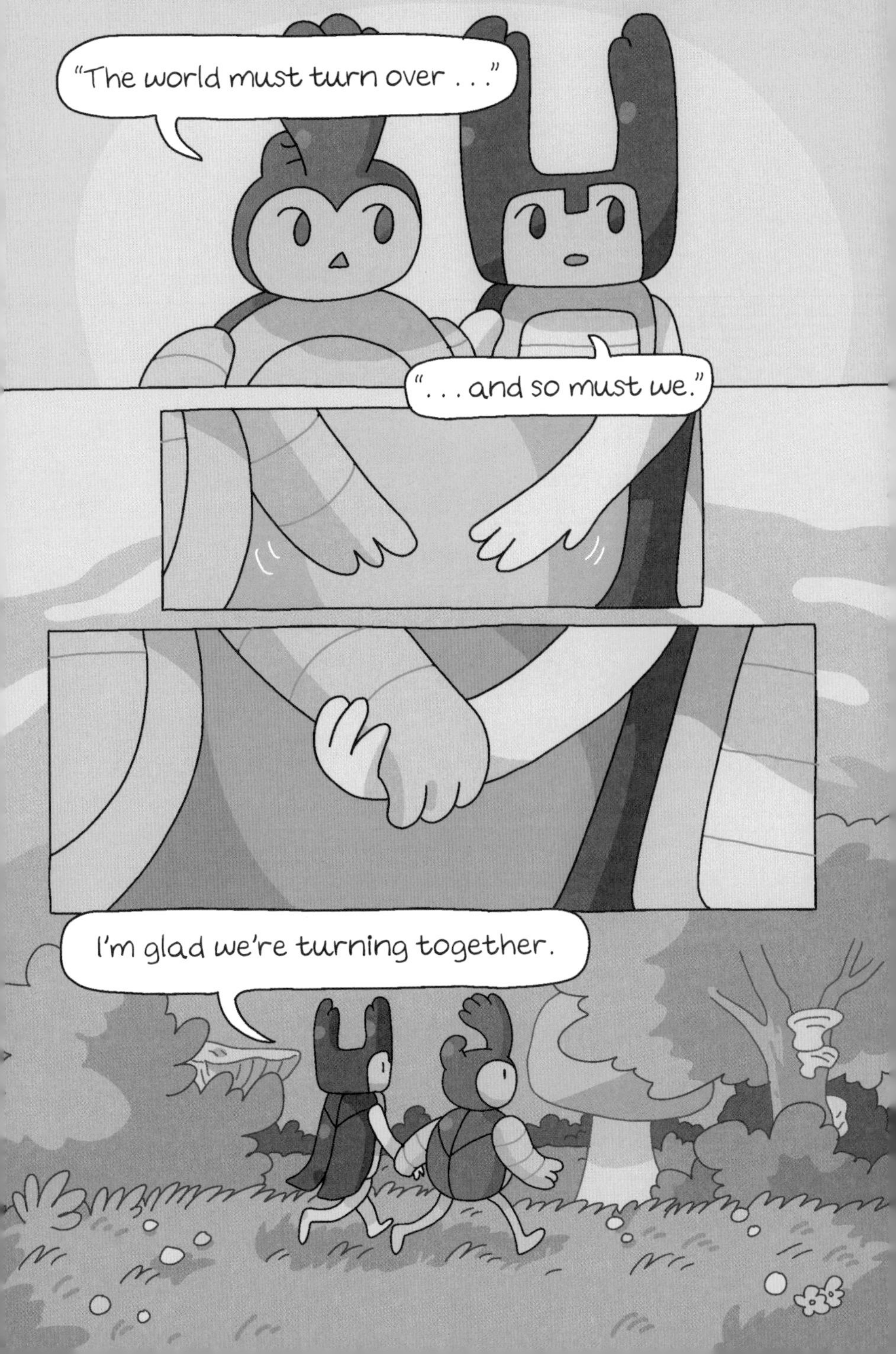
"The world must turn over . . ."
". . . and so must we."
I'm glad we're turning together.

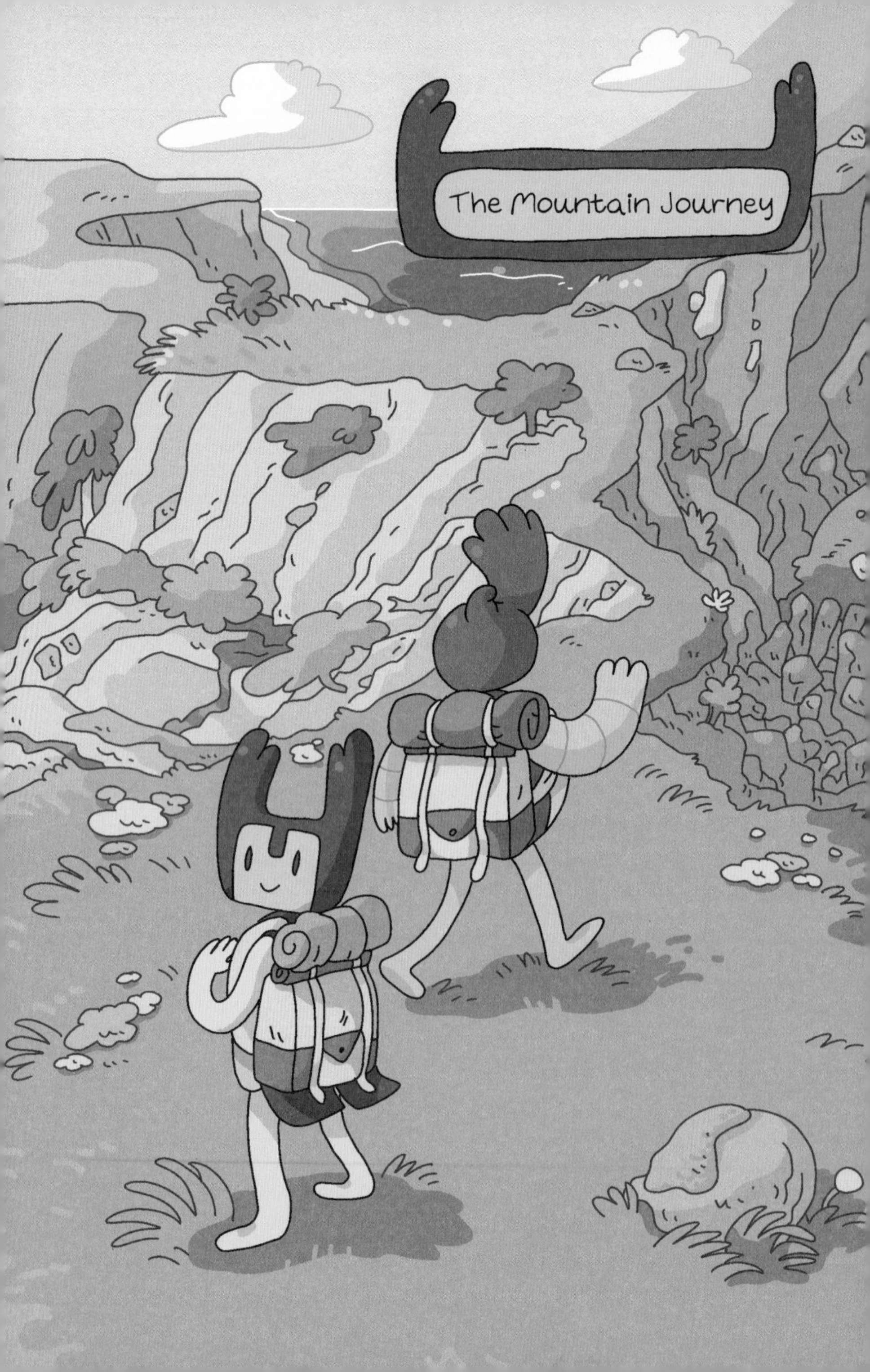
The Mountain Journey

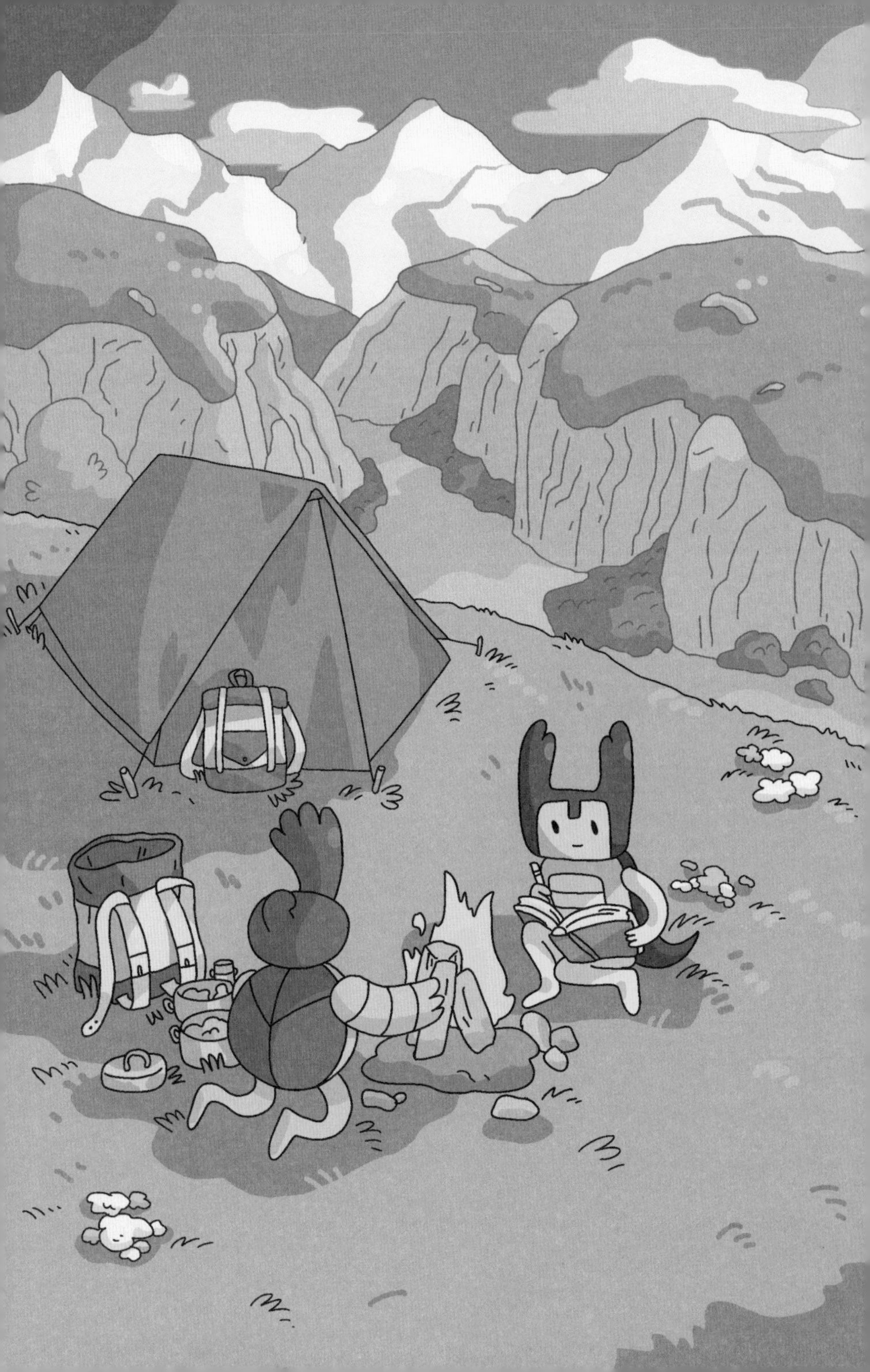

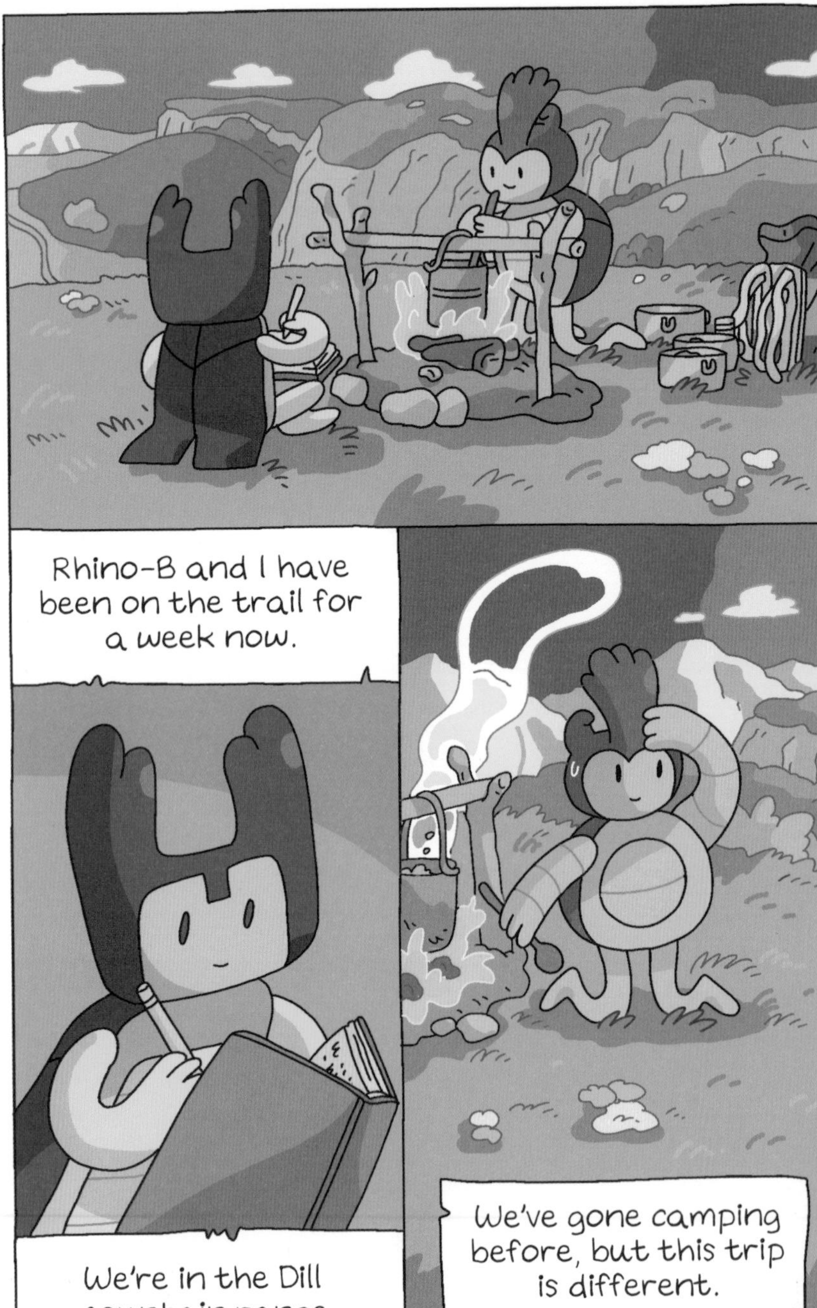
Rhino-B and I have been on the trail for a week now.
We're in the Dill mountain range.
We've gone camping before, but this trip is different.

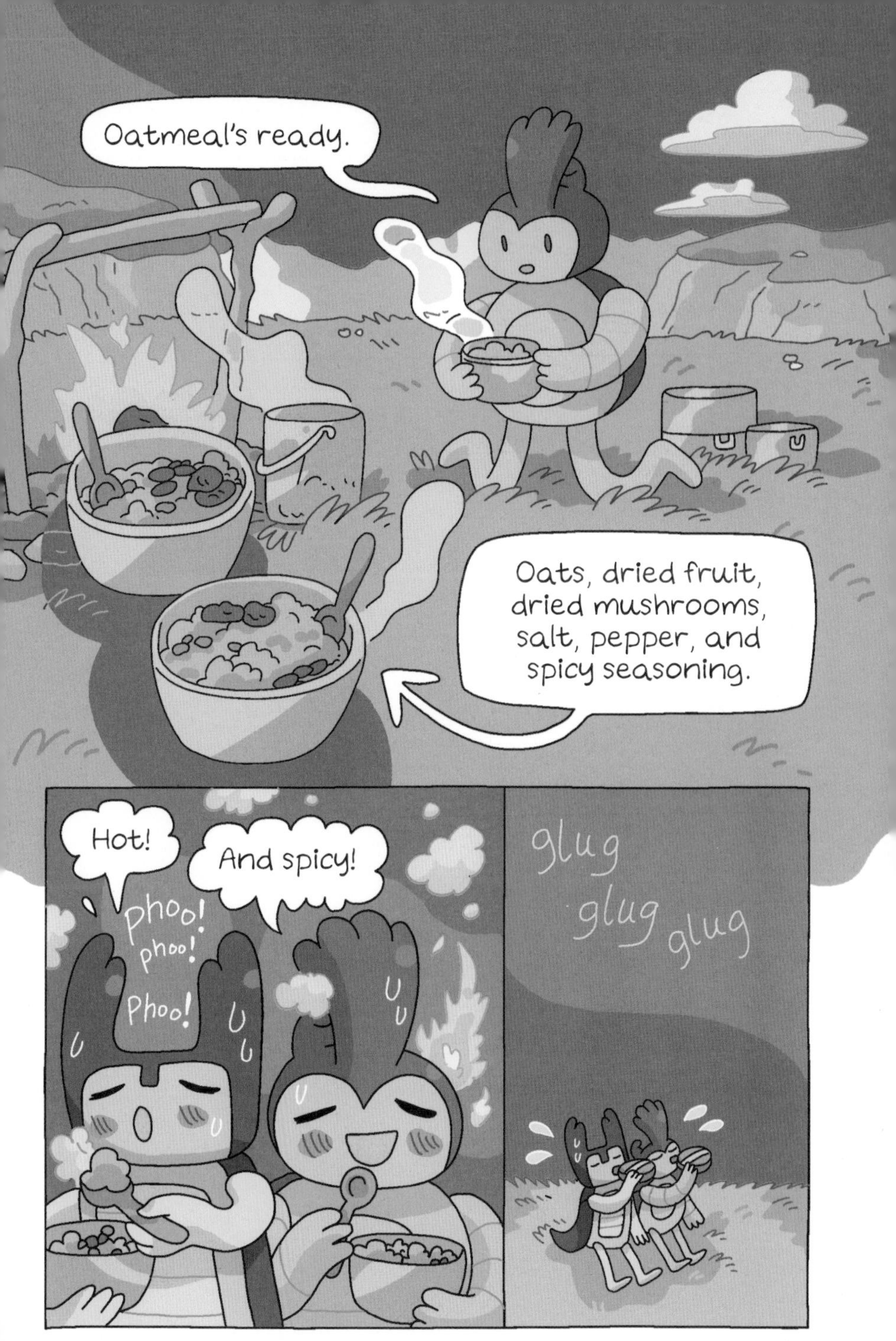
Oatmeal's ready.
Oats, dried fruit, dried mushrooms, salt, pepper, and spicy seasoning.
Hot!
And spicy!
phoo! phoo! Phoo!
glug glug glug

This is the vista that's our final destination before we turn back.
It's what I really want to see.
The maps always use this odd symbol for it and I don't know why.
The trail is about to get pretty rough.
Are you sure you still want to come? You can turn back whenever you want.
. . .
I hadn't even thought of it.

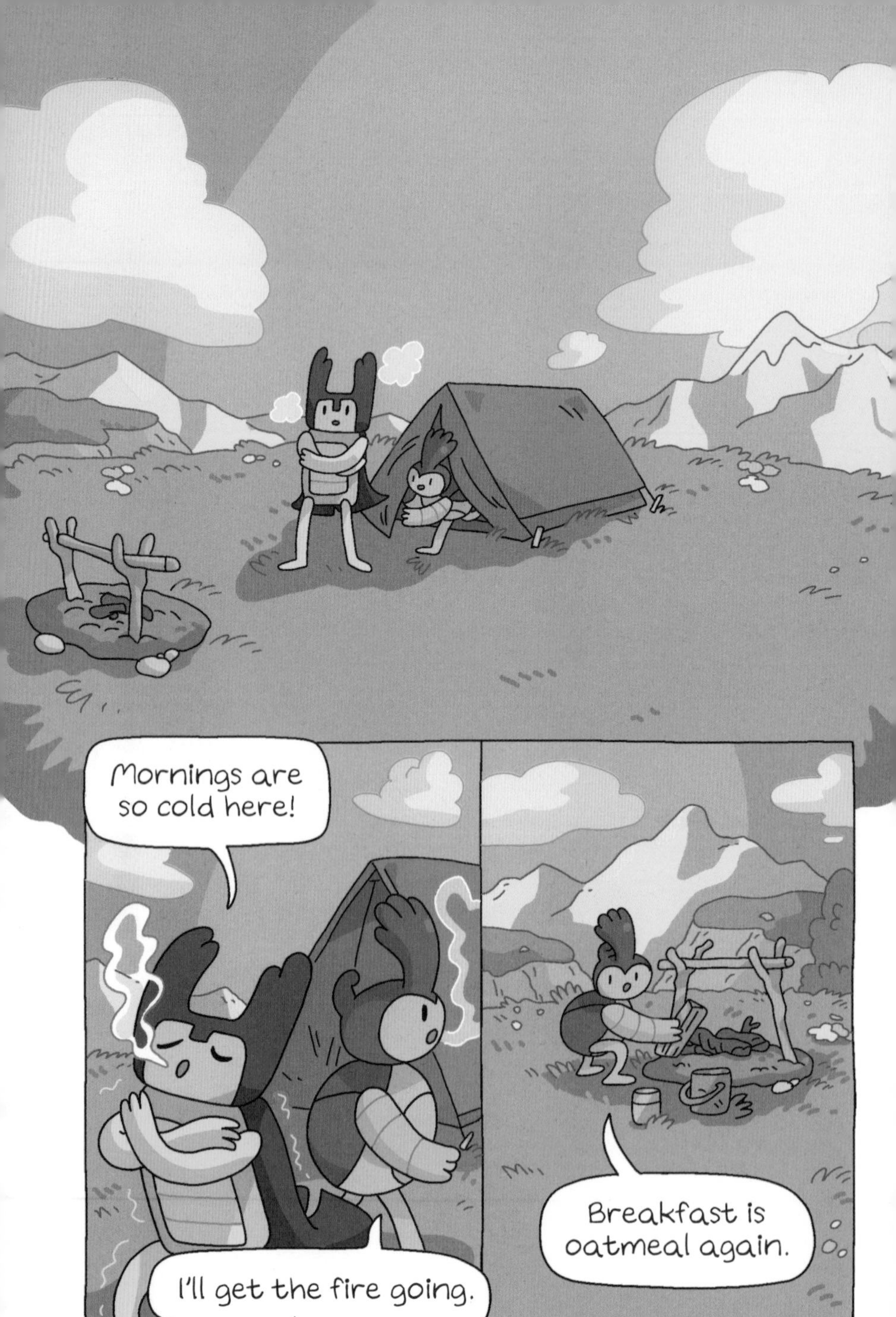
Mornings are so cold here!
I'll get the fire going.
Breakfast is oatmeal again.

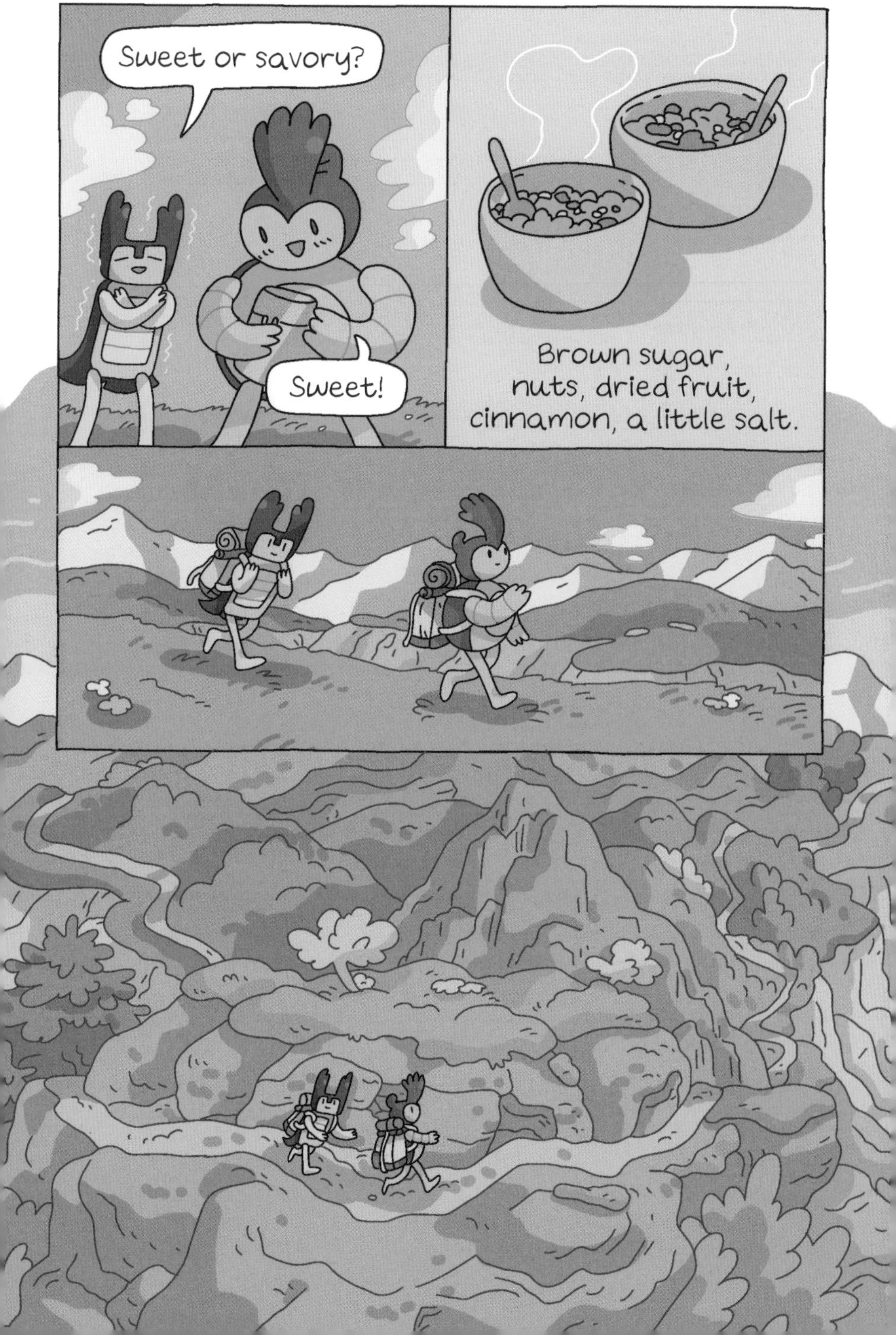
Sweet or savory?
Sweet!
Brown sugar, nuts, dried fruit, cinnamon, a little salt.

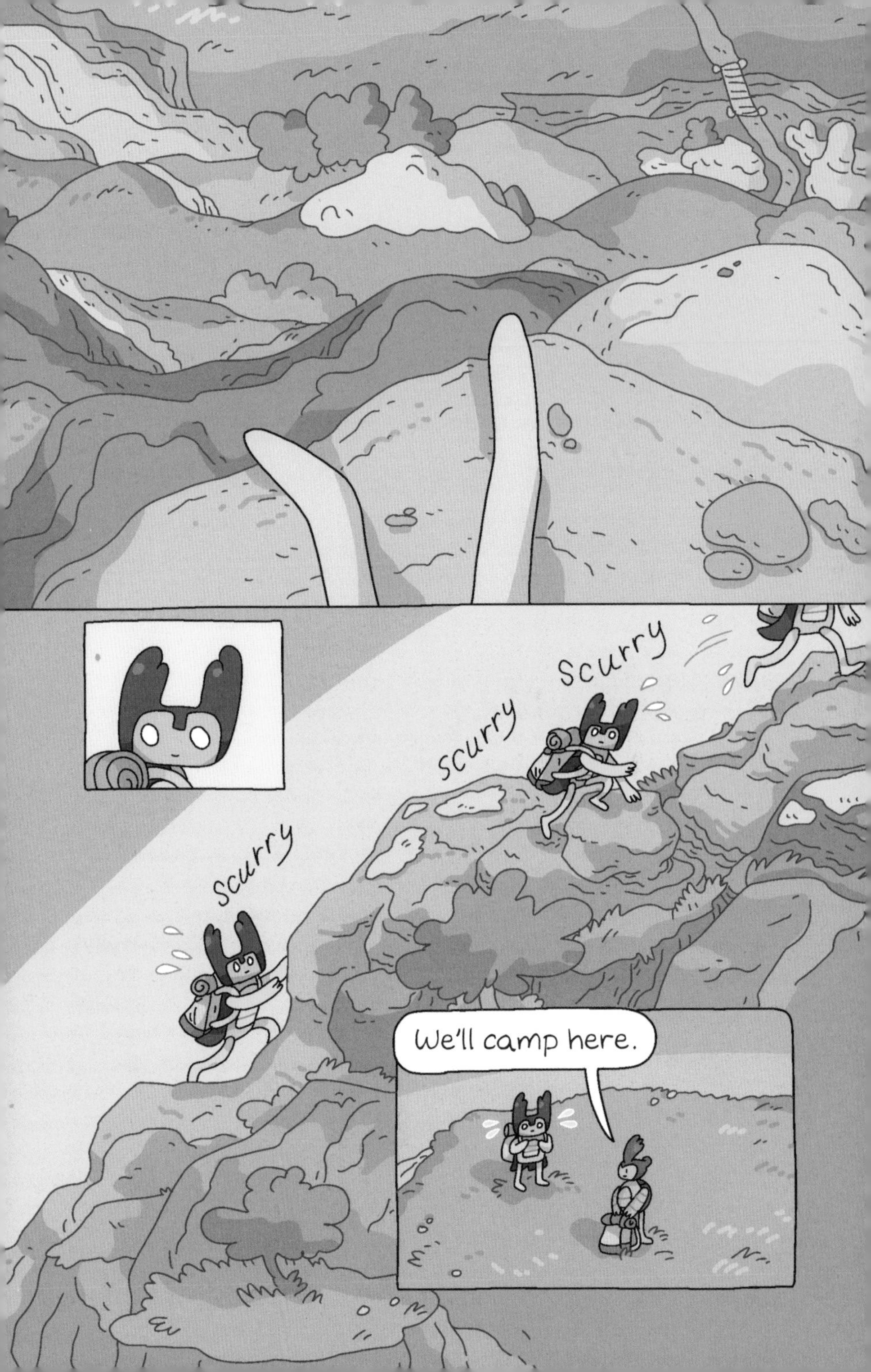
Scurry
Scurry
Scurry
We'll camp here.

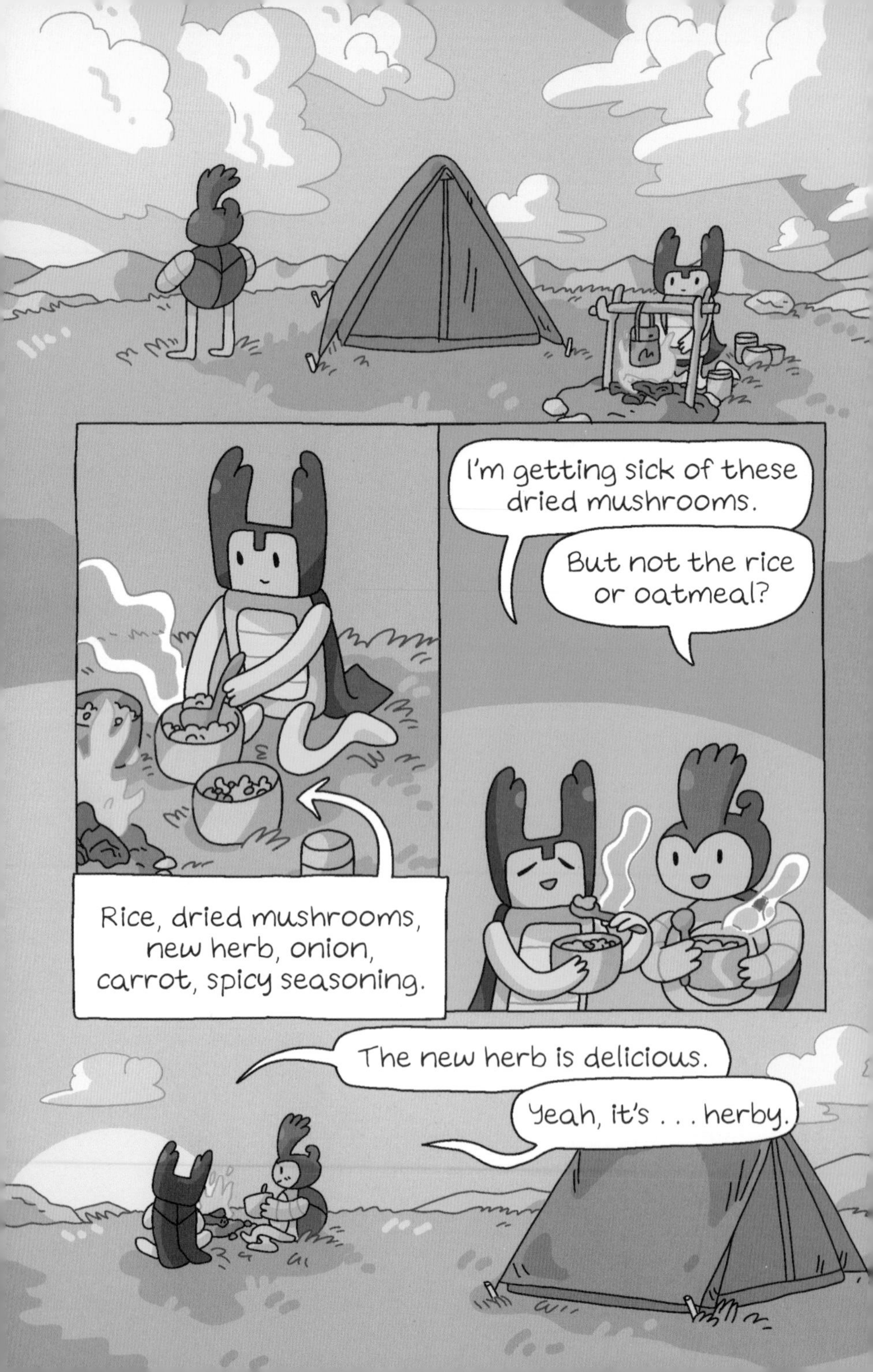

Rice, dried mushrooms, new herb, onion, carrot, spicy seasoning.
I'm getting sick of these dried mushrooms.
But not the rice or oatmeal?
The new herb is delicious.
Yeah, it's . . . herby.

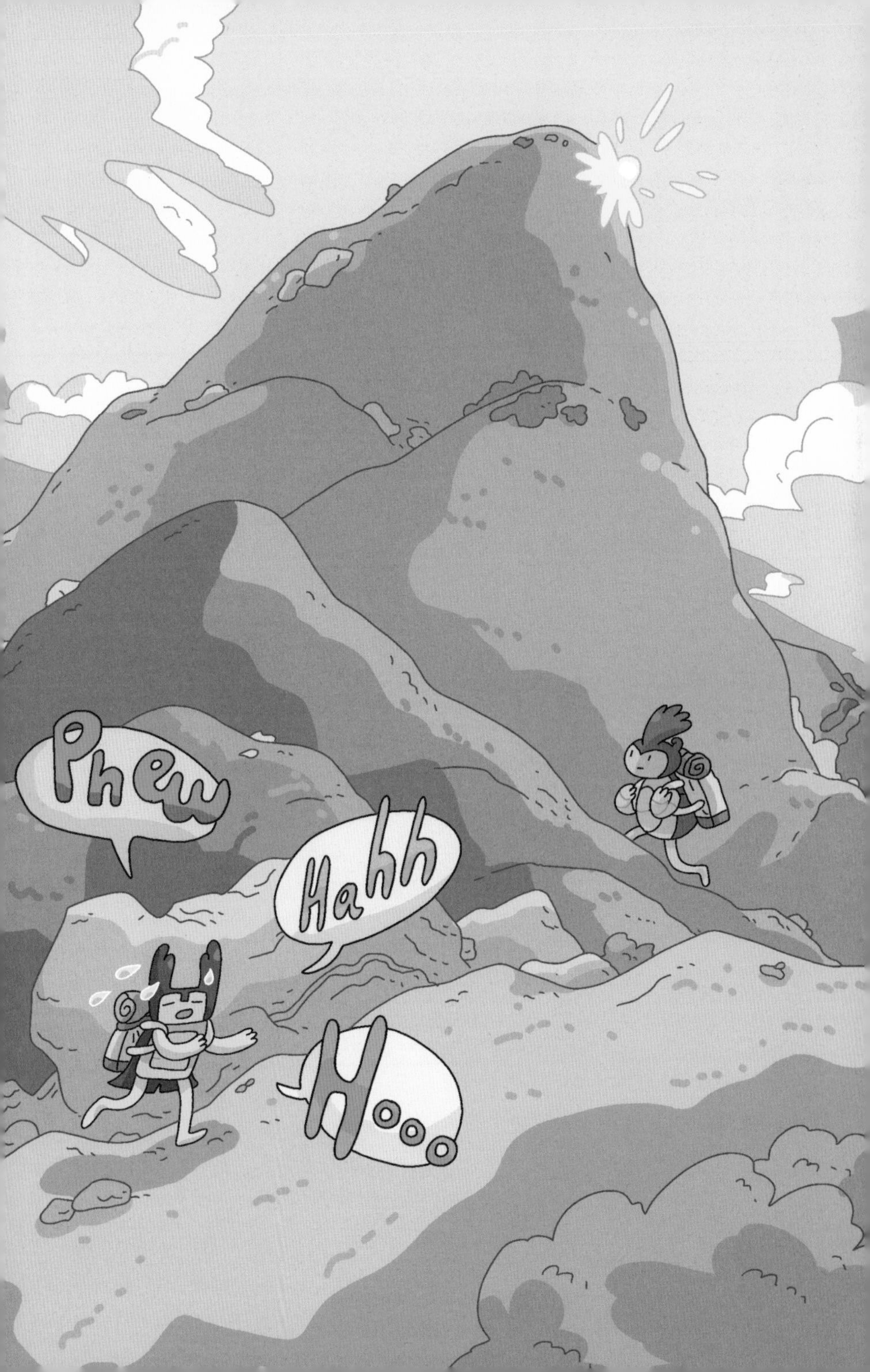
Phew
Hahh
Hooo

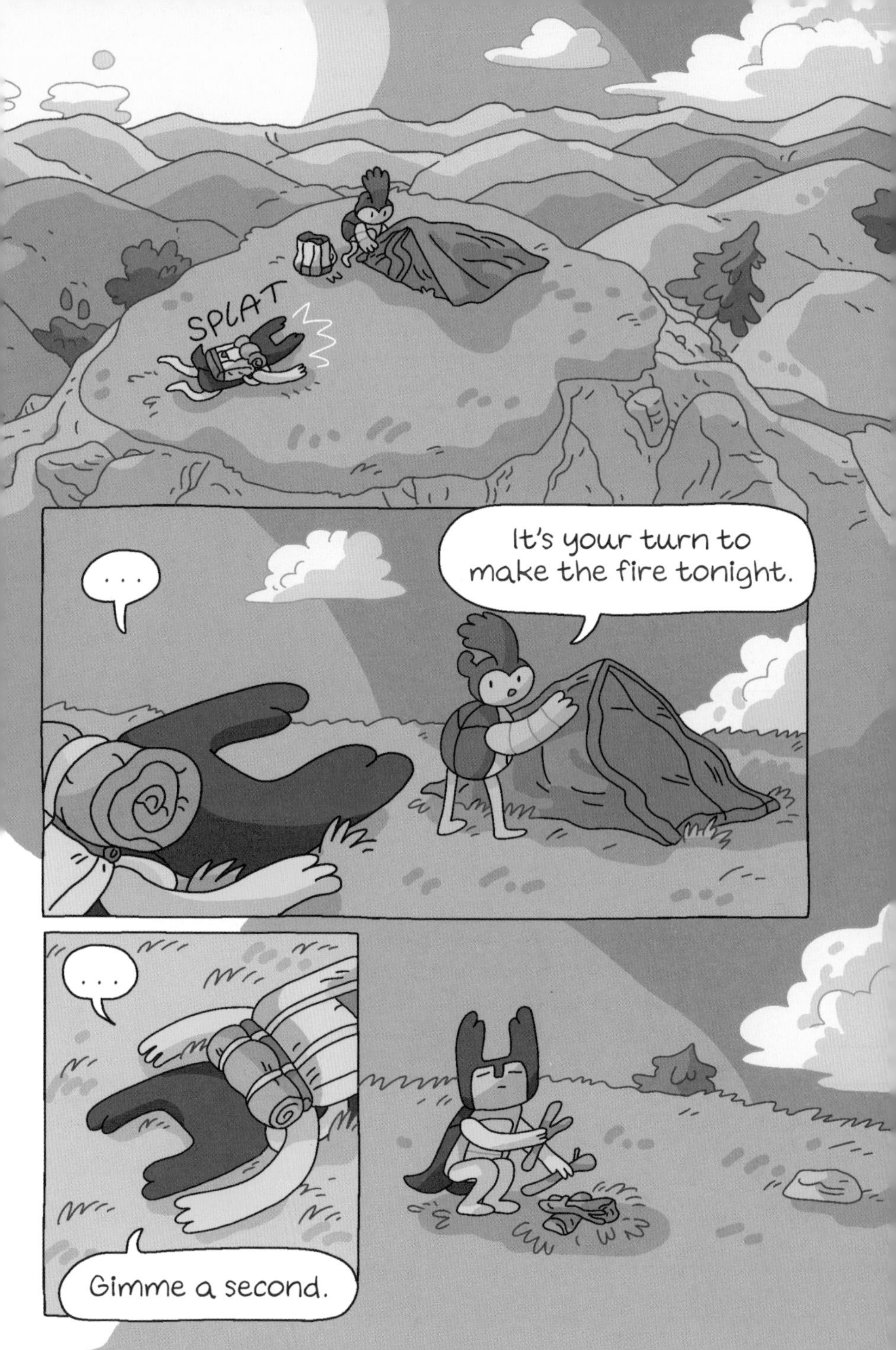
SPLAT
. . .
It's your turn to make the fire tonight.
. . .
Gimme a second.

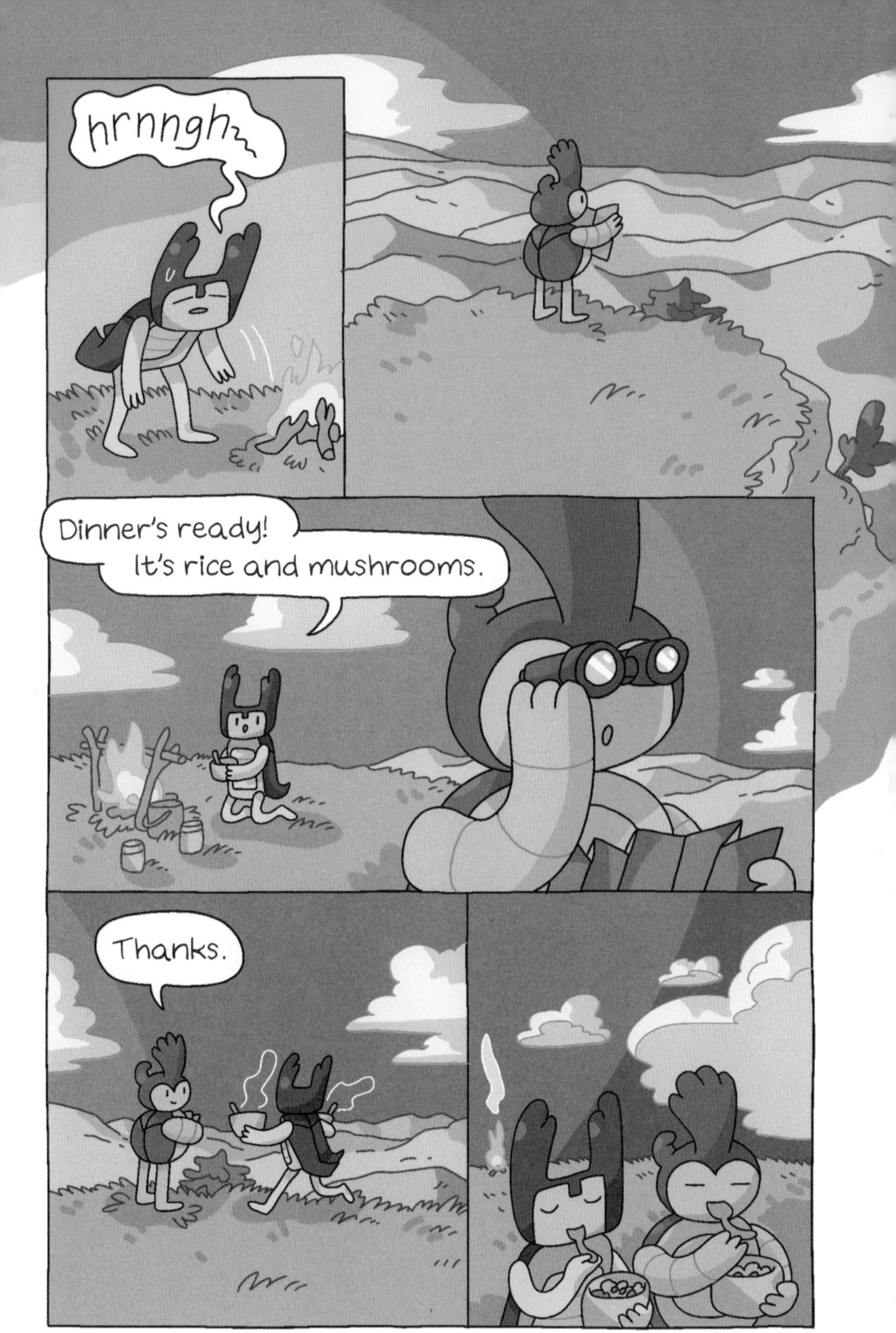
hrnngh
Dinner's ready! It's rice and mushrooms.
Thanks.

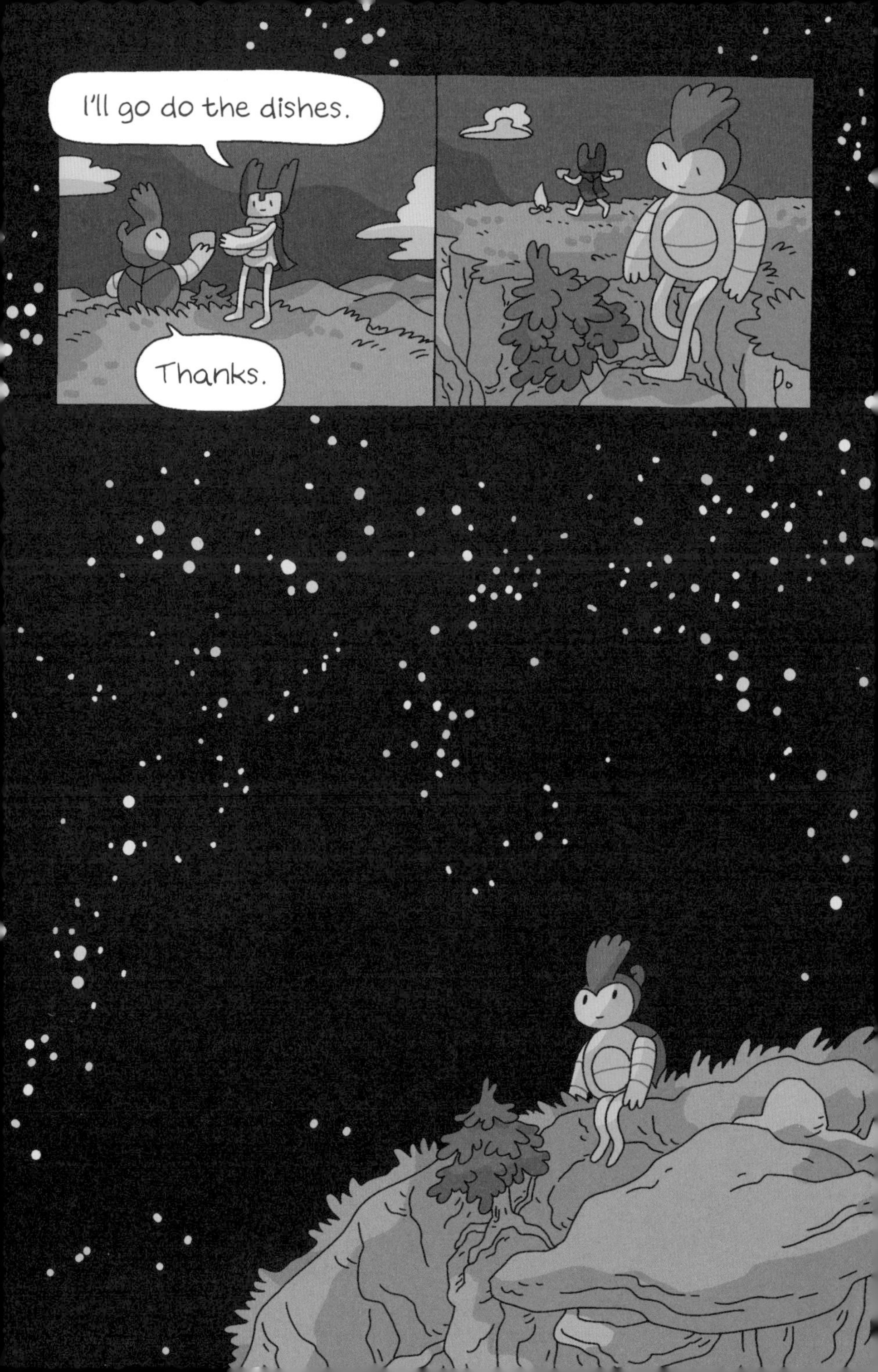
I'll go do the dishes.
Thanks.

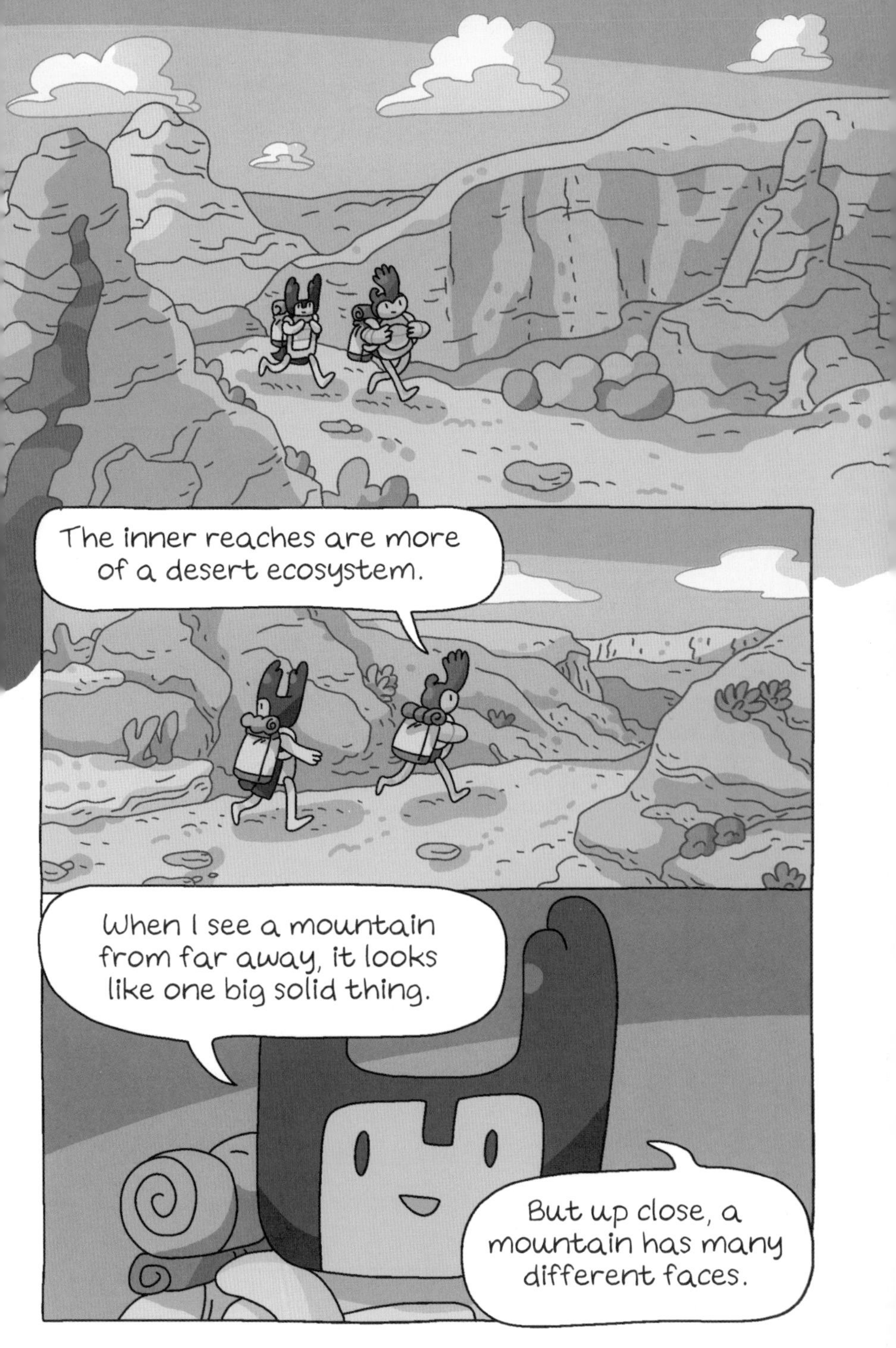
The inner reaches are more of a desert ecosystem.
When I see a mountain from far away, it looks like one big solid thing.
But up close, a mountain has many different faces.

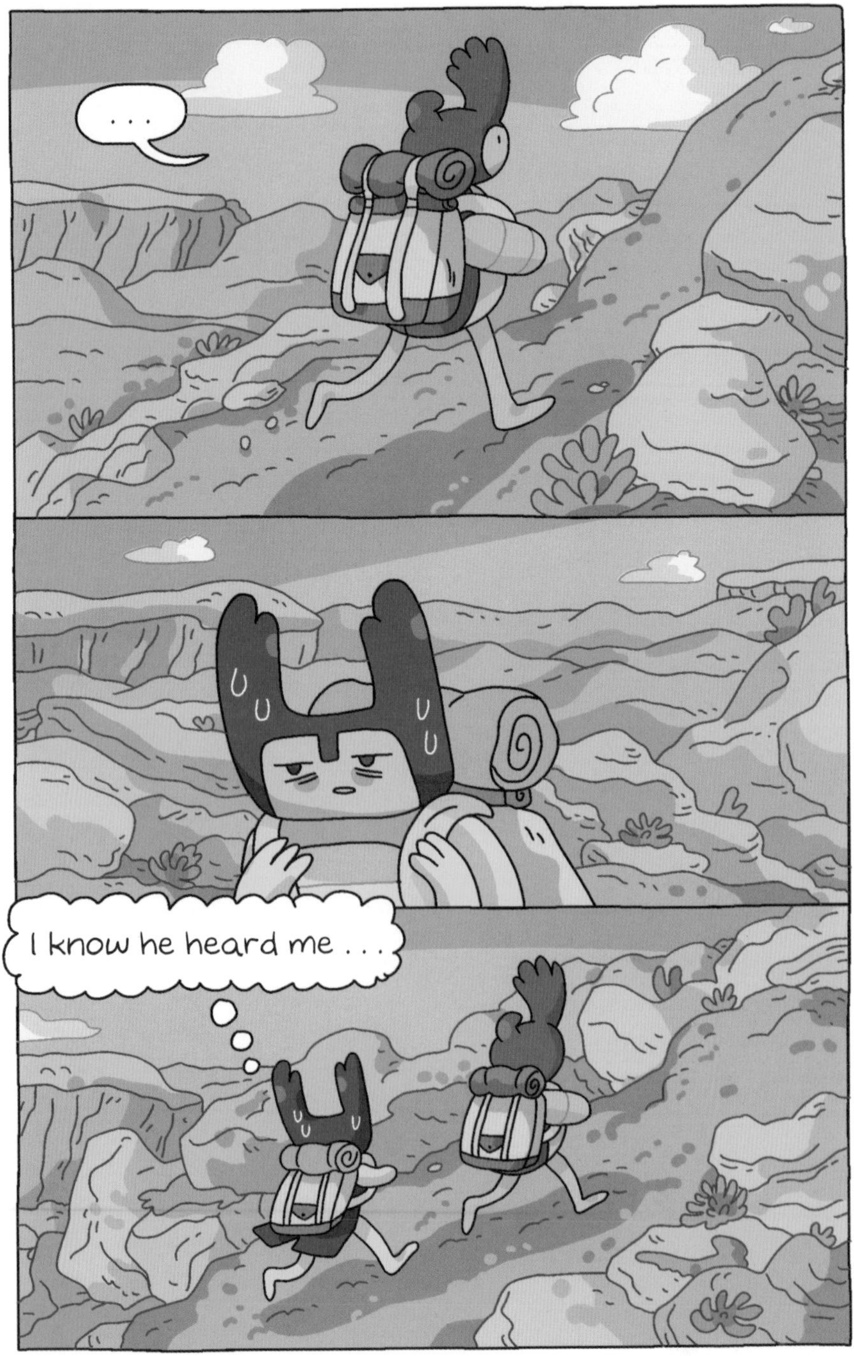
. . .
I know he heard me . . .

217

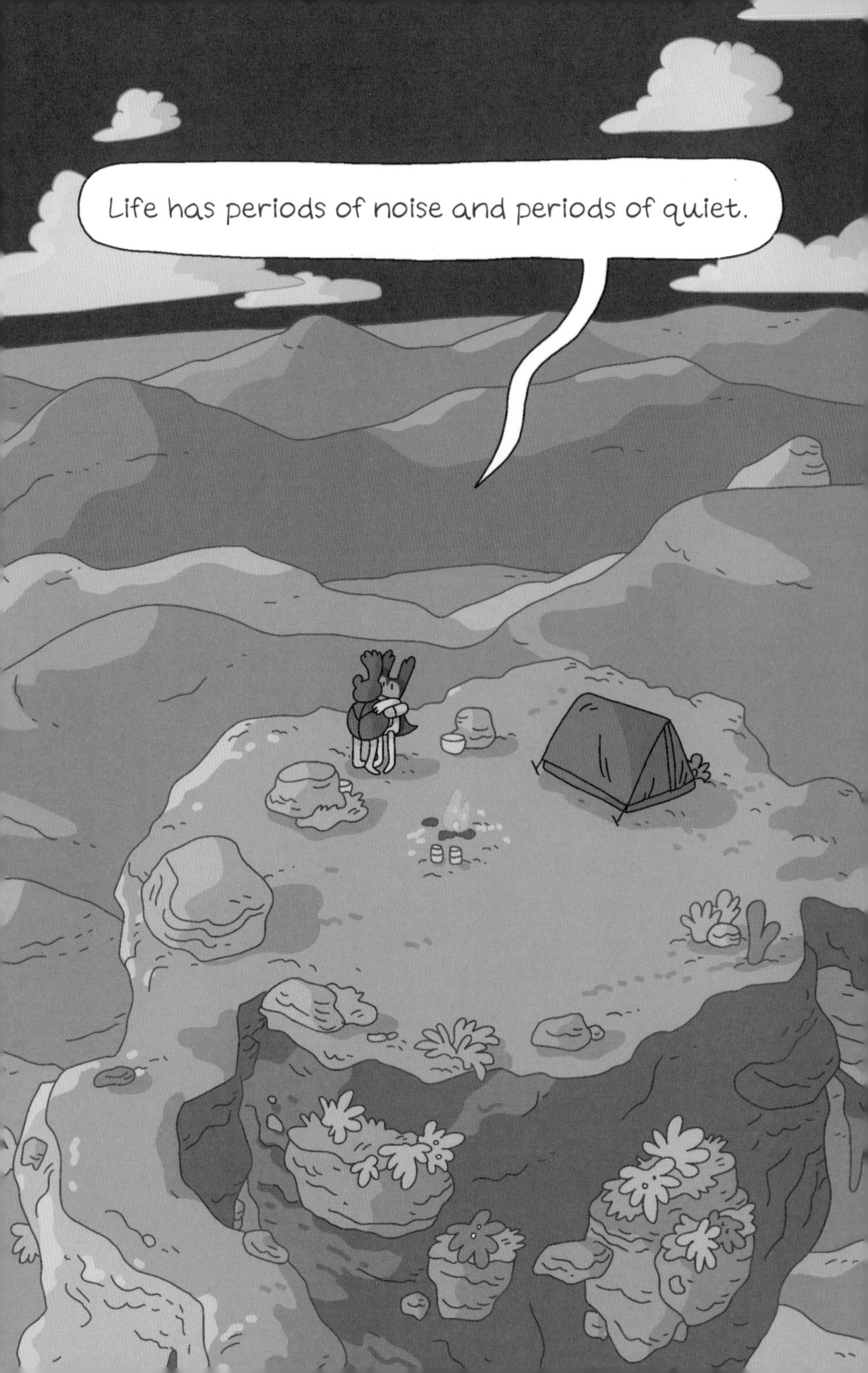
Life has periods of noise and periods of quiet.

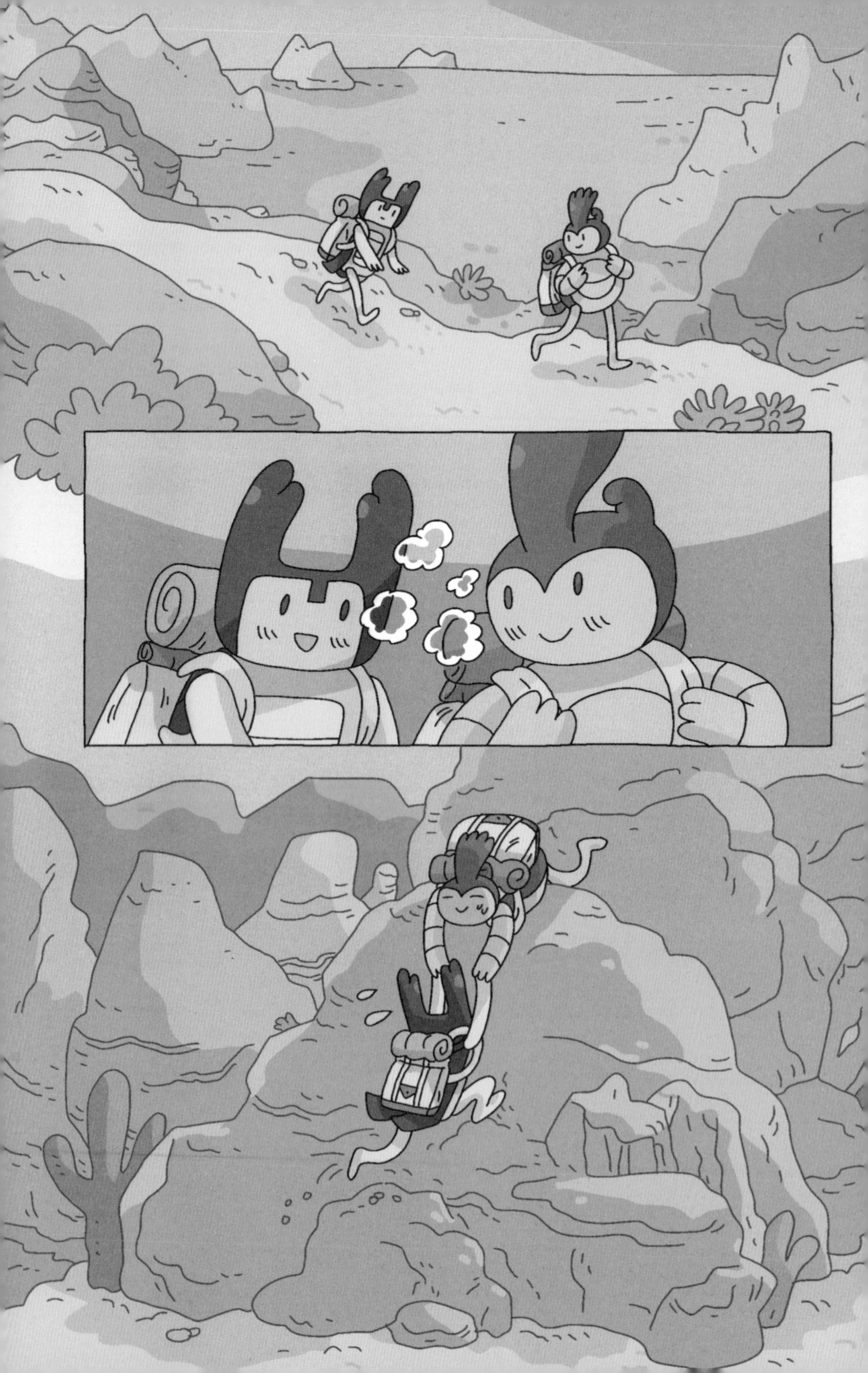

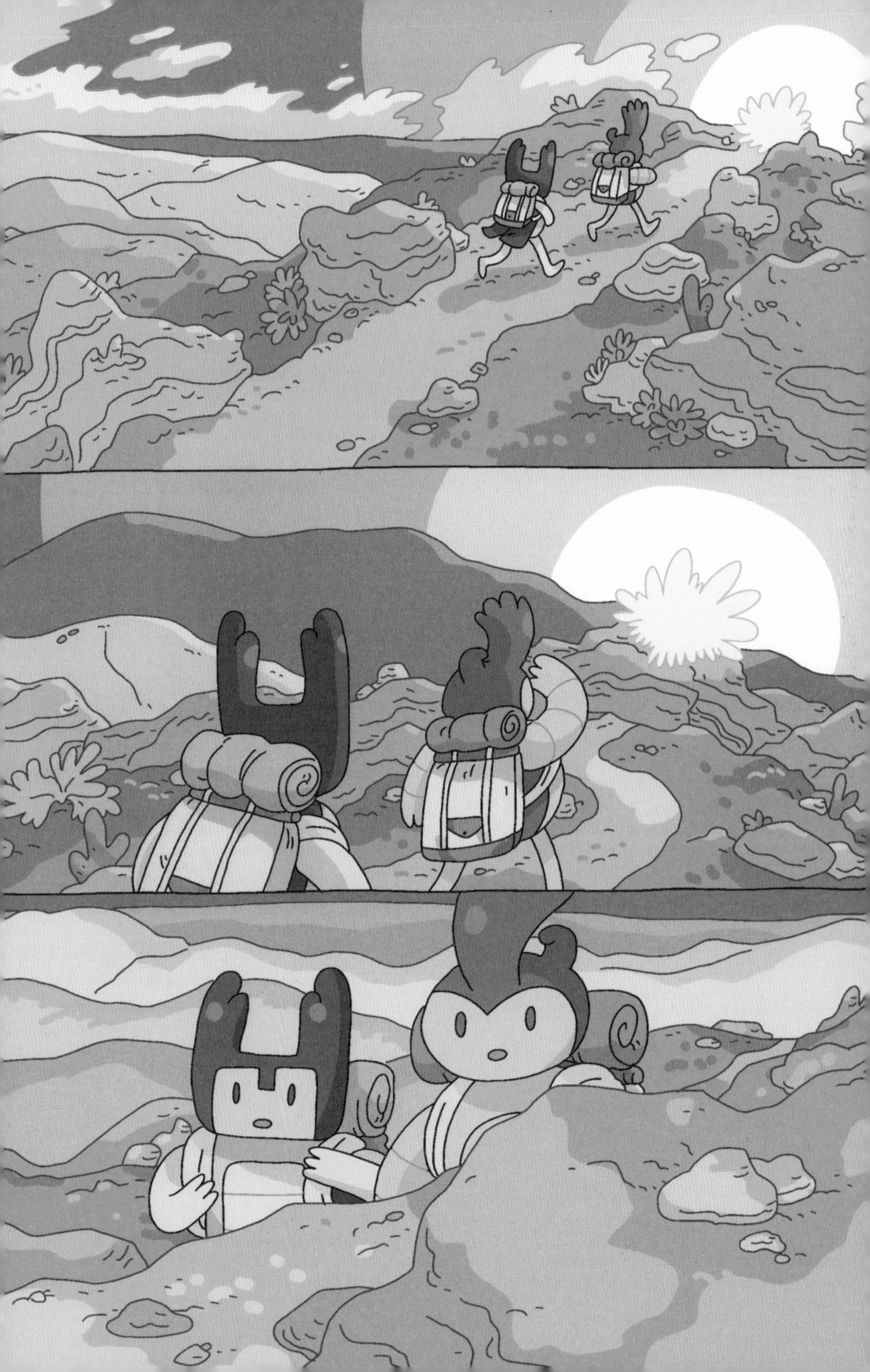

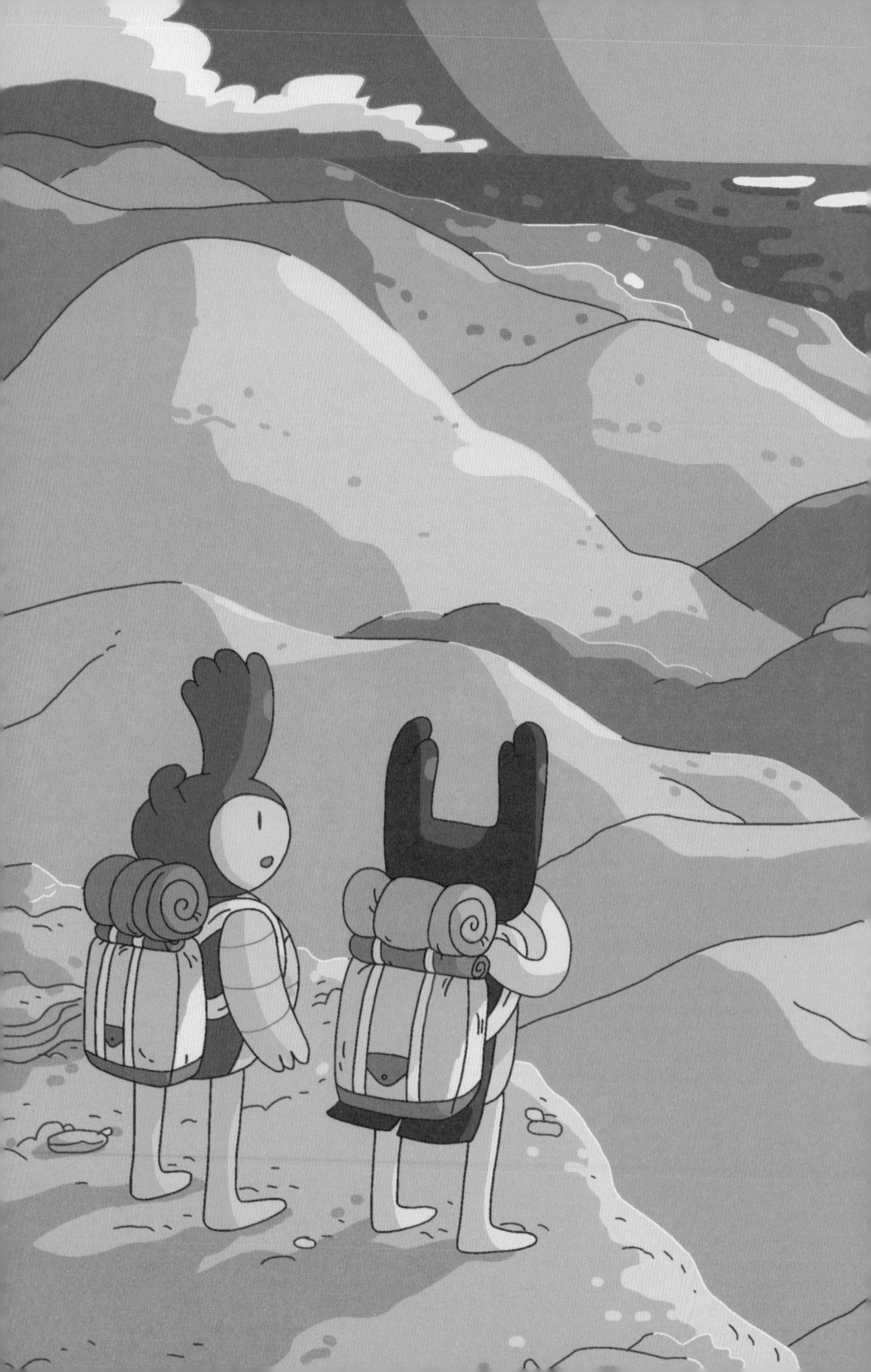

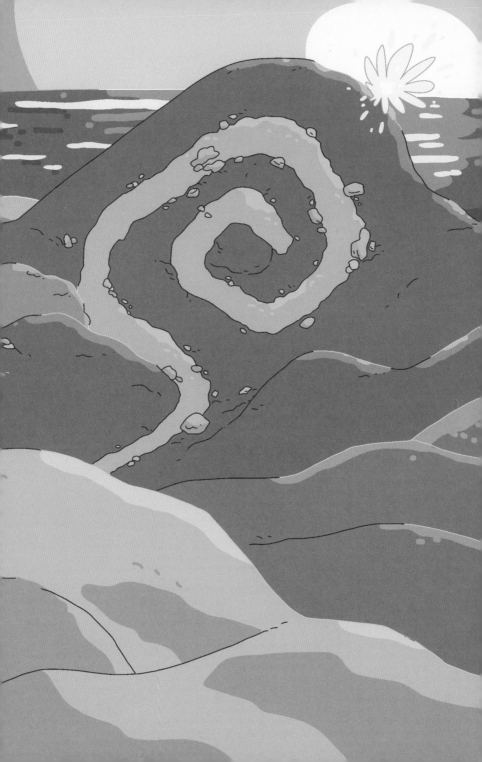

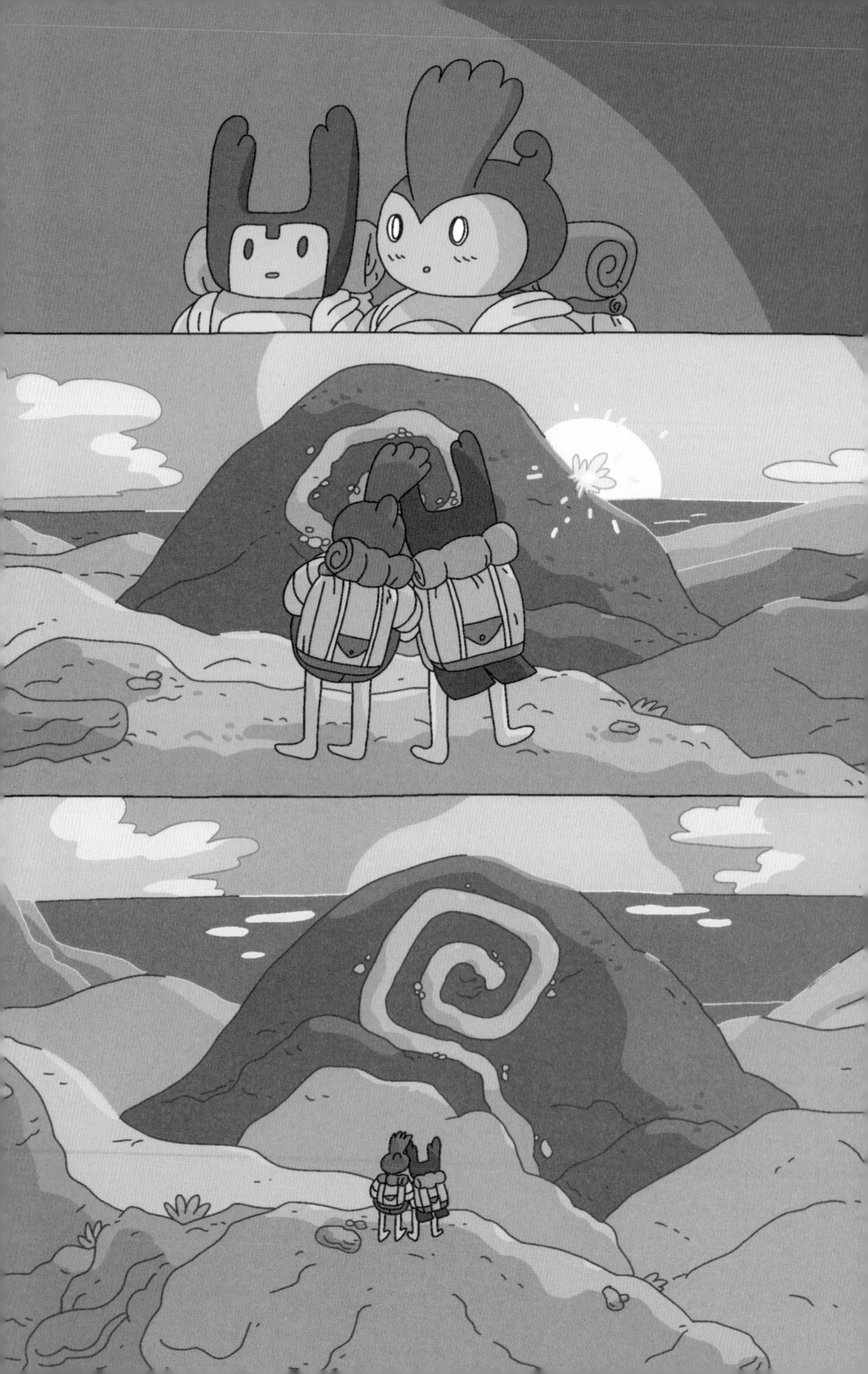

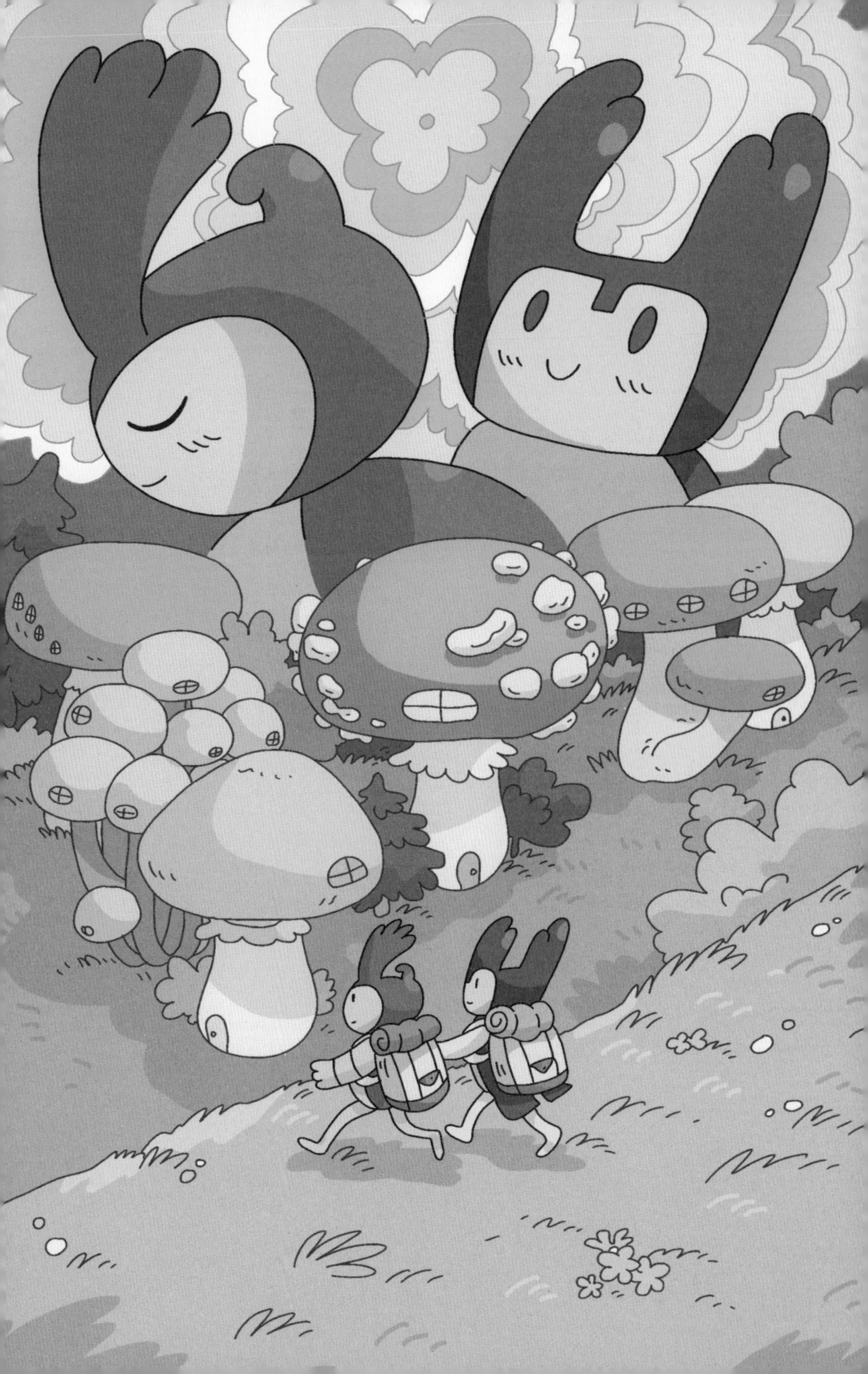

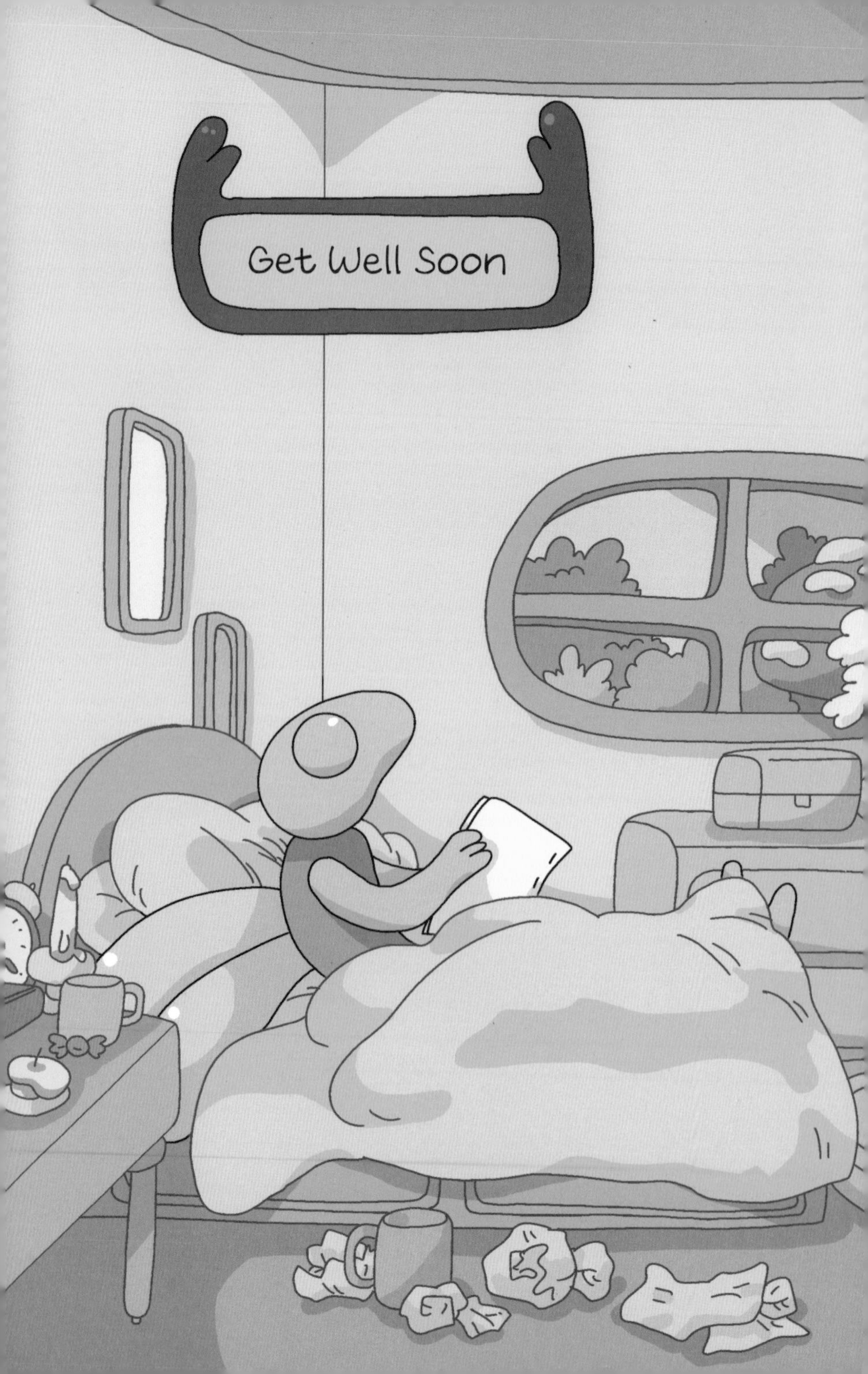
Get Well Soon

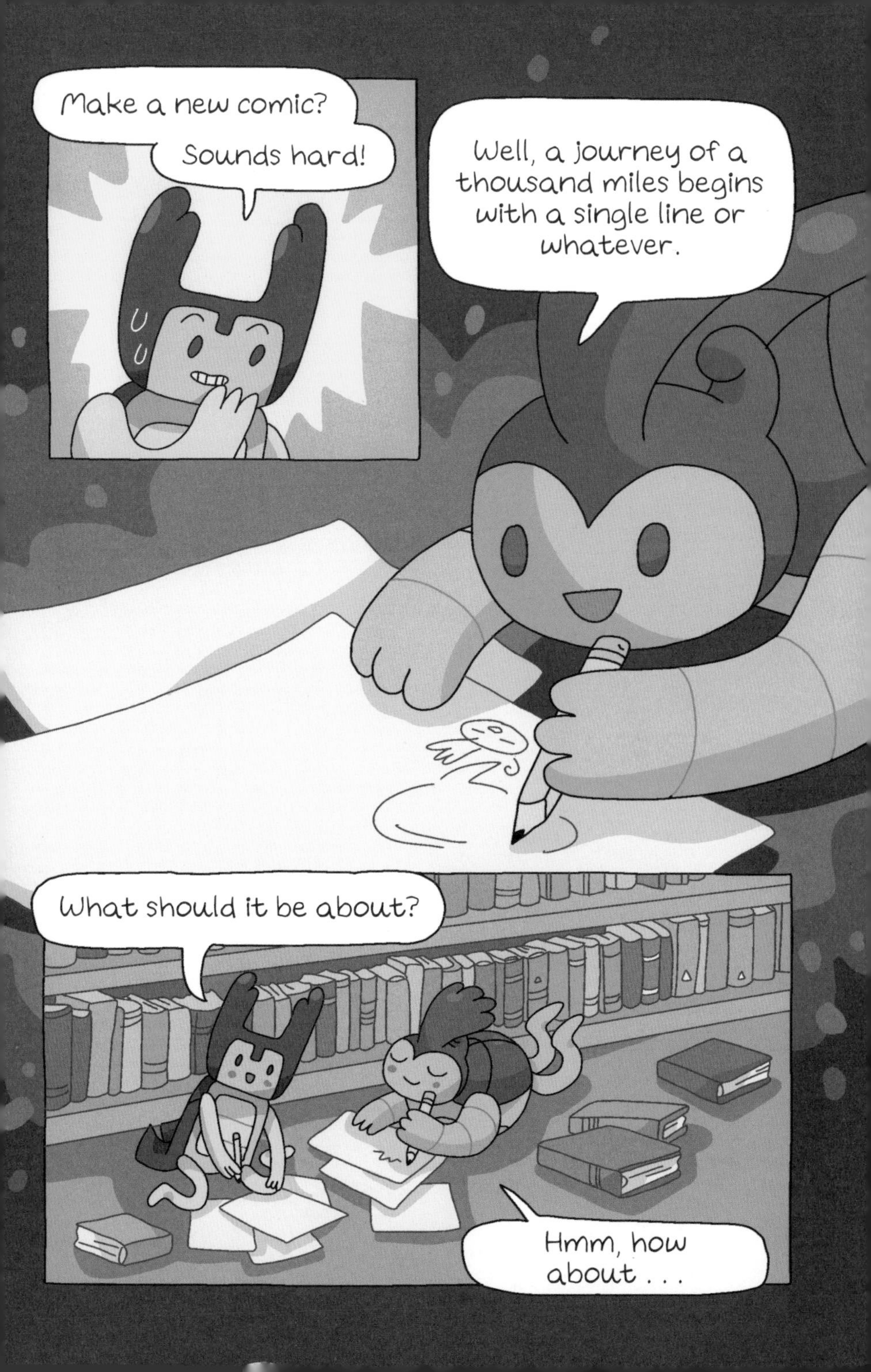
Make a new comic?
Sounds hard!
Well, a journey of a thousand miles begins with a single line or whatever.
What should it be about?
Hmm, how about . . .

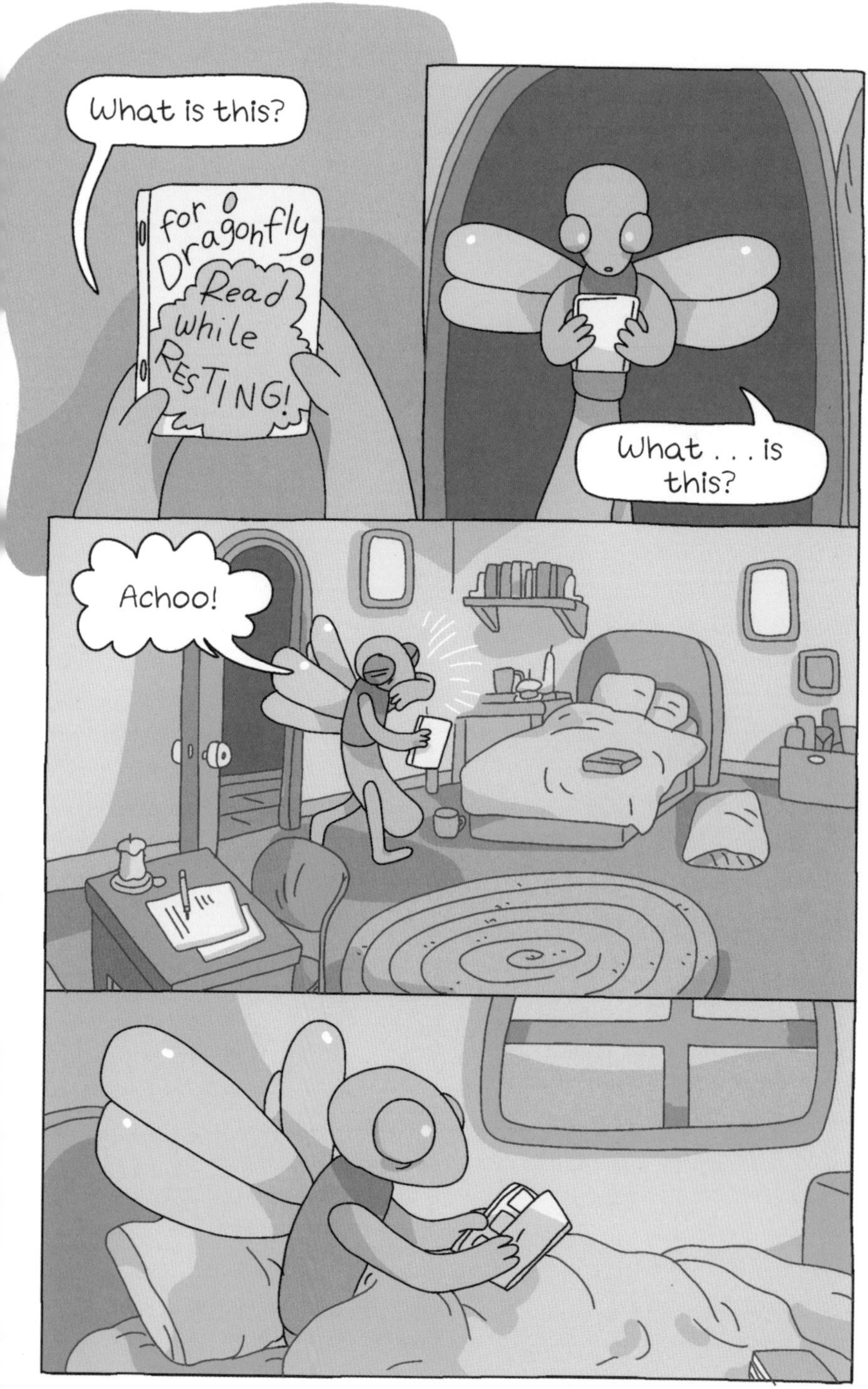
What is this?
for Dragonfly
Read while RESTING!
What . . . is this?
Achoo!

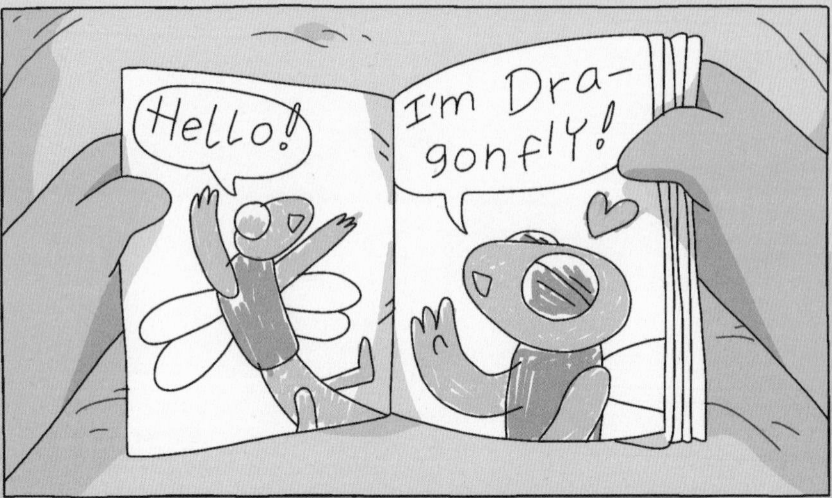
Hello!
I'm Dra-gonfly!
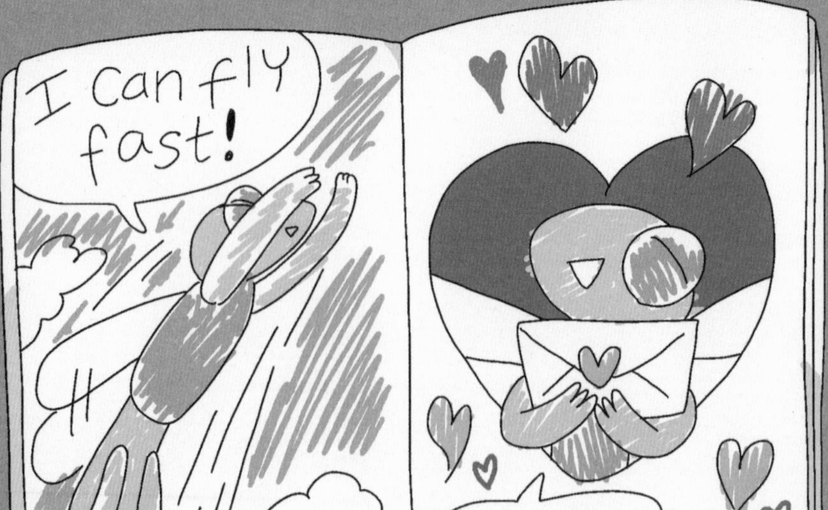
I can fly fast!
I love the mail!

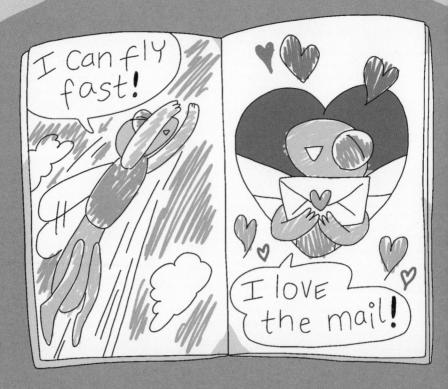

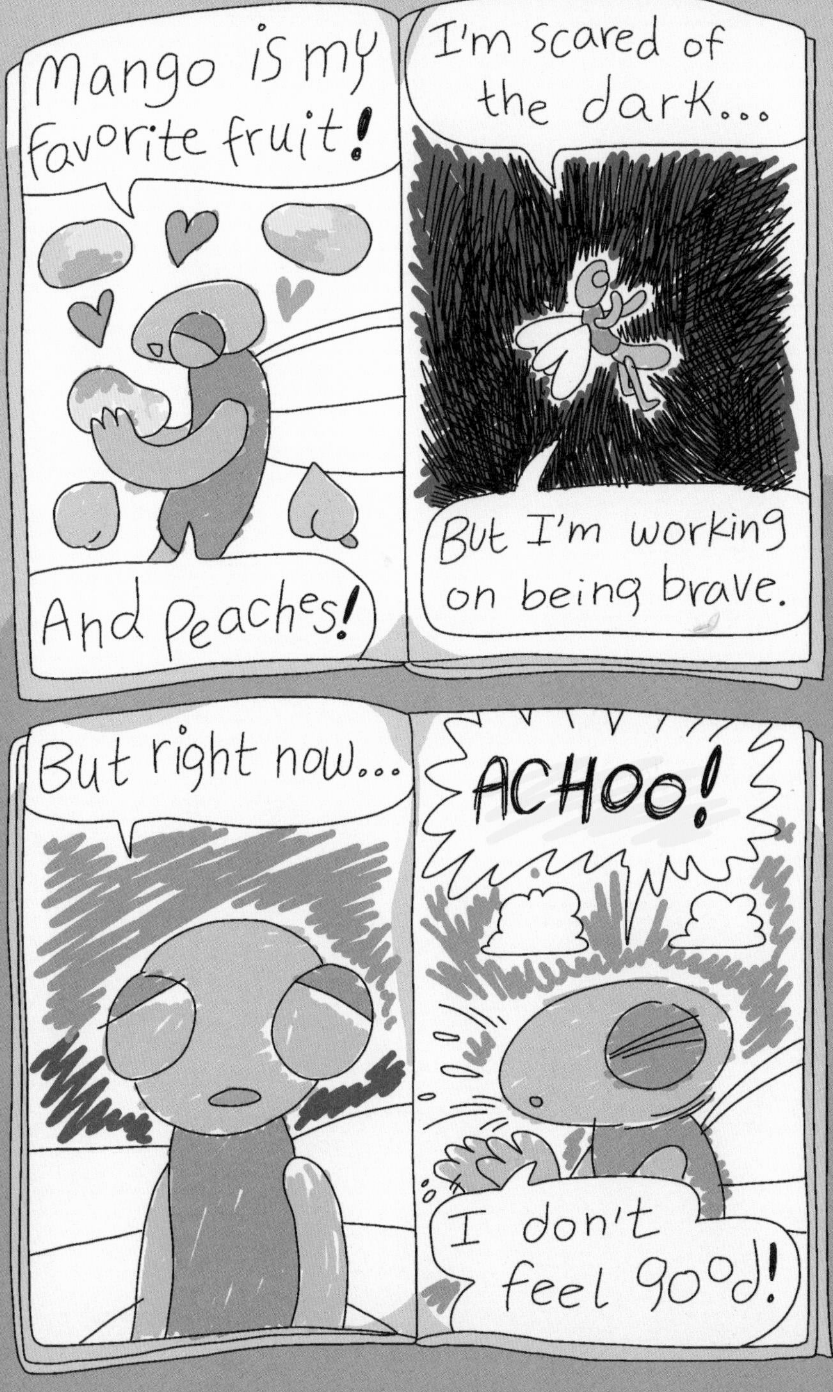
Mango is my favorite fruit!
And peaches!
I'm scared of the dark...
But I'm working on being brave.
But right now...
ACHOO!
I don't feel good!

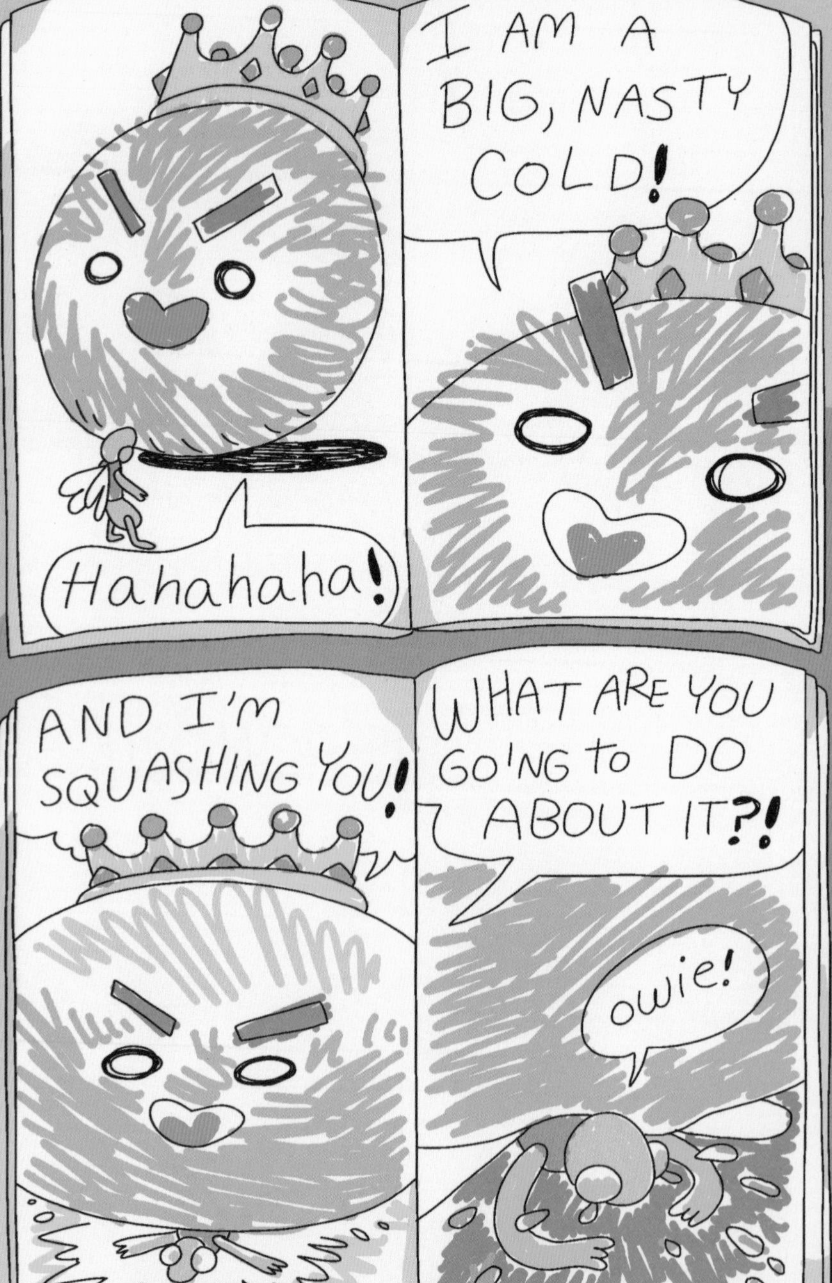
Hahahaha!
I AM A BIG, NASTY COLD!
AND I'M SQUASHING YOU!
WHAT ARE YOU GOING to DO ABOUT IT?!
owie!

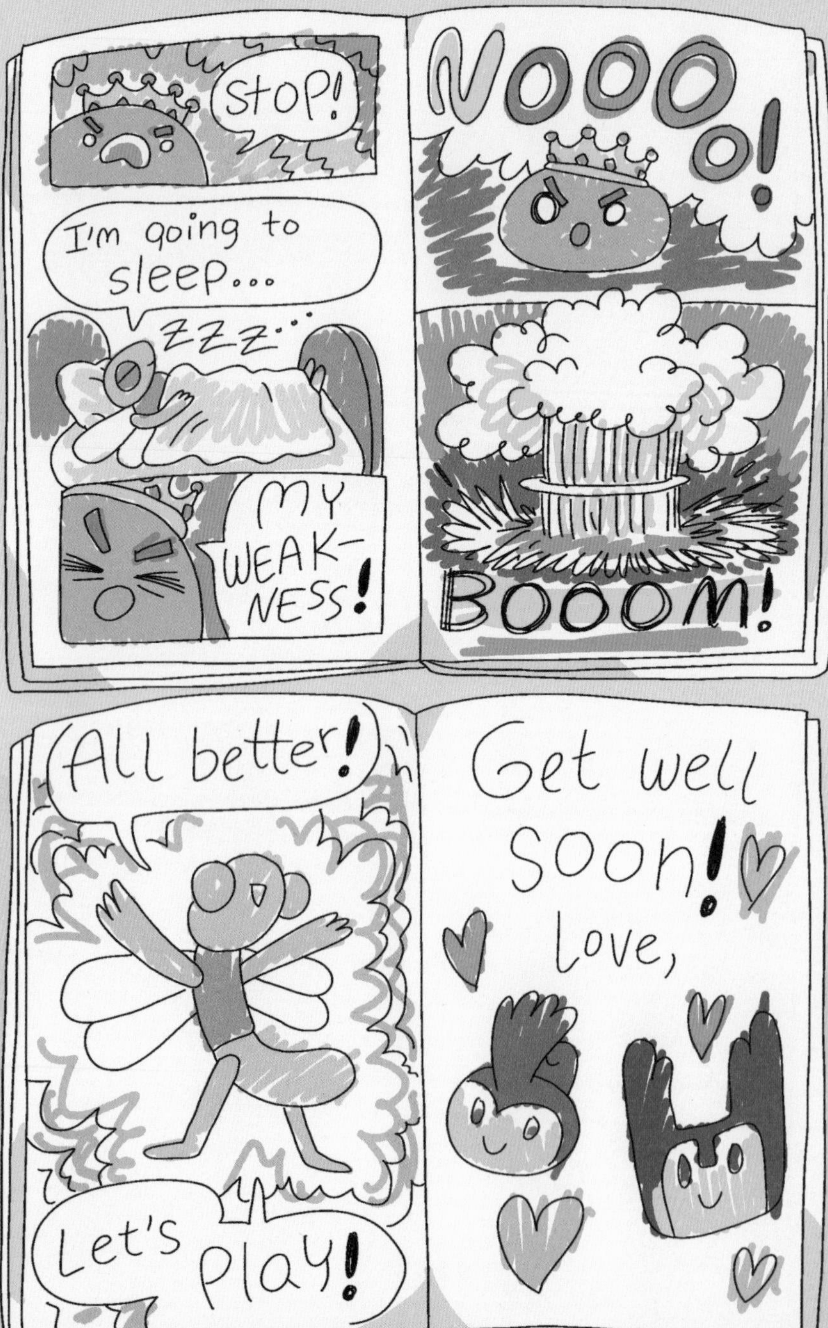
STOP!
I'm going to sleep...
ZZZ...
MY WEAK-NESS!
NOOOO!
BOOOM!
All better!
Let's play!
Get well soon!
love,

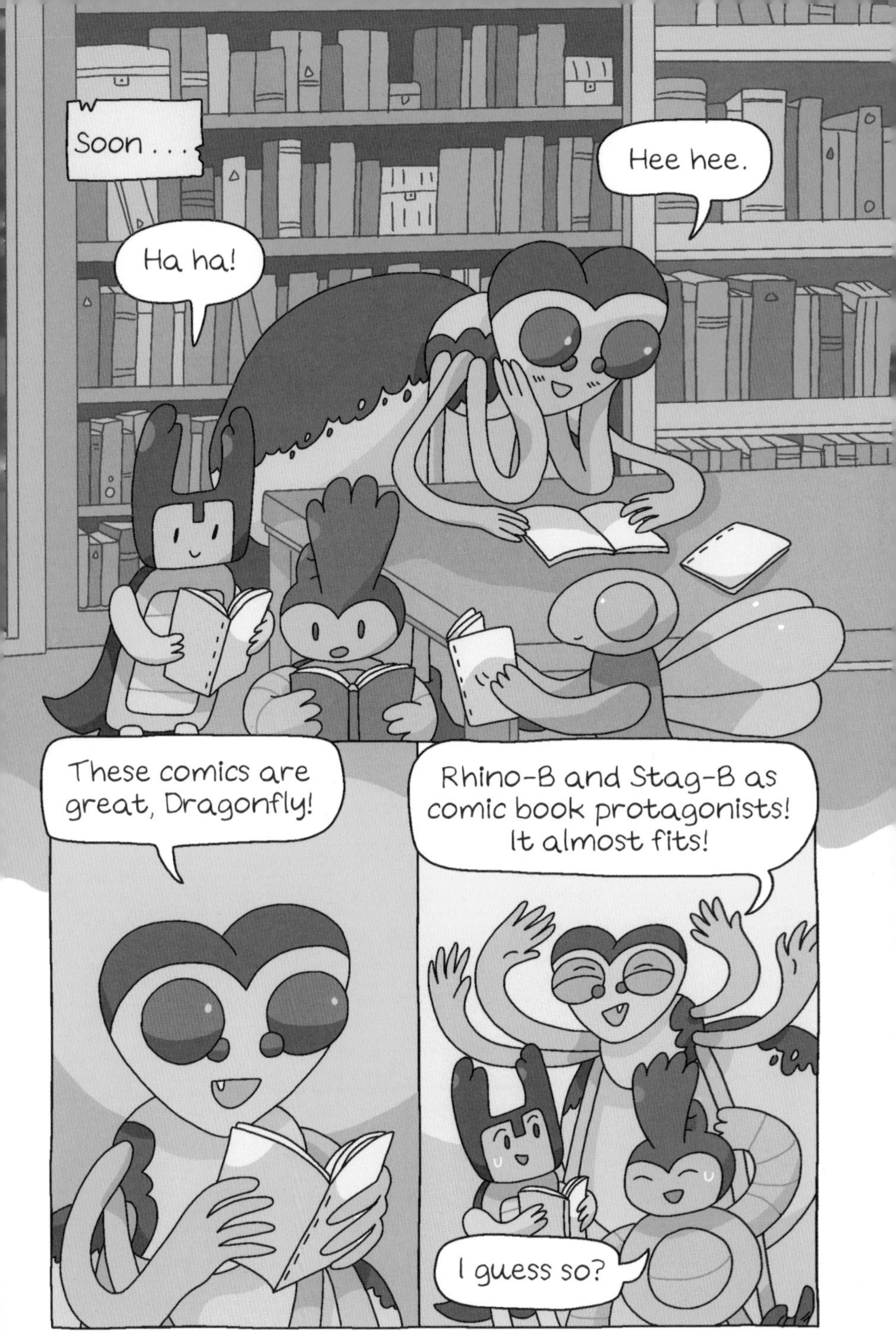
Soon . . .
Hee hee.
Ha ha!
These comics are great, Dragonfly!
Rhino-B and Stag-B as comic book protagonists! It almost fits!
I guess so?

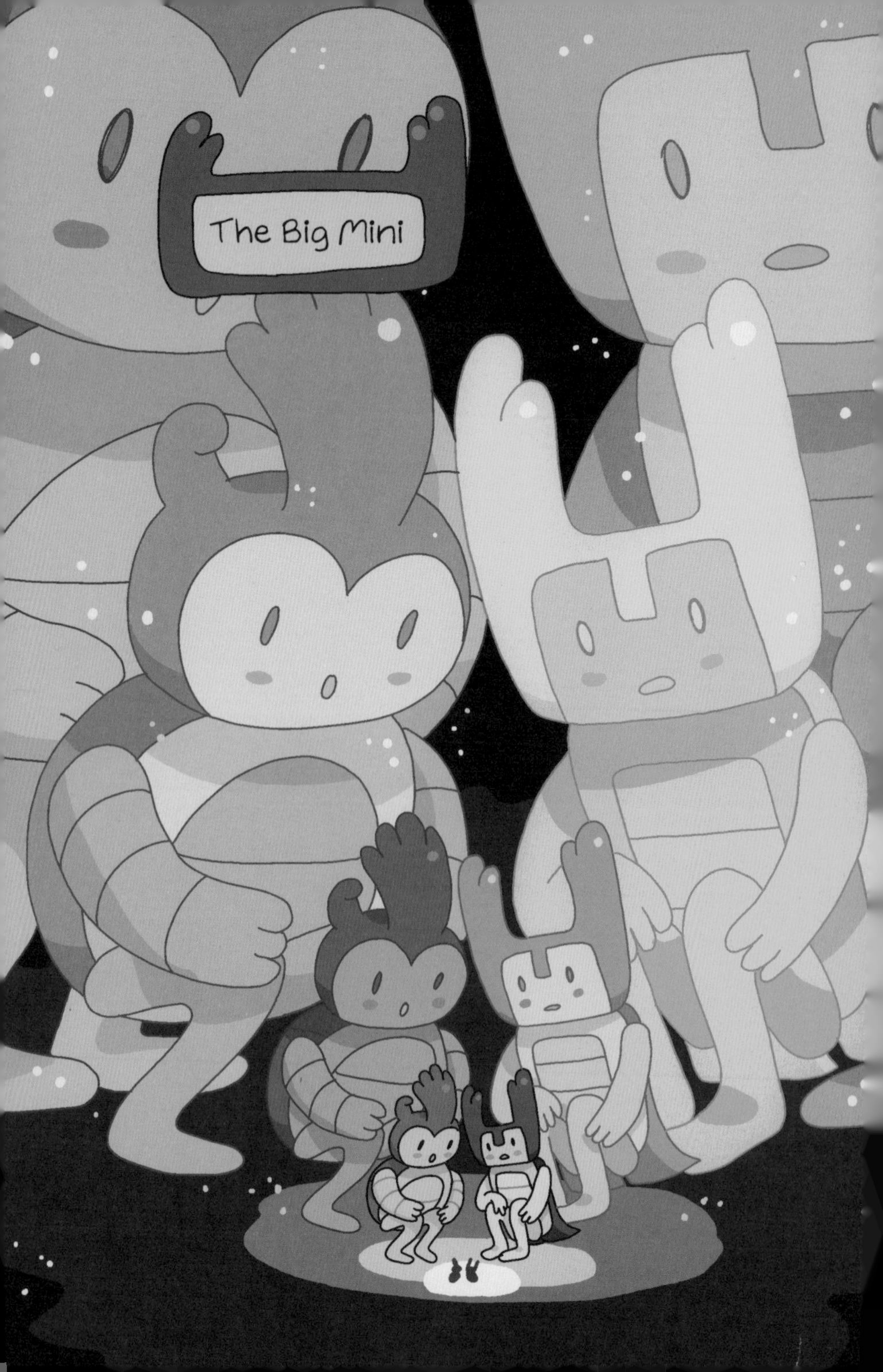
The Big Mini

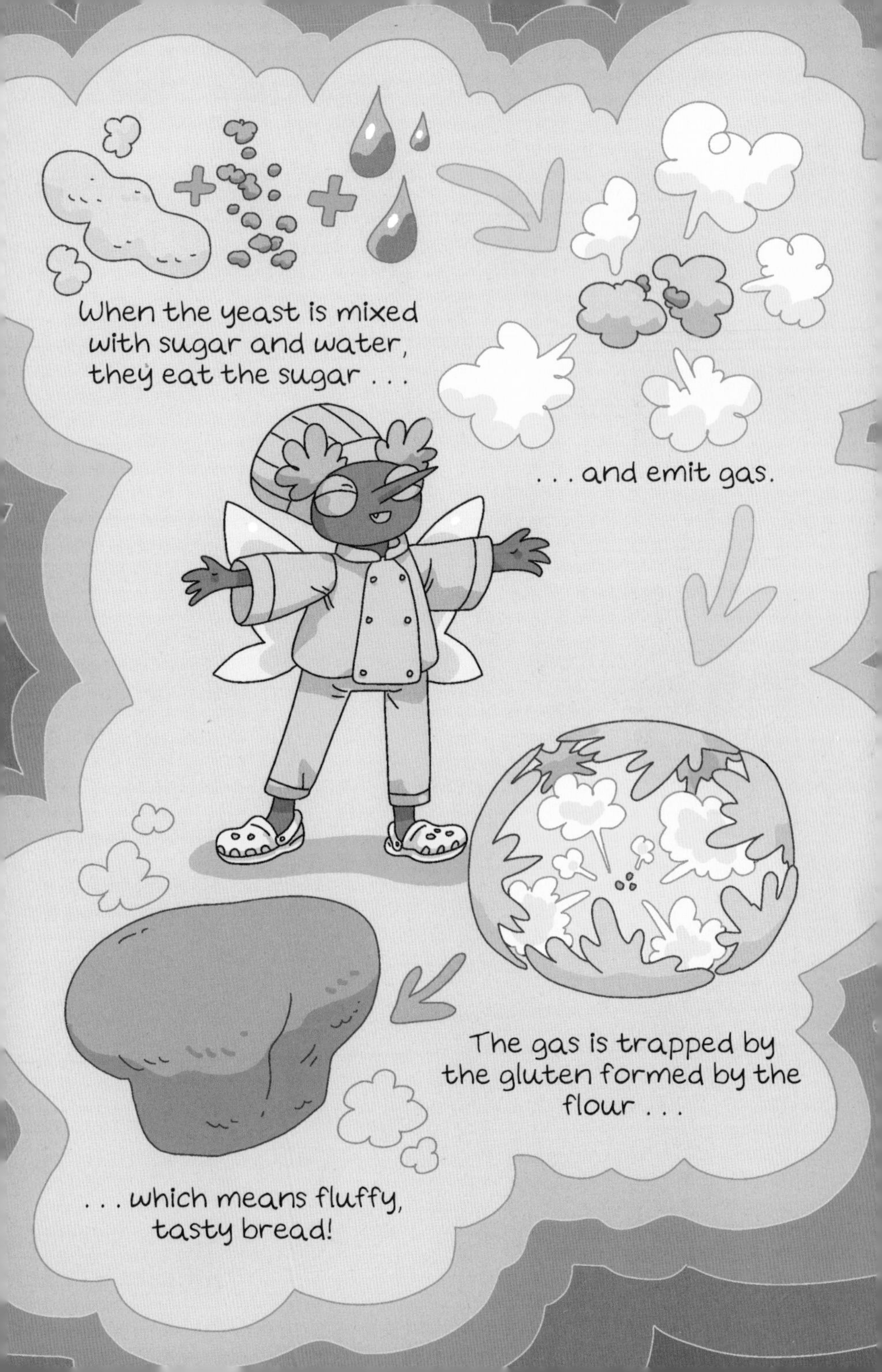
When the yeast is mixed with sugar and water, they eat the sugar . . .
. . . and emit gas.
The gas is trapped by the gluten formed by the flour . . .
. . . which means fluffy, tasty bread!

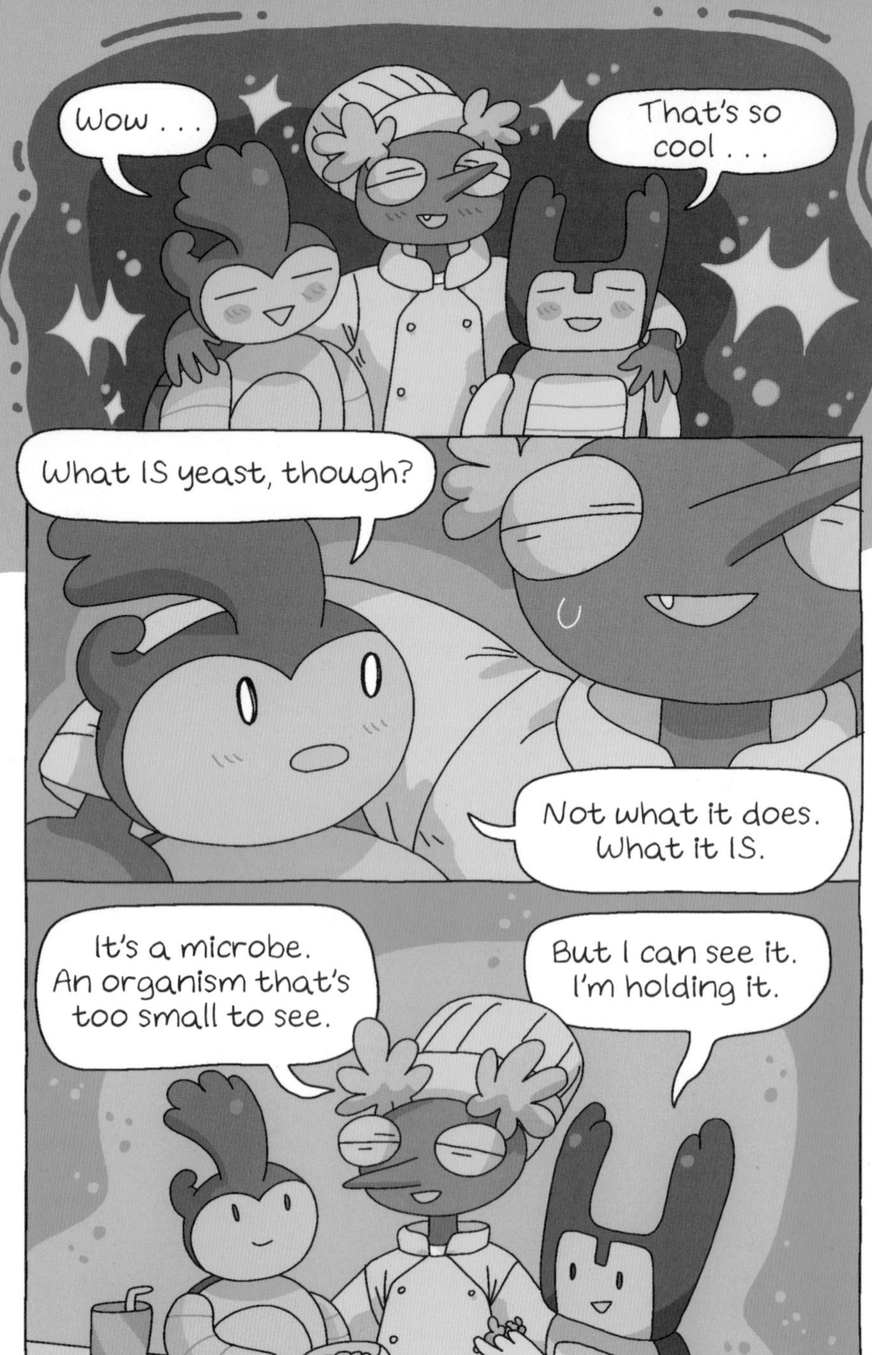
Wow . . .
That's so cool . . .
What IS yeast, though?
Not what it does. What it IS.
It's a microbe. An organism that's too small to see.
But I can see it. I'm holding it.

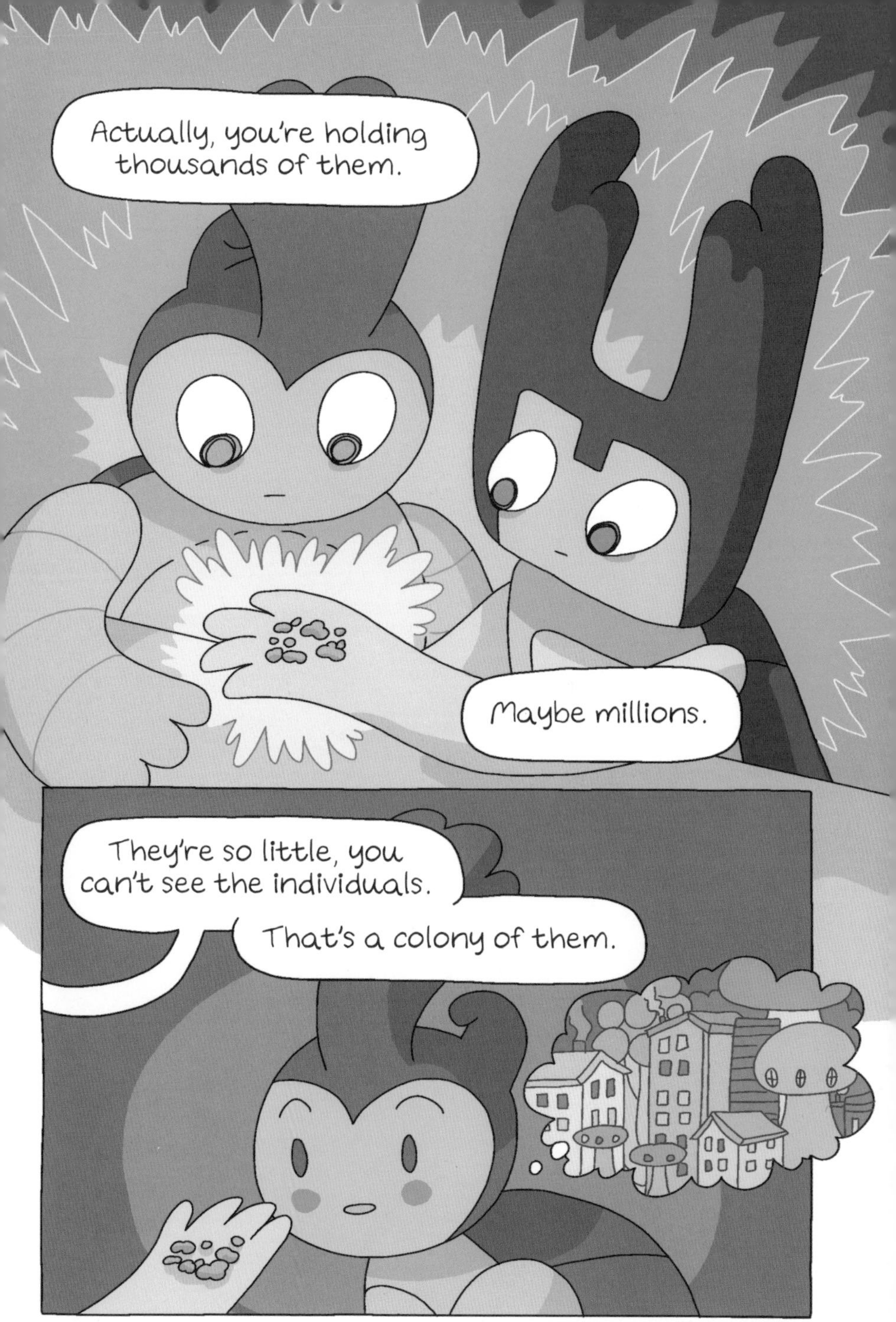
Actually, you're holding thousands of them.
Maybe millions.
They're so little, you can't see the individuals.
That's a colony of them.

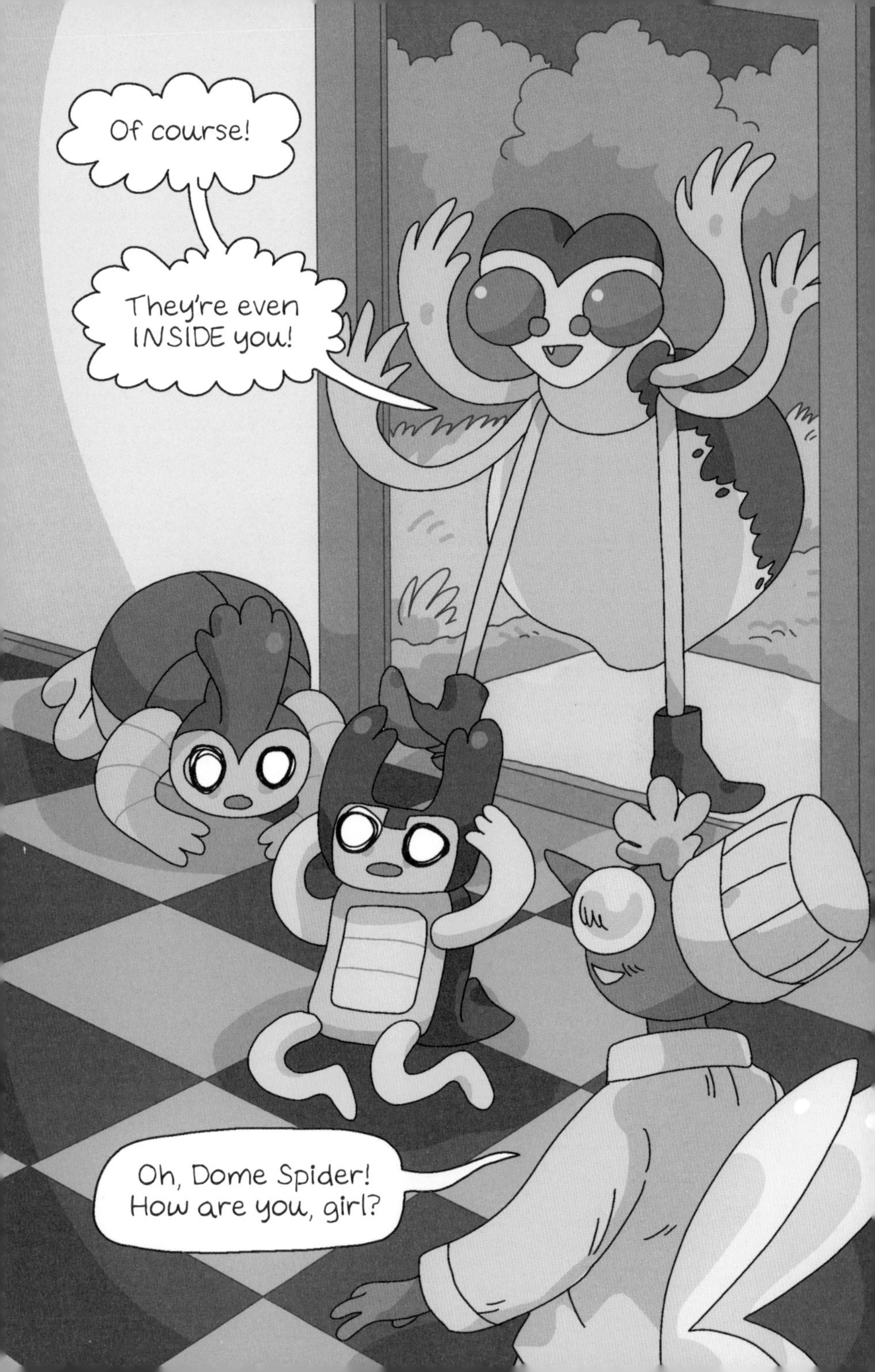
Of course!
They're even INSIDE you!
Oh, Dome Spider! How are you, girl?

Why do you wash your hands before you eat?
Uh . . . so you don't get in trouble?
Because adults say so.
How does a cold travel from one Bug to another?
Yes, but WHY?
Um . . . it just does?

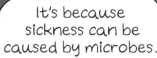
It's because sickness can be caused by microbes.

They might get into your body when you eat with dirty hands, for example.

They get us <u>sick</u>?

Can we get rid of all of them, then?

Good luck!

You'll need to wash everything in the entire world simultaneously, forever and ever.

But . . .

. . .
I'm thinking about microbes.
If I were big like a Giant,
I might not notice Bugs or any of the things they do.
Just like how I can't see a microbe.
They run the planet I live on, everywhere and invisible to me.

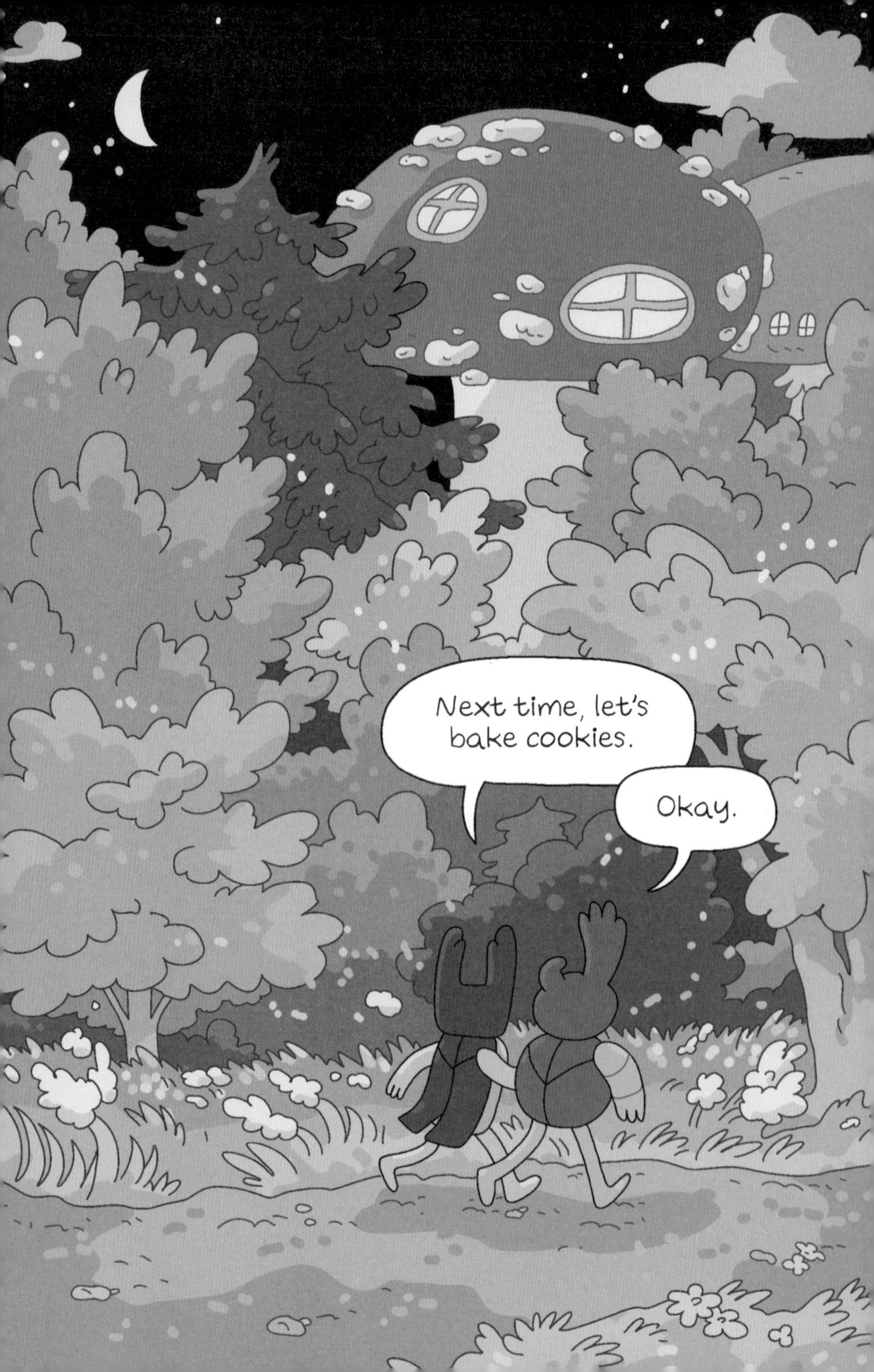
Next time, let's bake cookies.
Okay.

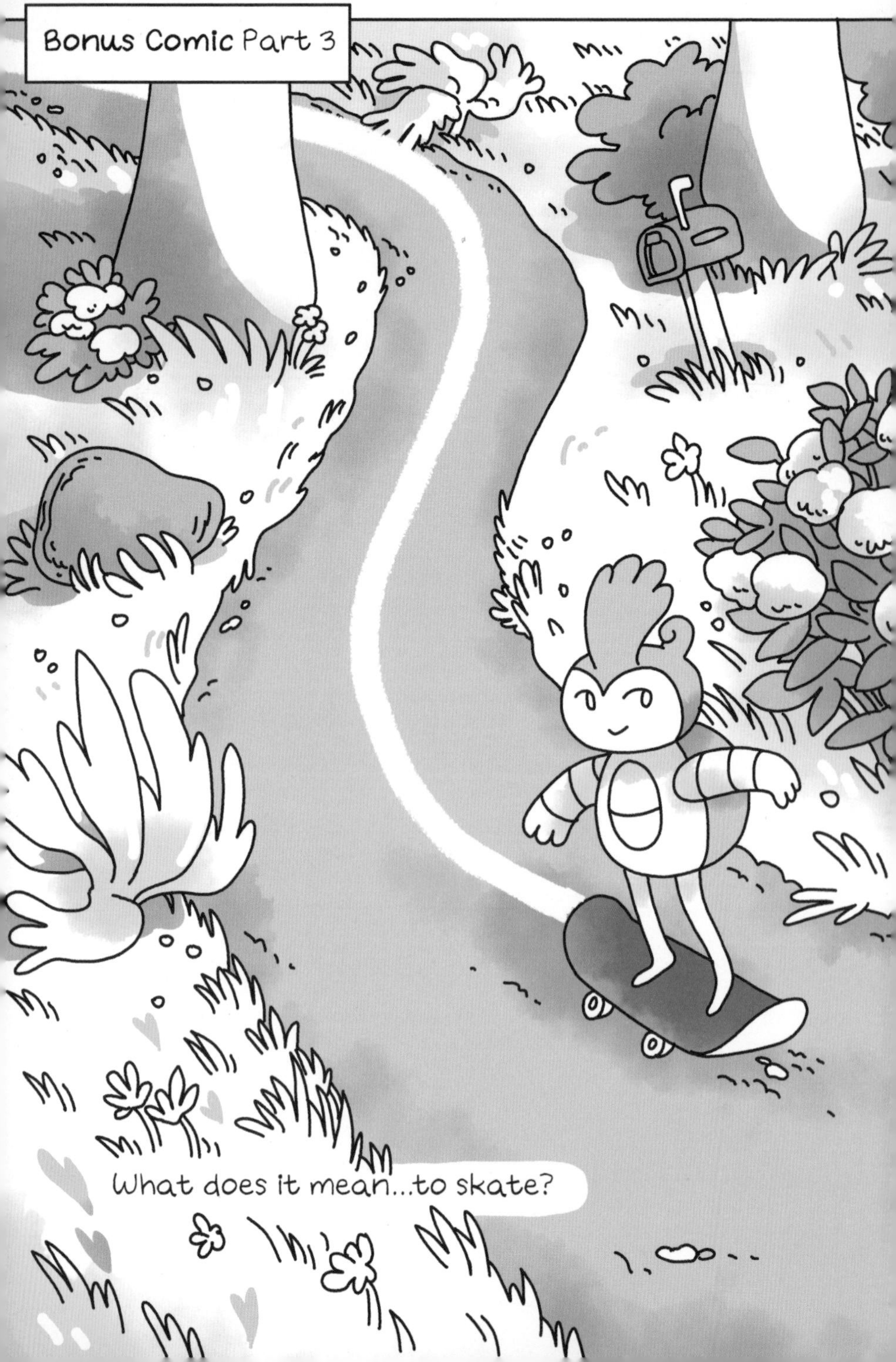
Bonus Comic Part 3
What does it mean...to skate?

Extra Art!

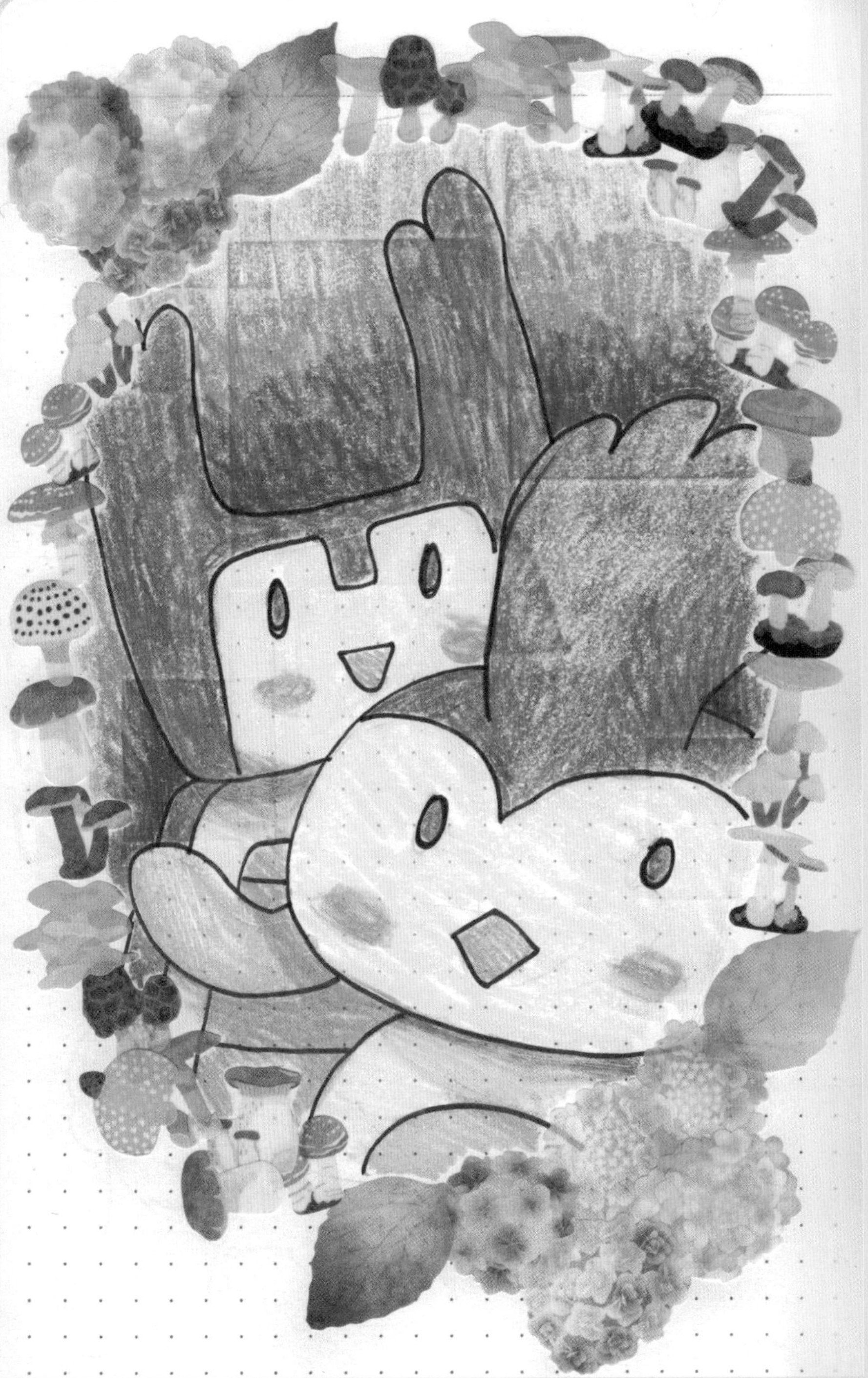

Early cover Sketches

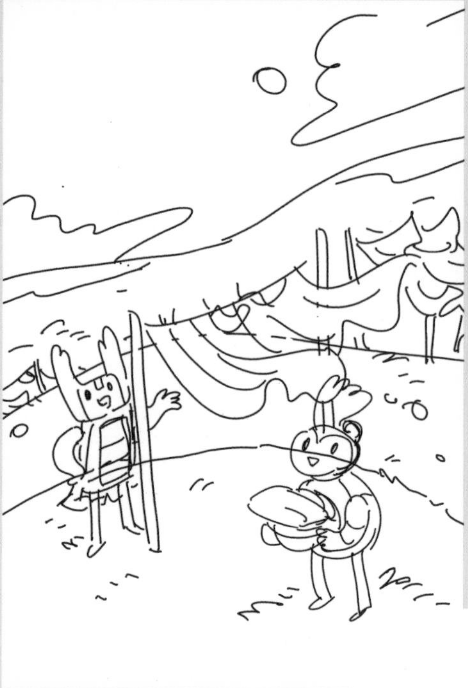

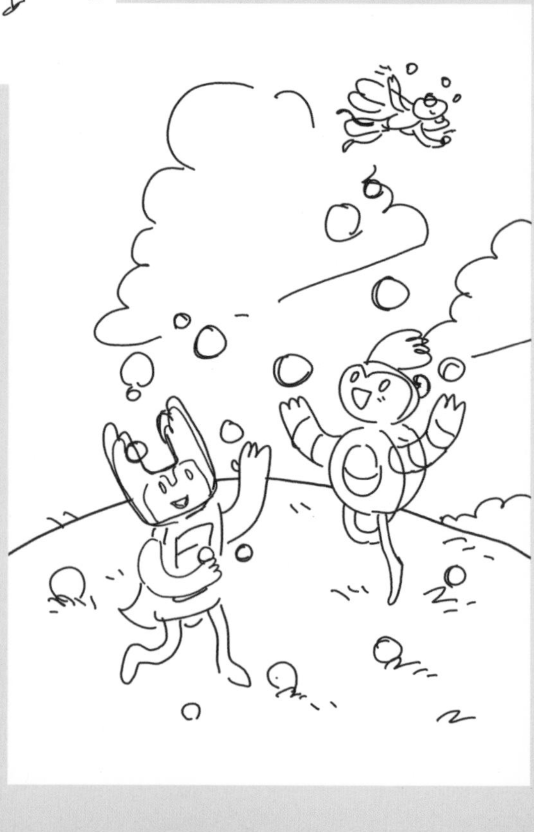

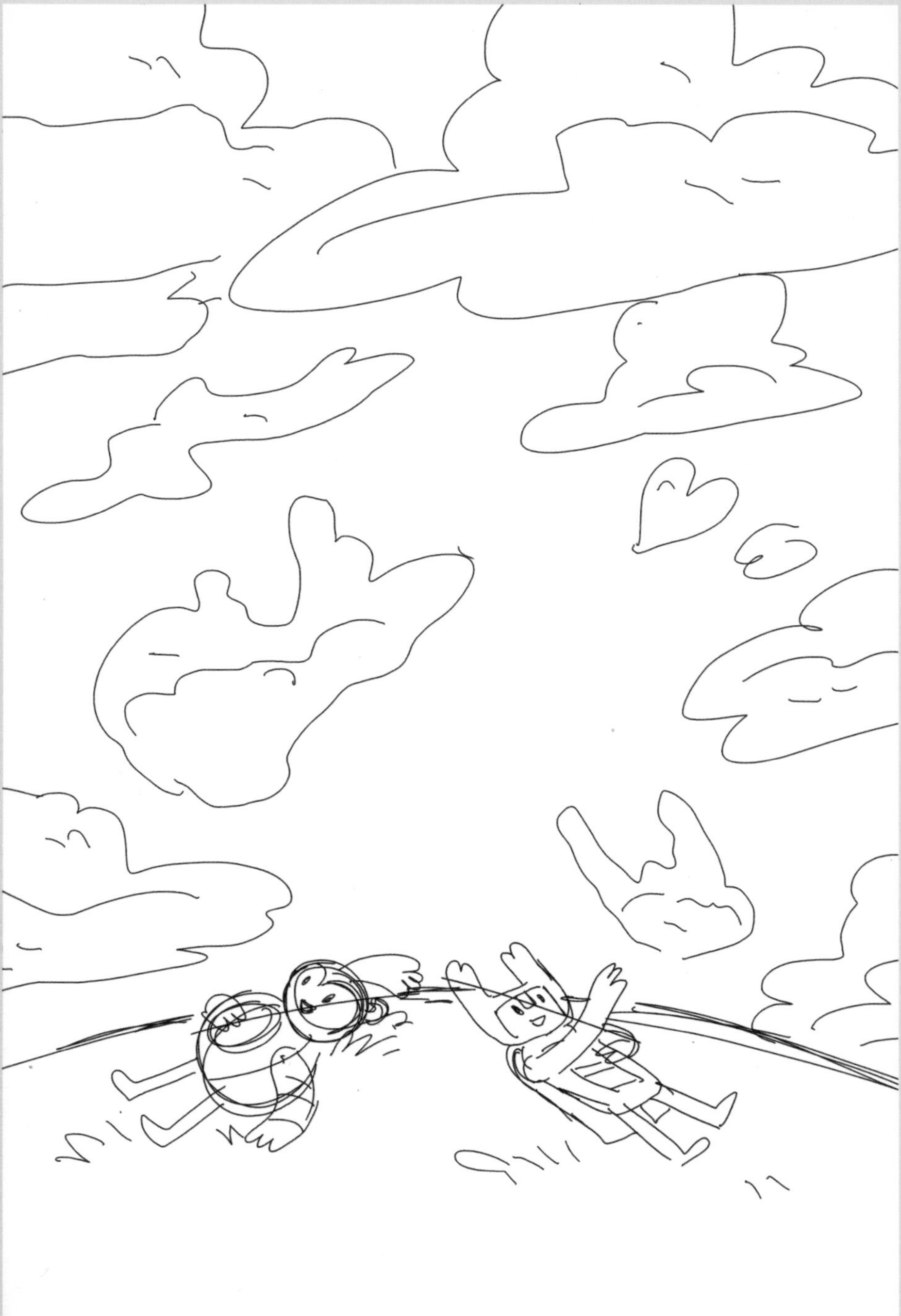

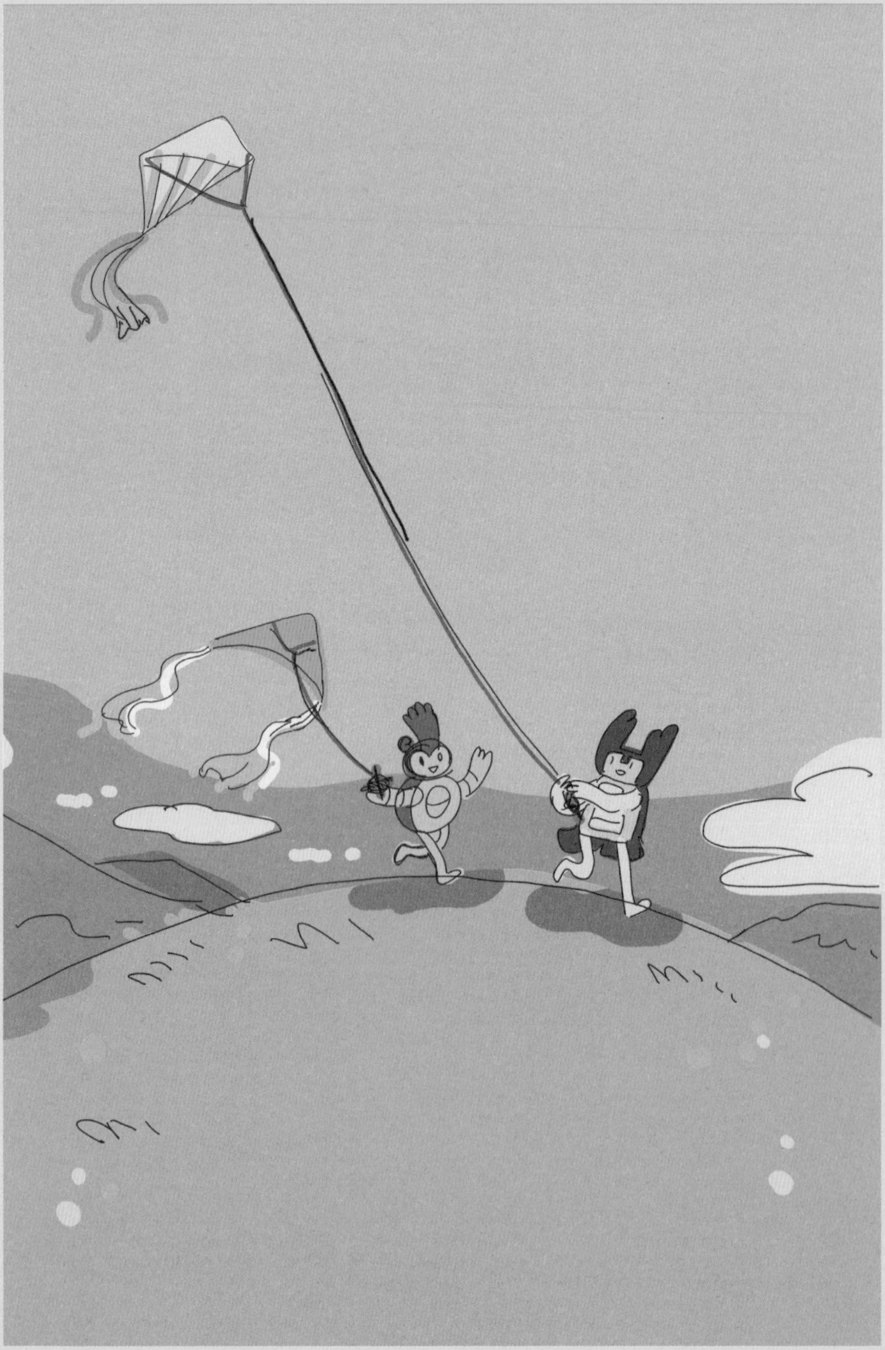

Laura Knetzger

grew up in Washington State, near Seattle. She wanted to be a cartoonist since she was eleven years old. She went to art college in New York City, and now she lives in Seattle.

She has a gray tuxedo cat named Chilly. Cats are definitely Laura's favorite animal.

Laura got the idea to make Bug Boys as she was watching a documentary about bug collecting called Beetle Queen Conquers Tokyo. She drew two cute cartoon bugs as she was watching the movie, then tried to make up stories about them.

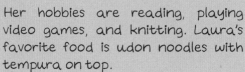

Her hobbies are reading, playing video games, and knitting. Laura's favorite food is udon noodles with tempura on top.